Ed Savage and the Savage Murders Trilogy

01/22/21

ED SAVAGE AND THE
SAVAGE MURDERS TRILOGY

THE SAVAGE SAGA

VOLUME 1

For Teresa

Many Thanks For My
Christmas Beer!
Hope You Enjoy The Thrill
Ride!

Best

Bryan Roberts

Bryan Roberts

ISBN: 0692539735
ISBN 13: 9780692539736
Library of Congress Control Number: 2015915669
Savage Roberts Publishing, Palm Springs, CA
www.SavageRobertsPublishing.com

This book is for every creative soul who dared to succeed in making a dream come true, and for all the contestants from every reality TV show pushing for their dreams. From the monster makeup artists, the clothing designers, to the obstacle course challengers to the ones I haven't seen. As I wrote this, through the highs and lows, watching you put yourselves out there gave me the *strength* to move forward. I'm looking at you—the ones sent home before reaching the end. Your passion fueled this writer when my clear path was suddenly overgrown with self-doubt wrought with thorns.

And for my mother, Susan, the strongest woman I know, and my late father, Harry, the bravest father a son could have.

And to my Uncle Bill and my Texas family, the closest people to my father—enjoy the scare ride.

A special thanks to my editors Amy, Lizzie, and Matthew—each in their own way brought out the better writer in me. And to my illustrator, Dave Seeley—I took one look at his portfolio and instantly knew he was the artist I needed to not only bring Ed Savage to life, but to pull the images from my novel to put the reader that much closer to the story. *Dave, I can't thank you enough.* Anyone needing artwork should check out his website at http://www.daveseeley.com because he is the man to bring your creations to life—big time!

CONTENTS

The Savage Family Tree · xi

Part 1 Ed Savage and the Mountain Murders—Killing Savage · · · · 1

Part 2 Ed Savage and the Black Ridge Cult—Surviving Savages · · 227

Part 3 Ed Savage and the Savage Hit—Saving Savage · · · · · · · · 361

A note from your author · 421

Author Biography · 423

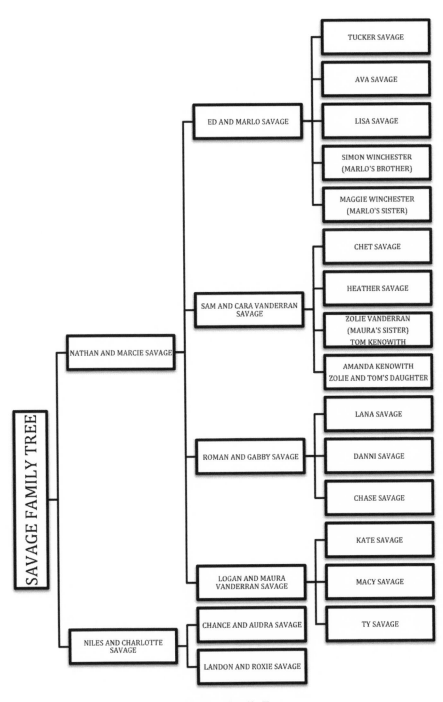

The Savage Family Tree

PART 1
ED SAVAGE AND THE MOUNTAIN MURDERS—KILLING SAVAGE

CHAPTER 1

E d Savage picked up the Black Ridge Falls Campgrounds vacation brochure from his desk and immediately felt that relief was on its way. But the computer's familiar chime alerted him that he had mail, and when he checked it, he wasn't happy.

Ed cringed when he read the e-mail from his agent. She had been warned that a tabloid story was coming out about the current bad boys of Hollywood and the nannies they'd bedded, along with other equally salacious stories. Twice before in his career, Ed had been maligned in such stories.

The first time—a setup by a former costar (if the guy could even be called one)—it'd nearly cost him his marriage. *Phantom Finders* had been fun when he was first asked to join the series all those years ago, but it quickly turned to shit. Ed's popularity surpassed the original actor's, and the guy's ego went straight into DEFCON ONE, plotting a character assassination of Ed. The second time (years later), his costar, Ellie Collins, got pregnant and asked to leave the series *Savage Strength* halfway through the season.

Both times, it was proved that Ed had kept it in his pants, but the shit being thrown in Hollywood sometimes sticks whether it's true or not, just like the Natalie Wood story. Now with the article outing the current guys, a brief history of the gossip over the years was added, and Ed Savage's name was there with the *Phantom Finders* and *Savage Strength* stories being rehashed.

He could just hear his wife Marlo's complaints: "I have to live with all the stares and the 'Look, her husband cheats on her' whispers." He loved his wife deeply and understood her wants more than anyone, but he hated it when she fought unfairly. But thankfully, all these stories were in the past, where they belonged, and hopefully they would stay there.

The argument a few weeks ago with Marlo had been a doozy, and he couldn't wait for a change of scenery. Everything had been going so well—he and his younger brother, Sam Savage, were excited about buying new extreme recreational vehicles, and the families were planning a wonderful getaway—until the script arrived.

Marlo Savage had just pulled into the driveway when the FedEx truck arrived, and she signed for the package. She knew exactly what it was, and her anger deepened.

Her career had never taken off after she'd met Ed, outside of a few lucky breaks. Perhaps she'd always blamed the pregnancy for her missing out on the career she'd wanted so much. To Ed, though, it was her acting that ended her career, although he would *never* voice such an opinion. After three children and a life of watching her husband shine on the big screen and now his several TV series, sometimes envy would rear its ugly head, and the fighting would begin.

Then there was their youngest daughter, six-year-old Lisa. Ed loved how she would always call him her "hero." On Sunday evenings they would sit together and watch his family show, *Archive Raiders*, where Ed would investigate the pyramids and the mummies, explore lost civilizations, and search for buried treasures. The show always included an animal segment from the location where they were filming.

The episode shot in Australia last year was Lisa's favorite because Ed had brought Marlo and two of their kids with them, and it included Lisa petting a koala in the segment about a sunken pirate ship.

To Lisa, it was like watching Jack Sparrow, and her father could do no wrong. Her innocence and love were all he needed to reassure him that he could get through any of his fights with Marlo. What hurt him most was that when they watched the Australian episode that first time, she had gotten so excited that her asthma kicked in, and it scared him. It was a bad attack, and he had to remind her, when she rewatched it from the DVD, to remember not to get too carried away and to always have her inhaler with her.

The trip to the mountains not too far from where they lived in Port Roberts, in Upstate New York, was a fresh escape the families had been looking forward to for quite some time.

Ed loved living up the street from his brother Sam in their quaint neighborhood, allowing their kids to grow up together. Sam also allowed their father to live with them, something Ed would never do after what had happened growing up. But time had a way of pushing the bad memories further away—if only time could erase them completely.

The fresh air would be great for all of them, and Ed thought the bad news Marlo had recently received would fade away as they reconnected as a family.

Downstate in New York City was the studio where he filmed for one of his series, and Ed liked being close to home when he stayed at their Manhattan apartment, as opposed to when he had to fly to Los Angeles for other work. On his last trip downstate, he had called his agent, Rachel Shepherd, about getting Marlo a part in *anything* just to give her a sense of what she missed so much. When a small part did come up, Ed had to promise a favor later on, and the audition was scheduled.

It was a disaster. Marlo was too excited and didn't remember her training from all those years ago, and she blew it big-time. And that was the day she drove home and intercepted the script. The explosion in the house was epic that day.

Ed shook away the thoughts and did an Internet search of Black Ridge Falls. Always the protective father first, he looked up the recent crime reports for the area, finding a few home burglaries and some livestock stolen from a farm nearby. He rechecked the reviews of the campgrounds, seeing mostly positive ones, and then noticed the sheriff's phone number for the area and jotted it down on a Post-it. He then picked up the phone and punched in the number from the brochure to confirm the reservations.

A deep-voiced man answered the call quickly. "Black Ridge Falls Campgrounds, Ranger Melvin."

"Hello. I'd like to confirm our reservations," Ed said, looking at the brochure.

"Yes, I can help you with that."

"Great. We'd like three spots; two we wanted next to each other, and the third we wanted about five sites away. Are you able to do that?"

"Shouldn't be a problem. I'll need your name."

"Ed Savage, and I'll be paying for all three spaces."

"Ed Savage. Got it. Yep, you got what you wanted, sir; have you in sites fourteen, fifteen, and nineteen."

On his desk was another brochure to Seneca Falls. Ed picked it up and threw it in the trashcan next to his desk, happy with the choice he had made.

CHAPTER 2

The sedan innocently driving down the expressway never saw it coming. The horrible act that occurred near that mountain town was in fact no accident. And those responsible who got away with it were going to pay. Fate can have a vicious way of waiting, prolonging the inevitable; it knows how to serve justice best, especially to those who deserve it most, and it never forgets. Even debts as old as forty years in the making will be paid in full; there is no escaping its reach.

Marlo's brother, Simon Winchester, knew all about this. When the person responsible for what happened to him all those years ago was finally caught, his murder was gruesome. Yet Simon was still having trouble, and his shrinks were helping with medications.

The same couldn't be said completely for Ed's father, Nathan Savage. He ruled Savage Construction like he had his home while his children were growing up—strict with a draconian flair no one wanted to go up against. His younger brother and partial partner in the company, Niles Savage, was no Prince Charming himself, and underhandedness was not a stranger to him.

The good days of the company started slipping around the time Nathan started losing it bit by bit, and it seemed to start with the dreams. Nathan would wake from the nightmares screaming for his life, and he would never tell anyone about them, except his brother, Niles.

Sensing the tables could finally turn at any moment, Niles dreamed of gaining more shares of the company and no longer living under his brother's thumb. But Nathan wasn't the only one having the night-mares. And although Niles would never admit to having a few fright-filled nights himself, he used it to add weight to his brother's guilt.

Fate's endgame originated the day of that horrible accident; it only kicked into high gear once the plan went into the works. And all it cost was a stamp…and luck…depending on *whose luck that was…*

CHAPTER 3

The summer had been long and hot, and the warm weather was not breaking in the northeast part of the country. And when the unexpected electrical repairs at their daughter's high school were more serious than first thought, a notice was sent out shortly after the new school year began. The school would be closing for the first week in October, and the time would be made up at the end of the year.

That was the week the Savages had scheduled their mountain adventure. There was just one hiccup in the plan—Sam's daughter Heather's seventeenth birthday party was on the Friday evening following the school's closure.

Wanting to get a jump on the vacation with some alone time with his family, Ed Savage loaded up their RV and left two days earlier, leaving their oldest teenage daughter, Ava Savage, with his brother, Sam, for her cousin's party.

He could tell things were going to work out due to the fun time he and Marlo shared in bed one morning before they left. It was as if she too wanted nothing more than to forget the silly arguments and enjoy their time together on the open road.

The brand-new RV glistened in the sun. From a distance, it had the brilliance of a gemstone, set in the beauty of the mountains. Moving down the highway, it gracefully wove its way along the curves, pulling the gray Range Rover behind.

The oldest of his four brothers, Ed was now in his early fifties— a rugged man, who was happy in his career away from the family business. He stared at the stunning mountain views and thought about the home he could build in this area. He certainly had the skills to make it happen. Even with the military background he was so proud of, there had been a very specific reason for his leaving West Point, where he'd studied civil engineering, for Cambridge. Architecture was his career of choice in order to follow in the family business of high-rise construction.

Keeping the RV at the designated sixty miles per hour, Ed scratched his face, feeling the bristles that rubbed his skin raw. As he looked into the mirror to see how bad it was, a movement in the rearview monitor caught his eye. Adjusting the camera to pan the back of the RV, he attempted to see what had caused the shadows, but there was only the familiar Range Rover following behind on the trailer. Then a motorcycle raced by at a high speed.

"Jackass," Ed barked as he glanced at Simon sitting next to him.

Simon, Ed's brother-in-law, was a harmless man, slightly on the thin side. Sitting quietly, whittling a stick with a plastic bag in his lap to catch the shavings, he looked over at Ed. "What?" he said, noticing the motorcycle speeding away.

Ed pointed to the rear monitor. "I could have sworn there were two motorcycles behind us, not just the one."

Simon looked to the monitor and then scanned the passenger-side rearview mirror. Not seeing anything but Mother Nature staring back, he turned back to Ed. "I'll go take a look."

Getting up, he placed his project on the floor and reached for his cane. For having a broken left tibia in a cast, he moved with ease.

Limping toward the rear of the vehicle, he passed by his sister, Marlo, who seemed lost in her own thoughts. She stared up at the TV and watched in awe as the station announced the preview of "What is to come on *Tycoon Wives*." The amount of in-depth concentration she gave to the silly show was equal to what a true patriot would give to the announcement "America is at war!"

She barely breathed as the coffeemaker filled the decanter on the counter. Simon sighed. "I'd shoot myself if I had to admit my sister was one of those crazy damn wives," he grunted, as he pushed forward to look out the back window.

Ed's wife shifted her eyes away from the screen as the much-less-appreciated ad for the latest dog food popped up, and she ran her fingers through her dark-brown hair. "Well, you may just have to get used to it. Cara sent in her audition tape, and they called her in for an interview. They offered her a spot on the show for next season. And I may want to do this, too!"

Rolling her eyes at the grunt she received, Marlo looked back to the screen as the preview began. Placing her steamy Zolie Vanderran novel, *Vander Place*, on the table, she picked up the remote and turned up the volume, so she could see and hear everything about a true Tycoon Wife.

Ed could feel the weight of the last argument percolate to the surface of his skin, and a flash of heat built up inside him. *She isn't over it,* he thought.

The preview was the best guilty pleasure that reality TV could offer—a ratings juggernaut that was an insult to some actor's in the industry that schooled hard and fought for every gig they could get. But television was changing, and so were the rules. Ed rolled his eyes as he heard the preview behind him.

"Look, Marilyn, I can explain," said a woman's shaky voice from the TV.

Marlo had a look of shock on her face as she watched the "other" woman get caught by her favorite Tycoon Wife and queen bee of the program, Marilyn Hart.

Marilyn approached a younger woman at a bar in her husband's office, picked up a glass of bourbon, and downed it in a hot second. The glare she shot could have turned the Arctic a hundred degrees colder. "Save it. You'll soon be back standing on your corner, you slut!"

A slap rang out, the younger woman's hair flew across her face, and the frame froze. "Next time on *Tycoon Wives!*" popped up in bold, money-green letters across a bright-red, newly slapped face. Marlo laughed out loud, causing Ed to look back at her with a grin.

When his gaze turned back to the road, he chuckled. "You're not serious about wanting to be on that show, are you?"

Marlo saw that the coffeemaker was finished, and she got up and poured a cup. "Why not? Cara and I think it would be fun to do it together. They offered her two hundred *thousand* for the season!"

Ed glanced back at his wife. "That's a high starting salary. Course, she is a Vanderran. They're probably hoping to get her sisters involved, too. Then their ratings would climb."

Marlo opened the refrigerator and grabbed a sparkling water. "Yeah, Cara and I talked about that. I know they wouldn't offer *me* that much, but it would be fun all the same."

Ed quickly turned back to the road; thoughts of the fights they'd had rolled around in his head for a moment, and he hoped she wasn't setting herself up for a fall. He looked ahead at the beautiful landscape before him and shook them away.

He heard Simon's laugh. "My crazy sister."

Ed watched in the mirror as Simon entered the back bedroom. As the door opened, he saw his daughter Lisa playing with her dolls on the bed.

Marlo took a drink of her water, grabbed the coffee mug, and made her way up front. "Coffee just finished." She smiled, handing him his mug.

"Thanks, sweetie," Ed said, placing it in the cup holder. "You enjoying yourself?"

Marlo rubbed his shoulder and placed a kiss on his cheek. "This was such a wonderful idea. We're not even there yet, and I already feel relaxed."

"I feel great; we needed this." He winked.

Ed's voice came from the TV behind them: "An old, charming house in need of repair in a brand-new neighborhood. What could go wrong? Find out this Wednesday at nine on *Savage Mysteries*."

Hearing the promo for his show, Ed grinned. "Would you turn that off? We're on vacation. What's Lisa up to back there, anyway?"

Marlo turned. "I'll go check."

Walking by the television, she glanced at her husband on the screen. A modern-day Indiana Jones type met her gaze, exploring a backyard. A headstone was front and center, with a creepy-looking house sitting just a few feet away. She smiled wide as she shut the set down, and she glanced into the back bedroom to see her daughter having a great time as she spoke to her dolls about safety in the mountains.

Making her way back to Ed, she sat down in the chair beside him. "She's having fun. But what's Simon doing back there? He's opening the windows in the back like he's going to jump or something," she said, laughing.

Ed glanced at the rearview monitor system again and grabbed his coffee. "Thought I saw something behind us, but then nothing. He's just taking a look."

Turning, Marlo watched Simon scan the road before she looked to her daughter. Lisa held the big, blonde doll in her right hand, and in her left, a doll with bright-red locks. She was holding them face-to-face as if they were having a conversation, while a third, much older porcelain doll with black hair lay on the bed beside her.

Lisa shook the blonde doll at the redhead, and suddenly it seemed as if the dolls were in battle. Marlo chuckled as little Lisa and Uncle Simon sat there and laughed when the dolls turned into their own version of *Tycoon Wives.*

Watching her little girl with her long, dirty-blonde hair, remembering her own hair was that color at that young age, wearing such a happy smile, Marlo's heart felt full, until Simon pulled back the curtain and looked out the window.

The memory came back in a flash—dropping her own doll at such a young age and seeing her brother in the window at *that place.* The scary sign that gave her nightmares, "Nettlewood Psychiatric Hospital," and the words he spoke to her that day: "You're safe."

Ed noticed Marlo deep in thought and called out her name.

When he finally got through to her, she seemed to blink a memory away. "Sorry, I was just…"

Immediately, he cut her off. "He's okay. He really is. That was a long time ago." Ed put his coffee down and reached for Marlo's hand, pulling her to her feet.

"I know." Standing behind the captain's chair, Marlo gave him a hug.

Limping up behind them, Simon retook his place in the passenger seat with a sigh. "No one back there, far as I can see," he reported. He looked ahead and grinned, pointing at the Black Ridge Falls destination sign. "Hey, we're almost there."

CHAPTER 4

Black Ridge Falls: 5 miles

Ed took the exit. Seeing a small gas station and garage, next to a café/general store combo that exuded that old, rustic feel of the mountains, Ed felt animated as their adventure began. He was immensely excited to arrive near the campsite, giving little notice to the rusted, shabby U-Haul with no license plate that started its engine on the far side of the garage as he pulled in for gas.

Stepping out from the RV, the crew stretched their legs and breathed in the fresh air. Ed sighed with relief that they were finally there. He noticed a section of the outdoor roof had come down over the café, there were a pair of saw horses and a buzz saw was next to some tools along with planks of plywood leaning against the building. He then went to the gas pump and noticed the sign to pay inside.

The sound of metal hitting the floor from the garage got Marlo's and Simon's attention, and they saw the back of an old school bus sticking out from the garage.

Lisa, of course, was scouting out things only a six-year-old would find important. She zeroed in on some horses tied up near the store and ran to them, just as the U-Haul pulled out, gunning the loud engine. Marlo turned immediately to see the U-Haul come dangerously close to her daughter, causing Lisa to trip and fall down, skin her knee, and start crying. Marlo screamed out and ran to her, and Ed just dropped his cash on the counter and ran out from the store to see Marlo picking up their daughter.

Ed saw the U-Haul speed away from the garage and disappear down the road as he ran to them.

"Shush, honey, you're okay," Marlo said as she rocked her child in her arms.

"It hurts!" Lisa screamed out as she gasped for air.

As her breathing became labored, immediately both parents thought of the inhaler, and Ed reached for his breast pocket to find it empty. His mind flashed to remembering leaving it in the console of the RV and raced back, nearly tripping up the stairs as he grabbed it.

"For God's sake, Ed, hurry!" Marlo yelled.

He raced back and placed it as quickly as he could to his daughter's mouth. "Take a breath, honey. Come on," he said as he depressed the inhaler.

Watching their daughter inhale the medicine to expand the pathways to her little lungs, both parents looked to each other in fear, and Ed saw the anger was back.

Simon broke up their stare when he noticed a woman with long, gray hair rushing toward them from the store. She had seen the whole thing and had a brand-new box of Band-Aids and a recognizable brown bottle of hydrogen peroxide in her hands.

"Hey there, is she all right?" the woman said. "Here, let me help you."

Marlo sat Lisa down on the ground, and Ed took the hydrogen peroxide from the woman and studied the label. He broke the seal of the new bottle and used the tail of his shirt to wipe the dirt from her knee. He then looked right into Lisa's wet eyes as her breathing started to come under control. "Watch now, little nugget; your knee's gonna turn white and bubble, and the hurt will go away; promise."

"No, Daddy," Lisa screamed as he poured the hydrogen peroxide over her knee.

Silently the group watched her knee as it turned white and bubbled, just like her hero said it would. Marlo then took the Band-Aids and tore a few open and bandaged Lisa's knee.

Lisa's crying slowed as Ed picked her up, and Marlo thanked the woman.

"Who was driving that U-Haul?" Ed demanded.

"I don't know. I heard the child cry out and followed you out from my store. I saw what happened and ran inside and grabbed what I could. Sorry I didn't see who was driving," the woman said.

"Thank you," Marlo said, noticing the "Patty's Specials" café sign behind her next to the entrance of the store. "Your store? Are you Patty?"

"Yes, this is my place, and welcome to Black Ridge Falls. Hope the rest of your trip is better."

"We do too; thank you again, Patty," Marlo said, rethinking the whole trip.

"I'll tell you what; let me make up an order for you while you fill up. It's the least I can do. I'll just be a moment."

"Thank you, but that won't be necessary," Ed said as he moved to take Lisa back inside the RV.

"No, I insist," Patty said, and she hurried back inside the store to prepare whatever it was she wanted to give them.

"Oh, come on, Ed; I'm sure the roadkill du jour will be delicious," Marlo said snidely once Patty was well out of hearing range.

Simon limped around the vehicle with his cane to pump the gas, and Marlo boarded behind Ed as a station wagon pulled up with its windows down to get gas near them.

"That was too damn close, Ed," Marlo said in a raised voice. "Let's just go home."

The woman in the station wagon heard her and turned to try and see what was going on.

Ed's heart ached for his little girl as he put her down on the sofa. "You'll be fine. See, it's already feeling better."

Lisa grabbed one of her dolls and hugged it tightly.

"She's fine," Ed said, looking to his wife and seeing that she was moving far from fine.

"Why you and Sam decided on this I'll never know," Marlo said, the anger and concern for her daughter still in her voice.

"Oh, come on; it's just a skinned knee. Besides, we're not far from the campgrounds. Once we get settled, she'll forget the whole thing."

The couple from the station wagon entered the store and made their way to the cold drinks while Patty finished packing up the food to go.

Marlo wet a paper towel and fussed with the bandage, wiping around her daughter's knee just as there was a tap at the entryway. Both Marlo and Ed looked to see Patty standing there with a bag filled with her special sandwiches of the day.

Oh great, I wonder if the tire marks are still on them, Marlo thought, as she smiled warmly and rose to move to the door to accept the gift. "Thank you."

"Pulled pork. Hope you like it," Patty said, staring at her for a moment longer than normal. She looked away in thought and then looked right back at Marlo. "*Skirt Squad,*" Patty said with an air of excitement. "That's it; that's where I know you from. Right? I loved that show."

Marlo's thoughts of the roadkill sandwiches suddenly turned into filet mignon, and she smiled brightly. "Oh my God, that was so long ago. How do you remember that?"

"Don't watch much TV now, but it was one of my favorites. I hated that it didn't last long."

Ed moved toward the woman and flashed his signature devilish grin, his trademark from his TV shows. She glanced his way but didn't pay him a second thought.

Marlo was beaming. "Well, thank you for the food; now I don't have to cook tonight."

"My pleasure. How's the little girl?"

"She'll live," Marlo said, feeling the celebrity high she hadn't experienced in years.

"They always do. Have a couple of my own, twins about her age," Patty said as she looked back at the store. "Now I have to get back inside; I'm alone today. You all have a safe rest of your stay now, and stop back by if you need anything."

Marlo watched Patty head back to the store and then placed the bag on the counter.

"Nothing's still alive in there, is it?" Ed joked.

Marlo gazed at the bag with a questioning look as they heard Simon finishing up with the gas. "Ed, that one show I did way back—I can't remember the last time that happened. And for once, it wasn't about you."

Together they shared a laugh, and Ed moved to his wife and kissed her.

Simon boarded and picked up the bag of sandwiches; opening it, he could smell the pork. "These are gonna be great."

"Well, then they're yours," Marlo said as she watched Simon put them in the refrigerator.

With the tank filled, Ed pulled the RV onto the road, and soon they found one of the two entrances to the park.

As they made their way into the campgrounds, Simon returned his whittling stick and knife to his backpack beside him and began reading the brochure all about the Black Ridge Falls area.

Marlo gazed out the side window, noticing several other campers departing and a family of deer in the distance. There were people building fires near their sites, while others were walking about. And through the trees, a lake could be seen that was an invitation to rest, relax, and enjoy.

"Can you imagine the fun we're going to have here?" Marlo grinned.

Ed nodded. "We're campsite number fourteen, so keep an eye out for our turnoff," he said, slowing the RV down.

Lisa walked up between them and saw the sign. As excited as a six-year-old can get, Lisa jumped up and down, ignoring her knee, pointing to the sign as her words rushed out. "Daddy, Daddy, that's it! Sites eleven through twenty! I can see the lake. Mommy, let's go swimming!"

Laughing at the continuous flow of words, Ed slowed down and looked to his daughter. "Good eyes there, nugget. We'll all go swimming tomorrow; I promise. But remember about getting too excited—you need to relax for a bit."

"I will, Daddy."

As the giant RV came to a turn, Ed saw the rangers' station and campsite rental agency that he must have called earlier that provided everyone with information. People were gathered around on the porch looking at maps, and Simon, with the brochure open to the lake rentals, got up to get a better look. "Ed, why don't you let me out here, and I'll go see about renting a boat."

Marlo sounded a bit worried as she looked to Simon and then to her husband. "Are you sure?"

Wanting to get out of the RV and grab some air, Simon reassured his sister. "I'll be just fine. I'll make it up to the campsite from here. Fourteen can't be all that far from eleven." He looked to Ed as a small, awkward silence filled the RV.

Ed smiled. "Good idea. And see how much the WaveRunners or Jet Skis are per hour. When the rest of the kids get here, it's a good bet they'll be on those all day long."

Bringing the RV to a stop, Ed watched Simon place his cane against the side of the cabinet and switch to his wooden crutches. Grabbing his backpack, he hobbled down the RV's steps.

Ed and Marlo watched him head to the rangers' cabin, working the crutches with a sense of rhythm and ease. Ed squeezed his wife's hand. "You worry too much," he said. Offering her a wink, he turned away from her slightly nervous face and threw on his New York Giants cap to shield him from the sun as he stood up and picked up Lisa. "How you feeling?"

"I'm good, Daddy."

Ed placed her in his seat behind the wheel. "All right there, nugget, I need you to keep guard while I go inside and check in."

"Yes, sir," Lisa said, moving to kneel in the seat on her bandaged knee to get a better view.

Ed smiled at Marlo, and they shared the thought that their daughter's latest trauma was well behind them.

Inside the cabin, Simon saw an open bag of candy on the first desk and grabbed a handful, tossing them into his backpack. He then went to the brochure rack as Ed entered the quaint cabin.

"Can I help you?" the ranger said in his deep voice.

Ed first noticed the guy's height—he was tall, at least six five against Ed's just over six-foot structure—and his beard. He then noticed his name badge and remembered the guy he had spoken to a few days ago.

"Hi, Melvin. Ed Savage—I have a few reservations."

Melvin looked out the window and noticed the one vehicle. "A few?"

"We're the first to arrive; the others will be here in a couple days."

"Oh, that's right; you booked three spaces, and we almost had to move you."

"Move us? We're still spaced apart like I asked, right?"

"Even better. We had a tree come down, closing an entire section, and we thought we'd have to move you all, but it just got cleared. So you and your group will have a nice, private area, for now anyway—no other bookings yet."

The thought of Simon in his tent and Lisa fast asleep and the alone time with Marlo excited him.

"Perfect. Do me a favor and direct any further bookings away; we can use the peace and quiet," Ed said, handing his credit card and identification to the ranger, who made a quick copy.

A female ranger heard Ed as she noticed Simon looking like he needed assistance.

"Can I help you?"

"How many Jet Skis are available?" Simon asked, moving toward the door to look down at the lake.

"You're not thinking of Jet Skis with your leg in a cast, are you?" the ranger said, looking the man over.

"Oh no." Simon laughed. "I'll be fishing from a boat; it's for the kids."

"Ah, all right then, come on; I'll show you."

Together they left the station, and soon Ed came out behind them, holding a map of the area. He boarded his new toy and handed Marlo the map.

"We're in luck; we have a whole area to ourselves."

"What'd you do? Reserve the entire section?" Marlo said, taking the map.

"Wish I'd thought of that," Ed said, giving her his signature devilish grin.

Marlo knew what her husband had on his mind, and maybe because of the compliment she'd just received, she was thinking the same thing.

"And to think that woman knew me and not you." Marlo laughed.

Ed was happy for her. The one series she had starred in just before they met so long ago...Maybe this trip would be better than he had hoped.

Lisa jumped down from Ed's seat, and soon the crew was on their way. Following the little arrows, he drove the RV through the woods slowly, pulling onto one road after another, heading deeper into the forest. They had seen the fallen tree on the side of the dirt road, and it seemed as if they had gotten lucky. The farther the arrows went, the quieter it became. The area looked as if they were the only campers there, as opposed to the small mob that had been located at the rangers' station.

Ed breathed another sigh; it would be so peaceful not to have campers surrounding them, partying loud in the middle of the night. This way, they could sit under the big sky and stare up at the stars...be lulled to sleep by Mother Nature and not kept awake by beer-guzzling vacationers.

As they climbed up the final hill, the road evened out in a clearing at a higher elevation than the campsites below, and Ed spotted the sign for campsite number eleven, then number twelve, and then number fourteen.

"Hey, they skipped the lucky number," Ed joked.

He didn't even notice Marlo's disapproving glare as he parked the RV in its dedicated spot, backed up the trailer a few feet, and unhitched the Range Rover.

Assembling the side awnings so they made the perfect overhead canopy, Ed secured them while Marlo set up a table and chairs underneath.

Lisa helped by pulling chairs out from under the RV's storage area, but as a chair got caught, she struggled. "Mommy!" she yelled out.

Lisa looked so cute tugging on the chair that Marlo couldn't help but laugh. "Hang on there; let me help you with that," she said.

As Marlo helped Lisa untangle the chairs, Ed smiled while he watched his beloved family.

When the wind began to pick up and whistle through the trees, Ed went and grabbed his jacket from inside the RV. Stepping back out, he saw the arrival of another couple taking a walk by their campsite with their young son and daughter in tow.

"Hello there," the man said, waving and smiling as he and his family got near.

Lisa looked up from getting another chair and shouted out a big hello back, offering a welcoming smile.

As Ed put on his jacket, he and Marlo exchanged smiles.

Reaching out his hand, the man introduced himself. "Ned Barnes."

"Ed Savage."

A whistle came through Ned's lips, and his eyes grew wide, checking out the brand-new RV. "That's some rig you got there. What is it... forty-feet long?"

Lisa raised her chin. Her voice took on the unashamed, snooty manner of a six-year-old, and she announced, "It's *exactly* forty-five-feet long. Isn't it, Daddy?"

The adults shared a laugh, and the kids wandered over to a wood-bin marked "Free Firewood" to start investigating the area while getting to know each other.

"Be careful, Lisa," Marlo said.

Looking back briefly, Lisa flipped her hair over her shoulder. "We will."

"Free firewood, huh? This place thinks of everything," Ed said, looking over at the kids.

"The scouts come up here and bring wood for the fires. They get a badge, and it's part of the fees. There are woodbins all over the place." Ned smiled. When he glanced at the woman standing beside him, he blushed. "I am so sorry," he chuckled. "I was so taken with your rig here that I forgot to introduce my family to you. This here is Genie, and the kids are Larry and Shelly."

They glanced over to the kids having fun by the woodbin, and Ed once again extended his hand. "Ma'am. Ed Savage, nice to meet you. And this is Marlo, my wife, and that bold little one over there is Lisa," he said.

Genie, clearly a bit younger than Ned, looked away from the children. "It's nice to meet you both. We were just talking about how beautiful it is here." She turned around and pointed back down the road.

"We're way down in the lower level at campsite number seven. Just up for a walk on this gorgeous day."

"How long have you been up here?" Marlo asked.

Ned, who was once again gazing at the RV like it was a castle in the air, broke away and turned to her. "Got here two days ago. Welcome to famous Black Ridge Falls."

"Thank you," Marlo said. "How did this place get the name Black Ridge Falls when it's so green up here? Do you know?"

"It's an old timber-and-coal town," Genie replied. "They used to mine the coal and send it down the log chutes. You can see them still, going down the side of the mountain. Some of the coal would spill over, and a black residue was left behind."

"Hence the name, Black Ridge Falls. Makes sense," Ned added, moving closer to the RV and glancing in the windows. "Hey, Genie, we need to get ourselves one of these. Trade in the old Winnebago for something like this, right?"

Genie waved her hand at the Savages and winked. "You bet, honey. We'll run right out and get one."

Lisa and Shelly screamed out, and the parents looked over, running to the children.

Larry remained bent over the wood as if searching for something, while the girls ran straight into their mothers' arms. Clutching Marlo, Lisa shouted, "There was a snake, Mommy!"

Ned furrowed his brow at his son. "Larry, what kind was it?"

Just as Larry kicked some wood chips out of the way, the small snake moved in the opposite direction. Moving fast, he looked like he was trying to escape from the frightening screams. "Just a garter, that's all." Larry grinned at his father.

Seeing the frightened snake, Marlo picked up Lisa in her arms. "It's going away, see? It's okay. He was probably just trying to find his own mommy."

Lisa stared in his direction. "I don't like snakes." Burying her face into her mother's shoulder, she started to cry.

Marlo patted her on the back. "I don't like them either, honey."

Turning back to the RV, she offered the adults a smile. "Nice meeting you. I'm going to take her inside."

Genie took her own daughter's hand and nodded. "We better get going, too; it's quite a way to go to get back down where we're at. Hope to see you again."

"Oh, if you see a man with crutches on his way up, tell him I'll drive down to get him if he's not back soon," Ed said. "We're farther from that ranger cabin than we both thought."

"Will do, Ed…like Ned—easy to remember." Ned Barnes laughed as they gathered up their kids and said their good-byes.

Entering the RV moments later, Ed smiled at his two girls sitting on the sofa. He joked, "My damsels in distress." When no smile was returned, he cleared his throat and turned around, realizing there was still a female "tragedy" being discussed. "I'll just go…check the slide outs… stabilize the RV."

Backing out of the RV, he laughed to himself. "Every woman's nightmare: a common garter snake."

Ed walked around the RV checking the extended slide outs and then went over to the woodbin and picked up a few pieces of wood. He brought them to the stone-circled fire pit near a picnic table a short distance from where they had set up the table under the awning. Some of the rocks had to be moved tighter together, and he adjusted them, getting everything just right, when he heard a rummaging sound in the short distance.

Ed got up, took a few steps in the direction of the sound, and peered into the woods; then he reached for a branch to a thick bush and moved it down for a better look. Not seeing anything but noticing his hands were dirty from the rocks, he headed back inside to clean up. Then he stopped and turned back to the direction of the noise he had heard. Maybe it was his military training, but he wasn't able to shake the sense that he wasn't alone.

He then went to the Range Rover, opened the front passenger door, and lifted the knob that raised the seat. Reaching underneath, he pulled out his towel-wrapped handgun he had kept there. Putting it in his jacket pocket, he ventured deeper into the woods.

When he came to the raccoon near the garbage can of the other empty campsite they had reserved, he sighed and headed back to the

SUV. He wrapped the gun in the towel, placed it in the glove box, and then went inside to wash up.

The raccoon watched the tall man retreat in the direction he had come from and then scurried down a path into the woods, not noticing the hunter as he stayed motionless and camouflaged in the brush.

CHAPTER 5

E d boarded the RV, took off his jacket, and went into the bathroom, placing his New York Giants cap on the counter to wash his hands and face. He grabbed a towel and was drying off when he heard his wife.

"Do you think Simon is okay?" Marlo finally asked.

Ed stepped out from the bathroom, tossing the towel on the counter next to his cap. "I'm sure he's fine. When dinner's about set, I'll go down and get him if he's not back yet."

Marlo nodded, looking back to Lisa, where she was "helping" fix up the salad for dinner.

Suddenly pausing, Lisa looked up at her mother. "Mommy, I wish Tuc and Ava were here."

Marlo stopped chopping the cucumber and looked down at her. "I do, too, sweetie. How about we take a photo and send it to Tuc right now?"

Lisa jumped up and down, sending some of the salad greens flying into the air. "No, Mommy, no! A video, let's send him a video."

Laughing, Marlo picked up her phone, "A video it shall be." Selecting the application, she aimed it at Lisa. "Ready?"

Lisa smiled and pushed a chair over to stand on, pretending to toss the salad like a head chef. "Hi, Tuc, I'm making dinner. I wish the war was over. I want you to come home. I miss you, Tucker." Lisa was waving to the camera and smiling when Marlo stopped the video.

Marlo sent the greeting to their oldest son and then placed the phone back on the counter. "Lisa, remember…Tucker is at sea on a big aircraft carrier. He's not exactly in a war," Marlo said.

Ed joined in, "Lisa, remember when we went and walked on the deck with all the airplanes before your brother and cousin Chet left?"

"Yeah." Lisa nodded, picking up the phone to play the video back.

Ed looked over her shoulder. "Your brother is going to love that, nugget."

Lisa laughed. "I miss him, Daddy."

As Ed glanced at Marlo, they shared the private worry they both held for their son, as well as Sam and Cara's son, Chet, who'd both joined the military after graduating from West Point.

"We do, too, honey."

Ed's brothers Roman and Logan each had a daughter just starting at West Point, so the military was certainly a background that the Savages were used to.

Putting the phone on the chair, Lisa went to the window to look out at the woodbin.

Seeing what she was doing, Ed grinned. "The snake's long gone, hon. He went home."

She shrugged her little shoulders. "I'm just making sure," she said, looking back at her father. "What time will Ava get here?"

Ed picked up the phone and placed it back on the counter. "Your sister will be here in a couple of days with everyone else. And she hates snakes too, so you can help calm her if she sees one."

Stomping her little foot on the floor, Lisa said, "Well, until she gets here, I'm not going *near* that woodbin."

Chuckling, Ed opened the refrigerator and looked inside, grabbing a beer.

Marlo looked over his shoulder. "I thought you put the wine in there. Or is it underneath?"

Closing the refrigerator door very slowly, Ed closed his eyes and sighed. "Oh, no."

Marlo put her hands on her hips. "You didn't forget it, did you?"

He paused. "I remember bringing it into the garage..." His voice trailed off. "Wait. Let me take a look." Placing the unopened beer on the counter, he exited the RV. Halfway down the side, he opened an underneath compartment where two ice chests were stored and opened them both. He sighed once again when he saw

the two containers filled to the brim with partially melted ice...
and nothing else.

Marlo stepped down from the RV, carrying plates to the table, with
Lisa following close behind. Seeing Ed and the empty ice chests, she
said, "No wine, huh? What did you do with it?"

"Ah shit, I forgot it in the garage."

"But I saw you carry it there when you were loading everything up."

"Yeah, I think Ava buried it under the clothes for the Salvation
Army. That was also when Sam called about the loans for the hotel and
housing project, and UPS delivered my new grill for the Challenger.
Sorry, hon, but I was distracted."

"You and that old car."

"It was more than the car. Ava clocked me when I tried to have a
father-daughter conversation about Jake. Why don't you call her and
have her bring it up? And I'll run back down to that store."

"So we'll be dining tonight with what? Boone's Farm strawberry
wine or some other hillbilly hideout moonshine?" Marlo shrugged.

Lisa looked up to her mother. "What's a hillbilly hideout?"

"It's where I met your mother," Ed said, shooting Marlo a mischievous look.

Marlo's mouth dropped; then she smiled. "Keep it up, Mr. Savage,
and it's going to be real cold for you tonight!"

Ed held up his hands in protest. "Wait! Can't have that! I'll be right
back!"

"Simon really should be up here by now. I hope..."

Ed interrupted her now-worried voice. Reaching out, he pulled
her into a hug. "I'll probably pass him on the way down. There's nothing to worry about; he's fine. I'll tell him to get his butt up here, or
we'll come back together," he said.

Marlo, with her head on Ed's chest, looked up at her husband. "I
love you," she said.

"I love you, too." Brushing her hair away from her beautiful eyes,
Ed planted a kiss on her lips.

Lisa was sitting in her child-size chair near the RV, pulling out the
doll with the porcelain face, when a rabbit appeared on the edge of
the woods. "Look, a bunny!"

Ed and Marlo watched their daughter jump up from her chair.

"I'll be back soon," he said, laughing as he watched his daughter sprint after the rabbit.

Lisa chased the bunny, which hopped its way around the RV, and Marlo followed after her. "Lisa, come back here and leave that rabbit alone."

Inside, Ed grabbed the Range Rover keys, leaving the RV keys in the ignition.

Stepping back outside, he picked up his daughter. "You help your mother, and I'll be right back, okay? And no chasing rabbits!"

Lisa stuck out her tiny lower lip and began to pout. "But I like the bunny; we can take him home," she said.

Ed shook his head. "We are not taking the bunny home."

"Uncle Sam was right; you're Edward Squidward."

Ed looked at this daughter and made a funny face. "Oh, I'm 'Squidward Tentacles,' am I? I'll show you how old Squidward takes care of naughty little nuggets." Ed started tickling her and raised her up high in the air like he was going to toss her into the twilight sky. Bringing her back down into his arms, he kissed her on the cheek.

Lisa hugged her father. "Yes, Daddy. No bunnies. I love you."

Ed responded with another peck on her cheek. Putting her down, he opened the SUV's door.

"Don't go, Daddy," Lisa said with sadness in her eyes.

Ed looked at his innocent child, and his heart filled with love. He kneeled down to her, and she hugged him. "I love you one more time," she laughed.

Ed patted her head and told her he loved her one million more times. Wearing a heartfelt smile, he stood up and got into the Range Rover, started it up, and looked over at Marlo. "Is there anything else we need?"

She held up her hand. "Wait a sec." Walking over to the SUV, she leaned in the driver's window and winked. Her voice and manner were alluring. "We've got plans after dinner…just wanted to let you know."

Ed's eyes lit up. "We do?"

"Right under the stars. Just like the old days," she said.

"Yee haw," Ed said with a mischievous smile, remembering the night they'd spent long ago in Santa Barbara. "Hold that thought, lady. I'll be back before you know it!"

Smiling, Marlo stepped away as Ed drove the Range Rover from the campsite and headed down the road. With his radio blaring and his voice happily singing along, Marlo knew her husband was in a great mood.

"I'm going to play, Mommy," Lisa said.

"Just stay close."

"I will."

As any six-year-old will tell you, whether it is light or dark…whether garter snakes are patrolling the area or not…finding a bunny is far more important than anything else in the world. Looking over at the woodbin, Lisa tiptoed to her dolls, picked them up with her backpack, and walked slowly to the edge of the woods to find the rabbit.

Lisa looked down the path and saw the movement of the small bush, and to her excitement, the rabbit hopped off. The radiant smile returned from her earlier pout, and she tried to catch the furry little creature, chasing after it with backpack and dolls in her hands.

Inside the RV, Marlo picked up her cell phone to call home. The coverage was so weak up in the thick forest that she moved to the front of the vehicle and adjusted the Wi-Fi in order to get a better signal. Looking outside at the beautiful waning twilight, she heard the click of the answering machine on the line.

"Ava, you're going to love it up here. It's beautiful. Just calling because your dad left the wine in the garage. It's buried under the clothes for the Salvation Army. Would you be a dear and bring it up with you guys when you come? I love you. Tell the family this is going to be great! 'Bye now. See you soon, and drive carefully."

Marlo hung up the phone and punched in Ava's cell. Wi-Fi adjustment couldn't help this time around, and with no luck, she hung up and rechecked dinner.

CHAPTER 6

s Ed parked the Range Rover at the little store, he opened the glove box and placed the gun back under the passenger seat next to him. He then reached over the seat and pushed the seat knob down to lower the seat over the gun. Getting out, he looked over to where the U-Haul had been earlier near the small garage on the property; the end of an old school bus was still sticking out from the open doors.

Closing his door and locking it with the remote, Ed entered the store, wondering why he hadn't seen Simon on the way down. There were people in line, and the woman they'd met earlier was behind the counter waiting on them; she looked up and smiled. Ed waved and grabbed a basket as he headed right to the wine section and spotted the chardonnay, transferring all the cold ones from the display to his basket. Just as he was about to head to the counter, he saw the bottles of Boone's Farm strawberry wine and grabbed one of those, too. Looking down at the label, he smiled.

When Patty finished up with her last customer in line, she greeted Ed with another smile. "So you did forget something."

Ed placed his basket on the counter. "Yeah, my bad. Oh, by the way, we didn't pay for the Band-Aids and peroxide you gave us earlier; go ahead and add it in now."

"Oh no, don't worry about it. It was the least I could do."

As Patty began to ring up the wine, Ed noticed that under the men's clothes she wore; the heavy, dark-framed glasses; her makeup-free face;

and long, salt-and-pepper hair pulled back under a scarf, she was an attractive woman. Beauty was definitely not something she dwelled on.

Patty then picked up the Boone's Farm strawberry wine and gave him a surprised look. "You're not serious with this, are you?" she asked.

Ed laughed out loud at her comment. "It's for the wife. Thought she'd get a kick out of it," he said.

With a shrug, Patty rang up the bottle and bagged it. "Well, you're in for a night, I'd say. With this gift and all."

Ed couldn't read her; was it sarcasm, or was she serious? "It's a joke," he added, eyeing the flowers on the counter. "Oh, by the way, do you have other flowers here?"

Ringing up the last bottle of chardonnay, Patty pointed behind him. "Against the wall near the end."

Ed glanced in that direction. "Thanks."

Walking back and grabbing some for Marlo, he turned to the counter, passing displays of potpourri and candy wrapped in gunnysacks of assorted sizes.

Patty's eyes followed him.

Ed saw Marlo and Lisa's favorite chocolate-peppermint candy and grabbed a bunch, bringing them to the counter. He then spotted the mustard pretzels he enjoyed and picked up a large bag. Patty bagged up his order and placed everything into a large gunnysack.

"One more thing, we've lost track of a family member since we've gotten here," Ed said, offering a smile, not wanting to make the woman uneasy. "I know this is a little far from the campgrounds, but I was wondering if maybe you saw the guy with us earlier or if he came back in here?"

Patty stood quietly, looking at him as if he were a bit of a lunatic.

Ed cleared his throat at the awkward silence. "Anyway...He's got his leg in a cast, using crutches. After we left here, we dropped him off at the rangers' information center."

Taking a moment, Patty finally nodded. "Yeah, there was a guy with crutches in here, asked about fishing."

Ed laughed. "I'm sure. He was really ready for that lake."

"Man just looked around and ended up buying some fishing line and some hunter's stuff."

"Hunter's stuff?" Ed questioned as he looked around the store.

Patty pointed to the display of fishing supplies and the small apparel section, where Ed saw the camouflaged items every local needed.

"Hmm…Did he say where he was headed?" Ed asked.

"No. He walked down the road. Looked like he was headed toward the lake. Do you want me to call a ranger to track him down for you? It's almost dark, and the man's leg might be really hurtin' him by now."

Ed shook his head and smiled. "Not a problem. Thank you. I'll be driving that way. Most likely I just missed him on the way down."

Patty remained silent as Ed turned to leave.

"Thanks a lot," Ed called back over his shoulder. "I'm sure we'll be seeing you again."

"Everyone always does," Patty said as the door closed behind him.

CHAPTER 7

Up at the campsite, the wind blew into the RV through the wide-open door, chilling Marlo to the bone. *It's cold up here for such a warm spell*, Marlo thought.

Looking up from the sink, she saw the trees blowing in the wind. Raising her voice, she leaned toward the open window and shouted, "Lisa, come inside; it's getting cold out."

Checking dinner, she closed the oven and looked out the open door. "Lisa, I said come in here," she yelled once more. Not hearing a sound from outside, Marlo moved to the door and searched for her daughter.

Stepping down from the RV, she looked to the table, where everything was still in its place. "Lisa, where are you?"

With no response, she walked to the end of the RV and spotted one of Lisa's dolls on the ground. As the wind blew against her back, goose bumps broke out on her skin, and she began to shiver. Rubbing her shoulders, attempting to warm up and not pay attention to the sudden hollow feeling of fear that was growing inside her gut, she called out again, "Lisa Marie Savage, stop playing around!"

No answer.

Marlo walked toward the main road and then stopped as absolute fear took over. About fifteen feet off the side of the road, Lisa's favorite porcelain doll lay in the dirt, as if her daughter had thrown it to the wolves.

Screaming at her own body to move, Marlo broke from the panic and ran to the doll. Picking it up and scanning every inch of road and forest she could see, she screamed, "Lisa! Lisa Marie!"

A branch snapped behind her. Whipping around and dropping the doll, hearing its face crack, Marlo wanted nothing more than to sigh in relief, but all she saw was the edge of the thick, darkening woods. With her voice breaking, she called into the darkness, "Lisa…? Is that you?"

Moving slowly toward the sound, Marlo began walking faster when she caught a muffled noise somewhere ahead; she suddenly thought that Lisa was hurt.

But…nothing.

All Marlo could feel the farther she walked into the trees was a set of eyes watching her, as if an animal was hiding behind a tree, waiting to attack and collect its dinner.

The fear was immense, and Marlo turned and practically raced back to the campsite. As she looked at the RV in front of her, the lights offered a warm glow through the windows, and the shadow of a figure was walking around inside. With a sigh of relief, Marlo could feel her heart rate begin to slow and return to normal. "Thank God."

Now that the "protector" in her had been silenced, Marlo felt the anger inside her grow. She marched to the RV and boarded. "Lisa Savage! Where have you been?" she yelled.

Silence.

She looked to the back of the RV. "Lisa, I saw you go in there. Hiding will not help you right now." Moving quickly, she swung open the bedroom door to see…nothing.

The sick feeling of worry was creeping back in. "This isn't the time for hide-and-seek," she said, her voice sounding like a whisper in her own ears.

As Marlo turned away from the bedroom, the bathroom door swung open with a loud crash, and a man burst out wearing a hunter's camouflaged hat and mask over his head. Marlo screamed as he grabbed her by the throat with one hand and covered her mouth with the other, pushing her into the bedroom and onto the bed.

She struggled, but the man's power was far greater than her own.

Panic. Surprise. Disbelief. *This is not happening.*

Marlo felt the fear grow inside her. Using that shot of adrenaline, she slapped the intruder, tearing part of the camouflage masking his face, and managed to kick him off balance to the floor. Getting up, she raced forward, trying to escape…trying to scream…trying to get away.

But she felt the arms enclose her from behind. Turning her around, the beast threw her to the floor, smashing her face into the glass coffee table and shattering it to pieces. Marlo rolled over, dazed. She tried to focus through the lines of blood that seemed to be running down her forehead and over her eyes, like a nightmarish waterfall.

She barely saw the movements as the figure pulled the black roll from his pants. She smelled the duct tape and tasted the chemicals as it was pulled across her mouth. Her hands were wrapped. Her head burned as she was pulled by the hair through the small hallway, picked up, and thrown back on the bed. A sharpened stick, what felt like the tip of a finely honed Bowie knife, met her skin as her shirt was pulled up from her waist, bringing forth warm droplets of blood. She struggled, and they both tumbled onto the floor next to the bed.

"Mommy!" came the scream from the distance through the open window.

The hunter pressed his hand over Marlo's mouth and nose, and Marlo's only thought was her daughter, so she played like she passed out.

When the hunter left the bedroom, Marlo watched in silence from her place on the floor. She could feel the blood still dripping, slowly, creating a warm line where the primitive weapon he'd used had torn her flesh.

She felt the breeze from the window. Her clothes were unbuttoned. The tape around her hands was slightly torn. She watched her attacker glance down at the blood on his hands and reach out, hitting the bathroom door with a loud bang.

She shut her eyes, and when she reopened them, Marlo watched him reach in to grab the towel her husband had used not that long ago. Ed's New York Giants cap was caught with the towel in the man's hand, and she watched him toss it to where Ed's jacket was on the sofa.

He wiped the blood from his hands and dropped it to the floor when they both heard her daughter call out for her mother again.

Lisa's voice sounded closer this time, and Marlo panicked, thinking her daughter was lost—but it would be worse if she came back now.

Hearing her daughter seemed to unnerve the man.

"They lost her," the man said to himself.

They? Marlo's blood froze as she thought, *There are* others.

As the man turned away from her, taking a few indecisive steps, he seemed panicked himself. She struggled to make out anything, any scar, a tattoo—*any* clue as to who the horrific creature was as he pulled the hunter's hat off and the torn camouflage masking came loose from Marlo's fighting. He pulled the remainder of the mask off, stuffing them into his pocket, and put on her husband's cap and jacket. But all Marlo could see was a mass of dark hair sticking to the skin on his neck where the sweat of his assault had taken its toll.

She wanted to get up, to scream out the window to see if anyone was walking by, anyone who could stop the man as he sat in the chair and turned the key that'd been left in the ignition. The RV came to life. Warning lights flashed, telling the driver that the slide outs were extended, and the vehicle should not be moved. Throwing the transport into reverse, the man with the Giants cap floored the machine, ripping it from its berth, backing it into something hard.

Marlo heard the smashing of camp gear and the scraping of the extensions against the trees. She could make out the awning as it came crashing down on the table outside. It felt as if the earth moved violently underneath her aching, bruised body. Marlo watched the contents of the RV begin to fall from the cabinets. The dishes, the groceries—everything flew onto the floor.

She needed to get out. She needed to find the strength to move, to defend herself. Her daughter was out there.

Marlo tore the tape from her mouth and started chewing on the bindings on her wrists, keeping her screams silent. The only way she could win was if he didn't know she was still a player in this nightmare.

CHAPTER 8

The weather report, coming through the speakers of Ed's radio before he tossed in the CD to shut the annoying man up, was for fierce winds and heavy rain. The reporter sounded like he was issuing the news with a smile on his face—happy that the excited campers would have a horrific night ahead and not the night under the stars they were hoping for.

The Range Rover lumbered across the small roads, heading back to site fourteen. Ed had done all he could to locate Simon, and as he stared up at the ever-darkening sky, with clouds slowly converging to cut off any light from the moon, he turned the corner.

He whipped the steering wheel, practically going off the road into the woods as he barely saw the lone motorcycle parked against the tree, left there by some idiot who apparently didn't care if his ride was turned into an insurance claim.

"Asshole," Ed muttered. Correcting his path, he headed back to his family, knowing that Simon, Marlo, and Lisa were most likely mad that dinner was on and he was late.

Reaching the even ground, Ed noticed the RV up ahead and slowed immediately. The huge machine rocked back and forth, as if caught in an earthquake that Ed could not feel. "What in God's name?"

CHAPTER 9

Marlo tore the last of the tape from her wrists and thought she heard the small, familiar voice outside the window. Was it her imagination?

Glancing out, she saw little Lisa, confused and scared, running in the dark down the road and directly at the RV. "Mommy, Daddy, where are you going?" she cried.

The man saw the little girl and flipped on the cruise control.

Eyeing a fallen frying pan, Marlo grabbed it. She stayed low, creeping up to the driver just as the headlights illuminated a deer in the road. The animal was so close to little Lisa, standing in the harsh brightness, completely afraid.

Marlo screamed out, "No!" Swinging the frying pan, she heard the violent connection with the right side of her attacker's head. Flying across the seat, the man hit the left side of his head on the driver's window. Marlo grabbed the wheel to turn the deadly transport away from her precious daughter.

But…It was too late. It was going too fast.

With the interior lights burning bright, the RV hit the deer, and as the man reached for her, Marlo heard her daughter scream. The RV sped across Lisa's backpack, crushing it, spilling her inhaler and all its contents across the road, and smashing a doll's head to pieces as the deer spun and landed half on the road and half in the woods, meeting his death on the path that would have led him to safety.

As the deer spun to the side of the road, barely missing Lisa, she tripped backward and fell down the small embankment, scratching and cutting herself on the ground as she rolled to the bottom. The little girl screamed for her father just as her asthma started up.

Sparks flew as the slide outs caught trees, and camping gear underneath the wheels grated against the road.

Marlo felt the grip of the man on her arm as she watched through the huge front window. She saw the horror play out as if it were a movie on a screen in front of her.

She saw the lights illuminate the drop-off.

The cliffs were there.

As if noticing the path of the runaway RV at the same time, the man pushed Marlo away from him and jumped out the RV's door. Marlo hit the far wall, falling to the floor as the RV went over the embankment. The hunter rolled safely into the brush just as the headlights from the Range Rover came dangerously close to the edge.

Ed stopped the Range Rover and ran to the edge to see the RV crashing down the steep embankment. The rig was rolling over and over until it finally stopped its deadly trip in a rock-and-dirt field.

He could hear the flying objects inside it hit against the now-shattered windows. And worse, he heard the familiar voice of the woman he loved screaming for Lisa.

Hearing his daughter's name, his heart dropped. Without thinking, Ed ran down the embankment, falling over steep boulders and going end over end, like the RV had just a moment before, cutting and bruising himself.

He was closer. He could hear Marlo, but Lisa's small voice didn't ring in his ears. That was when he saw the spark.

Marlo could hear the hiss. She could smell the gas.

Using everything her broken body had left, she desperately tried to climb from the front window that was now shattered; its glass decorating the land, and she heard him. The man she loved was calling out for her. The twisted frame kept her inside, and the only way out was the door. The oven caught fire, and it started to spread. Pulling herself up and out, crawling, attempting to stand on the side of the RV, Marlo moved to the edge just as the flames inside roared to life, exploding out the final window that was left in the completely twisted metal frame.

Screaming, she instinctively turned away covering her already bloody face as the gas line in the vehicle caught, and the ensuing explosion rattled in her ears. The power sent a side panel peeling back, hitting Marlo and blowing her off the RV.

The explosion stopped Ed in his tracks and the fell to ground.

He didn't get to her in time...and Lisa? He got to he feet as the thoughts made his soul erupt in flame, turning his heart to ash right along with the mammoth transport that had taken his family away from him.

Ed never had time to feel the rock that smashed into the back of his skull, knocking him out and sending his lifeless body rolling straight toward the fireball.

The hunter stood looking down at Ed and knew he was running out of time. Something had gone wrong. That damn little girl wasn't supposed to be there. The panic he had felt inside the RV when he heard her screaming was rattling in his head. He quickly took the jacket off and tossed it, along with the cap, closer to Ed, who lay unconscious atop the now-warm earth. The clean-shaven man smiled wide.

Wiping the sweat from his skin, attempting to catch his breath from the victory he'd attained, he hiked back up the steep cliff to the still-running Range Rover. A gift that'd been left for him as payment for all his hard work was his for the taking.

With the hunter's mask hanging out of his back pocket, he got in and drove back down the way they had come when his headlights spotted the deer. Quickly getting out, he spotted the girl's flattened backpack and spilled contents, including her broken iPod and an inhaler, as he went over to where the deer was and quietly looked down into the darkness.

The sounds of her gasping caught his ear.

CHAPTER 10

Nightmares were shared.

His gasping breath rang in his ears as the feeble old man urgently tried to make his way through the tall grass toward the bridge. Because of the abundant moonlight, he could see the figure standing there. It was an old woman dressed in an angelic white gown—long and flowing. She was calling out to him: "Nathan."

The old man stumbled and fell to the ground. He was frightened, yet he responded, calling back: "Marcie!"

He struggled as he managed to get back on his feet and look again at the bridge. The old woman was now farther across. Panic filled him. He worked up what energy he had left, trying his best to get to her, when a hand reached out through the tall grass and grabbed him. Turning, he screamed, seeing the hideous dead woman. Her face was decorated with shards of glass that stuck out from the gray, peeling skin. She was bleeding—her stomach was huge. Pregnant, she smelled of nothing but rotting flesh.

What looked like a twisted metal piece from the dashboard of an old car was emerging from her abdomen. She let go of him and stared over his shoulder. Following her gaze, he turned back toward the bridge, where a corpse of a man was now standing, blocking his way. His face was bashed in and scarred by burns. The wretched being pushed him back down to the ground.

The old man turned away and saw the child—the poor, innocent corpse that stood there. Wide-eyed and afraid, she gripped an old porcelain doll with a cracked face and wild hair with one hand while reaching out to grab him with the other.

He screamed out and crawled through the tall grass, managing to get to his feet one last time to see Marcie on the bridge calling back to him: "Why, Nathan? Nathan...why?"

His breathing became labored, and he clutched his chest. He took only a few steps toward her before rotting arms emerged from the ground beneath him; a cold, hard, muscular hand grabbed him and pulled with all its power. Falling backward, he turned his head to scream at the hideous, awful sight.

But no scream would come. It was him. The devil himself had him in his grasp. And judging by the eerie, sinister smile that adorned Satan's face, Nathan knew he was not about to let go, and when the evil one comes for a visit, he uses all his tricks.

Nathan Savage woke from his nightmare with a bloodcurdling scream, thrashing about in his bedroom, knocking over a photograph of his deceased wife, Marcie, onto the floor, and shattering the glass in its frame. He could no longer stand these dreams. Now a grandfather, after going through two heart attacks, Nathan could barely breathe at times. That was the reason. The fear. It was the only reason he'd chosen to come live with his son, Sam Savage, and his family.

Downstairs, his daughter-in-law, Cara, and her daughter, Heather, were in the kitchen. There were two caterers with them when they heard the terrifying screaming. Dropping what they were doing, they came running upstairs to his bedroom.

Cara reached the room first and saw Nathan sitting on the edge of the bed, holding the broken frame. "Dad, Dad! What is it?" she cried out. He was crying, and his hand was cut from the broken glass. He stared at the shard of glass as if in a dream, mesmerized by the sharp point sticking out from his hand.

Smartly dressed for school, this was not the sight Heather wished to see on such a big day. It was her birthday, a time for fun. But seeing her grandfather's injured hand, she forgot all that and gasped, "Grandpa! You're bleeding!"

Cara told her to grab a towel as she took the frame from Nathan's hand. "Dad, you're okay—just another bad dream," she said, trying to calm him. Cara placed the frame on the nightstand, and when Heather returned with a wet towel, she took it and wrapped Nathan's hand, being extra careful as she removed the glass from the wound.

Nathan rested his head against Cara and sighed. "I want to be with my Marcie."

The confession startled both girls, and they exchanged a disturbed look. Cara rubbed Nathan's shoulder, trying to shake him out of it. "Come on, Dad. Let's get you cleaned up." Able to get Nathan to stand on his still-trembling legs, Cara brought him into the bathroom to clean the cut.

The phone rang, startling everyone. Cara looked over her shoulder to Heather. She nodded and placed the broken pieces of glass from the frame on the nightstand, hurrying to her bedroom to grab the phone. The caller ID informed her it was her cousin, Ava.

"Hello."

"Happy birthday, Cousin!"

"Not really!"

There was a pause. "What's changed? I just left there."

"Grandpa had another bad dream."

"What happened now?"

"I don't know. Mom and I were downstairs talking about the trip, dealing with the caterers and all, when Grandpa started screaming from his bedroom."

"Is he all right?" Ava asked.

"I think so. Cut himself on some glass."

"I wish we knew what was wrong. He never talks about what makes him so scared," Ava said.

"I know. This sure killed my birthday buzz," Heather said, feeling a little deflated.

"Well, we're going to be late for school. I'm finished changing, and I'm coming back to get you."

Heather hung up the phone and went to the hall, pausing at the top of the staircase. She sighed as she looked down at the packed bags she had placed near the front door for what was supposed to be their fun trip to Black Ridge Falls.

CHAPTER 11

T he night in Black Ridge Falls had been eventful. The fact that the RV had crashed at a higher elevation, away from the rented lower campsites, didn't help the situation. By the time it was reported, it took longer than usual for responders to arrive.

By early morning it was buzzing with police, fire rescue, and paramedics. A tow truck was backed up to the point where the huge RV had gone over the mostly rock-and-dirt embankment. They were attempting to run cables down to the burned-out vehicle to try to pull it up. The fire was out now, thankfully; only some smoldering patches of ground remained for the firefighters to deal with. Police accompanied by their dogs were looking for any survivors, and a helicopter was in the distance helping from its perch up above.

Sheriff Arnie Mallard was interviewing Ned and Genie Barnes. The lawman was tall with dark hair, deep-set eyes, and a good start to a beard; he was sorely in need of a shave. Holding his pad, he looked over his notes and sighed. "One more time. Now, start over and tell me exactly what you saw."

Ned looked awful as he spoke briefly about meeting the lovely couple only yesterday, and now…this tragedy…He could feel nothing but shock. "Well, yesterday we went for a long hike. This whole section of the park was closed off when we got here. They had to move a tree that had fallen from high winds that was blocking the road. We decided to check out the other camping areas for our next trip up here. We met them at site fourteen."

Genie was equally distraught, speaking slowly and barely over a whisper. She nodded. "Site fourteen, that's where the rig was; they have the cutest little girl, spunky too, and that man in the Giants cap was looking for a guy on crutches," she said.

Arnie looked up from his notes. "Did you get the name of the man on the crutches?"

"No, they didn't mention his name," Ned said.

"Where again is your campsite?" Arnie asked.

"We're down in the lower level at number seven, but we have a clear view of the road back a ways," Ned answered.

"I know the spot." Arnie nodded, glancing to where Ned was pointing.

"Later on we heard a crash of some kind. That's when the rig raced by, lights inside blazing, on the open road back there. He was driving like a madman! What was his name, honey?" Genie asked, nudging Ned.

"Ed, like Ned—my name, remember?" he said.

"Yes, Ed was his name. Then he went right through the barriers toward the cliff. Then, well…You can see what happened from there." She swallowed hard.

Arnie looked at the couple intently. "There's no way you could see who was driving the rig from your campsite. Yes, you could see the rig, but not the driver. How are you so sure of what you saw?"

Genie looked to Ned, and he shrugged. Genie was even rethinking what they saw. "Sheriff Mallard, if it wasn't the guy we met earlier, then who else could it have been?" she asked.

Arnie looked from Ned to Genie. "That's a good question."

"Sure is," Ned answered. "All this seems a shame though—such a nice family and all."

From down below near the burned-out RV, another sheriff's dog started barking. Arnie moved away from Ned and Genie, carefully yet quickly, looking down the embankment to see what they'd found.

The dogs converged on a panel that'd been blown away from the vehicle. The sheriff watched his men lift the panel, but no one was there. He saw his officer shake his head. "Just a boot and some clothing," the officer yelled from below. As he dropped the panel, the dogs bolted left, barking wildly.

Going to investigate further, they found Marlo Savage. Standing in the woods against a tree, she was bleeding from under her hairline down her face; her clothes were torn, she was missing a boot, cuts and wounds showed, but…she was alive. Her facial expression was one of shock and desperation as she reached out to the officers and fell forward to the ground, passing out.

Completely stunned that any human could survive the tangled mess he saw, the sheriff shook the surprise from his mind and watched his officers turn her over and check her pulse. One of them soon turned and yelled up the embankment, "Medic! We have a live one down here!"

Hearing this, Arnie handed off the Barnes family to another officer, who had been questioning the woman from the station wagon at the gas station. A few feet away, the female ranger who had assisted the man with the crutches when the Savages checked in was talking with another officer. "Thanks, folks; just need to get some other information from you," he said. He then ran…fast, following the ambulance crew down to the woman who by all rights should have been dead.

Arnie paused briefly on his way down the embankment and glanced over at the other group of medics and officers who were placing a passed-out Ed Savage on a gurney and carrying him up to a waiting ambulance. Seeing the IV sticking out from the man's body, Arnie felt the chill once more. Yet again, he was completely shocked that another person had made it out of the wreck alive.

The others were working on Marlo; the first one grabbed his radio and barked orders into the mike. "Get that copter line down here now! Over!"

The helicopter pilot responded, "On our way. Over."

Arnie got to Marlo's side just as the helicopter arrived above them and sent down the cage. The ground crew worked at putting Marlo into it. They pulled her up, secured her, and flew off to the small local hospital.

"Sheriff!" Another officer yelled out over Arnie's radio. "You there? Over."

Arnie answered his radio. "I'm here. Over."

"We found something near the deer. Over."

"What is it? Over."

"You better make it over here when you can. Over."

Arnie moved carefully away from his men, and his heart dropped. The thought of the missing little girl's dead body chilled his blood. *The two most fragile*, Arnie thought to himself as he heard the helicopter in the distance. Taking off his hat, he said a silent prayer for the innocent.

Backing away, allowing the medics to load their gear, Arnie turned and just stared at the burned-out RV and shook his head in utter disbelief; then he made his way back up the embankment.

The male was identified as Ed Savage, and when he was being loaded into the ambulance, he woke to find himself handcuffed to the transport with blood on his hands and shirt, his vision blurred. He began pulling, fighting the bonds.

The officer with Ed, yelled over to Arnie, "He's waking up!"

Arnie's head was full; he had spoken with the woman from the gas station, who had heard the Savages arguing about something earlier when they pulled up for gas. This was before the accident, and then there was the report that he wanted to be in a *private* area of the park. Then there was what the Barns couple thought they saw. Something didn't feel right about all this, and he wondered what was coming next near the deer.

Sheriff Mallard rushed up to the ambulance, where the officer was holding several forensic-evidence bags; one held a bloodstained blue cap, another had a bloodstained inhaler, and the last had a torn, bloody scrap from a child's shirt. A second gloved officer was lifting long strands of hair from Ed's shirt and placing them into another forensic bag. "Sheriff," the first officer said, showing Ed's wallet and pointing to him, "it's that guy from those TV shows."

Arnie stared down into the wild, frightened eyes. "Marlo...Lisa... Where are they?" the man mumbled.

Arnie thought for a moment and then spoke. His voice was loud and gifted with the tone of authority: "Ed Savage, you have the right to remain silent..." Arnie stopped himself as he noticed Ed was out again.

"Get all his clothes in evidence at the station. I'm going to have a word with Mr. Savage when he wakes up," Arnie said, watching them load him into the ambulance.

Sheriff Mallard looked back at the scene below him. The brand-new and now destroyed recreational vehicle looked back at him, and it seemed to spite him. *Nobody spends that kind of money to cover up a murder,* he thought. *Of course, if he's some Hollywood crybaby, then anything's possible in this day and age.* He had a short time to hold him until charges could be brought, and Mr. Ed Savage had some questions he needed answers to.

Watching the ambulance drive away, he headed down the street to where the deer had been found. He dreaded what was waiting for him as he arrived by the side of the road.

"Down here," said the voice he had heard from the radio earlier.

Arnie made his way down to the officers collecting evidence and taking photographs. He was surprised when he saw nothing but blood splatters and torn child's clothing.

"Where's the girl?" Arnie asked, bewildered.

The officer nudged him and pointed to the bear tracks and one of the legs from the deer farther away from the blood splatters.

"Oh my God. No," Arnie said in shock.

CHAPTER 12

Ava pulled into the driveway of Heather's house in her red Audi convertible. There, the catering truck was parked on the street in front of the massive home, and a banner hung over the entryway that read, "Happy Birthday, Heather."

She got out from her car and was walking up to the house when the front door opened, and Heather appeared with a smile, moving her camping gear to the front porch. "Let me help you with that," Ava said, reaching for one of the bags.

Heather looked miles away in thought; she was obviously concerned about Grandpa Nathan. "Thanks," she muttered.

The cousins took the gear to the car, and Ava popped the trunk, squeezing one of Heather's bags in with hers. Seeing the full trunk, Heather paused. "I guess the backseat will do."

Ava opened the car door, and Heather placed the remaining bag in the backseat. The convertible top was down, making it easy. "We can drop these off at Nash's and just make class," Ava said.

As they stepped into the car, Ava could barely hear the phone begin to ring inside the house.

CHAPTER 13

Inside the Black Ridge jail cell, Ed woke up logy, not knowing where he was. His head was bandaged, and the pain was almost unbearable. "Marlo! Marlo!" Ed shouted, as he looked around and suddenly realized his surroundings and different clothes. "What the hell? Where am I? Why am I here?" he yelled. Trying to stand, he fell back to his bunk, rubbing his head.

Arnie got up from his desk and made his way back to the cells. The sheriff's office was an old-time station. From the front counter, you could see all the way back to where the jailbirds, usually the locals who had decided a drunken Saturday night was necessary, were being held.

Ed looked up at the man in uniform. "Why am I here, and where are my wife and daughter?"

Arnie paused a moment, thinking. "Mr. Savage, how are you feeling?"

Ed was sitting on the bed and started to stand, but he got a little wobbly and stayed seated. "Terrible, my head hurts like a…" He trailed off. "What am I doing here? Where's Marlo and Lisa?"

Arnie looked directly at him. "You don't know why you're here?"

Ed, being confused, hurt, and at a loss, raised his voice. "No, I don't know why I'm here!" When the sheriff didn't flinch, Ed tried to calm down and grasp his thoughts. "My wife…the flames…Where are my wife and daughter? Where is Simon? Would you *please* explain to me what I'm in here for?"

CHAPTER 14

On their way to their creative-writing class, Ava and Heather stopped at their lockers to get their books when their other cousin, Roman and Gabby's daughter, Danni Savage, came running up to them with gossip to share. She was still wearing her cheerleader outfit but wasn't as stuck-up as the rest of them. She tapped Heather on the shoulder. "She's back!" she said with a smirk.

"Who's back?" Heather said.

"Lucy! She was at our morning squad meeting and practice," Danni said.

"Did she spill?" Ava asked.

"Oh, yeah, girl spilled. I'm not going to spoil it 'cuz I know you have her in your next class. Just wanted to give you a heads-up." Danni winked.

"Thanks, can't wait to find out her side of things," Heather said, closing her locker. "By the way, I'm sorry you're not going camping with us."

Danni tucked her long hair behind her ear. "Yeah, Chase and I really wanted to go, but Mom and Dad planned a trip to visit Mom's family. Trust me, Chase and I have begged forever to go. But...not going to happen," she said with a deep sigh.

The bell for class rang, and Ava shut her locker. "You're coming to Heather's birthday party though, right?" she asked.

Danni nodded. "Oh yeah, grandparents or not, I'll be there."

"Great, see you then," Heather said.

The cousins hugged, and Danni rushed down the hall to get to her next class.

Walking in the opposite direction, Heather turned to Ava. "I would be totally pissed if I caught Nash with another girl!"

Ava side-eyed Heather with a grin. "I bet you would. But seeing that he's scared of you, I wouldn't worry about that."

When they arrived at the classroom door, they were laughing. Seeing Lucy sitting at their table with Mia, they walked over. On the blackboard was written: "Your life to music."

The cousins looked to each other with a sarcastic smirk. "Oh, this should be fun," Ava muttered.

Sharing a chuckle, they joined their friends.

Lucy Adams was the most popular girl in school and spoiled rotten at home. She had long, blonde hair and was the lead cheerleader everyone either loved or hated. Mia, on the other hand, had been a friend since middle school, a pretty girl from Colombia who'd somehow kept her accent after living here for quite some time.

The girls huddled, catching up, when their teacher, Mr. Wilder, entered the class and shushed the students. Lucy, who had a crush on the guy, like everyone else, sat down and watched the stud place a brown paper bag on his desk. Her attraction to older men was a thing of wonder, and when the Savage cousins' uncle Logan visited from across the pond, she always found an excuse to hang out—at their house. The things she fantasized letting their uncle do to her were indeed wild, but then again, so was Lucy.

"Mr. Wilder," Lucy said, loving the way his hairy chest was showing above his top button, "I know I've been gone a week, but are we still trying to write our poems into a song?"

"Good guess, Lucy. And you're first. Come on up and pull a music genre from the bag."

Lucy hated this class but took it to be in *his* class, and she went and dramatically pulled out a small piece of paper from the bag. "Really! A breakup song!"

The whole class roared, knowing Lucy had been out for a week due to a teenage drama involving her boyfriend and getting her parents to take her shopping in New York City.

Having heard the gossip, Mr. Wilder got the class to quiet down. "Lucy, if you want, you can pick another."

Thinking for a moment, Lucy changed her mind. "Screw it! I've got a song to write. God knows, I have enough fodder for it."

Watching her return to her seat, Mr. Wilder picked up the bag. "Okay, Lucy, Mia, Heather, and Ava, your group will work on that one. Now who wants to go next?"

CHAPTER 15

S heriff Arnie Mallard was conflicted with the entire case. Ed Savage's story never changed, not once during the entire inter-rogation. They had issued a warrant for the guy with the crutches, Simon Winchester, and Arnie even did some checking on Ed's ver-sion of the story. He hated playing the bad cop while questioning Ed, watching the pained look in his face as he answered the questions. No, his gut was telling him something wasn't right; he only had to wait for the test results to be sure.

All Ed could think about was his lost daughter alone in the woods without him. He couldn't explain how her inhaler wound up on his body when they found him, or her hair. And he wouldn't believe she was gone. He needed to get out of there and find her. He needed to go to the hospital and see Marlo. And where the hell was Simon? His mind ached with the ugly accusations thrown at him during the ques-tioning, and the horrific reasons why he was suspected of the crimes haunted him. Being caged and unable to search for his daughter, Ed Savage felt he was losing it. The pain in his head was throbbing, and no one would believe him or at least say they believed him. And as the anger and frustration built, the adrenaline spiked, doubling the pain. A paramedic was called, and they sedated him.

But he was still lying in his cell with his mind racing. He wanted his family. This had to be a nightmare…a bad dream. He couldn't keep his thoughts straight, and he finally drifted off. All he wanted was the darkness. All he wanted was to remember the good things that life actually had in it...the days when things were nothing but right. He thanked God he had been able to get through to his brother, Sam Savage.

CHAPTER 16

Ed Savage's acting career had started in school. He and some friends
went down to London on a weekend, where they saw a play and Ed
fell in love with the lead. A week later he saw an advertisement for
auditions for an upcoming play, and the rehearsals just happened to
be held on his days off from school. So he auditioned and got the part.
He met the girl, and they dated for a while. The relationship didn't
last, but the acting did, and Ed loved it. He loved life.

Graduating from Cambridge and coming home, Ed kept the acting bug with him when he'd joined the family business. But Nathan
Savage, his father, threw him to the wolves. Ed was given a high-ranking
title and started like a pro. Turned out, the only problem with "Daddy
dearest's" plan was that the wolves had actually liked him.

The project the family had had in the works was about halfway
complete when Ed finished school, and his father counted on the fact
that Ed, coming in as a higher-management officer, would ruffle a
few feathers. But not when it came to Ed: he knew how dear, old Dad
played the game just from growing up Savage, and he immediately put
his own plan in gear, befriending everyone at the company. He did it
not out of fear of not being able to do the job but because that was just
Ed; showing up his father was an added bonus.

A little over a year and a failed marriage later, Ed grew restless in
the business and Nathan noticed. And when the project he was working on was nearing completion, his dad told him to take some time off,
because the next job would be bigger. He did just that.

Never being the sit-around type of guy, he got bored three days into vacation time. It was that third day when he saw the article in the paper, just like the one he'd seen at Cambridge. A movie was being shot in town, and they were looking for extras. The open auditions were scheduled for the very next day.

He'd shown up at the hotel that morning and felt the excitement when he spotted the sign directing all the future "Meryls, Harrisons, and Denzels" to the banquet rooms. He followed along and came to the short line at the reception table.

By the time he got called to the table of three interviewers, the line behind him had grown. The casting subordinate he was directed to, Stacey McDaniel, asked him a few questions about his background— any acting gigs, his work schedule, anything and everything to see if he had the time free needed for filming, and if he had any knowledge of construction, which was part of the movie story line. He smiled wide, giving her a quick narrative of his accomplishments.

Sitting at the table in the center was the casting director, Carrie Archer. She was staring at the person who'd been in front of her talking, but her ears were listening to everything Ed was saying. When the man in front of her was finished, she smiled and sent him toward the banquet rooms. Carrie did not call another person from the line; instead she pulled out a script and circled a supporting character. Then when Ed was finished and sent to the banquet rooms, she huddled with the other two casting subordinates.

When Ed opened the banquet-room doors, he was stunned by just how many Meryls and Denzels were actually in there waiting. He moved over to the wall and leaned against it, rethinking the whole situation. Just as his mind turned to dreams of traveling someplace else for a few weeks of exploring, Carrie Archer tapped him on the shoulder.

"Mr. Savage? I'm Carrie Archer, casting director. May I have a word with you?"

Ed recognized her only as the woman sitting in the middle seat at the table. People nearby stared; the looks on their faces were a combination of smiles and frowns, from "Look at me" to "Who the hell is that guy?"

Carrie led Ed out of the room toward the reception table, stopping halfway there and handing him her card. "I hate cattle calls as much they hate waiting," she said.

Ed smiled and took her card.

"So…Ed, I'll cut right to it. I don't waste time. I have a part I want you to audition for. We have rented offices over at Bigelow Tower. Do you know it?"

He certainly did know *that* building. Jacob Bigelow and his unscrupulous sons were his family's biggest competition, and one son, Jeremy Bigelow, was no friend of Ed's. "Yeah, I know exactly where it is."

"Good. Be there tomorrow at one o'clock; wear jeans and a dark-colored T-shirt, not white, and don't shave. Oh, and don't bother going back in there. Enjoy the rest of your day, Ed Savage." Carrie ended the conversation with a smile. She returned to the reception table, where the people in line were all watching in awe as Ed walked past them grinning like a schoolkid with his first big crush.

That had been Ed's big break. He got the part and started getting acting roles over the years. Leaving the family business, he moved to Hollywood, which was harder than he'd first thought. He could have used his savings, and the family money was also there, but he wanted to make it on his own, so he'd taken some waiting jobs to make ends meet. That was when he'd met Marlo. She was a bartender waiting on her career to take off as well; it was meant to be.

Ed found another acting gig and quit the restaurant. Once the gig was over, however, it was back to work. As summer was in full swing, there were not a lot of waiting jobs to be found.

The satellite college near his apartment needed teachers for summer school. Ed, who had a knack for explaining things, took the job and loved it. There was just one new wrinkle: Marlo was pregnant with their first child, who became Tucker, or "Tuc" for short.

Ed was ecstatic. He was head over heels in love with Marlo, and she was with him, *just* him: not his family or the money, none of it. And he wanted to give her the best.

He had mentioned his family's business but never said just how big it was—again, that was just Ed, never one to brag. The restaurant and teaching work wasn't enough, and the acting gigs were unreliable, so Ed, with his pregnant new wife, returned home, back to the family business.

It was a year later that he got another big break after doing a shaving-cream commercial buck naked in the snow. His agent, Rachel Shepherd, had to talk him into it, and it paid off big. Ed was a buff guy to begin with, and the commercial had a black bear in it looking at him like he was crazy. The ad was focused on the "best shave in the coldest of climates" and offered up a split-second shot of both the animal and his "bare" side…which made his star status rise.

He got noticed and called on to star in a cop show called *Badges*. Now, in his early fifties, and looking a bit younger than his age, his rugged looks remained. The lines had gotten a little deeper, but he still was as handsome as ever. Ed ended up with several shows running in an arc at this time. They didn't have as many episodes as a regular series, but when one would end, another would begin.

He became the narrator for a show called *Savage Mysteries*, where he explained old crimes that spanned the decades, to an ever-growing fan base. A second special, which ran in a limited number of episodes and educated people on various careers, was called *Savage Life*. A cold-case mystery show called *Savage Cases* was also part of his repertoire, where he investigated cases from around the world, interviewing actual witnesses and sometimes finding new evidence to help in solving open cases. Ed also had a brand-new special in the works called *Savage Past*, which was a little darker than his family learning show that kids and parents loved, *Archive Raiders*, which aired on Sunday evenings.

Ed had built his life into a mirage of fun and entertainment. And although other shows had gone out of production, he still grasped a very full plate. His early years in TV after leaving the family business had offered him several movies, and he grabbed them with both arms, loving it, until the travel became too intense. At least that was what he'd told Marlo.

The year of that shaving-cream commercial was also the year his past had caught up to him.

CHAPTER 17

Ava and Heather drove home, talking about the songwriting assignment.

"It was actually pretty fun working together on that song," Ava said, glancing over when Heather's phone whistled like a bird, alerting her that she had a text from Mia.

Heather pulled out her phone and laughed while reading the message out loud. "Mia and Lucy just changed the lyrics; listen to this:

Have you been wrong before?

Could you be wrong now?

I stand here for you, right here.

I'm not going to ask.

How could you believe?

So strong and not look back.

I'm here for you, when you're done being you.

I'm here for you."

Ava passed her house on their way to Heather's; she loved living up the street from her relatives. She glanced over at her cousin. "That sounds good," she said, looking back to the road just as the catering truck and a police car passed them by. "Wasn't that the same truck that was at your house this morning?" she asked.

"Maybe they forgot something," Heather said, sending Mia a text.

Ava pulled into the driveway next to a light-blue Bentley and noticed that the "Happy Birthday" banner was gone from the front of the house. The front door stood wide open.

"Hey, something's wrong. What's Aunt Maura doing here?" Heather said, looking back to Ava. "She was supposed to be on her way to London."

Heather put her cell phone back in her purse as her voice turned worried. "I hope Grandpa is all right."

The cousins got to the open door and saw Cara's identical twin sister, their aunt Maura, carrying a tray to the kitchen. "Aunt Maura!" Heather and Ava both said, wide-eyed with wonder as their aunt broke a smile and addressed them in her calming British accent. "Hello there, girls."

As she carried the tray into the kitchen and placed it on the counter, the girls followed, and on the far side of the kitchen, they saw Cara on the phone, standing next to a framed newspaper article titled: "Vanderran Sister Takes Crown."

The headline was from her and her sister's life from years back. One twin sister, Maura, was wearing a crown and holding flowers; Cara was standing close by with tears of happiness, and their third sister, Zolie Vanderran, was also featured. The "British Babes," as they were once called in the tabloids, were all smiles.

The Vanderran sisters were quite the act to follow growing up in London. Hitting all the right parties and being seen out with the royals, these socialites were like a modern-day version of Hollywood's Gabor sisters. The Vanderrans were always in the tabloids with the men they dated, and when the twins married Savage brothers, it was quite the headline.

Zolie Vanderran was a successful writer of steamy romance novels and had acted in a few movies in her youth. Now on her fifth husband whom she remarried, an international construction tycoon, and countless novels later, she was finishing up a book tour to start a new venture planned with her sisters. They were opening a hotel in the States, along with a housing development, with the Savage family company.

Cara was listening intently on the phone, and when she saw the girls, she shot them a serious look.

Heather noticed the undisturbed bed tray from her grandfather's room and looked to Maura. "Aunt Maura, what are you doing here? I thought you were going to Aunt Zolie's wrap party in London."

Maura was facing away from the girls toward her twin, who wore a grave look on her face. Trying to alter her own nervous look, she smiled at the girls. "Come here and give your aunt a hug," she said.

Heather and Ava moved into Aunt Maura's open arms as she whispered, "I'm afraid Aunt Zolie's wrap party is going to have to wait." She then reached over to the tray to clear it.

"What happened to the banner? Where did the caterers go?" Heather asked, eyeing both her mother on the phone and a very oddly acting Maura. She took an uneasy step back toward the counter, wondering what the anxiety was that was building around them.

Hanging up the phone, Cara moved next to her sister. She looked to Maura and turned a shade of white as if she were about to faint.

Maura grabbed her, and Heather grabbed her other side, walking her from the kitchen to the great-room sofa. "Mom, are you all right?" a frightened Heather asked.

"No, I'm not all right," she replied, reaching up to rub the side of her face. "I feel flushed; can you get me some water?"

Ava, being the closest to the kitchen, turned to get a bottle of cold water and rushed back into the room. "Here, Aunt Cara," she said, handing it to her.

After taking a long, slow drink, Cara placed the bottle on the side table and looked up at Heather. She then looked to Ava with hurt shining in her eyes. "Oh, honey...I'm so sorry," she said.

Ava immediately got chills and could feel the weight of the room closing in on her.

Heather looked to Ava and back to her mother. "Sorry about what, Mom? You're scaring us. What's wrong?" she said, raising her voice.

"Girls, I want you to sit down. Something terrible has happened," Cara said.

Maura moved between the cousins and placed her hand on Ava's shoulder as Ava sat in the chair. "Is it Grandpa? Is he okay?" Ava asked.

"Your grandfather is fine."

At that moment, Sam Savage opened the front door and saw everyone there. His face fell, and he rushed to Ava's side. "Oh, Ava, I'm so sorry."

"About what?" Both cousins raised their voices in fear.

Cara looked to her husband. "Sam, they just got home. I was about to tell them."

"Oh God, give us strength," Sam said, letting out a breath as he moved to take Ava's hand. "How do I say this?" He paused. "Your parents...There's been some kind of accident. We don't know everything yet, but your sister is...well, your sister...Lisa is missing, and it doesn't look good, honey. There's reason to believe she may be...dead."

Ava could feel her throat close; it was as if the announcement were choking her to death. "What?"

Heather was just as stunned as she looked to her father. "What about Uncle Ed? Aunt Marlo? Are they..." She trailed off.

"No. Girls, look, we don't have all the facts yet," Sam said.

Sam pulled a shocked Ava up and into his arms, hugging her and trying to turn the now-pale girl warm.

Cara stood and hugged Heather. The news was horrifying for everyone. Maura sat on the arm of an overstuffed chair looking like she was doing all she could to stop the tears in order to be strong for Ava.

Ava barely felt her uncle wipe the tears from her cheeks; then he spoke. "Ava, your mom is in the hospital. She's in an induced coma to keep the swelling in her brain down. We don't know much more than that." Sam's eyes were wet as Ava stared into his face.

Her heart broke in half. "No! My God! No no no!" Ava's knees weakened, and she felt her uncle Sam place her down carefully into the chair. "What about my...What about Dad?" Ava cried out, looking up at him.

"He's all right. He has a head injury, but he's fine."

Heather's face was one of total shock, looking from her mother to her father. "But where is he? And where's Uncle Simon?" she asked.

Cara and Maura exchanged a disturbed look, and they both stared at Sam; Ava caught the strange movements. "What aren't you telling me?" Ava's raised voice raised the temperature in the room.

Her uncle touched her chin and looked directly into her eyes, searching for the words to tell her as gently as he could. "Believe me; I don't know what happened to Simon. I'm waiting to find out more. I told the police to have my brother call me back when he wakes up."

"The police? Don't you mean the doctors? Oh God, what else is it…Uncle Sam? What? What did my father say? We need to get there right away. *Please*, let's go now!" Ava shrieked, becoming distraught as the feeling of secrets and lies came over her.

"No one is going up there," Sam raised his voice. "It's just not a good idea right now."

"Why not, Dad?" Heather's voice had turned demanding. "Aunt Marlo is in the hospital. We have to. And why are the police calling? Where is Uncle Ed?"

Sam moved from Ava to his daughter. "He's…Ed's in jail," he said.

Heather was speechless. Ava stopped crying for a moment, absorbing the new piece of information. "Why is my dad in jail?"

As she looked over her family members, Ava knew that they were just as confused as she was. They simply did not know the truth, except what they had been told on the phone.

Sam's shoulders dropped. "A man named Sheriff Mallard called, and all we know is there was some accident up there last night. They said there's reason to think Ed may have had something to do with it," he continued. "I was then able to speak with Ed; he doesn't know how all this happened, and he's refusing to believe Lisa is gone. None of this is making any sense."

Ava went to her bag and pulled out her phone. "Give me their number; I'm calling my dad."

Sam's mind raced, knowing he had to tell them Ed's side of what had happened as he reached out to pull her to him. "Honey, your father was hit on the head, and he's out. I just called back a little while ago, and they said they would call me as soon as he's awake."

Ava backed away from him. "What about Simon? He went with them. Where is he?"

"Simon did go with them? Marlo didn't mention anything about that," Cara said, as she shot her husband a confirming look.

Ava nodded. "Yeah, he wasn't sure he wanted to go at first. They picked him up on the way there."

"Ava, Simon's missing as well; no one has seen him up there except when they checked in. Didn't he break his leg…or ankle?" Sam asked, wondering where he could be.

"Yes, he did, but I hadn't seen him since his surgery. But Mom said it would be good for him to get out and breathe the fresh air. I know they were supposed to pick him up."

"Dad, if this happened last night, when did they call?" Heather asked.

"Black Ridge police called this morning after you two left for school."

Ava turned to the window and looked outside at the Mercedes convertible that tore up the driveway with music pumping so loud it rattled the windowpanes. Nash Ryland was driving with his buddy, Noah, and Noah's girlfriend, Mia. He parked behind Ava's Audi next to the sparkling new RV Sam had left in the driveway on the other side of Ava's car.

As the music spread, Heather looked to the front door. "Oh no, they're here."

"The party is cancelled! I called Roman and spoke with Gabby to let them know," the tear-stained Cara informed Heather as a new thought occurred to her. "My God, it's going to be on the bloody news! I almost forgot. We need to call Ed's agent. And the studio. His new show premiers in a few weeks, and the promos are already airing. The press is going to be all over this," she said in a panic.

"I'll take care of calling Ed's agent," Sam interrupted, just as Ava turned a shade greener.

"Oh, I think I'm going to be sick. Aunt Maura," Ava said, clutching her stomach.

Maura took Ava's arm; she and Cara led her to a bathroom when the doorbell rang.

"I can't," Ava whispered.

"I'll handle this," Heather said, moving to the door.

The door swung open, and Heather stepped in front of her friends in order to stop them from coming inside. Stepping out on the porch, she closed the door behind her.

"There's my girl," Nash said, pulling her to him and trying to plant a big birthday kiss on her lips. Without saying anything, Heather saw that he noticed her red eyes and shocked expression. He backed up a step.

Mia noticed her disheveled look as well. "So what happened since class? Didn't get home soon enough for some quality mirror time?" she joked sarcastically.

Heather glared at Mia. "Zip it! This is serious!"

Mia's face turned to one of complete concern. "Sorry," she said.

Heather's boyfriend, Nash Ryland, was a football hunk with bushy hair and a smile that wouldn't quit—an eighteen-year-old from another wealthy family the Savages had known for years. "Heather, sweetie, what's wrong?" he asked.

"I was only joking," Mia said, now looking a bit guilty from her earlier comment.

Noah pulled Mia back slightly. "Easy there, Mia. Give her space," he said.

"I'm sorry," Heather blurted out with a look of panic. "Everything has happened today. Everything bad! My cousin, Lisa…She's missing, and they think she's dead. And my aunt and uncle are hurt, and we don't know what happened except some…accident. We just now found out."

Nash's eyes widened. "What? Where?" he asked.

Heather looked to him. "At that camp where we were all going after my party," she said.

Mia stepped forward and hugged Heather close. "Oh, Heather, I'm so sorry."

The teens clung to each other as the door opened, and Sam appeared on the porch.

Nash looked to Sam. "Mr. Savage, we're real sorry. Is there anything we can do?" he asked.

Sam motioned to the teens. "Come inside for a moment," he said. Inside, they saw Cara helping Ava onto the sofa. Maura was bringing a fresh washcloth, which Cara took from her sister, wiping her niece's forehead. Ava saw them, and she started to tear up as they gathered around.

Sam attempted to hide the pain as he looked at the startled faces of the teens. "Okay, the party today is canceled, of course. And as far as going to Black Ridge Falls tomorrow, that's canceled, too. Nash, I tried calling your parents, but I can't reach them. Where are they?" he asked.

"They left to run some errands before the trip. I noticed my dad left his cell on the kitchen counter, so you should call my mom," he said.

"I'll do that. I wanted to tell them the news and that you can't take the trip up there alone," Sam said.

"Why not?" Nash objected. "I mean, shouldn't we get Ava up there to be with her parents?" The teens exchanged looks as Sam stood silently, searching for words.

"Look…just know this. We're not all going up there right now. I'll take Ava myself when it's safe. But for now, for the rest of you kids, it's best if you all go home."

"Safe?" Ava said, taking the washcloth from her forehead. "What does that mean, *safe?* Uncle Sam?" she said.

Cara looked to her husband with a grave gaze.

"Sorry to be so cryptic," Sam said to his niece. "I'm waiting for a call from that Sheriff Mallard. Now, you kids should head on home. Heather, I want you to stay here with us," he added.

The teens moved toward the door, and Sam led them out.

"We're real sorry, Mr. Savage." A sullen Mia looked at him and then turned to Heather's mom.

Cara nodded. "Thank you."

Nash moved to Ava on the sofa. "Ava…oh, Ava," he said, putting his hand on her shoulder.

Heather could see that her father's patience was wearing thin, and she walked up behind Nash. "Come on, I'll walk you out."

On the porch they could see Noah and Mia getting in the car; there was a big present sitting in the backseat. Heather turned to Nash. "Whatever that is, I don't want it. Please take it back; I can't deal!" she said, close to tears.

Nash pulled Heather to him and wiped her face. "Okay, okay, just call me later. I have an idea…but I'm not sure yet, so call me."

Heather looked up to him, and he hugged her tighter. "Don't forget. Call," he said.

CHAPTER 18

The Ryland home wasn't as large as either of the Savages'; nonetheless, it was definitely upscale, just on a smaller footprint. Nash, Noah, and Mia pulled into the driveway and stared at the RV parked there. It was not as new as the Savages', but not that old either.

Just as they were getting out of the car, Jake Riker pulled up in his BMW convertible. His music was on, and he was in a great mood, until he noticed the group's somber attitude. He parked behind them, shutting off the music.

Jake Riker looked much older than his age and spent most of his free time at the gym or playing football with the guys. He thought he could have any girl he wanted but was head over heels for Ava.

Jake got out and walked up to them. "Where's Ava? I thought you were going to go get her and Heather. What's going on?" he asked.

"Life sucks for the Savages big-time!" Mia said, looking at the birthday present in the back of the car.

"Would you please shut up? God, where is your heart?" Nash said, slightly pissed off.

Turning, he looked up at the window of the RV and spotted his eleven-year-old brother, Eric. He was yet another who was in love with Ava; he had a secret crush on the girl. As he moved away from the window, Nash knew he was most likely listening from inside.

Irritated and confused, Jake interrupted the group. "Would someone please tell me what's going on?"

Noah, who was a little disappointed with Mia, looked to Jake. "Ava's family was in some kind of accident. Her little sister is missing, and they think she's dead," he said.

Wanting to speak, Mia added, "Yeah, and something really creepy must have happened, too; otherwise Heather's dad wouldn't have been so mysterious."

"What did he say happened?" Jake asked.

"That's it; he didn't. Just some accident, and Mr. Savage told us it's not safe to go up there," Mia replied.

"I'm going over there," Jake said, getting back in his car.

Watching Jake back out the driveway, Noah turned to Nash. "What do you think happened?" he said, pulling his backpack from the car.

"I don't know, but I say we go up there and check it out," Nash said.

Mia's eyes widened. "Mr. Savage will totally kill you!" she said. "He looked seriously creeped out over something back there, and did you see Mrs. Savage? She looked really scared."

Mia noticed a small movement inside the RV behind them and saw Eric's face plastered to the screen. "I think we have company," she said, motioning over to the window.

"Okay, little spy, out!" Nash said, quickly opening the door and causing Eric to stumble. But Nash, being the protective older brother, caught him and broke his fall.

Eric was holding a photograph of their gang and quickly stuffed it into his pocket. He didn't want them to see the small heart he'd drawn around the love of his life's face. "Is Ava okay?"

Nash was about to close the door when he saw the TV inside the vehicle. On the screen a banner ran across the bottom that read: "Accident at Black Ridge Falls."

"Quick, listen to this!" Nash yelled, rushing into the RV to turn up the volume.

As they piled into the RV, a TV reporter with blonde, highlighted hair, Wendy Storm, was standing at the remains of campsite number fourteen, where everything appeared to have gone to hell.

"This is all that remains of number fourteen. As you can see, what started as an outdoor family adventure turned into a nightmare that no family should endure. What we know is that a couple with a daughter approximately six years of age, and another man, pulled into the campgrounds yesterday in their recreational vehicle. By nightfall something so sinister had happened that this family was torn apart. Their vehicle was ripped from its campsite. What you see behind me are the awnings that came down from the RV as it pulled out."

Nash and the gang were shocked.

The cameraman moved the camera from Wendy's fake, overly concerned face to show more of the site before coming to rest back on the reporter. "We do not have names as of yet, but we do know the father is in custody, and his wife is lying at Pine Crest Hospital; no word yet on her condition." Wendy then put her hand to her ear, paused a moment, and seemed to listen to her earpiece. "Correct that. I'm just now getting a report from the hospital. The wife is in a coma but stable." She continued, "The little girl may have been lost in this tragic event. It has been stated that the RV hit a deer and possibly her as it sped away from the campsite. The RV then went through a railing and plunged over a cliff down an embankment, bursting into flames. The little girl is unaccounted for, and police are not giving out any further information at this time."

The footage was now showing the burned-out area where the RV had come to a rest. The towing cables were still there, as they had not yet been able to get the vehicle up to solid ground. The burned-out RV looked haunting beyond words.

Wendy continued, "The other man apparently had a cast on his left leg and is at this time missing. More on this breaking story as it unfolds. This is Wendy Storm, reporting live from Black Ridge Falls."

The news station told viewers to stay tuned for their local and national weather, and Nash turned off the TV.

Eric was scared and looked up at his brother. "Who was the other man, Nash? The one in the cast?"

"I don't know," Nash replied.

"You're not still thinking about going up there?" Noah asked, rubbing Mia's shoulders.

"I have to talk to Heather and Ava first, but...Yeah, I want to check this out," Nash said.

Mia was scared. "I have a bad feeling about all this."

CHAPTER 19

In the middle of the block between the Savage homes, Sam was walking over to his brother's house when Jake passed him by. Jake stopped the car and backed up to him.

"Mr. Savage, I just heard. Are you okay?" he asked.

Sam glared at him. "No, Jake! I am not okay!" Sam said. His shoulders immediately sagged, and his head fell as he looked back at the boy. "I'm sorry."

"I understand, sir. I'm sorry, too. Do you want a ride?" Jake asked.

"No, I'm just going over to Ed's. Go on, Ava will want to see you," Sam said.

Jake nodded and shifted the gearshift, driving down the street and parking where Nash's Mercedes had sat a short time ago.

When he knocked, Cara opened the door. "Sam, did you...? Oh, I'm sorry," Cara said. "Jake, come on in."

"Thank you, Mrs. Savage." He paused. "I am so sorry about... everything."

She nodded but remained silent.

"Where's Ava?" he asked.

"She's upstairs in Heather's room. Go on up," she said, closing the door behind him.

Jake ran up the stairs and stopped at Heather's door. Down the hall he could see their grandfather in his room watching TV from his bed. Not wanting to disturb him, he knocked lightly on the door and heard Heather call out, "Come in."

Opening the door, he saw Ava lying on the bed crying with Heather sitting next to her.

Ava looked up and burst into uncontrollable tears. He rushed to her. "Ava, I'm so sorry."

Heather smiled and immediately stood. "I'm going to give you some privacy while I go see when the doctor is going to get here."

Jake nodded and turned back to Ava. "I'm here now, honey, and I'm not leaving you."

He barely heard Heather's comment as she shut the door. "'I'm here for you when you're done being you,'" she snorted. "Stupid song."

Muttering to herself, Heather went down to her grandfather's room to check on him. "Grandpa, you all right?" she asked.

Nathan did not respond. He was looking at the TV and surfing with the remote.

She scanned the room and floor for any broken glass from the earlier nightmare. Not seeing any, she noticed the picture on the stand, minus the glass, and a present on his dresser.

She let out a sigh. "Some birthday," she whispered. Turning away, she moved down the hall. As she looked down the stairs, she saw her mother on the phone and Maura scanning her tablet for news.

But as she moved toward the first step, she heard the TV in her grandfather's room offering up a report. Standing still, she looked back and listened carefully, but the major news was ending...

"The search for the little girl continues. This is Wendy Storm reporting. Now back to the studio, Marcia."

Anchor Marcia Conti was the typical impeccably dressed woman in her fifties. "Thank you, Wendy. In other news, what would seem to be a Halloween prank and nothing more occurred when two graves were dug up in Century Town's cemetery. We go to field reporter, Sandy Storm, to bring us the news. Sandy."

Sandy Storm was Wendy Storm's younger sister, two reporters who remained in the shadow of their older, more accomplished sister, Halle, and forever trying to one-up her and each other. "Thank you, Marcia. Two graves were dug up sometime between last night and this morning, as reported by a caretaker who declined to go on camera.

What I was told is that both caskets were opened, and the remains were actually removed."

The camera showed the gravestone with dirt piled high around it.

"The names of the deceased were Earl Cullen and his wife, Amaleen Cullen. From what we can gather, they died within a week of each other over thirty years ago. More on this disturbing story as it develops. This is Sandy Storm reporting. Marcia, back to you."

"Thank you, Sandy. Now a quick look at your local weather," Marcia said.

The weatherman was already standing in front of the familiar green screen showing heavy showers. As his silly smile crossed his face, his calm voice took over: "Heavier than normal rain continues in the higher elevations of the state this evening, soaking the dry mountains. Mostly—"

Heather watched from the hall as her grandfather turned off the TV with the remote, cutting off the report. He looked to the picture of his departed wife, Marcie, picked it up, and held it to his chest. The slight cry was shrill in Heather's ears.

Her grandfather looked scared.

CHAPTER 20

nside his brother's home, Sam was looking around, not really knowing what he was looking for. He went from the kitchen through a TV room and into his brother's office. There hung a large, framed picture of the four brothers—Ed, Sam, Roman, and Logan Savage—dressed in their polo gear, leading their horses onto the field.

Sam stood there looking at the picture as a million scattered thoughts ran through his mind. "Oh, Ed, what happened up there?" Sam said out loud as he pulled the leather chair out and sat behind his brother's large desk.

Scanning the area, he read the memo pad, the calendar, and then the small stack of mail. There were brochures from Black Ridge Falls and an envelope addressed to Nathan at Sam's address. He picked that one up and studied it when the phone rang, startling him.

Sam saw his name on the caller ID and picked up the phone. "Hello."

"Sam, the doctor will be here within the hour; I want you to be here," Cara said.

"I'll be over soon. Give me the number to that sheriff, would you? I want to call him back," he said.

"Have you found something?"

"Maybe. I don't even know what I'm looking for."

"The number is…"

Sam wrote it down on the memo pad on Ed's desk. On a Post-it stuck to the Black Ridge Falls brochure was the exact same number. "Thanks, one call and I'll be home; love you," he said.

Sam hung up and peeled off the Post-it from the brochure to compare them, trying to figure out why a sheriff's number had been written down when a vacation was all that his brother had been going to Black Ridge Falls to enjoy. Just as he picked up the phone to punch in the number, he noticed the message light flashing. Sam hit the message button and heard Marlo's voice. As his grip tightened on the receiver, he held his breath and listened.

"Ava, you're going to love it up here. It's beautiful. Just calling because your dad left the wine in the garage. It's buried under the clothes for the Salvation Army. Would you be a dear and bring it up with you guys when you come? I love you. Tell the family this is going to be great! 'Bye now. See you soon, and drive carefully."

The happy voice ended, leaving Sam just staring at the phone. Rage consumed him as he punched in the lawman's number.

"Black Ridge sheriff's office," a vague voice answered.

"Sam Savage for Sheriff Arnie Mallard, please," Sam said.

"One moment," the voice told him.

Sam picked up the Post-it.

"Mallard here."

"Sheriff Mallard, Sam Savage. Any further news on my brother?"

"Well, we still have him, if that's what you're asking."

"Has anything changed since I last spoke to him? Have they found Lisa?"

"No, haven't found the girl; have a search going on but nothing yet. Your brother's story is different from witness reports collected. He hasn't changed it one bit, but something doesn't seem right."

"What do you mean?"

"It certainly looks bad for him, but this doesn't make any sense. Between you and me, he didn't do it, Mr. Savage. He was hit on the back of the head—real hard, too. But there are hair samples and blood on the inside right side of his hat. He has no trauma on the right side of his head."

"Can I talk to him?" Sam asked.

"He's out. Sleeping in the cell. Medics gave him something. Maybe his head will clear when he wakes up," Arnie said.

"Hey, Sheriff Mallard."

"Arnie."

"Okay, Arnie. Ed told me the inhaler was found on him, and if he says he didn't have it, he didn't have it. Now, I know he told you I was a lawyer—have you sent the hat for testing?" Sam said, looking at the framed photo of Lisa.

"Waiting for the results. Put a rush on it and will have them before his hold runs out. I must tell you, this is looking like a bad frame-up to me. Can you think of anything or anyone that could be involved in this? Someone who planned this?"

Sam searched his mind. Ed's past was deep, but it had been years since…No, he couldn't mention *that* part of Ed's past. "No, sir, can't think of a thing. By the way, did my brother call you prior to coming up there?"

A pause. "I never spoke to him. Why?"

"I found your phone number on his desk. I'm actually calling you from his house."

"That's strange. I'll ask around the office. And there's more I'd like to talk to you about, but not on the phone. When will you be up here?"

"It's getting dark so much earlier now: hopefully while it's still light out."

"Fine, I'll be expecting you."

"I saw the news. The guy with the crutches is Marlo's brother, Simon. Have you found him yet?"

He could almost hear the concern and interest on the other end of the line grow bigger. "No. I haven't."

"Arnie, there is something you should know about Simon."

"Then I guess you'd better tell me."

CHAPTER 21

Not long after the call, Sam got home with the framed photo of Lisa and some mail from Ed's desk. The doctor was just descending the stairs from Heather's bedroom, where Ava was now calm and lying down.

Heather, Jake, Cara, and Maura were downstairs waiting for news. "How is she?" Jake asked.

Doctor Daniel Clark, a family friend, kept his voice calm. "Physically, she's fine. Emotionally, it's going to take time. She needs to be with her parents. That's all she wants. I wanted to give her something to help quiet her, but she refused," the doctor said, handing the pills to Sam.

He read them out loud. "Xanax and Ambien?"

Laughter from Cara suddenly changed the mood in the room, "Bloody hell. Doesn't every home keep those in stock like scotch and coffee? *I* could have given those to her. Raise teenage daughters, and you'll have them too," she said.

A few actually smiled for the first time in hours, and it was a nice feeling. The doctor nodded, offering no judgments. "I'd keep an eye on her for now. Don't let her be alone, and let her get some rest if she can," he said, heading to the door.

Maura got up and grabbed her bag. "I should be going, too. Call me as soon as you know anything."

Sam and Cara walked them out. "We will," Cara said to her sister, watching Sam and Daniel walk outside.

The twins hugged and then looked at each other, remaining quiet. It was as if by remaining silent, they could each hear what the other was thinking. Maura finally nodded and walked out to her Bentley.

Inside, the phone rang, and Cara could hear Heather grab the receiver. "Nash," she said. "Yes…No…Okay."

Cara looked back inside and stared at Heather with a questioning look on her face.

"It's Nash."

"Is everything all right?" Cara asked.

"Yeah, Mom," Heather replied.

Cara watched her turn away and run up the stairs to be near Ava, missing completely the huge grin plastered on her daughter's face.

CHAPTER 22

lackness.

BThe sound of someone moaning in pain could be heard…a muffled voice…a scraping sound in the darkness. The dim light was glowing and growing in the old stone fireplace, as orange and red-hot embers bloomed. Within the fireplace were some broken sticks and a torn board that had not yet sparked. The glowing embers were warming it…*pop*! The embers ignited the sticks, and the frayed board caught quickly, illuminating small bits of plaster. The sticks were broken pieces of a crutch, the plaster remnants from a cast. The flame threw out light into the black room.

Within the light you could barely see a man lying on the floor with a camouflaged hunter's mask over his head. The fire lit the darkness, and the other, unbroken crutch was visible next to the man, as well as a few candies thrown about as if the remains of a piñata had been broken while children cheered.

The fire glowed brighter.

CHAPTER 23

The fire crackled with life in the Ryland family room. Nash, Eric, Noah, Mia, and Jake were there talking around a billiard table. Outside, night had fallen, and the almost-full moon had risen to illuminate their small world.

Pouring soft drinks behind the wet bar for the guys, Mia handed one to Jake. "So how was she when you left?"

"Not saying much," Jake said, taking his drink. "She wouldn't take any of the meds the doctor left for her to sleep."

Noah stopped racking the pool balls. "I would have. I don't know how she's holding it together. Do you think her sister is alive?"

Nash cued his pool stick. "God, I hope so! The not knowing is driving me nuts, so I can hardly imagine what it's doing to them."

"Nash, you really think it was that Simon guy?" Noah asked, lifting the rack from the table.

"He was committed once," Nash replied.

Hearing that, Eric got excited and blurted out, "Let's go find that freak, *Uncle* Simon, and kick his butt!"

"For once, that little brat has something worth saying," Jake said, taking a drink.

Eric, being eleven, gave Jake a goofy look. "I'm not a little brat, you big brat!"

"Shut up! Both of you," Nash said, slightly irritated.

"He does have a point," Jake mentioned.

"You mean you want to go up there?" Mia said in a worried tone.

Jake put his drink down and stood near the pool table. "I don't know. This sounds too weird; maybe we should wait, like Mr. Savage said. I don't want to piss him off."

Mia moved from behind the bar. "If it is him, and they haven't found him, then he's still out there: in the woods...lurking...like that hockey-mask-wearing guy in the movies."

"He's not a movie character, Mia," Jake said, rolling his eyes.

Eric was paying close attention and getting more scared by the minute.

"Look, I've met the guy; he's nice. Okay...so he was institutionalized, but that doesn't make him a serial killer. I just can't figure out why they can't find him," Jake said.

"So why was he committed?" Mia asked.

"Good question," Noah added.

Jake leaned against the pool table. "I don't know for sure. One time I was over visiting, and he was there. Later, when Ava and I were by ourselves, she mentioned it. Something happened when he and her mom were kids that really screwed with him mentally. She doesn't know the whole story; her parents wouldn't ever tell her about it," Jake said.

Nash put down his pool stick, no longer interested in playing the game. "Why don't we go get them and all of us go up there tonight?" he asked the group.

"I don't know," Mia said, looking to Noah.

"Let's vote on it," Nash said with authority.

"Let's vote on what?" The voice came from outside the window, causing Mia to scream and everyone else in the room to jump out of their skins. They looked to see Ava and Heather outside the window moving toward the sliding doors.

Taking a deep breath, Jake rushed to open them. "Jesus, you scared us. What are you doing here?" he asked, taking Ava into his arms.

Ava had a duffel bag with her, and she dropped it to the floor. "Sorry for scaring you. We didn't want to ring the doorbell incase your parents were home and the back gate was open. We were going to stay home until we went to my house," she said. "I needed to change. Besides, I wanted to pack some stuff for my dad."

Heather gave Nash a hug. "Mom and Dad let us go together. Ava went upstairs to get her dad some stuff, and I looked around. When she came back down, she asked if there were any messages," she said.

Ava added, "We went into my dad's office and played them. There was one from my mom asking me to bring the wine in the garage. That was the last thing she asked me. After hearing that, I went to the garage to get my dad's duffel bag, and I remembered him giving me that stupid grin he does on TV for his fans when he tried talking to me about sex. We even talked about wishing his old Challenger would now come in a convertible while he was packing for the trip Lisa was so excited about. Those were my last thoughts of my parents and my sister…Right then I just knew I had to go there…do…something," she said, holding back the emotion.

"So we came over here. That should speed up the plan you mentioned on the phone," Heather said to Nash.

Eric was excited and jumped up. "We're going to Black Ridge Falls to kick your crazy uncle's butt!"

"What? It was Simon?" Heather said to the group.

"No way," Ava spoke, slightly annoyed at the silly notion.

"We don't know that," Noah said to the cousins.

"So you were just going to drive up there and…do what? Go traipsing through the woods looking for him?" Heather said sarcastically.

"With my luck I'll find the Blair Witch," Mia half joked.

"You are the Blair Witch." Eric laughed.

Mia sneered at him.

"Nash, just what is this plan of yours?" Ava asked.

"I don't know exactly. It's a long drive. We can figure it out on the way up there. Anybody else have any brighter ideas?" he asked, looking to each of them in turn.

"My dad will kill us," Heather said quietly.

"And so will Simon. Simon says die! Mwahahaha!" Eric laughed.

Jake interrupted, shutting Eric's ridiculous display down with a look. "Ava, it could be dangerous," he said. He turned to Eric. "And *you're* not going."

Eric pointed at Nash. "No way! It was my idea! Tell him, Nash."

"Ava, are you sure you want to do this?" Heather asked.

Ava looked at her cousin. "I'm sure. Look, our stuff is still here, right?"

"Everything is still packed up and ready for tomorrow's trip," Nash said.

Ava looked at him and turned to Heather. "Then I say we go. We have our cell phones with us so when Sam and Cara wake up tomorrow and see that we're gone, they'll call us. They're not letting us all go tomorrow; this way they'll have to. We'll just be a little ahead of them is all."

Heather's cell phone started to ring, and everyone went silent, watching Heather dig in her purse for her phone. "Okay, but we're going to hear it big-time over this! Hold on."

"Hi, Mom," she paused. "Ava wants to stay over here for a while longer." Another pause. "Yes. Okay, we'll be home soon. Get some rest. See you in the morning." Heather hung up her phone and returned it to her purse. "I hate lying…and we're so in trouble." She looked right at Ava. Her cousin knew hell would have to be paid. She just didn't know how much the debt would be.

Nash grinned at his girl with pride. "Nicely done!" he said, kissing Heather on the cheek.

"Okay, Nash, we're in. Now what?" she said.

"Let's go!" Nash clapped his hands together, and the group headed out to the RV.

Completely sad and more than a little angry, Eric sat down quietly in a high-backed chair.

Jake picked up the duffel Ava had brought, and they moved to the driveway. Nash started the vehicle up and got the lights turned on as everyone settled in for the trip.

"Where's Eric?" Nash asked.

"He stayed back inside when we left," Noah told him, as he tossed his backpack inside the back of the RV.

"I'm going to go talk to him; be right back," he said.

Still in the chair, Eric was looking at the picture of the group with a heart drawn in red felt-tip pen around Ava's lovely, smiling face. Nash stood behind the chair, looking down at the picture in his brother's hand. "She's pretty, huh?" he said.

"If you tell, I'll kill you," Eric said, immediately hiding the photo.

"I'm not going to tell anyone. She *is* pretty."

"I know…and she likes Jake." He stared up at his brother with sad eyes. "Are you *sure* I can't go?"

"Eric, Mom and Dad would kill me if I brought you. They'll be home any minute, and I want to be gone before they get here. Tell them I'm with the gang, and I'll see them later. Okay?"

"Please let me go."

"Sorry. Now do what I asked you, okay?"

"Fine. Be careful," Eric added.

"We will," Nash said.

Rubbing his brother's head, he messed up his hair and went out to join the others. Nash stared up at the moonlit sky, wondering, very briefly, if their trip was such a good idea.

CHAPTER 24

In the ICU, Marlo Savage lay in a coma as a fan blew back and forth in the small room. The guard outside the door left his post and went down the hall to the vending machine.

Seeing the perfect opening, dressed like a competent and loving nurse, the figure entered Marlo's room. She was impressed with her own luck. By stealing an identification badge some nurse was now searching frantically for throughout the hospital, she could easily blend in; she'd volunteered there off and on and knew the hospital well, and knew exactly who was in that room.

She was in and out...there and gone.

When the assigned nurse arrived for her rounds, she found a surgical blade on the floor near the head of Marlo's bed; she looked at it oddly. Putting on a glove and picking it up, she placed it in the sharps container, raising her eyes at the sloppiness and wondering who it was that was obviously doing such a poor job.

The nurse then took the glove off, threw it away, and resumed checking on her patient just as the guard arrived at the open door, holding a can of soda.

"Did you see who was in here last?" she asked.

"I just got on shift and no one's been here. Is there a problem?"

"No...long day. That cold drink sure looks good; think I'll get one myself."

"Let me get one for you."

"Thanks, I'm almost done here."

The guard left to get another beverage, and the nurse hurried to finish. She checked the monitors and scribbled something down on the chart, but it was her own heart that fluttered. The man was certainly something she wanted. Smiling, she adjusted her hair and took a quick look in the mirror. The sound of the blinds hitting the window made her jump. She walked across the dimly lit room and stared out the window. She was amazed that someone had also left it wide open. Yet another flaw in the idiot that left the blade on the floor, she thought to herself. Slamming it shut against the rain, she left the room and returned to the nurses' station with Marlo's chart in hand ignorant of her own sloppiness: she hadn't checked her patient's identification bracelet because if she had, she would have noticed it gone.

The bandage on Marlo's head remained, yet now her hair was pushed up out of the top of the covering. Clumps of hair rested on the pillow and decorated the floor between the bed and the window. The nurse had never even noticed it.

When the guard appeared at the nurses' station with her beverage, the nurse set down the chart and walked him back to Marlo's room, wanting to find the perfect, quiet place to flirt for a while.

Sandy Storm came around the corner and saw the two moving down the hall and the timing was perfect. Approaching the nurses' station, she looked down and found exactly what she was looking for. Without catching anyone's attention, she opened Marlo Savage's chart, took a photo with her phone, and was gone in the blink of an eye.

CHAPTER 25

Noah pulled the pot of coffee from the maker. It was mostly dark in the vehicle now. The lights had been dimmed, so the girls could go to sleep in the back bedroom.

After checking on them, Jake had quietly closed the bedroom door and made his way up to the front of the RV. "They're asleep," he said.

Noah picked up his coffee mug. "Good. Come on, let's try to make some sense of all this," he said.

Jake grabbed the pot of coffee, and he and Noah brought it up front to refill Nash's mug, noticing that the speedometer was practically trembling at eighty-five. "Hey, slow it down; you're flying," Noah said.

Nash looked down and back to the road. "It's fine; we can say it's an emergency," he said.

Jake raised his eyes. "It *is* an emergency. But us being killed or locked up isn't going to help. Pull over, and I'll drive for a while."

Yawning, and admittedly a little tired, Nash glanced at his coffee mug. "I can use a break. I'll pull over at the next exit," he agreed.

"So, what's first when we get there?" Noah asked, staring at the open road.

Nash picked up his mug. "First, we find the sheriff's office. Ava needs to see her dad. We can talk to him and see what happened. Or we can take a look at the campsite, see where all this happened first, and then go see her dad. What do you guys think?"

"I say we see where all this happened first—that way they can't tell us not to go; we're already in enough trouble. But more importantly, if it gets weird, I say we drop the hero act and get the girls out of there," Noah said, looking over to Nash for an answer.

"Agreed. We need to do this for Ava. Our families are close, and I want to help out." He nodded. "Exit up ahead. Jake, you sure you're okay to drive for a while?"

"Yeah, no problem," Jake said. "Guys, I need you to listen. Ava is all I think about, and Mr. Savage was worried about something back there. The girls' safety has to come first."

"Fine, first the campsite, and then we go see Ava's dad. Then what?" Nash said, as he put on the turn signal to exit the freeway.

Looking out the side window, Noah saw nothing but dark woods and felt a chill run down his spine. "I don't know…find Simon," he said.

"But where?" Nash asked, coming to a stop sign.

"I don't know. Maybe they've found him by now," Jake added.

"Fine. But if some Hollywood psycho-slasher does get anywhere near us, we're out of there," Noah only half joked.

"It's not going to be like that," Jake said, returning the coffeepot to the coffeemaker, getting ready for his turn behind the wheel.

The cabin grew quiet. They each prayed that no matter what was hiding up at Black Ridge Falls, Hollywood would *not* come a-callin'.

CHAPTER 26

The early-morning dew on the grass sparkled in the sunlight as it lit up the cemetery—a different-looking cemetery than the one shown on the news, far more upscale.

Nathan Savage was kneeling at his wife's grave. He had flowers in hand and was placing them on the ground. His younger brother, Niles, now a grandfather himself, was standing behind him. Parked beyond them, the black limousine waited silently as distant storm clouds began to gather.

"Oh, Marcie, how I miss you. I don't know what I've done. The dreams aren't just dreams, are they? It's the future...my future in hell. The evil one is coming for me, I know. You forgave me, but God Almighty has not. How could I have been so stupid? This is my fault. Now our little Lisa is with you. Dear, sweet girl," Nathan said, staring at her grave.

Niles Savage, a small-framed man with light-brown hair mixed with gray, had an air of refined self-worth about him. "It was an accident, Nathan. You must remember that!" Niles barked.

Nathan left the flowers and stood slowly to face his brother. "Damn you! Like it was an accident that I let you do that. Think about that poor girl. What she saw. What she must live with. Her mother was pregnant. An accident? Damn you, Niles!" Nathan growled.

"I had to." Niles went quiet and then loud; his voice was one of an unforgiving man who was sick of standing in the presence of a lesser one. "There was no other way."

"You could have used your head, Niles. You weren't forced to do it."

"And you weren't forced to take the blame for my actions."

"But I did, little brother; I *did*. I had to. It was my fault to begin with," Nathan added, his voice trailing off into sadness and guilt.

"Could we risk letting anyone find out? I did you a favor. If the truth ever came out that you were the father of her redneck bastard right after Sam had been born, it would have ruined Dad's political career. Mom and Dad, rest their souls, knew you gave me my alibi. And it was brilliant! Dad paying that family off to point to some homeless jerk to take the blame—it worked. End of story. Period!" Niles said.

"Is it? Wait until the dreams come to you, my dear brother. Just wait," Nathan warned as he brushed past his brother to the car and looked up to the sky. The clouds were gathering, and it looked like rain. A chilling breeze knocked over flowers in the cemetery lines, one right after the other...as if a quiet army were falling.

CHAPTER 27

In the bedroom, Cara woke up next to a still-sleeping Sam; a bottle of scotch and two glasses were on their night tables. Getting up from the bed, she put on her robe and saw the two Great Danes asleep on their own giant-sized beds. Their eyes opened slowly with her movements.

"Come on, Whisky, Dewar's—outside," she said.

The two Great Danes yawned and got up, walking slowly over to the sliding glass door. She opened it, and the dogs ran to the balcony, down the stairs, and into the backyard to do their morning business.

"A dog's life," Cara said as she watched them run past the pool. She then smiled back at her handsome man as she made her way to check on the girls.

Cara moved down the hall, passing Nathan's room, not noticing his door was cracked open and his bed made. She got to Heather's bedroom door and knocked. Opening the door, seeing the bed empty, she thought that the girls had stayed together in the guest room, until she discovered that room was empty, too.

Panic started creeping up into her heart as she hurried to the top of the stairs and looked down. "Heather? Ava? You here?" she called. Not getting an answer, she rushed down the stairs and searched the house. She saw the housekeeper in the kitchen.

"Edith, have you seen the girls?"

"No, ma'am, and Mr. Nathan is out too; I just made his bed," she said, getting breakfast ready.

Surprised, Cara rushed back up the stairs to Nathan's room. Her soul screamed in fear as she saw that he was gone as well.

The panic inside her was climbing faster, and she raised her voice as she went down the hall. "Sam! Sam, wake up!" she said as she got to their bedroom.

Sam was stirring, and she sat next to him, rubbing his shoulder. "Sam, wake up. The girls are gone. So is Dad."

Sam opened his eyes. He saw the empty scotch glass on his night table and shook off his alcohol-driven sleep. "What? Huh?" he said, waking up completely.

"The girls aren't here. Dad is gone."

Sam threw back the covers and got up, picking up his boxers and putting them on. Leaving his robe behind, he marched down the hall, yelling and feeling the dryness of his raspy voice, "Heather? Ava? Dad? Where are you?"

Cara followed him. "Sam, I'm scared." Her voice trembled.

"Has Edith seen them? Is there a note?" he asked.

"No, and I didn't find one. Call them!" Cara said.

Going back to their bedroom, Sam picked up the phone and punched in Heather's cell number. Listening to the many rings fueled his rage.

He slammed his hand on the dresser. They were far more than just "in trouble."

Parked in the rest area, the RV was almost silent, with everyone sleeping from the long travel the night before. Heather's purse was on the floor near the bed the girls were in and her phone was ringing.

Hearing the sound, the girls stirred and slowly began to wake, not knowing where they were and looking out the windows for information. Ava was the first to reach for the phone. Still half asleep, she saw Heather's screen and the caller ID. She was nervous as she answered, "Hello?"

Sam's angry, panicked voice met her ears. "Ava, where are you?" he demanded.

Heather was now fully awake and making gestures at Ava, wide-eyed and knowing trouble had arrived. Worried, Ava chose her words carefully. "Uncle Sam...Hi. I'm with Heather, and we're fine. Hang on," she said quickly before letting Sam get a word in edgewise. She handed Heather the phone.

"Gee, thanks," Heather said, shooting Ava a look. "Hi…Dad?"

"Where the hell are you?" Sam barked in a dry husky tone from his night of drinking.

Knowingly, Heather deflected, "I'm not sure where we are, exactly. We're in the Rylands' RV, though," she said.

"Parked in his driveway. Right?"

Heather sighed. She knew her father already had the answer. "Um, Dad…We should be near the Falls."

"What?" Sam barked louder. He went past pissed to full-on anger. "You little…damn it, Heather! We told you not to go up there. Who is there with you?"

"Bloody hell!"

Heather heard her mother's worried voice in the background and knew she was in a whole lot of trouble. "Everyone's here, Dad, so there's no need to worry. I'm all right. Ava, Jake, Nash, Noah, and Mia are with me."

Ava looked out a window and saw the sign. "Tell him we're in a rest area. I'm not sure where, though."

"Dad, we're at a rest area; everyone is just waking up."

"Heather, we don't know what's happened up there yet. I spoke with Sheriff Mallard, Arnie Mallard."

"Mallard, like the duck?" Heather said, trying to sound goofy in order to calm her father. But no humor came from the voice on the other end of the line.

"He's a lawman, Heather. And he suspects something happened up there, or is *still* happening, that could be dangerous. You kids could be in danger. Now, I want you to get to the nearest police station up there and call me from inside. Do you understand me, young lady?"

"Sheriff Mallard. Got it. We'll find him, Dad, and we really are okay. But what sort of danger are you talking about?"

Her words made everyone in the RV move closer to Heather's side.

Her father's angry voice was now mixed with fear. "Heather, I don't know for sure. I believe someone up there caused all this to happen, and *that* someone is most definitely not locked up. I don't want to worry about you. Now, *please* do as I ask."

"Yes sir, everyone is now up; I'll tell them."

"And Ava?" Sam asked with worry.

"Ava's fine…all things considered."

"Hang on, your mother wants to talk to you," he mumbled.

Heather rolled her eyes, getting ready for blast number two.

"Are you all right?" Cara asked.

"Yes, Mom, we're fine."

"Where is your grandfather?"

Heather paused, completely confused. "Huh? Grandpa's not there?"

"No! You don't know where he is?"

"No, Mom, I don't."

"Well, that's just bloody brilliant! No bloody note, no nothing! You petulant imps do as you please; your grandfather just decides to disappear. What else is…?"

Heather waited as her mother seemed to stop, collecting herself.

"I'm sorry; I'm so sorry, but something's not right," she continued. "Please, do as your father told you; am I clear?"

"Yes, Mom, I'm sorry," Heather said. "We'll call you from the police station just like Dad told me; love you." Heather hung up the phone with everyone staring at her.

"Oh, this was so not a good idea," Heather said with a sigh.

"What did they say?" Ava asked.

"To get to the nearest police station as soon as possible and call them. Dad said we could be in danger."

"What do you mean, danger?" Jake said, raising his voice.

"Dad thinks someone up here caused all this to happen and that the guy is still out there. Ava, what are we getting ourselves into?" Heather said.

"I just want to see what happened and get to my dad. He'll explain everything; then we can go see my mom." Ava's mind was clearly set. It didn't matter if there was a killer on the loose; she was going to get to her parents no matter what it took.

"We need to find Sheriff Arnie Mallard. He's been talking with my dad, and I think he believes *your* dad is innocent."

"Of course he's innocent!" Ava shot Heather an angry look but stopped to take a breath. She stared out the window, looking at the endless woods, thinking of her little sister out there amid the dangers. She imagined a fiend behind every tree and large boulder, and put her arms around her shoulders. "But that leaves the question: who exactly *is* guilty?"

CHAPTER 28

About an hour after the call, Sam was getting dressed for the day, and Cara, already dressed, brought him another cup of coffee from downstairs. Placing it on the dresser, she heard the front door open.

She rushed from the bedroom and felt a sigh of relief. "Dad! Where have you been?" she said, coming down the stairs.

He was startled at first and then took off his coat. "I'm sorry. I went to visit Marcie early this morning. I didn't want to wake you."

Sam appeared from upstairs, thanking anyone who could hear him for his father's safe return as he headed down the stairs.

"How did you get there?" Cara questioned him.

"Niles came and picked me up. Now…Why all the fuss?"

"Dad!" Sam said, looking directly at him. Nathan took a step back; he could see his son was upset. "With everything that's happened, *please* don't go off on your own without telling anyone or at least leaving a note."

Nathan nodded. "Any word on Ed?"

"Nothing since yesterday. I haven't called today yet. We're dealing with waking up to an empty house here. No notes…not knowing where anyone is."

"Where are the girls?" Nathan asked.

Cara picked up her tablet to check for any e-mails or messages from Heather. "They took off for Black Ridge Falls with Nash and their friends last night. They had better listen to you, Sam," Cara said.

Hearing the words "Black Ridge Falls" surprised and frightened Nathan. "No! They must not go up there."

Sam and Cara both stared at the man's sudden fear. "Dad, what is it? Did the sheriff call with any news?" Sam asked.

"The phone hasn't rung all morning; I would have heard it," Cara said. She turned to her father-in-law. "Now, Dad, what do you know?"

Black Ridge Falls was close to where…No, it couldn't be, he thought. Confused between his guilt, the dreams, and the nightmares playing out in front of him, Nathan looked completely lost. "Nothing. I don't know anything. I'm just worried."

Sam glanced at the brochures sitting on the table that he'd retrieved from Ed's house. "Dad…Have you ever been to Black Ridge Falls?"

The reply was immediate. "No, why do you ask?"

"Then how did you hear about it?"

"I haven't." He paused, apparently realizing the lies that had come from his own mouth. "Until…Ed said something about it when he was planning the trip, but I thought he'd decided on Seneca Falls instead; that's where I told him I'd rather go."

Now Sam knew the reason Ed had chosen Black Ridge over Seneca Falls.

Sam went over to the table and picked up the brochures. "Then why, exactly, are these Black Ridge Falls brochures that were in Ed's house addressed to you?"

Nathan looked down at the brochures in Sam's hands but did not touch them. "I know nothing of these."

Cara tossed her tablet onto the sofa and went over and took the brochures from Sam. "Wait a minute…Sam, a few of weeks ago, I remember getting these in the mail. Ed and Marlo were over, and we were talking about the new RVs we were buying and looking through the different brochures. They could have gotten mixed up with theirs when they left," she said.

Sam kept his focus on his father's odd face. "Dad, are you *sure* you didn't call anywhere for vacation brochures?"

"No, Sam, I didn't call and ask for anything!"

"Then who sent these to us?" Sam said in frustration.

The realization of another clue of malevolence at work sent chills though Cara. "Oh, God! Are you saying this was deliberate? This was no bloody accident? Is this some sort of *scheme* to hurt us? Who sent these damn things?"

"That's it!" Sam was done. "Cara, call the Rylands, see if they know anything, and tell them to get over here. I'll call Black Ridge police."

"First, I'm calling Heather," Cara said, picking up the phone and calling her daughter. Getting the familiar recording—that the call would not go through due to coverage—Cara slammed down the phone. "Ugh! I can't get through; they must be on the road."

"We'll keep trying. Now call the Rylands," Sam said.

Cara punched in the number and looked outside to see the two Great Danes at the sliding glass door; it was their breakfast time. Their faces were grim as the rain began to fall.

CHAPTER 29

Nash and the gang pulled into Black Ridge Falls with the sky above beautiful and sunny. They knew there were more heavy rainstorms approaching, as seen by the distant clouds, but they hadn't yet arrived to spoil the excellent camping day.

Although quiet inside the RV, each member of the crew had something to do. Mia was putting away dishes, and Ava was wiping down the table, while Heather was searching on her tablet with no luck. There was still no service. She checked her phone and saw she had one bar. "I can't get Internet to look up where the sheriff's station's at," she said, looking from her phone to see the Black Ridge Falls sign on the road. She turned to Nash. "I thought we were going to the police station first."

"We're going. I just want to take a quick look around here. Besides, we don't even know how to get to the cops, and the GPS in this thing is not pulling anything up," he said. "Good thing I was looking at the directions last night, or we never would have found this."

"I want to see where all this happened, too," Ava agreed quietly, looking ahead down the road.

Driving the RV farther into the park, they came across a rangers' station. Mia eyed the wooden building with hope. "Let's ask a ranger where the police station is; maybe they know something that can help us."

Seeing the camp nearly empty of RVs, Noah got an uneasy feeling. "Where is everybody? And where are we supposed to park this thing?"

Ava spoke without turning away from the view. "My parents were in space fourteen. Nash, your parents were supposed to be in fifteen with Sam and Cara. We were booked farther up in number nineteen."

Nash brought the RV to a stop near the information station, and Jake and Ava were up and out the door. "We'll be right back," Jake said, closing the door behind them.

Inside the cabin, a female ranger stood talking to some guests, explaining the way to a hiking area seen on a large wall map of Black Ridge Falls. Farther back in the office, another ranger was taking a pill and washing it down with a bottle of water. In front of him was a map laid out on his desk next to the pill bottle. Jake and Ava went straight for him, and he quickly folded the paper map and placed it in the desk drawer with the pills for his heart.

Ava stared at the plaque that sat in front of the man introducing him to visitors as Ranger Melvin Galloway Jr. She practically gasped when he stood up to shake their hands. Ranger Melvin was one big guy. At six feet five, he was rugged, with black hair, a black beard, and the blackest eyes she'd ever seen. He was wearing the typical ranger's uniform—a dark-green shirt, khaki pants, and a hat and boots, and his initials were embroidered on the shirt pocket.

"M. J." wore a smile plastered on his face. "Good morning," he said, looking from Ava to Jake.

"Morning," Jake replied. "Can you tell us how to get to campsite number nineteen?"

The ranger stood completely still, yet Jake's words seemed to grab his full attention. He shifted his eyes from Jake to Ava once again. "Sure. You just passed the sign back there, about one hundred feet or so. Just turn around and follow the markers."

Ava lifted her head from looking at his desk. "Can you also tell us how to get to the police station?"

"What seems to be the problem?" Melvin said.

"Oh, my parents were here and—"

Jake cut her off. "And they made friends with the sheriff."

Ava looked to Jake and then quickly back at the ranger, who seemed to have caught the odd movement.

"Yeah, they told us to stop by and say hello when we got here, right, Ava?" Jake said, hoping Ava would follow.

"Yeah," she said. "That's right."

Melvin smiled and looked at Ava for what seemed like a long time. "Ava? That's a pretty name." He paused. "Well, get back on the highway the way you were going, and up ahead there'll be a turnoff for Old Mills Road; take that exit, and you'll see the station."

Jake eyed his shirt. "Thanks, M. J."

Melvin seemed to look into Jake's very soul like a shotgun sight being aimed at a deer.

"Yeah, thank you," Ava added, leading Jake to the door.

"Just drop on by anytime. We're here till five daily," Melvin told them, tipping his hat in farewell.

Hearing him over her shoulder, Ava turned back, smiled, and waved as they got to the door.

Outside, with the door to the office now closed, Ava turned to Jake. "What was that all about?"

"Wait until we get inside."

Heather was standing outside the RV with the door open, waiting for them. "What's up?" she asked.

Jake shot Heather a serious look. "Get inside, now," he ordered.

The three climbed aboard, and Jake shut the door, locking it. Everyone was looking to him as Ava pulled on his arm. "Well, what was that all about?"

"What happened in there?" Nash asked.

"We got the information we needed," Jake told them.

"But why did you stop me from telling that ranger who I was?" Ava said.

Jake was surprised no one else had thought of it. "Because of what Heather's dad said about danger. Even you have to admit something was off about that guy. I thought it best not to say anything until we get to Ava's dad at the police station."

"Who are you? NCIS?" Mia joked.

"Hey, it doesn't hurt to be careful," Noah said.

Jake took off his jacket and looked at Ava. "Besides, I didn't like the way he was looking at you in there."

"I know…He gave me the creeps," Ava finally admitted.

Mia moved toward Ava. "What did he do?"

"All Jake did was mention my name, and he said, 'Ava; what a pretty name.' Then he just…stared."

Nash grinned. "Well, Ava, you do have a way with the guys. Just ask my brother when we get home. He's got a picture of you with a heart drawn around it. Don't tell him I told you."

Heather smiled. "Aww, he has a crush on you. I think that's sweet."

Mia let out a sigh and looked back out the window toward the station. "Is that dude in there a psycho or not?"

Ava and Jake stared at each other and shook their heads. "I don't know," Jake replied.

Mia clutched her cardigan. "Enough of this, guys. Let's just hurry to the campsite, so we can get to the cops. This TV teen-mystery stuff is working my last nerve."

CHAPTER 30

Deep in the woods an older cabin, with a separate garage, sat alone. In a strange way, it was a foreboding sight—an unwelcome feeling lingered around it. The garage's barn-style doors were closed, shut tight to the prying eyes of the world. There was smoke coming from the chimney of the cabin, however, and a light was on in the kitchen window. The light exposed a small kitchen with a cutting board on the counter, covered with carrots waiting to be hacked to pieces with a large, silver kitchen knife that sat beside it. On the stove, a pot boiled. And a bluish-tinged light beamed from a TV set that seemed to be lost in another room.

Decorating the walls leading from the kitchen to the living area were old family pictures. Covered with a dusty sheen, the faces of a man and woman holding a little girl stared out. Beside that frame, in a straight line, came two younger boys who were dressed alike at about five years of age; another of a girl, just a few years older, sporting long, black hair and sitting astride a horse; and lastly, a group of grim-faced miners covered in black soot.

The TV ran *Play Misty for Me*, and Jessica Walter held up a knife.

Poor Patty Galloway never had a chance. Sitting in the cabin, her home now, taking notes from an old Clint Eastwood movie...The whole scene was sad.

Even before she'd lost her parents, life had been hard. Being born a girl was a problem right off the bat: her father, Melvin Sr., wanted all boys, rejecting her female DNA before she'd even left the hospital. Even though she had an older sister, Stevie, poor Patty Galloway always felt like the targeted one. Even then she was wrong.

A commercial came on, and Patty went to the kitchen. She started chopping away at the carrots on the cutting board. And when the commercial ended, a promo for Ed Savage's new show came on.

Patty winced at the sound of the man's voice. Gripping the knife, she turned and went back to the TV to see Ed Savage standing in an operating room dressed in full scrubs and mask. A surgery was taking place, with a well-oiled team moving about behind him. Savage made his way to the outer glassed-off scrub sink area to remove his mask, and the camera followed him like a dutiful puppy as Ed walked through the hospital, offering annoying narration on the scene.

"A tragic accident occurs, and you depend on these highly educated individuals to save your life. As the season nears an end here on *Savage Life*, we'll be looking at the careers of every person associated with saving *your* life. From the medics who arrive on the scene to the orderly who wheels you out of the hospital after your recovery, you will meet them all."

Ed passed the whiteboard with patient names, which had been blurred per the Health Insurance Portability and Accountability Act.

"You will know what jobs will be available to you as a high-school graduate in the medical field and all the way along your college educational path, as you earn your degrees. We will show you what jobs you're working so hard for and what pay you can expect: from the entry-level position, to the surgeon, all the way up to the CEO."

Ed hit a button on the wall, which opened the electric double doors to the recovery room used for the gurneys.

"It's a *savage* world out there, friends," Ed said as he walked through the double doors. "Will your education lead you here?" Ed looked right into the camera with his signature devilish grin. "I'm Ed Savage. Join me for *Savage Life*, Wednesdays at eight, and catch our new episodes of *Savage Cases* premiering soon."

The TV promo ended with Ed's smiling face and a wink to the viewers, when an X-ray tech handed him a large chest X-ray film. "Learning improves you," Ed said directly into the camera and taking the film and moving toward a recovering patient and handing it to their doctor.

Patty Galloway almost threw up in her own mouth at the sight.

She returned to her work at the kitchen counter, just as the sound bite of Wendy Storm's latest report began.

The steam rising from the now-boiling pot was fogging the window that Patty was staring out of. Without noticing, she held a death grip on the knife and began stabbing the sharp tip into the cutting board.

On the TV, reporter Wendy Storm was rehashing the horror: "Again, the woman in the accident is still in intensive care, and her husband is still being detained by the sheriff; nothing further has been released. This is Wendy Storm, reporting live with—"

The TV shut off, turning to a black, silent screen.

She had no recollection of coming back, but Patty stared into the set with the remote in her hand, pressing the old VCR's play button. On another VCR, she hit record. And as the VCR started to play, Patty began humming to herself the tune of "London Bridge."

The VCR tape was of an old home movie, not filmed very well and transferred to tape long after its time. The cameraperson was shooting the porch of an old house when the front door was hit open with a kick, and the door hit the wall.

Patty stared at the TV in a daze, and when the little girl in the video spoke, Patty stopped humming and changed her voice to that of a little girl. She did the same for her parents as well, so the narration would fit the picture, just like she did every time she watched it, remembering that horrible day.

"Hey, be careful," Patty said as her younger self.

It was then that her father, Melvin Galloway Sr., and a very pregnant wife came out the front door. He was carrying an overnight bag, and she had her housecoat draped over her arm.

"Oh, come on, darling, get in the car; you can film later. It's time. Hurry along now." Patty narrated her mother's words.

"Momma, we'll get you there in time."

"Don't get your mom going off now, Pat. Get in the car," Patty said to the TV, mimicking her father's deep, gruff voice.

"Yes, sir." And the Galloways are off to the hospital! "Momma, you want a boy or a girl?"

"Whatever the good Lord wishes for our family is what I want," Patty said as Rose, who was looking at Melvin with an odd sort of worry written all over her face.

It was no secret that Melvin Galloway Sr. wanted only boys. After their first two daughters, Stevie and Patty, the latter of which Melvin Sr. always referred to as "Pat," they had the twin boys, Melvin Jr. and Leroy. Melvin Sr. wanted more of only their kind.

"A boy," Patty said in her most chilling tone for her father's reply. "Now, Pat, I said get in the car."

As Patty got in the backseat of the sedan on the screen, the camera angles got tilted, revealing Rose and her highly concerned look.

While still holding the camera, the young Patty lifted her mom's long, gray hair over the seat. "Momma, hand me your hairbrush. I can't make you a big movie star with your hair like this."

"Big movie star? I'm about to give birth, and she's worried about how I look?" Patty said in her mother's sweet voice.

Melvin started the car and put his hands together to pray. "It's our special day. The Lord has smiled upon us, and we are about to be new parents again. I love you, Mrs. Galloway," Patty said as her father.

Rose told him she loved him, too, and he leaned over to her, placing a kiss on her lips. Melvin then looked back to their daughter, who was holding the camera on them. He took the camera from her and filmed her with it.

Patty was a thin girl, all smiles, with long, black hair. "Let's go, Dad!" Patty said as her young self.

He handed her back the camera, and outside, her older sister and twin brothers were standing at the front door waving. Patty aimed the camera at them.

"Okay, we're off," Patty said as her father when Melvin shifted the car into reverse and backed out of the drive.

Rose looked out her side window; her smile turned sullen as she waved good-bye to the other children.

The boiling pot in the kitchen continued to steam the window, and the kitchen timer went off. Patty looked toward the kitchen, still in her daze, choosing to ignore real life completely.

The pot boiled over as the little girl in the video was filming the traffic on the busy expressway. The other lanes were busy, but the speed was good. Melvin looked anxious to get to the hospital, and Rose was fanning herself.

Patty resumed humming her tune and watching the video when they passed a gasoline truck and other traffic as they approached an overpass. The large rock dropped from the overpass at the exact time Melvin's sedan passed underneath, slamming directly onto the windshield of the driver's side: a moment in time that was no accident.

Patty stopped humming when the camera in the video was dropped to reveal her younger self, screaming in silence. Patty remained standing in front of the television, frozen as she watched the hideousness play out. The Galloway car swerved into the other lane, clipping another car, which sent it rolling over and over, like the video she was now watching, throwing the camera from the car window while it went on recording after landing right side up.

The gasoline truck they had just passed tried to turn away from the accident, but in doing so, it overturned and burst into flames. The Galloway car finally came to a stop, upside down and on fire.

Melvin was dead; his face had been bashed in by the rock and sliced with shards of glass and metal fragments, and what was left of his skin was covered in blood. Rose was still alive...but barely. The windshield had exploded in her face, and a jagged piece of twisted metal from the dashboard was jammed into her abdomen, as if she were a pig on a skewer. She was screaming as little Patty Galloway came crawling out the broken back window and around the side to her mother. She was hurt, cut, and crying.

People from other cars ran to help; a few even passed the camera to get to Patty, but someone running kicked the camera, finally shutting it off.

The TV went to static, returning to the blank screen. On the now-darkened area, for just a split second, a scary reflection of Patty appeared...an old face, possessed with revenge, stared back at her.

Patty pressed the stop buttons on both VCRs. Still in her trance, she dropped the remote on top of the single manila envelope that rested on one of the machines. She then moved to a door in the house and opened it to descend into the cellar below.

Patty made her way slowly into the dark, dank space and pulled on an overhead light string. The single bulb barely lit the drab cellar. Up against the wall, she came to a dresser. Taped on the mirror was a yellowed newspaper article with the headline: "Young Homeless Man Arrested for Dropping Rock over Expressway—Killing Two." Sitting on the dresser below the article was a pile of old, weather-beaten books pertaining to the subjects of witchcraft and voodoo and one entirely unique tome made of skin stitched together. Strange symbols decorated the cover, with no words at all to let the user know what oddities could be found within its pages.

Without a thought, Patty opened a drawer of the dresser and stared down at the dead contents. Inside, there was a doll made of rotted animal parts. Spoils of human hair and nail clippings were clumped together with black wax and tied with Marlo's hospital identification bracelet. The burned remains of the hospital badge she had stolen were on the floor next to the dresser.

Patty tilted her head back, remembering her mother on that ugly day, and mumbled something in Latin. "*Ex morte matris meae. Maledictus matris tuae vitae.*" *From the death of my mother's womb. A curse on your mother's life.* She then thrust her hands into the drawer and dug in deep, extracting another manila envelope—this one was addressed to Marlo Savage at the hospital.

CHAPTER 31

Nellie Larson took the call in the maternity ward on that fateful day that started a ball rolling, a ball that would grow larger and larger until it turned into a nightmare for the Savage family.

Niles Savage had started dating Nellie for the sole purpose of getting information. He called her many times a day at work to flirt, around the time Rose Galloway was due. On the day of the accident, he was on the phone with her, and she put him on hold at the nurses' station to answer another line. When she returned, she told him she had to go and call the doctor to let him know he had a patient on the way in.

Niles teased her about the mayor's wife, who was also due, but Nellie joked that it was those Galloway "hicks from the sticks," as she called them. She had no idea she was being played when she let him know that Melvin Galloway had phoned, telling her that his wife had gone into labor and that he and his family were on their way in.

Niles felt lucky that day and had said he would call back, but he lied when he told her they were on their way to the airport for a last-minute family getaway. The truth was, he had a plan, an ugly plan at that, and he'd hung up the phone with a smile, happy.

After his horrible deed had been done, he and his brother, Nathan, did go out of town. It was just later then he'd alleged, and when he got back, he dutifully dumped Nellie Larson from his life, using the excuse that his ex-girlfriend was pregnant, and he had to do the right thing…as a gentleman.

The truth had always been that Niles's ex-girlfriend had lied. She'd later said that she lost the baby, crying at all the right moments to be believable, in order to get the large sum of money that he'd promised her. It was great having so much money that you could pay people off with.

It was Nellie who'd been hurt that day, yet she still had never put the clues together.

CHAPTER 32

At Heather's house, the Savages were loading the RV when the Rylands arrived.

Parking their Cadillac, they popped the trunk. Asa and Rayna Ryland were just grabbing their bags when Sam stepped out from the RV. "Asa, Rayna, just in time—let's go," he said.

As the couple boarded, they saw Cara and Nathan waiting inside for a journey that no one understood or could possibly fathom was about to begin.

CHAPTER 33

Nash had parked the RV at campsite number nineteen. It was eerie—the silence all around. Perhaps it was paranoia, but it felt to him as if eyes were watching them from deep inside the woods.

Further down the road at campsite number fourteen, the teens arrived at the taped-off area where Ed and Marlo had set up their camp. There was a sign posted: "Police Scene, Do Not Enter." But Ava stared at something that sat well beyond the tape.

Looking at the group, she lifted up the fragile barrier and passed underneath it. No one moved as they watched her go over to an object encrusted in the mud. She picked it up, revealing the doll that had belonged to her sister.

Heather recognized the doll immediately. "Oh God, that's Lisa's!" Heather lifted the tape and went to Ava; the others followed behind.

While looking at the mud now crusted solid in the doll's hair, a tear came down Ava's face. "Mom, Dad, what happened?" she whispered.

Jake put his arms around her from behind. "Are you all right?"

Clutching the doll and looking at the remains of the campsite, she burst into tears and turned into Jake's arms.

Mia was hanging on to Noah and looking around like a deer caught in headlights, wishing she had never come on this journey.

Noah noticed the tire tracks leading to the road. "Hey, it went this way," he said.

Ava looked up from Jake's chest and held back her tears. "Where?"

Moving to where he pointed, she began to follow the tire tracks.

Jake and the others caught up to her, and they went down the road, coming past the numbered campsites one by one, until the tracks forked. It was this other trail that the Savages' RV had taken. The road was narrower than the other and not as well maintained.

Farther down on the side of the road, they found the nasty carcass of a dead deer. Animals had torn into it, and crows and ravens were picking it over, but the scavengers flew off with the sudden appearance of humans, scaring the teens and causing the already on-edge girls to scream. The guys put their arms around their girlfriends to calm them, but to be truthful, they were more than a little spooked themselves.

Up ahead they could see the broken barricade where the RV had gone over, the lonely cables left from the tow truck, and the snapped branches of trees.

When Mia saw this, everything became too much. The dead deer remains, the dark woods, and now the crash site—she no longer could hold herself together. "Ay, no no no," Mia chanted, taking steps backward while shaking her head. "No more. I don't want to see any more. Let's go back to the RV," she pleaded.

"No. I want to see this. We'll be okay." Noah, still curious, tried to sound assuring.

Jake looked back to Mia. "We have to get going soon, so let's check this out; then we'll head to the police," he said.

Mia folded her arms. "Fine, you guys go. I'm going back to the RV," she said, adjusting her backpack. Turning away from the group, she hurried away from the scene that she knew would stay in everyone's nightmares.

The five of them watched her go as a squirrel ran across the old road past the deer and disappeared into the brush. Scurrying away, the squirrel stopped dead still. There was movement just beyond the bloody remains of the deer—another animal carcass was being held up in a tree as someone quietly enjoyed his meal while he watched the scene play out down below. He kept silent, staring at the kids as they walked around slowly, masks of fear on their faces, searching for answers he knew they would never be able to find.

As the teens made their way down the embankment and reached the burned-out RV, they saw the carnage everywhere. The first thing they noticed was the personalized mud flap in shiny chrome—"SAVAGE 1"—hanging from the back end of the destroyed RV. It was like a name on a gravestone, and Ava and Heather hurried past it and made their way to the front and saw the destruction. The driver's side was smashed into the earth, and the windshield was cracked and broken in places, covered with a black burnt film from the fire inside. There was no way a person could get inside the RV through the windshield, and Ava clung tightly to Heather.

"Oh my God," Heather whispered in complete shock.

Ava started to shake with fear, thinking of what her mother had gone through.

As the boys came around and witnessed the wreckage, the feeling of absolute horror raced through their souls.

Noah spoke. "Mia was right. I'm going with her."

Jake noticed the blown off panel and moved towards it. "Noah, we'll be up in a little while."

"Ava, Heather, I'm really sorry for you," Noah said quietly, making his way back up the hill to go after Mia.

CHAPTER 34

Wendy Storm drove into the news station's parking lot to see her sister, Sandy, standing outside smoking a cigarette, waiting for her arrival.

She was pissed after getting that information from Marlo's chart. Dropping her cigarette to the ground right next to an available ash-tray, she put it out with her high heel.

Wendy tried to ignore her sister's rage as she gathered her things from her car. But when the sound of Sandy's spiked shoes met the pavement, the *clack, clack, clack* made it clear to her that there wasn't the slightest chance to avoid the confrontation she knew was coming.

"Why didn't you use it?" Sandy shrieked, flipping back her blonde hair and nearly pushing Wendy back against her car.

"Back up with your satanic heels, bitch! It wasn't time!" Wendy snapped back, pushing Sandy against the other parked car.

Storming up the sidewalk and into the office, Wendy could feel her sister's gaze and winced from the daggers being shot into her back.

CHAPTER 35

The clouds at the campsite had grown dark by the time Mia arrived at Nash's RV. The wind had picked up speed, and she took a moment to look around. Mia was more than confused, swearing she could hear the notes of "London Bridge" being hummed by the large, frightening trees all around her.

Hurrying to the RV, she pulled on the door only to find it locked. "Damn!" she said as the cold wind blew around her. Pulling off her backpack to get her cardigan, she dug for her cell phone to call Nash.

The man moved closer.

Mia looked up and checked her surroundings as she pulled her pink phone from her backpack. Seeing she had no coverage, she went to the front of the RV. Looking farther up the road where it curved, she spotted a ranger's jeep parked on the side. "Nice to know someone's working around here," she mumbled.

Dropping her backpack and tying her cardigan around her shoulders, Mia knelt down and dug for her notebook, tearing out a page that had the song from class written on it. She turned it over and pulled out a pen, writing the note to her friends: "RV locked, going to ranger."

She heard the stick snap close beside her. The sound alarmed her. The birds taking flight from the trees turned her anxiety into outright fear. Seeing the flock, Mia grabbed her backpack, passing to the other side of the vehicle, where she looked down and saw the open window. She breathed a sigh of relief.

Hurrying, she ran to the RV where the slide out had been extended at the bedroom. She dropped her backpack on the ground and placed her foot on a large rock next to the vehicle to climb up.

Mia punched the screen of the open window, denting it inward and knocking it to the floor. She then lifted herself up and got her one arm and head in, struggling to climb inside.

The giant hand slammed down on her back, causing her to hit her chin on the windowsill.

Biting her tongue almost in half, Mia spit out blood.

Pulling her by her shirt and hair, scraping her face on the ledge, he pushed her to the ground.

Mia rolled over and saw the giant man wearing a camouflaged hunter's mask over his head and tried to scream, but all she could do was cough up blood from her wounded tongue.

The thunder rumbled, and lightning flashed above them as the man looked up into the sky.

Adrenaline flowing, and seeing this small window of escape, Mia turned and crawled under the RV.

When the man looked down, she was gone. Squatting, he tried to grab her, but she was too fast. He saw her get to the other side, crawl out, and run into the woods, dropping her cardigan along the way. With a deep sigh, he got up and ran around the RV, chasing after her.

Running ahead of him, Mia was trying to scream, but nothing would come out.

It took only moments before the man caught up to her, and with the open palm of his hand, he smacked into her back, pushing her forward. "Run a little faster, bitch!" he yelled.

Mia's body went faster than her feet; tripping, she fell forward and down a slope of rocks to a ledge. She tried to keep from going over but couldn't. With nothing to grab on to but the loose rocks and some forest growth, she went flying over the side. Landing about twenty feet down, hard on her side, she heard her arm break with a *snap*, and she rolled over in excruciating pain.

The hunter got to where she'd fallen and placed his large boot on a rock near the edge to look over; the rock moved slightly from his weight, and he caught on to a tree in order to stay upright.

Mia looked up from where she'd fallen to see the man standing there, looking down at her as if she were a treasure he would not lose. Mia's eyes widened as the man pushed his big boot down on the large rock, displacing it and sending it over.

The thunder crashed, and the lightning crackled when Mia screamed out, trying to move, putting weight on her broken arm and falling back as the large rock hit her square in the face before rolling away.

In the distance, Noah was calling for Mia. And to the surprise of the attacker, Mia stirred on the ground. Her face was broken, bruised, and bloody; she was choking on blood and dirt, and the man knew he had to follow her down in order to finish what he'd begun.

Noah was near Nash's RV. "Hey, Mia, I'm back!" he yelled.

Lying on the ground, bleeding and in pain, Mia heard Noah. She tried to move, but it was no use. The man appeared from above holding a sharp stick in his hand. And before Mia could make another sound, the man squatted down, grabbed her by her hair, and jabbed the sharp stick into her throat.

Her death was quick—and silent. He twisted the stick, pulling the carotid artery and causing it to snap back and hang from her neck listlessly, still pulsing with blood. Mia's body convulsed and then stopped—dead.

Pulling a small bush from the ground, he threw it over Mia's face and the growing pool of blood. The note was still clutched in her hand.

The flashes of lightning struck across the sky as Noah searched around the vehicle. He saw a movement as the wind blew the trees and bushes. "Mia, you over there?" he said, seeing nothing but the dark woods in front of him.

Cold and scared, he was about fifteen feet from the RV door when he fixated on it and moved quickly. It was locked. He pounded on the door. "Mia, it's me. Let me in. I'm sorry I didn't come back with you. Now, open the door," he begged.

No answer. He stopped pounding and looked down along the RV, noticing the disturbed ground. Quickly moving around to the other side, he spotted Mia's backpack, and his pulse began to beat out of control.

Rushing to pick it up, he noticed the dirt and the large boot prints beside it. He then stared at the open window...and the line of blood that painted the side of the RV and left a trail on the ground.

Scared, Noah stood and yelled, "Mia!"

Racing away to look for help, other campers, anyone he could find, Noah moved fast toward the road and heard a branch snap.

Halting in place, he turned toward the sound. "Mia?"

Moving toward the noise, he spotted Mia's cardigan on a hiking trail and ran to it, picking it up, finding more blood. Knowing Mia was hurt, he dropped it and ran down the path, coming to the edge of the embankment. Stopping, he looked down.

It was a Hollywood movie: *this could not be happening.* Seeing Mia with the bush sliding halfway off her face in the wind, he panicked.

Seeing the trail, he rushed down to her. He got to her, yelling, "Mia, are you...?"

Shock settled in as he saw her beautiful face, now bashed in, and the stick in her throat. He jumped back in fright, tripping and falling just as the bushes in front of him started to move.

Terrified, he got up and climbed the path he'd come down when a small rabbit leaped from the bushes.

Getting to the top of the trail, he ran back toward the RV but stopped dead in his tracks. Mia's bloody cardigan was now hanging on a stick that'd been planted right in the middle of the path.

He could barely breathe...barely swallow. He took off running as fast as he could, never seeing the man's large arm swing out from behind the tree, hitting him in the upper chest and knocking him to the ground.

A large figure wearing a camouflaged hunter's mask on his head stomped out from behind the tree. Placing one giant foot down on each side of him, he squatted over Noah and grabbed his throat with one hand while pulling a large, frightening knife from his back belt with the other.

Noah was choking, gasping for air as he stared up in total fear at an attacker who was about to end his life while humming a children's song.

Noah looked into the slits of the mask and saw the killer's dark, cold, lifeless eyes looking back at him. The man then plunged the knife into Noah's chest...over and over and over again...all the time humming that stupid song into his ears.

Noah cried out, and the sky joined in; thunder boomed and lightning flashed.

Blood was splattered on the man's camouflaged shirt, the ground, the boy, and the brush...everywhere when the hard rain began to pound.

The killer looked up into the sky and yelled. The sky sent an echo of thunder that sounded like the gods themselves congratulating him for his hard work.

The killer dragged Noah to where Mia had gone over the edge. Watching Noah gargling blood and digging his hands into the dirt amused him. Grabbing Noah by his shirt and belt, the monster picked him up, throwing him over the edge headfirst. Noah landed on his head, snapping his neck. His spine severed; it poked out the right side of his neck as he landed next to his dead girlfriend.

The note from Mia's hand was gone.

The hard rain pooled in the hole where the rock had been and filled with mud, which began flowing over the edge.

The rain quickly started puddles near the RV as well, and the blood spatter under the window washed down the side of the mobile home, erasing Mia's fate.

The hunter moved back toward the RV with Mia's note in his hand, pulled the cardigan with the stick, and threw it into the brush. He then hid in the woods, pausing to see the movement near the jeep parked up the road.

Ranger Melvin Jr. had heard the strange mix of cries and thunder, and the sounds resonated in his ears as he got in the jeep away from the rain. Closing the jeep's window, he shifted the gear, putting on the wipers. Glancing in the direction of the cries, he drove off in the other direction.

Down at the crash site, the downpour began.

"Oh no!" Heather said, moving closer to the RV to avoid the powerful storm.

"Wait! What was that noise?" Jake said, looking up toward the embankment.

"Thunder?" Nash said.

"No, before that."

"I didn't hear anything," Ava said, dropping the partly burned book, *Vander Place*, and joining Heather.

"We've got to get out of here; come on!" Jake said, waving to the group as they joined together and ran from the RV back up the embankment.

The four were soaking wet when they arrived back at the Rylands' RV, and Jake tried opening the locked door. He pounded on it, yelling, "Guys, let us in!"

Nash remembered the keys and started digging them out from his pocket. Getting them, he unlocked the door just when the thunder decided to boom overhead.

The four boarded the RV, thankful to be out of the storm.

Jake, still thinking the RV had been unlocked when they'd left, went to the back bedroom's closed door. "Thanks a lot, guys!" he yelled.

Heather grabbed a towel from a closet to dab at her hair when Ava noticed the note on the windshield. "What's that?"

Jake turned and went back to the front, staring at the note now stuck on the windshield and getting soaked.

Nash opened the door and ran to retrieve it.

Shrugging his shoulders, Jake went back and opened the bedroom door to have a word with his friends. It was empty: the screen was on the floor, and the rain was coming inside.

He closed the window as Nash returned, closing the door behind him.

"What is it?" Heather asked Nash as he unfolded the note.

Jake came out from the bedroom holding the screen.

"RV locked, going to ranger," Nash read, holding the note in one hand and the keys in the other. They all looked to him, and he shrugged. "I forgot it was locked."

"They left!" Ava said.

Jake lifted the busted screen to show them. "They tried to get in through the window in the back."

"Why didn't they just wait?" Heather asked.

Nash turned the note over, seeing the song lyrics. "Better yet, why didn't we see them on the way up here?" he said, placing the note on the counter.

Nash took a towel from Heather and wiped the rain from his face. "Come on, let's get down there and get them," he said in what was now a completely annoyed voice. Getting in the driver's seat, he started the vehicle. As he held down the buttons, the slide outs moved back into place.

And as the rest of them changed into dry clothes, he drove back out to the road.

CHAPTER 36

"Lorna, your order's ready," the pharmacist called out to the heavyset woman down the aisle in the small store. She moved to the counter, placed her large purse on it, and began to dig into it for her money. "This prescription's new for you all. Do you know how to use it?" the silver-haired man in the white apron behind the counter said.

"Thanks, Pete. Yeah, Charlie used to have it when he was a kid. Seemed to go away, but he had an episode mowing the lawn and fell to the ground. Scared me half to death. He knows how to use it," Lorna said, paying the man and placing the little white bag into her purse.

At that moment, Sam and Cara entered the pharmacy and didn't see any employees up front, so they made their way to the back, where they could see the man behind the counter.

Lorna finished with her business just as they approached, holding flyers in their hands.

"Excuse me, sir. Would you mind if we post a flyer in your store?" Cara asked, holding up the flyer with the photo of Lisa that Sam had retrieved from Ed's desk.

The pharmacist took one look at the flyer and immediately agreed. "Yes, of course, I'm so sorry. Is she a relative?" he asked.

"My niece," Sam said, moving the "Free Kittens" flyer on the bulletin board near the counter.

Lorna looked back at them posting the flyer and made her way out from the store, where she noticed the unmistakable extreme RV, with the personalized mud flap under the rear with "SAVAGE 2" in shiny chrome, parked a short distance away from her nasty-looking, tan van. She got in and threw her purse to her husband. "It's inside," she said.

The man in the van opened her giant ratty-looking purse and pulled out the small white bag.

Lorna got in and noticed the couple inside the store moving up toward the front with Pete, and they taped one of the flyers to the window. "Hey, Charlie, they're looking for that poor little girl in the news."

Together they watched the couple leave the pharmacy and board their fancy-looking ride.

Sam pulled out and made his way onto the main road to the highway, with Asa Ryland in the passenger seat. His mind was alert to the storm, and the visions he had playing behind his eyes of the children being in harms way in such a horrendous downpour kept him in a state of worry.

Nathan was half asleep, leaning back on the sofa, when Sam applied the brakes at the stop sign before the highway on-ramp. Nathan woke with a flinch.

"Hey, Dad, why don't you go in the back and lie down? You'll be more comfortable there," Cara suggested to him.

Without a noise, Nathan nodded and got up, making his way to the bedroom.

Cara and Rayna sat at the table looking out the window. Although there was a deck of cards between them, they were not interested in playing. Their visions were the same as Sam's—hoping and praying silently that the kids were all right.

Innocently lying next to the cards was the box of flyers they had made, with the reward for the safe return of Lisa Savage.

CHAPTER 37

Heather sat up front beside Nash, continuing to try her phone. Still having no luck, they drove down to the rangers' station. Ava was quietly staring out the window from her place on the sofa as Jake picked up Mia's note. He turned it over and looked at the song lyrics.

Driving far to meet you.
Wonder and delight.
Not knowing what was coming.
How could I be not right?
Stupidly and selfish.
I messed up big and then.
I'm sent home all alone.
And here I start my fight.
How could I be so wrong?
I'm sorry now.
But that was not me at all.
One day you'll see.
How could you believe so strong?
And not look back.
I'm here for you.
When you're done being you.
I'm here for you.

Jake was smiling at the paper when Nash slowed the RV down. He then looked over at Ava. "Hey, this is pretty good."

Ava looked back at him and forced a smile. "Yeah, back when my life was normal, if it ever was."

"But I thought Lucy caught her dude with some sophomore; the way this sounds, Lucy messed up," Jake said.

Ava thought for a moment. "Huh, you're right."

Nash stopped near the station, and Ava looked out at the cabin with dread. "I don't want to go in there," she whispered.

Jake joined Ava on the sofa and looked out with her. "You're not," he said, standing and putting on his jacket. "You girls, stay here. Nash and I got this."

Nash took his damp shirt off and switched to a dry one; grabbing his hoodie, he followed Jake out the door.

Heather locked it behind them and went to join Ava on the sofa to watch. Outside, most of the few remaining campers were leaving just as fast as possible.

Jake and Nash ran over to the cabin and entered. Seeing it was empty, they stopped at the first desk, which had an open gunnysack of candy sitting on it. Farther back, near the same desk Jake and Ava had been at earlier, they saw a bathroom off to the side. The door was ajar, and the light was on. Someone was in there.

"Be out in a minute," a man's voice called from the bathroom.

Jake was keeping an eye on the door, just as Nash looked around to see the dripping-wet hat and coat that hung on wall hooks beside the desk. He nudged Jake in the side and pointed them out.

The tall man with the black hair came out of the back bathroom with his shirt unbuttoned, holding a hand towel. He had spots of shaving cream on him, and he wiped his face, throwing the towel into the bathroom hamper.

They could see this guy worked out just by the size of his muscles as he started to button his shirt. He stopped to close the bathroom door, and when he turned, Jake noticed a bandage on the right side of the man's head.

"Sorry, got caught in the rain, so I showered."

"Hi, remember me?" Jake asked, looking at the man as if something was different.

The ranger paused for a moment. His stare was completely blank. "Ah, yeah, it's been real busy today with the rain; it's a bad one. What can I do for you?" The man sat down and rubbed the right side of his head.

Nash looked from the closed bathroom door back to the man. "We're looking for two friends who were on their way down here: Noah and Mia. Where are they?" he asked.

The man shifted his eyes from Jake to Nash. "Sorry? Nobody's been here," he said.

Nash motioned to the wet hat and coat. "You just said you got caught in the rain, and it was busy."

Almost looking as if he was working hard to hold back his temper, the ranger glanced over at his wet belongings. "True. I left. And when I got back, the *other* staff was busy with the phones. Several people have been in and out of here, but nobody said they were going to be waiting for anyone," he said.

Jake continued to stare at the man. "You shaved your beard. That's what's different."

"Yeah, I do that," the large man said as if studying them.

"Anyway, we're looking for our friends. One is a Latin guy a few inches shorter than me and thinner. He would have been with a girl named Mia—curly, dark-brown hair, hot accent, from Colombia?" he said.

"Sorry, no one like that has been through here that I've seen. I'll call around, though. Are you reporting them lost?" the ranger asked.

Nash and Jake answered simultaneously, "Yes."

Jake stared down at the desk. A few pictures and a spindle with three pink message sheets stuck to it were all that was there. The man reached to the spindle, which sat next to a photo of two young boys dressed alike, with an older girl standing between them. He then grabbed the message notes and spread them across the desk. Nash and Jake could clearly read the messages, and there was nothing about Noah or Mia to be found.

"See, guys, no notes," the ranger said.

Nash and Jake looked at each other as the man pushed back his chair and stood up, motioning them toward the front door. "I'll put a call out. What campsite are you in? And do you have a cell-phone number you can leave, so we can contact you when we find them?"

Standing at the front desk with the candy, Nash eyed a pen and paper and reached for them.

"Yeah, we're in number nineteen, and I'll write down the number, but the service up here sucks!" Nash said. Scribbling the contact information, he handed it to the ranger. "Have them call us as soon as you find them," he said. "Okay?"

"Will do." The man looked at Jake and smiled. "Oh, right...I did meet you earlier. Now I remember, you and your girlfriend," he said. "Pretty name."

It was as if a chill had suddenly entered the dimly lit room. Nash opened the station door.

Leaving fast, running out into the rain, they left the ranger standing and watching them through the window, smiling wide.

Seeing the guys running toward the RV, Heather got up and unlocked the door to let them in. "Where are they?" she asked.

Nash was taking his wet hoodie off. "They're not here, and the ranger hasn't seen them," he said.

"I don't know about that," Jake said.

Ava jumped off the sofa. "Why do you say that?"

Jake looked troubled. "I don't know...It was strange. I don't believe that he remembered me," he said.

Nash was puzzled. "What do you mean? He said he remembered you and your girlfriend."

Jake shook his head and looked out the window at the rangers' cabin. "It was the same guy Ava and I saw earlier, all right, but something seemed *off* about him," he said.

"He told you he shaved his beard," Nash said.

"Yeah, but that wasn't it," Jake replied, trying to think of what his gut was telling him.

Ava moved toward the door. "Like what? I'll go in and see," she said, reaching for the door.

Jake grabbed her wrist. "Ava, he was lying when he said he remembered me, and you're going in there with Heather." The three looked at Jake. "Ava, do you remember him having a bandage on the side of his head?" Jake asked.

Ava thought for a moment. "No. I remember he was wearing a hat, he had a beard, and his initials on his shirt were M. J."

Another RV moved past them, catching Heather's eye. "While we were waiting, several other campers were leaving, like that one," she said. "And *why* am I going in there with Ava?"

Jake smiled. "I've got a plan."

Inside the cabin, the ranger was on a radio back at his desk when Ava and Heather ran inside, startling him.

Stopping quickly, Ava looked at the large map on the wall near the brochures, while Heather went right up to the clean-shaven man in the back of the office.

The man turned off his radio and smiled. "Hi there," he greeted her.

"Hi, it's me again," Heather said. "I have another question."

"Sure thing. Ava…right?"

"Right," Heather said without skipping a beat.

Ava quietly joined Heather and looked right at him. The ranger looked over to her, clearly not recognizing her at all. When he turned back to Heather, Ava noticed the bandage and then the messages spread out on his desk.

"Did you find your friends?" he asked.

"No, not yet," Heather said. "I just wanted to ask about this rain. Do you know how long it's supposed to last?"

He smiled. "They say through the night, and it could even go on and off over the next few days."

Heather smiled back at him. "Thank you." Looking at Ava, she nodded. "Come on, Heather," she said as she moved toward the front of the cabin.

Ava looked at the ranger quickly, nodded, and then followed Heather out.

Back in the rain, they ran to the RV.

Ava was first. "Jake, you were right; he acted like Heather was me from earlier."

"Yeah, and he *is* creepy, bandage or not," Heather added.

"I didn't remember him having that. Jake, maybe he hit his head and can't remember me?"

Nash moved up to the driver's seat. "So what do you think?"

"I don't know, but we better get to the police station now," Jake decided.

As Nash started the RV, Heather picked up her cell phone and breathed a sigh of relief, seeing she had coverage. "Hey, my phone's working. I'll call Mia."

The phone rang and rang before going to voice mail. "Mia, where are you? We got your note and can't find you at the rangers' station. We're going to the police station now. Call us as soon as you get this."

Nash pulled the RV away from the ranger's small jeep that sat parked in the lot.

Down the road, the bearded Melvin Jr. saw those troublesome kids leaving the information cabin and quickly got into a different jeep parked in the dark shadows of some trees. He picked up the binoculars on the seat next to him, the strap knocking a backpack onto the floor, spilling its contents as he watched. Smiling under his beard, he knew those know-it-all teens had just met his brother, Leroy Galloway. He glanced down on the floor beside him and saw the pink cell phone blinking. Apparently, Mia had a message.

CHAPTER 38

Sam and Cara Savage asked the store clerk if they could post the reward flyer for Lisa Savage's safe return on the store's bulletin board. The clerk was helpful in allowing them and sorry that he had not seen the girl. He told them it was the talk of the area and everyone was keeping an eye out for her. Sam and Cara thanked him and boarded the RV just as Asa Ryland finished gassing it up.

They had left a few extra copies to keep at the register, and the clerk was taping one to the back of it as he watched them board the vehicle. Moving to the door, he watched the brand-new RV leave the store, noticing the license plate and the customized mud flap.

The rain started hitting the windshield hard when Sam and company drove down the highway. No one was talking as they listened to the radio, all thinking about getting to their children as fast as possible.

Nathan Savage napped restlessly in the back bedroom. Sam and Cara knew that Nathan was keeping something from them, but they truly had no idea as to the extent of his secret.

Sam shook his head, thinking back over his father's life and lies.

Nathan Savage was a retired air-force colonel and a businessman you didn't want to cross. He'd played dirty his whole life; a mean alcoholic, he was not one to back away from taking off his belt to deliver an unfair punishment to his boys, Savage style. It had been a tough conversation Sam had had with Ed when he told him he was allowing their father to live under his roof. To this day, Ed would never forgive his father for what had happened.

When Ava was young and Marlo was pregnant with their third child (one she miscarried), Ed had a moment with dear old Dad that Sam still remembered to this day. Nathan had a small dog at the time that he loved with all his heart—he seemed to love that dog more than he loved his own children. One day in the garage, Ed walked in to find Nathan smacking Ava with a rolled-up newspaper because she'd dropped her chocolate ice-cream cone in his newly detailed Cadillac and made a mess on the carpet.

That was the last day Nathan ever hurt a child.

Ava had run to her father, who told her to go inside to her grandmother. That was when Ed picked up Dad's little dog by the neck with one hand and pinned his father against his own car with the other. "If you ever lay another hand on my child or *any* of the other kids, I'll choke the life out of your little dog here, Dad!"

Nathan had looked his eldest son in the eyes and knew the tables had finally turned.

The dog was yelping helplessly. Nathan nodded, staring down at his pet. "Put my dog down," Nathan said, controlling his rage.

Ed had shoved the dog into his father's chest, letting go of both animals at the same time. "I remember, Dad. I remember when you put Roman and Logan in the hospital. I'll never forget it!"

That was a long time ago, and even though Ed was now cordial with their father, those memories were still there, resting on the back burner in all four of the Savage brothers' minds.

Sam had always been the softhearted one. He was the one who always broke up the quarrels the brothers would get into while growing up.

He felt kindness toward his father as he aged. After their mother's death from a brain aneurysm, Nathan had spiraled downward, having two heart attacks and going through three home-care nurses by scaring them off with his antics. It had been Sam to the rescue.

It wasn't the money either, although the Savages always had money growing up. New cars, the big house, money to burn—but the boys did well for themselves despite living under Nathan's thumb and overbearing rules.

Sam was destined, after mediating his brothers' silly fights, to become a successful lawyer. He had done just that. He stayed on in

Nathan's construction business as a construction contract lawyer and later joined an outside firm for a chance at trying criminal cases.

Roman and Logan had used their construction backgrounds to get into real estate, and together the brothers formed an invincible team while staying with the family business. Roman kept his office at Savage Tower in the States, and Logan set up shop in London.

And Ed, well...Ed had made himself into a star.

With their mom deceased and Nathan's age and manner changing from long hours at the office to a simple life of building birdhouses and hanging them in the backyard, Sam decided to take him in. Ed, Sam's closest confidant, had warmed up to their father over time, but he had never forgotten the past. It was this bond that these two brothers shared—and Sam knew Ed's other secrets too.

Sam shook his head as he stared out between the raindrops, thinking of the past and wondering what on earth had happened to Ed. How was he going to fix this one?

As he glanced into the rearview mirror at the closed bedroom door, he wondered exactly what the patriarch of the Savages was so afraid of. Why was he acting like he'd traveled to Black Ridge Falls before?

On the other side of the door, the dream was heavy. Nathan's body twitched as his mind looked back to a past he so wanted to forget.

The scene was familiar. A late-twenties Nathan was looking for his brother, Niles, in a park near a few acres of trees. Next to the park was a lowered expressway with a bridge over it for pedestrians and bicyclists, leading to a library.

Nathan was calling out for him when, up ahead, he spotted Niles crossing the bridge. Near the base of the steps leading to the walkway were rocks in a garden. One of the largest rocks had been wedged free from its berth. It was easy to see the hole that now sat in the middle of the otherwise well-maintained landscape.

Farther out, in the middle of the bridge, Niles could be seen standing alone, holding the missing rock on the railing and watching the cars pass beneath.

When Nathan got to the bridge and saw the traffic, he called out to his brother, begging him not to do it, just as Niles let the rock fall. The two watched in silence as it smashed into the sedan below.

The car smashed into other cars, and a gasoline truck crashed into them, bursting into flames.

Nathan ran to Niles and grabbed him, pulling him away from the railing. As if running for their lives, they raced into the park to hide in the woods just beyond the horrible mess.

On the other side of the bridge, a couple walking away from the library heard the crash, sending them running to the bridge in panic. They saw the backs of two young men fleeing into the woods.

Nathan could hear Niles running right behind him. He slowed to turn around and…screamed. It wasn't Niles chasing him. The devil had found him instead.

It was time to pay.

Nathan woke in the back of the RV and clasped his hands over his mouth; he stopped himself from yelling out, just as Sam changed lanes and moved forward through the rain.

CHAPTER 39

Nash was pushing the speed limits back to the highway, completely ignoring Jake's concerns coming from the passenger seat next to him. Ava and Heather sat as close to them as they could. They were all looking ahead at the heavy rain beating against the windshield. The wipers were on at high speed when Nash pulled up to a stop sign. Beyond the sign, the road passed a little store and garage before coming to the highway. "Okay, which way?" Nash asked.

"We go right," Ava said, pointing.

"Are you sure?"

"Jake, you remember what he said, don't you? We go right," Ava said, putting her hand on his thigh.

A car behind them honked, and Nash drove the RV through the intersection and into the little store parking lot next to the garage.

"Jake, what's up?" Ava asked.

"Do you remember exactly what he told us?"

"Yeah, he said go right at the highway." She paused a moment. "No, wait, he said something else…What was it?"

Jake spoke, "He said, go the—"

Remembering, Ava jumped back in, "Go the way you were going!"

Heather tugged on Ava's shoulder. "Please tell me you told the big creep which way we had come from."

"No, we didn't," Jake informed them.

"Then, how did he know?" Ava said.

"So, which way?" Nash asked again.

Heather and Ava both shouted at the same time. "Go left!" they said.

Jake looked over and noticed the store. "Screw this; let's ask here. Besides, I don't remember seeing any police or sheriff signs posted on the highway when we got here."

Nash turned off the wipers, missing the small jeep as it pulled into the parking lot and headed inside the garage. He started to mess with the GPS system on board, which had been pretty useless this entire trip.

Jake started to look at the GPS with him when the girls got up and went to the store. Thinking he'd better go with them, he followed them out.

The bell on the door rang as the three entered. There were no other customers inside, and in the back, where a deli/café seemed to be, was a woman busy making sandwiches.

"Welcome. I'll be right up to help," came the slightly raised voice.

"That's okay; we'll come back to you," Heather answered.

They got to the deli, noticing the sign "Patty's Specials" on the counter and a display of backpacks and assorted camping accessories next to it. A backpack was on the counter, and the worker was cleaning off a knife. Her hair was pulled back in a scarf, and she looked up with a smile.

"Can I offer you one of my specials today, kids?"

"Hi there, Patty; can you tell us how to get to the police station?" Heather asked, noticing her name on the specials sign.

"Oh, sure, go up to the highway and head right. Next exit is Old Mills Road; the sign says 'Sheriff,' not police. You folks in some trouble?" Patty asked.

"Oh no, my…um…My folks are camping up that way, and we're going to catch up with them. Thank you," Heather said.

Patty smiled. "You're welcome. I love easy questions. Be careful with the rain." She laughed.

Thanking her, they walked out the door.

Jake opened the RV, and they piled in, getting Nash's attention. "So which way?" he asked.

"We go right. Just like we were told," Ava said. "We're overthinking this," she added with a sigh. "But I'm totally spooked. How did that ranger know which way we were going? And where the hell are Mia and Noah…Why haven't they called?"

"Maybe he took a good guess," Nash said.

"Mia was right; this teenage-mystery thing isn't as fun as it seems on TV," Heather reminded them.

"Come on, let's just go," Jake said to Nash, who was still looking at the GPS. "Any luck with that?" he asked.

"Nope," Nash said, putting the RV in drive and making his way out of the parking lot.

The rain seemed to fall even harder as they drove back onto the highway. And up in the mountains, above the campsite, the pools of water slowly began to form a mudslide.

CHAPTER 40

When the teens pulled into the police-station parking area, the rain had let up almost as quickly as it'd started. They piled out, excited and worried to finally be getting to Ed.

Being the last one out, Nash closed the door and tried it to make sure it was locked. "Hey, guys, we're locked up here." he said on his way up the steps to join the others.

The sheriff's office was an older, more rustic jail, like one you would see in an old western. There was a counter with a lift that separated the entrance from the back, with a newspaper centered in the middle of it. Beyond the counter were a few desks, and to the right and down was the row of cells. An officer, his name tag reading "Carl Rumple," was seated at one of the desks, talking on the phone, while Ed Savage lay on a bed facing away from the front of the office.

Ava spotted his head; it was bandaged.

"Daddy! Daddy!" she shouted.

Ed turned to see them, and Officer Rumple jumped up, dropping his phone on his desk. He hung it up and dashed to the counter.

Ava, seeing the counter lift, went to pull it up, but the officer put his hand over it, pushing it back down with authority.

"Let us pass, damn you! That's my father!" Ava demanded.

"Ava! Heather! Oh, thank God!" Ed said; he was now slowly standing in his cell and facing them.

The girls stared at Officer Rumple, noting that the small-town lawman was most definitely one of a kind. Although he had slicked-back, dyed-blond hair and wore the requisite brown, mirrored, gold-framed sunglasses, he had a weird sort of power coming from him. He was more than authoritative at six feet four, but his too-tight uniform and tightly trimmed, dyed-blond goatee pretty much said it all: jackass!

"Just a minute here, miss. You'll calm down or find yourself in a cell next to him," he said.

The sneer Ava gave Rumple was priceless, looking him up and down as if he were some sort of circus freak.

The jackass picked up the counter phone and punched in a number.

Taking off his sunglasses—which he was wearing inside on a rainy day—the man eyed the teenagers like they belonged on the FBI's "Most Wanted" list.

The group exchanged looks, and Ava rolled her eyes, dismissing the jackass and speaking to her father. "Daddy, are you okay?"

The jackass held up his hand to silence her. Ed, who had been dealing with this idiot, just nodded.

"Hey, Arnie, our guest's family has arrived," Carl said. "Uh-huh, will do." He hung up the phone. "Just a moment."

A car could be heard pulling in behind the small station, and soon the backdoor opened and Arnie Mallard walked in, putting his cell phone in his pocket on his way to the counter.

"Sheriff Arnie Mallard," he said, greeting the teens. "And you all are?"

"I'm Ava Savage, and *that's* my father," Ava said, pointing. "This is my cousin Heather, and Jake and Nash. Now can I please go to my dad?"

Arnie shifted his eyes from Ava to Heather and zeroed in on her. "In a minute. I've been expecting you, young lady. Your father called and told me you were all coming up here after being told not to. Anything to say about that?" Arnie's voice remained that of a seasoned cop as he looked at the others. "And where are the other two who supposedly came up with you?"

Nash said, "That's just it; we don't know. We thought they would be here."

"They're missing!" Heather blurted out. "They walked back to where we parked by themselves, and then it started raining. When we got back to the RV, they were…gone."

"Come on back." Arnie sighed heavily, moving the newspaper and lifting the counter, putting it in the locked position. He then looked to Officer Rumple. "Open it up," he said.

Carl stared at his superior while moving his hand dramatically to his holstered gun. "Are you sure, sir?" he said, looking like a fool.

Arnie looked at him with wonder. "Just do it," he said.

"Like this is a jailbreak. What a dick," Ava muttered under her breath.

Carl pulled his oversized key ring off his belt and slowly moved to Ed's cell, opening the door. The girls were right behind him and rushed into Ed's arms. For the first time since this nightmare began, Ed Savage smiled and held his family tight.

Feeling a little overexcited and flushed from his head wound, he sat back on his bunk. "Careful there," he said.

Ava and Heather sat next to him, holding his hands as if he would somehow disappear, Arnie pulled up some extra chairs near the cell, motioning to the boys. "Here, guys."

Pulling the cell door all the way back, Arnie leaned against it.

Ava looked at her father's bandaged head and saw he was in pain. "Daddy, are you sure you're not hurt?"

"I'll survive, sweetie. Now, better question, what are you kids doing up here?"

"That's my fault, Mr. Savage," Nash said, shifting uncomfortably on his chair.

"My brother is going to kick your—"

Ed stopped and looked up at Arnie. "Sorry."

"That's fine. I would kick his ass, too," Arnie said, offering a grin.

Ava nudged her father. "How's Mom? Have you heard anything?"

Ed pulled his daughter closer. "Your mother's condition has stabilized, meaning she should wake up soon. That was what they told me earlier."

"And Lisa? Have they found her yet? Or Simon?"

Ed shook his head. "They're still searching for her. Right?" he said, giving the sheriff a look that demanded an answer.

"Weather's turning bad; not sure how much longer the teams will be out," Arnie said, knowing in his gut that the man in front of him was innocent, but also thinking the girl was dead.

"And still nothing on Simon?" Ed asked Arnie.

"Nothing. I made a statement to the media; we're looking for both of them."

"But what happened, Uncle Ed? Why are you here?" Heather said. Her voice shook, as if she was scared to hear the answer.

"I was driving back from this little store when I saw the RV go tearing up the road," Ed began, swallowing his emotion as he continued to relive the nightmare. "We had just got here! I couldn't believe what I was seeing. I followed and saw it go through a barricade. It went over a cliff and crashed down an embankment. I got out and started down after it, but…It exploded. Then something hit me from behind. I remember being loaded in the ambulance and then waking up here. That's it."

Ava hugged her distraught father. "Dad, who was driving the RV?"

"I don't know. They think it was me," Ed said and looked to Arnie. "But I'm telling you it wasn't."

Ava's eyes were getting red as she held back her tears. She looked down and wiped her face, staring up at the man in charge. "Why are you keeping him here? We should be with my mom, or looking for my sister."

"They don't believe me," Ed said, holding his daughter.

"Why not? How could you drive *both* vehicles to the cliff at the same time?" Jake demanded. "I would call that impossible."

"The Range Rover wasn't there when we found him, son," Arnie said.

"Dad?" Ava looked to her father.

Ed's frustration was clear. He was sick and tired of telling the same story over and over and feeling like the nightmare would never end or be believed. "I left the keys in it! The engine was still running. Someone must have stolen it," he said.

The lightbulb over Ava shined bright. "Yes. The same someone who hit you in the head. Sheriff, please, we're good people; *please* believe me," she said.

The horrific static finally cleared a bit on the radio. A voice could be heard offering up a report of a mudslide happening in the local mountains, just as a new officer entered through the front door. The report said they could lose power. As if God wanted to prove the voice wrong, the police fax machine rang, and a fax was transmitted.

The second officer came around the counter and picked up the fax; he glanced at it and waved it in the air. "Sheriff."

Arnie looked over and left the family reunion, taking the fax from the officer.

"Oh my God, Dad. Lisa…Is she really? She's…" Ava started to cry into her father's shoulder.

"No, Ava," Ed said sternly. "I won't believe it, and I'll find her if it's the last thing I do." He glared over his daughter at the sheriff reading the fax.

"But the news—it sounds awful," Ava cried, leaning against him.

Ed's eyes were filled with hurt and pain, but he tried to be comforting. "Hang on, honey. We all have to hang on."

Arnie appeared back at the cell with the fax. "So you were saying when you walked in that your other friends were lost?"

Jake eyed the fax. "Yes, sir. We don't know where they are."

Arnie remained quiet, studying the others.

Heather reached up to her uncle's bandage where it was coming loose and tucked it behind his ear. "We were at your campsite, Uncle Ed; then we walked down toward the crash site. Well…Before we got there, Mia got scared and went back to Nash's RV by herself. We were parked up in number nineteen. We went to where Aunt Marlo crashed the RV," she said.

"Your aunt didn't do it, Heather," Ed said, raising his voice.

"I'm sorry. I didn't mean—"

Heather looked down at the floor; the redness filled her cheeks.

"I know. I'm sorry, too," Ed said, pulling her to him.

"Noah went back up after Mia," Nash said to Arnie. "We stayed and looked around to see if we could figure out anything, but then it started raining. So we went back…And when we got there, they were gone."

"That's when we found Mia's note on the windshield," Jake continued. "It said that they'd found the RV locked, so they were going to the ranger station. We went there and were told they hadn't shown up. I think that ranger knows something, though."

Ed looked from Ava to Jake. "What do you mean?"

"It was just so weird, Dad," Ava said, pulling herself together and wiping away her tears. "Jake and I went in there earlier and asked him for directions. When Jake mentioned my name, he looked at me funny. Even said I had a beautiful name. But later, when we came back to see if Noah and Mia were there, he acted like he didn't know me."

"It's true," Heather added. "When Ava and I went in together, he had never seen me, but he believed I was Ava. Like I was the one who'd spoken to him."

"He sees a lot of people, campers during the day. He was probably just mistaken," Ed said, looking from Heather to Ava.

"Mr. Savage," Jake added, "when I went in, he acted the same with me. He also knew which way we were headed on the highway before we even told him where we were coming from."

"Which ranger are you talking about?" Arnie asked.

"The tall one with the big beard," Ava said. "Except he later shaved it off. He also had the initials 'M. J.' on his shirt."

"Oh, that's Melvin Jr. He's been around for years; he's harmless," Arnie assured them.

"Wait a minute," Heather added. "Why don't you ask the store clerk where Ed was at? They can tell you where he was when this all was happening."

Ed grimaced. "I asked them to do just that," he said. "This woman, Patty, at the store: I spoke with her, so she *would* know. She had long, grayish hair, and she dressed like a guy."

Jake raised his voice, looking at Arnie. "That's the same lady we just saw at the store."

Arnie nodded. "And I did speak with her. Problem is, she doesn't remember seeing Ed there. And I can forget about asking for video, because that store hasn't had surveillance in years. And Ed here paid in cash," the sheriff said, sighing heavily. "In other words, there's nothing to support his alibi."

"Then how did he know she had long, gray hair?" Ava demanded.

Ed smiled, as if proud of his daughter for catching that. "Honey, I mentioned that fact, too," Ed said. "We even had a conversation about Boone's Farm strawberry wine, a joke bottle I bought for Marlo." A look of sheer pain came across his face as he spoke his wife's name. "That woman is lying," Ed said, looking right into Arnie.

Everyone looked to Arnie, who agreed. "Yeah, Patty's had it hard. She lost her parents when she was young, and, well... Sometimes she isn't all there. I even asked to pull the register tapes to see what was sold, but she told me it was jacked up and was ringing up everything on one key; she even showed me. But, like I told your brother Sam, I don't believe you were involved. But I needed this to be sure," Arnie said, holding up the fax. "This is something we've been waiting for."

Arnie looked down at the fax. "The DNA found in your hat is not yours, Mr. Savage. Someone else was definitely there. I'm sorry to have held you. You're free to go."

The teens cheered around Ed as they rose and walked him from the cell.

"Another thing, Ed." Arnie patted him on the shoulder. "How did you folks come about picking Black Ridge Falls for your family vacation?"

"My dad sent away for brochures," Ed replied, glancing over his shoulder as they headed for the counter.

"No, he didn't," Arnie said, putting the fax on his desk.

The group stopped at the odd comment and turned back to him.

Arnie shrugged. "Sam called earlier saying he found the brochures on your desk addressed to your dad, but your father swears he never heard of Black Ridge Falls or called for any vacation brochures for that matter. Someone wanted you here, Mr. Savage," Arnie said. "And I need to find out why."

The group looked to each other for support at hearing the disturbing news.

"One more thing," Arnie said, "Sam said he found the phone number to the station on your desk. Did you call up here for something?"

"No," Ed said. "I meant to—was going to ask about the campgrounds."

Arnie opened a drawer in his desk and removed a manila envelope with Ed's name on it. He handed it to him. "Here's your wallet and personal items. Again, I'm real sorry about this. But I have to tell you: this isn't over," Arnie said.

Ed opened the envelope and pulled out his phone; it was dead. "Someone call Sam and tell him we're going to the hospital," he said.

Heather had her phone out and was already calling. "I've got this," she said.

Ed pulled out his wallet and opened it to see if anything was missing before realizing he was still in his assigned clothes.

"Can I get my clothes back?" Ed asked, motioning to what he was wearing.

Arnie cringed. "Sorry, Ed, they're not back yet. But I tell you what; I'm parked around back. Let me pull my squad car around, and I'll lead you directly to the hospital. Least I can do," Arnie said, holding up his keys.

Ed nodded, stuffing his wallet into the suit's single, breast pocket. "Thank you."

"Dad, it's cold outside. I packed you some clothes and a coat. You can change in the RV," Ava said to her father.

Ed smiled and gave her his devilish grin.

Ava actually smiled back, unbelievably happy to be by her father's side. "Nope, not working!" Ava said with a wink.

Ed smiled wider and pulled her close as they moved through the open counter.

Heather's phone call to her father went directly to voice mail and then dropped...just as the lights went out in the station.

Even though the rain had let up, the dark clouds in the sky were foreboding, not allowing very much light to enter through the frosted-glass windows of the door.

Officer Rumple stood and told them not to worry; the emergency backup lights would come on. They didn't.

The officers immediately turned on their flashlights, and Arnie moved over to the electrical box on the side of the wall. He opened it, saw everything was in the on position, and then gave it a good whack. The emergency lights flickered first and then flooded the station.

"Thank you, Officer Rumple," Ava said, making a face as the guys started laughing.

Even Ed grinned as Arnie put on his hat. "Old-fashioned ingenuity is still the only thing that works in this modern-day world."

Arnie headed to the back to get his car. "We better get going. Stay close to me; the roads could be bad, but I'll get you there."

Ed led Ava past the counter. "I pray to God you can," he whispered under his breath. He could feel the pain meds he had taken just prior to the kids arriving as he took a last look at the cell he had been in and gritted his teeth. "I don't want to see this place ever again," he said. He then checked the envelope to see that it was empty and tossed it on the counter. Watching the envelope glide to a stop, a feeling of déjà vu came over him, remembering back to when he was younger than Logan, to an old situation he'd had in a similar setting; it hadn't ended well. Ed put his arm around Ava, his mind strangely on that long-ago nasty experience.

They were the first to open the door of the station to freedom, as Heather tried her dad again.

CHAPTER 41

Standing against the outside wall of the station, waiting with her trusty microphone, was Wendy Storm; her cameraman was beside her. She surprised everyone as she jumped in front of the little gang.

"Ed Savage, what will happen to your career when the whole world finds out you tried to murder your wife?"

As she shoved the microphone in Ed's face, he was blindsided. He had a massive headache from his injury, and with his mind on that long-ago situation (and the meds), like a premonition, he flashed back to being mauled by a reporter during the *Phantom Finders* mess, eerily on location at an old jail. Even the reporter back then had similar blonde hair like the shrew attacking him now.

He blurred the memory away of his younger self, jolted as history seemingly was repeating itself. He'd been through a lot. His head was foggy; he was happy to finally be free and with his family, and now... this.

Wendy pushed forward, knocking him back into Jake. Ava shoved Wendy hard against the wall, ready to rip her apart, and it was all caught on camera. Ed grabbed his daughter off Wendy and pushed her along down the steps toward the RV. But Wendy was on fire; she screamed at Officer Jackass to arrest Ava immediately.

The second officer came from inside. "No one is being arrested," he shouted, watching Wendy follow the group to the RV while waving her arms and yelling about her constitutional rights as a member of the press.

"I'm going to break this story tonight!" Wendy shrieked, running toward them and getting Ed and Ava to look back at her just as they were in front of the RV.

Ava lunged, but Jake and Heather stopped her movement and turned her around, and in the commotion, Heather stopped the call to her dad in order to try to save her cousin from being on a tabloid cover with her dad for the rest of her life.

Ed got around the RV to find Sandy Storm with her own microphone and a second cameraman blocking the RV's door. "Are you having an affair with your pregnant, slutty little costar, Ellie Collins, whom you used to work with? Is that why you did it?" she blurted out, shoving her microphone in his face.

"Get that away from me!" Ed yelled, raising his arm up to bat the microphone away from his face. He looked right into the camera, putting his hand up and knocking it down.

"That's private property!" Sandy screamed.

Ed got to the locked door. His frustration rose.

Wendy came around the back of the RV. "Is it true that little girl, whom you know will never be found and is probably dead, was not your biological daughter? Did that have something to do with your actions?" Wendy said, shoving her microphone at him.

Ed had never hit a woman in his life, yet looking at this insane bitch, all he wanted to do was punch her. He raised his arm and knocked the microphone from her hands, just as Nash pushed through with the keys and unlocked the door. He opened it fast, blocking Wendy and her cameraman, and they all piled in—closing the door and locking it behind them.

"Get us out of here," Ed demanded, falling exhaustedly onto the sofa.

Nash jumped into the driver's seat and started the RV. Throwing it in reverse, he backed out, barely missing one of the cameramen. When he was able to turn out, Arnie pulled around with lights flashing.

But Wendy and Sandy Storm followed the RV, with their cameras in tow, before stopping. They turned to the men to report their story with the RV speeding away behind them. The perfect shot had been claimed, as the women stood beside each other blathering into their microphones; each one attempted to prove that she, and only she, was the perfect reporter. Her sister be damned.

Arnie saw the commotion and eyed the two pain-in-the-ass reporters, hitting the siren in order to interrupt their story.

The reporters were more than angry, as Wendy pointed to Arnie's car and screamed, "Film him!"

The cameramen pointed their cameras in unison at the cruiser, and Arnie floored it, turning close enough to Wendy and Sandy that he hit the huge puddle dead on and sent mud splashing all over them. He laughed to himself, happy as a clam to have *that* caught on film.

"God, I hope it was this hard for our bitch sister Halle," Sandy snapped.

Inside the RV, Ed was trying to focus with all the commotion going on and the meds doing their job. He remembered the last time he had held his beautiful daughter. Picking her up…her kissing him on the cheek and him planting one on hers. His eyes started to tear up, and he put his hand up to wipe them away. The thought of his little nugget and how she loved her old man, how she teased him by calling him "Squidward"—it was starting to feel all over as his hope slid further away. Ed's eyes blurred, and he shook it away, searching for his strength to believe.

As he watched from the window, Arnie's police car pulled in front of the RV to lead them to the hospital, and Ava got the duffel bag she'd packed for her father.

"Dad, isn't Ellie Collins married to a woman?" Ava asked, handing the bag to her father.

Ed took it, sighing and nodding. "Yes, she is. Where the hell do they get this stuff?"

"Uncle Sam will have a field day with these two bitches."

Ed winced at his daughter's choice of words but silently agreed as he pulled out his own clothes to change into.

CHAPTER 42

The bearded ranger, carrying his backpack, made his way through the woods to the familiar cave. He pulled out his flashlight and entered the harsh darkness. The deeper he went, the darker it became, except for the thin beam that he used to carve a path.

Water from the heavy storm was seeping through the mountain-side and dripping inside the cave. As he walked along, the flashlight's beam moved from side to side, revealing the walls. It highlighted the old mining track and the long-ago discarded miners' items scattered about, before finally coming to rest on the back of the small, eerie shack that'd been built inside the cave long ago.

The shack was two stories tall, with the slanted roof following up the angle of the cave slope. He directed the beam of light to the lock on the door and pulled out a key. There were broken tables and chairs scattered around the doorway.

He pushed it open, and in the blackness he could hear a moaning and scratching noise.

The backdoor opened to a kitchen, where he put the flashlight on the counter and reached for a lantern. Finding the box of matches, he lit the lantern, and the soft glow brightened the room, slightly revealing the contents of the forgotten, broken-down mining shack.

The kitchen was fairly large for its location; it had been used for feeding the miners when the industry was going strong. To the left, from the faint glow of the lantern, he saw the entrance to the dining room. To the right was a side hallway with an office off its far side, where old mining tools sat in a corner. The ranger took the lantern, pausing and shining the light into the old office area, before continuing on.

Down the side hall, he walked along the wall of the staircase leading upstairs to the larger main room, where the front door was located directly across from the foot of the stairs. The dining room also led around the other side of the staircase to this main room with the stone fireplace.

The moaning and scratching had stopped, but he could still hear the sound of labored breathing. Melvin Jr. lifted the lantern, and the light shined on the broken crutch that'd somehow escaped the fire uncharred. "Where are you?" he said, turning from the fireplace. Against the wall was the man; sitting on the floor, he had a camouflaged hunter's mask over his head.

The man was bound with rope from behind, and he had managed to roll over and pull himself up to sit against the wall. Melvin dropped the backpack to the ground next to him and put the lantern down. Opening the backpack, he pulled out a sandwich.

He then grabbed the man by the back of his head and listened to the frightened scream as he shoved the sandwich into the slit of the mask. The hooded man on the floor choked, and Melvin let him fall forward, laughing. "Eat up! It's almost carving time," he sneered.

The man on the floor was struggling when Melvin stood and kicked him in the stomach with his big boot. The man recoiled and screamed out, spitting bits of sandwich and listening to Melvin's laughter. "If it were me, you'd be dead already. But rituals require you to stay alive," Melvin said, as he picked up the lantern and looked back to the beam of the flashlight he'd left in the kitchen.

Without another word, he returned to the kitchen and blew out the lantern, leaving it on the counter and picking up his flashlight. He closed and locked the door behind him; he laughed yet again as he heard the man inside moan and thrash about—looking for freedom he would never be able to achieve.

CHAPTER 43

With the rain still at bay, Nash and company followed Arnie in his cruiser. The sky promised that more storms were on the way as they drove down the road behind the somehow comforting red-and-blue flashing lights. When the cruiser slowed to a stop, Nash stopped twenty feet behind him, staring at the patriotic beams that lit up the forest on each side of the road.

Arnie got out from his cruiser, and Nash put the RV in park. Everyone was watching Arnie as he walked up to the front of his cruiser, shaking his head.

Nash turned the high beams on, and Ed stood up. "Girls, stay here. Jake, you're coming with me," Ed ordered, moving to the door.

They stepped down to the road and met up with Arnie, leaving the others to watch from inside.

Arnie heard them and turned, letting them see that the road was out. A large chunk of asphalt had broken away, making it impossible for them to go any farther. Arnie could see the sadness written on Ed's face. "I'm sorry; we have to go back," he said.

Ed put his hand to his aching head. "There has to be another way, Sheriff. I'm not waiting another minute to get to Marlo."

"There is a way," Arnie said. "Back on the highway. It's another hour to a road that's mostly gravel and dirt, but it connects to the road going to the hospital. Problem is, it'll probably be worse than this one. The other main road is clear on the other side of the mountain. Take you about two or three hours to get there on the highway with traffic."

"Should we wait for Heather's dad or just go? What do we do?" Jake said.

"Well, there's a side road we passed back there. That will take you to that little store you were at earlier, or you can come back to the station and sleep there," Arnie said.

The idea of going back to the station was not one Ed wanted to consider, but he had to. "Do you have generators and hookups for the RV?" Ed asked.

"Have a generator but no hookups. You can sleep in the cells," Arnie said with a shrug. "The doors won't be closed this time."

Ed gave Arnie a look like he was crazy.

"The campgrounds have generators and hookups. Should we go there?" Jake said.

Ed was surprised. "No way," he said.

Arnie agreed, "I don't think that's such a good idea. But next to that store where you got the wine is a garage. They have hookups, and maybe their power is on," he suggested.

Ed turned angry. "*Now* you believe me about buying the wine there?"

Arnie nodded. "I always did, Ed."

Moving past them, Arnie opened the door of his cruiser. "I can get turned around here, but the road is too narrow for the RV. Back it up slowly; there's a warehouse with a driveway not too far back where you can get turned around yourselves."

Ed and Jake went back to the RV as Arnie turned around.

"There's something about the woman in that store that he's not telling us," Ed said to Jake as they neared the RV.

"Mr. Savage, I think there's a whole lot that he's not telling you."

CHAPTER 44

Nathan had closed his eyes again after his nightmare had passed and finally found some sleep, until the sound of a motorcycle's engine met his ears and woke him up.

He sat up in bed and looked out the window to witness a motorcycle driver wearing a red helmet with a black-tinted shield. Bits of long, gray hair came from the back of the helmet and blew in the wind as the driver looked directly into the RV's window at Nathan. The driver nodded slightly. In that moment, Nathan's mind flashed to Rose Galloway and the long, gray hair she'd had. Then the motorcycle accelerated, passing the RV and leaving it far behind. A creepy feeling that reached his soul spooked Nathan, and he yelled out, "No!"

Cara rushed through the door. "What's the matter, Dad?" she asked.

Nathan turned from the window. "That...that motorcycle." Nathan got up from the bed and made his way to the front of the RV, standing between the two front seats. "Where is it? The motorcycle—where is it?"

"What happened?" Sam looked over his shoulder at Nathan and then back to the road. "Sit down, Dad. Cara, help him sit down."

Nathan leaned toward the windshield, trying to find the mystery motorcycle. "No, no, something's wrong."

Sam glanced at Asa. "Help get him to sit down," he said.

Asa got up from the passenger seat and put his hands on Nathan's shoulders. "Come on, Nathan, over on the sofa."

Rayna got up to help Cara as Asa moved his hands to Nathan's forearms and tried to push him back in a safe position. With the passengers worried, Sam wasn't concentrating as well as he should have—he never saw the old school bus that came speeding up behind them. The four of them were standing, trying to get Nathan to sit down, as the bus pulled up next to the RV.

"Let me go," Nathan yelled out, causing Sam to look back at just the wrong moment.

Without warning, the bus turned into the side of the RV, smashing into it. Sam was caught off guard, and the RV swerved to the right, throwing everyone but Sam to the floor. Nathan turned in the fall, landing face-first, hitting his forehead and busting his nose.

Sam panicked. He turned the RV to the left, back to his lane, as the bus slammed into them a second time, pushing them all over the highway. The women were screaming as the RV sped toward a deep ditch next to the road.

Sam saw it. "Hang on!" he yelled, turning the RV into the bus in order to stop them from flipping over. Sam couldn't see who was driving, as the bus swerved to the left and accelerated. Speeding ahead, Sam floored the RV, following it at top speed.

Rayna and Cara were on top of Nathan, and Asa was knocked head-first into the door. Getting up and shaking it off, Asa stood carefully, attempting to balance himself in the now-speeding RV. Cara rolled over and extended her hand to him. As he helped her up, Rayna looked to them and then to Nathan. She was shaking him, but the old man wasn't moving. Rayna screamed out, "Help me roll him over. Watch his neck."

The three of them rolled him over and saw his bloody nose. Rayna quickly checked his pulse.

The RV, being a top-of-the-line model, was much faster than the bus, and Sam was catching up. Unfortunately, just as the bus's brake lights came on in front of him, an old U-Haul, rusted and shabby-looking, slammed into the rear side panel of the RV.

The RV's rear swerved to the right; as Sam corrected the steering wheel, he rammed the back of the bus. Asa and Cara fell forward, but Rayna was able to stay at Nathan's side.

Swerving to the right, Sam floored it, pushing the bus forward as the RV broke away from the relentless vehicles that seemed to want nothing more than to kill the Savages in the middle of nowhere.

Up ahead, Sam saw the exit. Getting alongside the bus, he turned the behemoth of the RV into its side, seeing the black clouds of smoke appear from the rear exhaust where the RV had hit only moments earlier.

Hitting the bus just as they drove under an overpass, Sam saw the vehicle swerve to the left, slamming up against the cement support columns at the front driver's seat and bounce back into the lane. He heard the bus driver's scream and spotted the figure wearing a ski mask as he doubled over in pain. The U-Haul then pulled between them as if to protect the bus, and its driver was also wearing a ski mask; looking over at the bus, he did not count on the exit.

Sam waited until the last possible second and turned hard starboard to escape, catching the exit to escape the highway. Cruising at their high rate of speed, the bus and U-Haul missed the exit completely.

Leaving the highway, Sam saw a church. Behind, there was nothing but trees—a large area to park where they could find some sort of cover.

Asa and Cara got up and looked back at Rayna, who was holding Nathan, trying to get him to respond.

"Dad! Dad!" Cara screamed out. She went to him and took his chin, slapping his face in an attempt to get him to move.

Nathan stirred, coughing up blood.

"Jesus, what the hell is going on?" Rayna shouted out.

Sam pulled the RV behind the church, threw it in park, and jumped back to join the others.

"Dad!" Sam yelled. "Asa, help me get him up!"

Together, Sam and Asa pulled Nathan up on the sofa, as Cara grabbed a towel out of a drawer and wet it in the sink.

Nathan was badly bruised, bleeding from his nose and his mouth. Cara handed Sam the towel, and he wiped his dad's face as Nathan opened his eyes. Pupils wide and full of fear, he could barely speak.

Immediately, Nathan began thrashing his arms about. He screamed, "Get away from me. Don't hurt me!"

Sam pulled the wet towel away from his father as the four looked at him in complete confusion.

Nathan seemed to be experiencing some kind of psychotic episode. He was acting as if he were ramping up to take a final curtain call for a role no one knew anything about.

They could not see the horror he witnessed. In Nathan's mind, he was alone in the RV; in front of him stood the dead couple with the little girl. The pregnant woman with the twisted piece of metal sticking from her stomach pulled a shard of glass from the man's face. The little dead girl was laughing, giggling, holding her hands to her teeth, as Nathan screamed out and began convulsing, throwing himself from the sofa to the floor.

Sam, Cara, Asa, and Rayna looked on in shock and tried to keep him from hurting himself.

But the dead woman with the shard of glass had center stage. As she plunged the weapon into Nathan's chest, all three of the corpses screamed out: "We have your soul!"

Nathan was locked in terror. From underneath the floor of the RV, giant, clawed hands punched through and grabbed him; the devil's face followed, staring into Nathan's eyes and laughing. "Mine!"

The demon bit him on the side of his head and began pulling Nathan through the floor of the RV, into the bowels of hell.

Nathan reached up; his eyes seemed to focus for a brief second, and he grabbed Sam's hand. He screamed, "Don't let him take me! It wasn't me! It was Niles! No!" Nathan continued to yell, to beg, to confess sins to the confused family, as his eyes glassed over and refocused on the laughing little girl. Happiness flowed through her as the devil pulled him away from the earth.

As suddenly as it had begun, it ended. Nathan stopped convulsing; his body stopped thrashing. He turned stiff on the floor of the RV with a look of fear frozen on his face. Nathan Savage was dead.

The blast from the shotgun to the back window sent glass exploding into the RV. The women screamed, and the men grabbed them, throwing them to the floor. Cara landed between the front seats and got behind the wheel. Without a thought, she put it in gear and floored it.

The RV squealed around the church to witness the U-Haul pull up behind the bus—completely blocking the exit to freedom and safety.

Sam, Asa, and Rayna crouched near Cara, staying low.

Sam saw the blockade. "Do it!"

Cara floored the RV and aimed between the U-Haul and the bus. "Hang on!" she screamed out.

When Cara neared the barricade of vehicles, movement could be seen inside the U-Haul cab. The driver was trying to get to the passenger seat, just as the RV smashed into the driver's-side door and the back of the bus. The RV moaned and groaned as it crashed through between them out onto the road. Everyone was rocked back and forth, but Cara kept her head clear and sped to the highway on-ramp.

"Everyone okay?" Cara shouted, glancing back.

"We're fine!" Sam yelled. "Keep driving."

Rayna looked over to Asa, who had taken the fiercest hit of glass. "You're bleeding."

Asa put his hand to his face and felt the tiny glass bits scratch his skin. "I'll be all right," he replied.

"Cara, keep going. We're close to the Falls exit. Take it," Sam said, looking over to Rayna, who tended to Asa's cuts. "I'll get the first-aid kit," he said.

Sam moved to the kitchen and opened the pantry door. Pausing, he looked down on a father he would *never* be able to get answers from—the answers they needed.

The man in the U-Haul was bleeding. When he tried to move away from the approaching RV, his left hip had hit the steering wheel right as the RV smashed through. He lifted his shirt to see that his lower left side was bruised and swollen. His left elbow had been cut and fractured from the twisted frame of the driver's-side door exploding inward.

The passenger door was jammed, and he kicked it open and slid to the ground. Removing his ski mask, the clean-shaven man silently wondered whether the bandage on the right side of his head was still intact.

Melvin Jr., with his ribs hurting from the bus crash, came around the corner, holding a shotgun, to help his twin brother, Leroy. Melvin could see he was hurt and knelt down beside him. "We're not done yet, brother."

Leroy raised his arm slowly, so Melvin could help him stand. The fractures in Melvin's ribs cracked with pain. "You, too?"

The twins were a sick, sad, and sorry excuse—a complete failure at the job they'd been ordered to do.

Patty was going to kill them.

CHAPTER 45

The clouds were getting heavier, promising that more hell was coming. Parked between the store and the garage, Ed and the teens stood outside the RV near Arnie's cruiser—still running with the door open.

Ava and Heather were trying their cell phones constantly, with no luck; they couldn't get even the slightest reception.

"Nothing," Ava said.

"Me either; I keep getting one bar, and then it disappears. We should have called my dad from the station," Heather said.

Arnie was walking up to the garage past the gas pumps when his car radio called him back.

"Sheriff...Are you there? Over."

Getting into the car, Arnie reached over and answered the call. "What do you have? Over."

The static from the radio was erratic. "Shots fired...Timberland Church. MVA...hurt...one hurt. Can't...ambulance...road outage. Weather grounding...air...no rescue, can you...there? Over?"

"Ten-four, Dispatch. On my way." Arnie tossed the radio as he shut the door. His window was open, and he looked to the group. "I'll swing back by after I deal with this."

"We'll be fine," Ed said, looking from the store to Arnie.

The sheriff nodded. Pulling the cruiser away, Arnie went out on the road and floored it, siren blazing, squad lights casting colorful beams in the dark, threatening sky.

Ed looked back over to the store where he'd bought the wine on that miserable evening. The red, electric "OPEN" sign was flashing intermittently. "Come on, let's get hooked up before it starts raining again."

Leading the teens over to the store, Ed pulled on the door only to find it locked. They looked in through the windows but couldn't see anyone.

"Maybe the garage?" Jake suggested.

They walked over to the garage, past the gas pumps. On the side were the RV hookups for power. Ed got to the door of the garage cashier and pulled on it; it was locked up tight.

"Mr. Savage, the battery is getting low, and we'll need to recharge soon," Nash said, looking through the glass window of the garage.

Ed shook the door handle. "How's the fuel?"

Nash pulled back from the window. "It's getting down there."

"Dad, what are we going to do?" Ava said, looking back at Jake, who was over at the pumps.

"Pumps are off!" Jake yelled out, replacing the pump and moving toward the others.

Ed's experience had taught him many things, and getting the pumps on would be easy once inside the garage. He peered in through the window and saw the electrical boxes and switches laid out against the far wall. "Nash, stay here with the girls. Jake, come with me. We'll try the garage and the backdoor. Maybe one is open," Ed said, looking at Ava and Heather. "If anyone—and I mean *anyone*—shows up out here, yell! Come on, Jake."

As he led Jake around the garage, they proceeded to check the garage doors first. They were all locked. They went around the corner to the backdoor. Ed pulled on it, but there was no give. Someone had locked up the little station in the middle of nowhere as if the contents of Fort Knox were buried inside. "Damn it!" he said. Turning around, they went back to the others.

"Any luck?" Heather raised her voice as Jake appeared around the corner; seeing her angry uncle behind him, she knew the answer.

"All locked up," Jake said, joining the others.

Ed went over to the garage window. Outside were two metal chairs and a table with a dirty, overfilled ashtray, where the employees would obviously spend their time hanging out, waiting for customers. Ed picked up a metal chair and, without warning, smashed the window in.

Hearing the glass break behind him, Jake jumped and turned back to see Ed kicking away the remains of the window.

"We have a way in," Ed announced to the teens.

He cleared the remaining glass away and stepped inside. Going to the front door, he opened it. "Wait here; I'll have the pumps on in a minute," he said.

Ed moved past the counter to the garage area where the electrical boxes sat and flicked on the switches to power up the station; the lights at the pumps lit up. Next to the boxes was a larger switch, which he raised in the air. Listening to the sound of the pumps coming online, he smiled. He then went to the cash register and entered two hundred dollars' worth of gas as paid in cash.

They watched Ed step from the register and were excited to see him come out from inside. "Nash, fuel up while I go take a look at the hookups around the side."

Inside the garage was a rack of snacks and cold drinks. Ava and Heather looked at the bounty and then turned to each other, grinning. They went in and raided what was there.

Ed saw the connectors were ready and was walking back around when he saw Heather and Ava come out of the garage carrying their score—just as the power went out. The flashing "OPEN" sign went dark, and the sound of the pumps slowing to a stop made everyone angry.

"Damn it!" Ed yelled. He ran over to Jake and tried to help with the gas. "How much did we get?"

Nash turned the key in the ignition, looked at the gas gauge, and stuck his head out the side window. "A little over a quarter full."

"That won't keep us going long," Ed said to Jake when the girls arrived with their snacks.

Kicked down again, Ava sighed. "So much for that idea."

"What about the campgrounds?" Jake said, pulling out the fuel pump from the RV's tank.

"I don't want to go there," Heather said in a scared voice.

"Me either," Ava chimed in. "Besides, if the power is off here, it's probably off there, too."

"Not necessarily," Ed said to his daughter. "The campgrounds have gas generators in some of the spaces, for emergencies. I booked one where you kids were going to be parked, just in case."

The sound of the bird whistle announcing an incoming text on Heather's phone startled them all. The familiar automated sound effect she'd selected specifically for Mia's texts made her shout with joy. "Mia!" Heather dropped the snacks and dug for her phone. Seeing the text, Heather read, "Got lost and dropped my phone, breaking it. Can't hear. Found Noah at the ranger's cabin, can't tell if this is working."

"Mine has no bars at all," Ava said, showing them her phone.

"Same here," Nash and Jake agreed.

Ed reached his hand out. "Let me see that." Ed looked at the text message and then scrolled up to see the previous messages. They each had a time stamp, with this one being written an hour ago. "It just came through. The text is an hour old," he said. Seeing she had one bar on her phone, Ed punched in Sam's number and crossed his fingers. Ringing once, the call dropped, and the bar disappeared. Ed offered up a frustrated sigh. "Now we can't stay here. We have no choice; let's go."

The four of them boarded the RV, and Ed stopped at the door. "Hang on a minute. Stay here." Jumping down, he headed back into the garage and looked under the front counter. Not finding what he was looking for, he moved into the garage and grabbed a heavy wrench, heading toward the locked store.

He was more than angry. And even though he knew the kids were watching his definitely juvenile, irresponsible actions, he didn't care. Going up to the front door, he smashed in the glass with the wrench. Kicking away the rest, he entered the building.

Inside, he got behind the counter and looked down under the register. He smiled. "Come to Daddy," Ed said, pulling out the requisite gun that all shop owners made sure to have in case of emergency. Behind the gun was a box of bullets, and he grabbed them, too.

Standing up, he noticed the phone and picked it up, but the line was most definitely dead.

As he boarded the RV, he held up the gun. "Not taking any chances this time. Now, let's go."

Nash smiled. "I like the way you think, sir."

Nash pulled the RV out and headed back down the road to the campsite. The sky was getting darker, and the rain started to once again hit the windshield. They didn't even notice the emergency pay phone at the far end of the store with a direct power line leading to the utility pole.

The outdoor covered café area's roof was still being repaired, and lumber and boards were leaning against the phone, obscuring it from view.

CHAPTER 46

With the rain increasing anew, Arnie drove more carefully down the highway to reach the motor-vehicle accident where gunshots had been heard at the local church. The road turned slightly to the right and sloped down into a large dip. The lanes in the opposite direction were higher, and between the lanes sat a copse of tall trees.

It was at times like this that Arnie hated these backwoods areas. Although lovely for the tourists, it was impossible to see what was coming directly at you when on the lookout for a suspect.

As the highway lanes merged back near each other going in the opposite direction, Arnie noticed the emergency flashers on a station wagon on the far side of the road. He picked up his radio and called for another car.

The people in the station wagon saw his red-and-blue lights and now had hope that help would be on the way, not like the assholes in the brand-new, smashed-up RV that had passed them by moments ago, leaving them on the side of the road.

CHAPTER 47

T he rain continued as Nash pulled the RV into the campgrounds. Heather was sitting up front with him when they drove up to the familiar rangers' station that was now all blacked out.

She stared at the gloomy building through the rain. "Why aren't they coming out?" she said nervously.

Ed looked out the window and got a bad feeling. Something wasn't right. He got up and opened the RV's door. "Wait here. I'll get them."

He stepped out, pulling the gun from his belt, and made his way to the station to retrieve the kids.

Ava watched her father closely. "Mia must be scared to death in there."

The light from the RV brightened the front porch, and Ed looked in the window; he could barely see inside. He knocked and then tried the door. Strangely, it was open.

Ed felt a little wary. After all, his work was mostly done in the daytime when it came to exploration, and his film crew was always with him, usually having permission to access places. He even had security when he was filming. Yet now, when he stepped inside, the reality of true fear and loneliness hit him—but he had trained for that. Hearing the RV running behind him and thinking of his family, he yelled out for Mia and Noah.

Everyone in the RV was watching, and when he turned from the dark cabin, he headed straight to the passenger window where Heather was sitting. "Hand me a flashlight," he said.

Heather reached down and grabbed the flashlight in the console, handing it to her uncle. Ed turned it on and went back to the front door. Shining it inside with one hand and raising the gun with the other, he walked in. He saw a light switch and tried it. No luck.

He then moved all the way to the back, found the radio, and tried to turn it on, but he heard nothing other than the clicking sound of the device.

As he turned to leave, he noticed the bathroom door. He aimed the flashlight and opened the door wider, peering inside. It was empty except for one wet, dirty, stained, long-sleeve camouflaged shirt on the floor.

Heading to the desk, he shined the light on it, looking for notes. Not finding anything, he went up to the front desk and shined the light there. Seeing no clue whatsoever, he paused. Ed felt as if he had stepped into some sort of strange trap. He looked back to the RV as worry invaded his skin, and he left the station just as thunder rocked the sky. A few seconds later, the lightning flash followed. "They're not here," he said boarding the vehicle.

"Dad, your bandage is soaked." Ava handed him a towel.

Drying his face, Ed caught the bandage as it came off with the towel; he patted the back of his head to dry whatever wound was there. "Don't think I'll need that anymore," he said.

"Maybe they got a ride or something?" Ava said.

Ed sat there thinking about Ava's comment; not wanting to worry them further, he played it cool. "Maybe they did—I wouldn't want to wait around this place."

"Now what? Wait around here?" Jake suggested.

Ed played the scenario out in his mind. The text had led them here, so "here" wasn't a good idea. "No, better we go back to the gas station and wait there, closer to the highway. Nash, get us turned around," he said returning the gun to his belt.

As Nash turned, the wind became fierce and slammed into the RV, causing it to rock back and forth. The rain came down harder, and Nash slowed. It was hard for him to see; he stopped short of the exit from the campgrounds and looked back to Ed. "We can't get back this way; look," he said.

Ed moved up between the seats and looked ahead. The mudslide had moved over the road, bringing with it mounds of debris that had created a perfect roadblock.

"Is there another way out?" Nash asked.

Ed knew of another; he had looked at it on a map prior to driving up. He just couldn't remember exactly where it was, and with all lights in the campgrounds out, it would be almost impossible to find. The road that led to the campsites where they had the generator was still passable, and as much as Ed did not want to go back up there, they had no choice. They were low on fuel, and he didn't want to risk running out of gas. "We're not far away from your campsite; we'll go there and hook up. We stay inside all night, though. No one goes outside for *anything*. I'll hook up the power, and in the morning we leave." Ed patted the gun in his belt, happy for insurance.

As Nash backed the RV to the turnoff and made his way slowly up the road to the campsite, Heather thought she saw someone out the side window. She immediately put her hand to the glass to shield the inside light and thought she saw someone move behind a tree.

"What is it?" Nash barked, feeling his own fear build seeing her look out her window.

The wind blew the bush behind the tree, and Heather saw its movements and figured it was just her imagination. "Nothing, I thought I saw… nothing." Heather sat back in her seat, imagining an evil killer within the trees…watching…waiting. If only she could be sure she was wrong.

Into the dark woods they drove, the headlights cutting through the storm as best they could. It was the terrible neon-yellow tape that let everyone know they were almost there. The police tape spoke of a tragic accident, and the campsite felt as if it were giving off a scent of pure and utter evil.

"Keep going," Ed said, looking out the window with Ava.

Nash kept driving, never taking his eyes from the road. "Don't worry, sir."

Ed thought of his baby girl out there, and it scared him. He knew it didn't look good, but he would not accept her being gone until he absolutely knew one way or another, bitchy reporters or not. Then there was Simon and what had happened to him all those years ago.

Ed forced the images out from his mind to think his nugget could be at the hands of fiends.

The RV made its way deeper into the woods and up another hill, finally arriving at space nineteen.

Ed got out and hooked up the RV to the generator. The inside lights glowed brighter with the surge of power, and at that moment a feeling of relief came over them.

Getting back inside, he began to look around. "Anything to eat in here?"

Jake almost whimpered, "Why did you have to mention food? Now I'm starving."

Nash pointed to the refrigerator and grinned. "It's stocked."

Ed opened it, saw it was full, and practically cheered.

"Dad, let us do that," Ava said, moving over to pull things out.

Ed spotted the beer and grabbed one, holding it up. "And what is *this* doing in here?" He stared at the guys.

Nash looked guilty as hell. Knowing he was caught, he tried humor to keep from getting in any serious trouble. "Oh, that's…um, my dad's. That's it, yeah. My dad must have put that in there by mistake."

"Um-hum," Ed said. Glaring at the boys, he placed the gun on the table in front of him.

Ava laughed. Opening a drawer, she handed him a bottle opener.

Gratefully, with a small smile aimed at his daughter, Ed popped the cap and took a long drink. He had other things to think about.

CHAPTER 48

Cara pulled the battered RV off the highway exit in the rain and arrived at the store and garage.

The emergency lights inside the store were intermittently flashing on and off. They could see no one was there, although there were signs that someone had broken in. Staring at the shattered glass, Cara picked up her cell phone.

Now with a few dried cuts on his face, Asa peered out the side window. "Nobody's here. And the windows at the garage are broken out, too," he said.

A worried Rayna moved from window to window. "Oh God, now what? Where are Nash and the others?" Her panic was reaching its top level.

"Damn!" Cara hung up her phone. "I still can't get through."

Sam picked up his and stared at the screen. "The storm, most likely. Or there's actually no service out here." He saw a call had come from Heather's phone. "Looks like Heather tried calling us not more than an hour ago."

"Did she leave a message?" Cara asked, filled with hope.

Sam shook his head and tossed his useless phone on the console.

Outside the storm raged on; the rain and wind continued to grow in power as the lightning flashed all around. Rayna noticed the lumber blowing over near a pay phone that was situated at the far end of the store. "Look!" She excitedly pointed it out to the others.

"I'll go try it," Sam said, reaching into his pocket.

"I have some change in my purse." Cara stopped him, getting up to reach for her bag.

"First, aim the lights at the phone. It's too dark over there," Asa said. Cara handed her purse to Sam. "Back pocket inside."

With the RV now aimed directly at the pay phone, Cara put on the high beams. The headlights on the driver's side were broken from the bus crash, and she flipped on the driver's-side searchlight and aimed it at the phone.

With the others watching, Sam exited the vehicle and ran over to the pay phone. Picking it up, he heard the tone and gratefully fed it some coins. He called Heather's cell but heard the recording of "no coverage" speak back to him. Hanging up, he called the operator.

"Operator, this is an emergency. Please connect me with the sheriff station at Black Ridge. I need to speak with Sheriff Arnie Mallard," Sam said, happy to get through.

"One moment," the woman said. After she worked the only magic that never seemed to fail, an officer came on the line: "Black Ridge Sheriff."

Sam was excited to finally be getting somewhere. "Hello! Sheriff Arnie Mallard?"

"Sorry, he's out on a call. What can I help you with?" the officer answered.

"My name is Sam Savage; my brother Ed is there. We're in danger, sir. Somebody just tried to run us off the road...They're shooting at us."

"Mr. Savage, your brother was released a while ago. He left with the kids who came to get him in their RV. Who ran you off the road? Where are you?" the officer said.

In the RV, Sam could see Rayna now sitting up front next to Cara, watching every move he made. Even Asa was scanning the area as the wind blew over another of the boards that leaned against the building. Asa pointed out the windshield.

As the RV's door opened and Asa appeared, running to the board, Sam saw what he was doing. He hung up the phone and helped Asa with the wood. Getting to the RV, completely soaked through by the rain, Asa placed the board down against the counter in the kitchen.

Sam picked up a towel and wiped the rain from his face. "Tried calling Heather's cell: no service. Then I called the sheriff. Ed's been released, and he's with the kids."

"Oh, thank God!" Cara said, putting her hand to her chest. "Where are they? At the hospital?"

Wiping his head with the towel, Sam tossed it into a chair. "The roads are out leading up there: mudslide," he said.

"Then where are they?" Rayna said, looking at Sam with worry.

"They should be here, but with the power out, I can only think of the campgrounds," he told them.

Rayna became a little hysterical. "No, they wouldn't go back to that horrible place. Not on a night like this."

"The power is out. The cop said even they were on a backup generator. Which means the only place they can hook up around here *on a generator* is up there," Sam said.

"Sam." Asa kicked at the board. "Do you have anything that can secure this to that blown-out window?"

Sam pointed to the cushion of the bench seat. "Under there," he said.

Asa moved the cushion, finding tools and a roll of duct tape.

Cara got up from the driver's seat. "I'll help him with that. I don't really want to drive," she said.

Sam helped Asa lift the board to the blown out window, and the women followed to help. Putting down the board, Sam barely glanced at the bed where Nathan rested with a blanket over him.

His father's corpse was something he simply couldn't deal with right now.

CHAPTER 49

Nash's RV glowed warmly as the five of them sat at the table finishing up a meal.

Heather looked to her uncle. "Uncle Ed, who is doing this?"

Ed took a swig from his beer. "I wish I knew," he replied.

Ava pushed her plate up. "Dad, what happened to Simon all those years ago?"

"This has nothing to do with Simon," he answered quickly.

"Then where is he?" she asked.

"I don't know." Ed paused. Sighing heavily at the worried, confused faces, he decided they should all have every bit of data he could give them—no matter what they thought of Simon in the end. He just had to keep his thoughts of Lisa out of it. "I guess it's time you knew," he whispered. "What happened to Simon almost happened to your mother."

Everyone was looking at Ed as he began. "When they were kids, they were playing in a park when their ball went into the parking lot. Your mother chased after it, and the ball bounced against a van; there was someone inside it," Ed said.

Outside the thunder boomed, and the lightning seemed to ricochet off the trees. Everyone was startled, but they hung on every word. "The van door slid open, and a man grabbed your mother. Simon was chasing after the ball behind his sister and saw what happened, so he jumped on the man, who quickly dropped your mother. But the man threw Simon into the van and drove off," Ed said quietly.

Ava's mouth dropped. "I had no idea."

"Simon had it bad. He was seven years old when that happened. The guy abused him; he beat the hell out of him, choked him, and left him for dead in the woods only a few miles away from their home. Thankfully, some joggers with their dogs found him shortly after. From then on, his whole life, he's been in and out of hospitals."

"Poor Simon, I had no idea. I told you guys it wasn't him," Heather said, standing up to clear the plates. "Did they catch the freak who did it?"

"Worse," Ed said, picking up his beer. "The guy abducted and killed another child, not knowing the father was a wayward motorcycle-gang member. And when the search was on, the gang came full force and found him first, before the police did." Ed took another swig of his beer and continued. "They took him out to the desert and kept him alive and tortured him. No one knows how long they did it, but when they found him, part of his body had been dissolved, and his junk was sewn into his mouth.

"Gross!" Ava said as she picked up her dad's plate to help.

"The guy deserved it," Nash said.

"And Simon knows all this?" Ava asked, looking disgusted.

Ed nodded. "This is why we never told you."

Ava nodded back to her father. "I'm glad you didn't, but I'm now glad you did. I think knowing this now helps explain the fights you and Mom were having a while back. I think I now know where some of her anger comes from."

Ed smiled at his amazingly brilliant daughter, and his heart filled with love.

Ava put Ed's plate in the sink, and Heather saw she was hiding her face from her father. Knowing the subject needed to be changed, Heather reached for Jake's plate. "Uncle Ed, I know we talked about this at the jail, but I think that ranger has something to do with this. He sure acted weird."

Feeling the meds lingering in him, Ed put down his half finished beer. "Well, tomorrow we'll get out of here and go see how your aunt is doing."

Heather placed the plate in the sink. "Sounds good to me. Mom and Dad should be getting here soon, too. Everybody, try your phones again," she said.

Outside the rain came down harder; they could hear it pound on the RV's rooftop. It sounded like the rapid fire of an AK-47, with the bullets beating against the metal roof. Lightning struck, and a tree went down somewhere up the hillside right above them. The noise was so sudden and so close that the gang froze.

Heather was the first to notice the strange sound. Crashes commenced, as if a giant were walking through the woods, destroying it all with every step he took. "What's that noise?" she shouted in panic.

Everyone in the RV stopped talking and went silent to listen. They all could hear it. Everyone rushed to look out a window. It was Heather, however, who spotted the huge, frightening stream of mud and grabbed Ava's hand. The girls watched the river of debris coming at them and screamed out, just as the mud slammed into the side of the vehicle.

The RV's front end turned with the power of Mother Nature and began to slide sideways, listing to the driver's side. More mud slammed into the RV, and the driver's-side wheels got pushed down a slope. As the RV turned over, the power cords from the generator snapped, causing sparks to fly and dimming the inside lights as the RV slid down toward a ridge where it finally—thankfully—came to a stop.

Everyone was tossed into the side, but all were okay. The battery had charged long enough to keep the lights on.

"Everyone out!" Ed yelled.

With the RV on its side, the exit was just above them. Ed got to the door and pushed it open. The muddy rain came pouring in. "Ava, Heather, you two first," Ed shouted. The guys helped lift the girls.

Heather got out on top and looked down, reaching to help Ava. The lightning flashed again, and the fallen tree, which had gotten stuck against another, came crashing down toward them. They got Ava out, and the girls moved to kneel on the side, looking down into the RV, reaching for Nash, their long hair soaked and dripping from the rain.

Grabbing him, they pulled him up just when the tree slammed into the RV. Heather and Ava lost their balance and their grip on Nash, falling backward off the side and into the moving mud, which pushed them into thick bushes and trees. They held on as Nash fell back inside the RV as it slid over the ridge.

Instantly the RV rolled over, and Ed grabbed on to a handle next to the door, using his other hand to reach out to the guys. Jake grabbed for him, but Nash fell farther into the kitchen as the RV rolled back up and the door swung open. Ed hung on the handle, shoving Jake out first before the RV rolled again.

Ed looked back for Nash and spotted the gun as it fell near him. He grabbed it as the RV made another roll. Still hanging on to the handle, when the RV righted itself, he yelled for Nash and stuffed the gun in his belt. Nash was farther back by the bedroom and worked hard to climb the inside wall, reaching out for Ed.

The twisting structure of the RV popped the microwave loose, connecting with Nash in the side of his head and knocking him back as the RV rolled up and over once more. The door swung open, and the handle broke off in Ed's hand, sending him flying toward the far wall. He slammed into the side and pushed himself up, and dove for the doorway. Grabbing the edge of the door, Ed was thrown from the vehicle into the moving ground, yelling for Nash.

His body began to slide.

The RV rolled down to a steeper ridge, gaining momentum, as Ed managed to stop his own slide and watch Jake, up above him, clinging to the moving ground for some sort of support. Jake couldn't keep up and came tumbling down on top of him.

The RV hit the steeper ridge, and the rolls increased at a higher speed. Nash was still trapped inside, being tossed around like a rag doll in a dryer full of sharp, broken debris.

At the bottom of the ridge, the RV rolled to a stop, upside down on the road below. Nash crashed through a window, getting stuck in the glass and twisted frame; he took his last breath as his blood painted the side. Debris from the RV flew forward into the mud, and a sharp, twisted piece of metal got caught, sticking up in the mud, pointing away from the RV. As the lights went out, the mud slowed behind the doomed vehicle.

Up above the girls were screaming down into the darkness. "Dad! Dad! Jake!" Ava's voice could be heard.

"Nash! We can't see you!" Heather yelled.

Ed and Jake could hear the girls, and Ed yelled back up to them. "Get away from the edge! We're climbing up!"

Ava and Heather started to climb up the small slope that the RV had first slid down before going over the ridge.

Above, the clouds parted slightly and allowed the moon to shine a light down upon them. There were many clouds in the sky, so their light was temporary, but the hard rain stopped as quickly as it had started.

The girls got to the top and saw the sparking hookups. They looked down into the blackness toward the men when they heard something behind them.

A strange sort of humming met their ears.

Hmm, hmm, hmm, hmm, hmm, hmm, hmm...

"What is that?" Heather said, looking to Ava.

"It sounds like a child!" Ava shouted back, gripping her cousin's arm.

They both turned, seeing the man coming toward them from the woods at exactly the same time. The lightning flashed, illuminating a strange mask covering his head. The girls suddenly knew: he was coming for them.

Ava screamed out, "Daddy! Someone's up here! Help us!"

Heather grabbed Ava by the arm. "Run, Ava!"

The girls ran screaming into the woods, and Ed and Jake climbed up the muddy hillside as fast as they could.

The hunter slipped in the mud and fell forward, sliding to where Ava and Heather had been standing near the edge of the ridge. The lightning flashed again, and Ed and Jake were seen climbing, staring up and spotting the camouflaged hunter looking down at them.

Stopping his climb, Ed raised the gun and fired, clipping the man in the right shoulder as he pulled away from the edge.

Getting up, the man turned and went after the girls.

Ava and Heather ran through the woods on a path that they could barely follow. The earth was wet and muddy. As they were running, the ground sloped slightly, and they tripped into each other, stumbling forward into the mud, landing on the bodies of Noah and Mia.

Both screamed in terror as they backed off the bodies stuck in the swamp-like terrain.

Coming closer, they could hear the psycho tune being hummed by their attacker's lips.

Ava got up first, grabbing on to Heather. "Come on, hurry; he's coming," she screamed.

Seeing the man behind them, they ran farther into the words, finding another path as the ground sloped once again. Their feet hit something that sounded almost hollow, and they crashed through an open space, feeling the wind meet their skin as they fell into the bowels of the earth.

Heather landed hard on her side, falling to her right. Ava fell to her left, hitting what felt like a floor. She moaned as the strange surface crumbled underneath her and sent her falling another ten feet before coming to a stop on the hard floor below.

Heather screamed for Ava. But when she listened for her reply, all she could hear was a desperate moaning and a scratching sound that reminded her of a corpse struggling to rise from its grave.

CHAPTER 50

The cabin was clean and spotless. Patty's table was perfectly set for three. Two of the place settings had child cups at them—perfect for the dinner guests. Children's laughter could be heard from the cellar.

The four children enjoyed playing four square in the cellar. A young Patty was laughing as she hit the ball to her older sister, Stevie, and the twins. Laughing innocently, playing as they did before, Patty hit the ball over Stevie's head into the dark corner of the cellar under the stairs; still laughing she watched her sister run into the darkness to get it and disappear.

When the ball slowly rolled from the dark corner, her sister was not there.

"Stevie? Stevie?" The young girl called for her sister, taking a few steps toward the darkness and turning to look for the twins, who were also now gone. Patty's young face turned sad, and she went to get the ball where it sat at the edge of darkness. As she reached for it, the old man's hand reached out and grabbed her.

"No, Mr. Cullen, no," the girl screamed, pulling away from him as the cellar room blurred to the shack in the mining cave. Little Patty was in the living room near the stone fireplace. The man picked her up and took to the stairs, and she grabbed on to the railing, screaming for help, seeing his wife, Amaleen Cullen, move from the dining area to the kitchen, not giving a damn. The little girl screamed as her tiny fingers lost their grip on the railing. The *thud, thud, thud* of his heavy work boots echoed in her head as he took her up those nasty stairs.

Patty Galloway sat in her cellar in the center of a pentagram on the floor. The black, clumpy mixture of dead creatures and the soot of the newly drawn pentagram stained her hands. Her hair was wild, and her stare was fixated on the corner under the cellar stairs as she remembered the ugly life that had befallen her after the accident. Tears stained her hard face as she stood, and she hummed her favorite tune as she stumbled toward the dresser where the bowl with the foul mixture sat.

She looked to the filthy mirror and grabbed the yellowed newspaper article with the headline: "Young Homeless Man Arrested for Dropping Rock over Expressway—Killing Two." She placed it between the open pages of the strange, skin-covered tome among the black lit candles.

Standing in her outdated, long, gray dress, she tilted her head back, closed her eyes, and spoke in the oldest, most powerful language in the world. Her voice quivered, her eyes rolled back to their whites, and in her mind the rage inside blew, sending the vibration, which shook the room, cracking the mirror in front of her. *She was there...*

The cracks from the cartilage in her neck were loud and frightening as she rolled her head forward and stared into the cracked mirror. Her eyes glazed over, and she reached for the candles, lifting them and turning them upside down, dripping the black wax into the bowl and extinguishing them in the remaining black mixture.

Patty's mind blurred, and she heard the twins behind her, seeing them in the filthy mirror, but when she turned...nothing. Then she looked to the empty stairs. "I see you!" she screamed.

Moving away from the mirror—which was filthy but intact, without a scratch—she went after the "boys" in her altered state. Up the stairs she went to find the twins sitting in their rightful places at the table, still making a fuss. In her mind it was as before those nasty Cullens came and took them after the accident. She was such a young girl taking care of the boys, alone after Stevie ran away. But the twins were still making such a racket.

She moved over to the boys and slammed her hand down on the table. "I said behave," she spat.

The boys immediately looked up at the young girl, wide-eyed and scared.

"That's it," she said as her young self.

Patty moved into the kitchen and picked up the pot of stew. She then returned to the table humming that silly song and threw the slop down on the plates with the ladle, making a mess on the lovely table-cloth in the empty room.

Stopping, her vision once again blurred, and her state of mind flexed. The boys were at it again, laughing and throwing stew at each other. Patty dropped the pot, hitting the table at an angle, spilling the stew down the side and onto the floor.

Patty screamed, "I said behave!" She turned, walked quickly to the kitchen, and grabbed a wooden spoon from the counter. Returning, she could see the fear in the boys' eyes.

"No, Patty! No, we'll be good," they begged.

Patty grabbed one of the twins by the arm. "I know you'll be good."

The child whimpered as Patty struck his legs with the wooden weapon. She let go of the child and went for the other, screaming, "I raised you since the accident! You *will* behave!" As she rounded the table to grab the other twin, her vision blurred yet again. She stopped and swooned, tilting her head back and uttering strange words. Her trance was fading in and out.

In Patty's twisted mind, reality and memory merged, and she stared at the mess she'd made on the table in the empty room; then her vision blurred, and the twins returned. Patty dropped the wooden spoon, and she lifted the table, throwing it backward and spilling everything to the floor. The two chairs went flying. "Clean up this mess!" she screamed. Turning, she leaned against the mirrored sideboard and lowered her head to see the empty pill bottles. She batted them off the sideboard, sending them across the room.

Patty slowly raised her head to stare into the sideboard mirror. Her state of mind was returning. All that was left was the woman she was today. Her hair a fright, she raised her hands and tried to pat it into place. Patty was truly a sick girl.

She looked down and opened the large drawer of the sideboard to see the syringes, a rubber tourniquet, and more pill bottles. Below them were the envelopes. She removed two thick manila envelopes and one letter-sized envelope; taking them with her and passing the mess she'd just made, she walked to the front door. Her raincoat was hanging on the coat tree, and she grabbed at it, putting the envelopes down to put it on.

Picking up her delivery, she pulled keys from her coat pocket, opened the front door of her solitary cabin, and walked out into the wet, frightful night.

The rain had stopped, and her slow steps turned to a hurry as the rage inside her grew. She pulled open the garage doors and saw Ed Savage's Range Rover, parked, with all the windows down. The license plate read 2SLA102, and for some reason the vehicle seemed to spite her. She got in and started it. The engine roared to life, and she turned on the lights.

The tires squealed off the paved garage floor onto the wet dirt drive and raced down the road as she drove off into the night. Not far from her cabin, she slammed on the brakes under a streetlight flickering intermittently between a tree and a mailbox. The Range Rover slid a little in the mud, and the envelopes flew off the seat next to her and onto the floor next to a single bottle of Boon's Farm strawberry wine.

Patty grabbed the three envelopes, jumped out, and dropped them into the mailbox, slamming it shut; then she raced back to the still-running Range Rover.

The flowers Ed had bought for Marlo were still in the car, their petals now crushed into the floorboards among a few bottles of wine and scattered peppermint chocolates. Patty gunned the engine as she sped away and heard the sound of something clinking near her. She looked to the seat next to her with suspicion. Slowing, she looked to the backseat and saw two other bottles of wine partly under the front passenger seat. She reached for them, pulling one free and throwing it out the window, ending that annoying sound.

CHAPTER 51

A t the church parking lot, Arnie was looking inside the smashed cab of the U-Haul with his flashlight, staring at the blood on the seat. He walked back to his car and got in, picked up the radio, and noticed there was no license plate on the U-Haul. "You still there? Over."

The static had cleared, and the second officer from the station answered back, "Yes, sir. Over."

"Who was it that called this in? Over."

"Negative. The caller did not leave a name, sir. Call came from a pay phone in the church parking lot. Over."

"Has Ed's brother called or arrived yet? Over."

"Yes, sir. Just heard from them, said they had been nearly run off the road...and, sir, they said they had been shot at. Over."

"Give me Sam's number. I need to speak with him. Over."

"Just a minute sir. Over."

Arnie scanned the area and looked over at the pay phone.

"What is going on tonight?" he said out loud as the officer returned to the radio.

CHAPTER 52

The storm and mudslides had made quite a mess of the campgrounds. Signs had blown over, roads were washed out, and intermittent power sparks caused the road lights to either be completely out or flickering, resembling strobe lights that had once decorated the local bars.

There were two entrances to the campgrounds. One was now blocked with mud and debris. Finding the other, Sam drove into the campsite and came to a fork in the road. On the right he could see the broken stub of a street post sticking up. Tree branches had come down on it, sending it down a slope. He slowed the RV to a stop and used the driver's-side manual searchlight, panning the area for any sign of life.

The road to the right had a broken tree lying at an angle across it. The road to the left looked passable. He panned the light up the road farther and saw another RV in the distance. Sam turned, keeping the searchlight on as the headlamps below were broken, but as he came closer to the vehicle, he realized it was upside down.

Sam slowed to a stop and looked to his wife in horror.

"Why have we stopped again?" Rayna asked, getting up from the table to take a look just as Sam aimed the manual searchlight on the upside-down RV.

The spotlight moved from side to side and stopped directly on the broken window. The now-very dead yet familiar body of Nash was lodged within it.

Seeing her son's body hanging through the glass and twisted window frame of the RV, Rayna screamed, "Oh dear God…No!"

Asa ran up to look, passing her to see what could possibly have made her go completely pale. He saw the destroyed RV holding his dead son just as Rayna opened the door and ran out to her child. He turned and chased after her.

As Rayna ran toward her dead son, she slipped and fell forward onto a sharp piece of metal that'd broken off from the RV. It pierced her thigh, and she screamed out hysterically. Asa was right behind her, and he could see the twisted piece sticking out from her leg. He tried to pull it free, but she screamed and fell back into the road.

Watching the horror play out in front of them, Sam and Cara went for the door when the ring of a cell phone stopped them in their tracks. Sam and Cara froze and looked to each other. The cell phone rang again, and they both moved to search for it. Cara found it, answering the call with fear and panic in her voice.

The phone was full of static as Cara tried her best to hear. "Hello. Hello!"

Headlights appeared from behind the RV, and Sam and Cara saw them. The cell phone went dead. "Damn it!"

"Come on!" Sam yelled.

Cara dropped the phone, and the two of them raced out from the RV. They turned to the left and got around the front just as the headlights came speeding up the road.

Sam and Cara were about to step past the RV to the other lane just as Patty came speeding past them in Ed's Range Rover. The open windows were blowing her hair in all directions; it was like a cloud of smoke flying out behind her.

Sam threw his right arm out, blocking Cara and pushing her back out of the way of the speeding vehicle. He yelled, watching the headlights of the Range Rover illuminate Asa and Rayna. They were like the innocent victims standing in front of the devil himself as the Range Rover headed straight for them, running them over. Their screams combined with a demonic female laugh as the driver sped off without a care in the world.

The crush of Rayna's skull was audible. Her death came instantly. As if in a horror movie, Asa's arm was torn from his body, and the back tire crushed his throat. Their bodies were buried in the muddy ground just a few feet away from their beloved son.

Seeing the whole thing as if it were playing out in slow motion, Cara screamed, "She didn't stop! She didn't stop! That bloody bitch!" She dropped to the ground crying, and Sam knelt down and held her in his arms.

Burying her head into his shoulder, Sam just stared in complete shock at their murdered friends.

CHAPTER 53

The hunter was panting as he continued his search. He would not slow his stride as he chased through the woods, searching for the girls who'd somehow gotten away.

He stopped and fell to the ground from the sudden shot of pain. Lifting his shirt, he winced at his left side that was now bruised black and bleeding. His left elbow, now with a rag tied around it, was stained red with blood. He hunched over in pain, putting his right hand out to stop himself from falling over. He screamed from the bullet wound that'd torn into his right shoulder, courtesy of Ed Savage, and arched his back to keep from falling over into the mud.

Getting up slowly, he looked around and heard a girl's voice call out, "Ava!"

Moving down the path, he finally spotted a strange hole that'd been dug into the ground. He crept up to it, seeing nothing but blackness below.

Heather sat in the musty darkness. Her side hurt where she had landed, and she could feel the broken floor beside her, just ready to take her down farther into the earth. She had a little moonlight coming from above, but the rain had started again. It was a light mist coating her skin. She continued to call out for Ava, moving to the edge where her cousin had disappeared and fallen even farther. She stopped to listen for a reply. All she could hear was a moaning voice followed by a scraping sound, as if fingernails were desperately trying to claw their way up to get her.

"Ava, is that you? Why don't you answer me?" she yelled. "Who's down there? Ava!" Heather screamed into the quiet depths of the black hole.

The lightning flashed again, and the mist turned back to heavier rain when Heather spotted Ava's small body lying on a floor beneath her. "Ava! Ava, wake up!" Heather screamed.

She watched as Ava stirred slightly as the rain hit her face. Her eyes were slow to open, and she was more than disoriented as she looked above her and met Heather's gaze.

She screamed, "Heather, look out! Above you!"

Heather looked up and saw the man with the camouflaged rags over his head reaching down into the hole to grab her. Blood dripped from his wounds and hit her in the face. She screamed, backing away from the edge where Ava had fallen through, only to find a staircase leading down that she hadn't seen before. With panic racing in her blood, she moved away from the attacker and tumbled down the rotted staircase. The stairs broke and crumbled one by one as her body made contact.

Hitting the side wall at the small landing where the stairs turned to the front door, Heather bounced off the wall and crashed through the rotted railing, tumbling over the sideboard and into what felt like a dining-room table. Debris from the railing fell onto the sideboard, nearly knocking over a lantern hidden under an old curtain. A can of lighter fluid sat below on a shelf with a few old mining helmets shoved in next to it.

She could hear Ava scream, and she watched her cousin as she crawled over to her. Hugging, thanking the good Lord that they were once again together, they got themselves up and attempted to move out of sight of the monster above.

The lightning flashed again, and their hearts seemed to stop. The scene they now looked at was more frightening than anything they could imagine. Two skeletons dressed in rotted clothes sat at a dining-room table covered with a rotted tablecloth.

The girls screamed and backed away from the table into the main room. On the floor was a man tied up and moaning. Tripping over him, the girls fell, and Heather hit her head on the fireplace, slipping into her own blackness.

Seeing the man, Ava grabbed the fireplace shovel. The man, in his struggle, had managed to scrape the hunter's mask up off his face just a bit, and when the lightning flashed again, Ava saw the familiar face of Simon and managed to stop her brutal attack before it was too late.

"Simon!" she said, dropping the weapon and pulling the mask off his head.

He looked as if he was having one of his convulsions. She'd seen them before, and now she played witness to the torture he'd been through. Not understanding what she was looking at, Ava attempted to untie him just as a rotted board from the stairs came loose and fell beside her.

Ava jumped at the sound, pulling Simon with her away from the tumbling wood. Leaving Simon on the floor, she then made her way to the dining room. Avoiding the skeletons, she glanced up only once and saw their attacker above move away from the opening of the hole.

The rain kept coming as she looked to the table and grabbed the tablecloth. When she pulled at it, the old fabric ripped in half, sending dust-covered plates, a candelabra, and wine glasses crashing to the floor.

She balled up the tablecloth and soaked it in the rain. She then moved back to Simon and squeezed it over his face, wiping the cool rainwater across his overheated skin.

Simon stopped convulsing and opened his eyes. He spit up blood and soon recognized his niece. "Ava, thank God," he gasped.

Ava tried her best to locate a smile somewhere in her nightmare. "Simon, what's happening? Heather, it's Simon! He's here!" Ava said, looking toward the far end of the room and adjusting her eyes to the darkness. "Heather?" Ava said, gently lowering Simon's head to the floor and moving closer to her cousin.

Seeing that Heather was passed out, Ava listened to her steady breathing and looked at Simon. "Simon, she won't come to! Heather!" she said, shaking her cousin.

"Untie me quickly before they come back," Simon spoke.

"Before who comes back?" Ava moved to Simon and started freeing him from the ropes. "What happened, Simon? What is going on?"

Simon tried to catch his breath and did his best to tell the tale. "I was walking up to the campsite…There was a ranger on the side of the road with the hood of his jeep up. I asked if he needed any help. He said he was fine, so I went on my way, and next thing I know—*bam!* Everything went dark."

"I almost have it," Ava said, focused on the ropes and his story.

"Ava, my leg was in a cast, and it hurts like a mother. I'll need my crutches to move," Simon said.

"Got it!" Ava said.

With the ropes untied, Simon pulled his arms forward in pain. He was sore from having had them behind his back for so long. "Light, Ava…They have a light in here somewhere…maybe a lantern. I could hear the gas from it. Find it," he said.

Ava was beyond overwhelmed. "Where? I can't see anything!"

Simon reached out to her. "Ava, focus. You can do this!"

Ava nodded and got to her feet, stumbling in the direction of the large opening. Pausing under the hole they'd fallen through, she looked up in the rain and saw that no one was there. The clouds moved, covering the moon, and the sky turned black. Moving slowly into the next room, she kept her hands on the walls, trying to feel her way around.

The thunder boomed, the lightning flashed, and the spark allowed her to see a counter. Ava reached for the lantern that was there and bumped the box of matches into the sink, where a few plates sat as if a meal had just been eaten. A few of the matches stayed on the counter, and she felt for one. She felt for the box, lit it on the first try, and tried to open the lantern, but by the time she got the lantern's small door to give, the match went out. Feeling for another, she lit it and placed the glowing little piece of wood into the lantern, allowing the room to grow brighter.

Ava could now see that the room she stood in was an old, dusty kitchen; takeout trash was thrown on the counter, the plates in the sink had food scraps on them, and weird bugs crawled all over, clearly enjoying the leftovers. She moved with the lantern past the skeletons and back to Simon. She saw his bare leg where the cast had been and gasped at the bleeding. "Simon, your leg…"

"I'll be fine," Simon said. The light from the lantern shined on Heather and the fireplace. They could see part of a broken crutch that had been burned, while the other lay just a few feet away. "Hand me that one."

Ava placed the lantern down on the floor and grabbed the crutch. Handing it to Simon, she then went to Heather's side. "She's still out."

Holding her cousin in the dark, she wanted her father like she did when she was young, scared of the closet monsters in her room. Like her sister, Lisa, Ava needed her hero on this savage night.

CHAPTER 54

s the rain finally came to a stop, Ed got to the top of the ridge and
looked around for the man he had shot. The wind was blowing,
making him question every movement. He then extended his arm
down to pull Jake up beside him. Both men looked around, calling
out for Ava and Heather, but all they could hear was the sound of the
storm that would not go away.

They were dirty and scraped up. Jake had cuts on his cheek, and
he could feel blood under his pants at his knee. "Which way?" he said.

Ed's shirt was torn; debris filled his cuts and bruises. He motioned
Jake to a path. "Come on," he said as the wind hit them again.

Jake saw a movement over Ed's shoulder but figured it was the
trees moving in the wind as he turned and limped behind him on the
path, not seeing the menacing figure in the distance.

The figure in the trees moved again. Melvin Jr. had his rifle pointed, and Ed was in his sight.

Jake stopped on the path near a tree and turned, leaning against
it to rub his knee. Stopping his trek, Ed moved back to him. He stared
down at the swelling.

Jake spoke quietly, completely exhausted. "I don't think I can walk,
sir."

As Ed lowered his head to look at Jake's knee, the strong winds
blew the voice into his ears, and he could almost swear he heard the
words "A father for a father," just as the thunder boomed, and the shot
hit the boy right in the face. The back of his head exploded out onto

the tree trunk, and his lifeless body fell to the ground, knocking Ed over.

Ed opened his eyes to see Jake's bones protruding from his face, a face that now held only one wide eye staring back at him. "Dear God, no!" He rolled away from him and aimed the gun in the direction of the shot.

Crawling up the path, staying low in the brush, he slid on the mud down to the landing where Noah and Mia had been dragged to. He could see the stick in Mia's throat and her bashed-in face. He saw Noah's spine protruding from his neck, and Ed's eyes widened as he backed off from them and looked for the killer with the rifle. "Ava, Heather!" he called out into the night, wanting so badly to not be the only survivor in a place that a serial killer seemed to know like the back of his hand.

Anger filled his body; he crawled away to what he thought was a safe distance; then he got up and ran to circle around to stalk the killer himself, finding himself back where Nash's RV had slipped into the darkness.

Below him at the remains of the boy, the sound of the thunder had masked the gunshot above them, and after dragging Asa and Rayna from the road over to the upside-down RV to be near their dead son, Sam and Cara leaned into each other. "God, take them home," Cara sobbed in Sam's arms. "And, God, please let the girls be safe," she added.

"Cara, we have to go," Sam said, pulling away from her. He lifted her chin and kissed her. "The girls are fine. They need us."

The dark look came over her face, a mother lioness preparing to kill the evil villain that was threatening her cubs. "That bloody bitch is *dead!*" Cara announced.

As she grabbed Sam's hand, they ran to the RV and drove off after the Range Rover.

Farther away, the Range Rover was parked behind the jeep on the mountain road. Patty left the knife on the floorboard and moved to the back of the SUV, pulling out a flashlight and a shotgun she had placed there earlier. She then entered the woods, stepping on a branch and snapping it in half on the same path that she knew a ranger with a backpack had taken.

"Over here."

Patty turned to see Melvin Jr. fall to the ground near a tree. He was holding his left side; it was clear that it was extremely hard for him to breathe. With not a note of sympathy in her voice, the orders came out: "Get up. Now. There's work to be done!"

Melvin got to his feet immediately, completely out of breath.

Patty noticed his movements. "What happened to you?" she spat.

"I got hit...in the bus. Think my ribs are broken...It hurts to breathe," he said.

Patty looked at her brother in utter disgust. "You're such a failure. We're not done yet! They have to pay for what they did. Taking Ma and Pa from us...Every one of them must pay! And she'll pay like I did. She'll grow up with the pain just like I did, if she lives. Now come on! Unfortunately, I can't do this without you!"

Turning away from him, she headed into the cave. "I'll show them I finally did right," she whispered, knowing that the skeletons of those evil miners that had put their hands on her after her parents were burned in the fire resided in that miner's shack, because she had placed them there herself. Between the Savage family and the Cullens, her payback list was long and overdue. And she could finally prove her worth to her father, all in one night.

CHAPTER 55

The night was filled with movement. Simon was up on his crutch, and Ava still held her passed-out cousin in her arms. "Uncle Simon, what is this place?" she said.

Simon turned away from the skeletons and back to Ava. "Part of an old coal mine. The place is supposed to be full of tunnels. I was talking to the boat attendant when we first got here, and she told me this place used to be a big coal town. As far as how to get out of here—that I don't know. Where's your mom and dad?" he asked.

Ava realized Simon didn't know what had happened with the crash and Lisa. Not wanting to add panic to the already insane situation, she deflected, "Dad was with us; then we got separated, and that freak with the mask chased us. Uncle Simon, we have to get out of here."

Simon stared down at the floor, watching the small bits of debris suddenly fall from up above. In a shot, he looked up, ready to take on the evil being that'd put him here, yet what he saw made his heart relax.

"Ed! Ed! Down here!" Simon yelled at the familiar figure up above that the lightning had illuminated.

"Simon! The girls? Ava and Heather are lost."

Hearing her father, Ava yelled, "Dad, help us; Heather's hurt!"

"Hang on, Ava! Simon, shine the light up here; I'm coming down."

Grabbing the lantern, Simon did his best to light the way into the dark and dingy space.

Ed reached down and pulled on the roof and siding still against the cave walls, and it crumbled in his hands. He paused and then began his descent.

Simon held his breath, watching Ed as he used everything from the rock in the cave walls to the siding of the odd shack's roof to lower himself down, dropping where Heather had landed earlier. The musty, damp dust from the old shack filled his nose, and he coughed it away. He then navigated the broken stairs until they gave way further, sending him down in a cloud of dust to the first floor. Ed got up, brushing himself off, and coughed out the dust, eyeing the can of lighter fluid that was knocked from the sideboard to the floor with him. He then spotted Ava holding Heather on the floor and raced to them. "Ava, thank God," he said with relief.

Ava reached for her father and held him as if he were a lifeboat in a raging storm. "Dad, she fell and won't wake up."

Ed checked Heather's pulse and listened to her breathing; then he looked into his daughter's eyes. "Are you all right?"

"I...I don't know. I guess? Where's Jake and Nash?" she asked.

Ed bit his bottom lip, and he saw that his daughter realized the truth beaming in his saddened eyes. She put her hand to her mouth and started to cry.

Seeing Ava lose it, Simon limped over to them. "We have to get out of here, Ed."

Ed looked to Simon. "Can't get up the way I came down; everything is rotted. What's down here?"

Simon shook his head. "I don't know; when I woke up, I was here."

"Was that after you went back to that store?"

"I didn't go back there, Ed. I got bushwhacked and woke up here."

"More lies," Ed said, staring at Simon, wondering when the time would come when questions stopped and answers arrived. He looked over to the table with the skeletons, noticing them for the first time. "What the hell?"

"Don't ask," Simon said, throwing up his arms.

The lightning flashed above, illuminating the muddy boot prints leading away from them as they planned their escape.

The monster that had made the prints was hurting. The hunter stumbled in pain, falling and hitting his bad elbow. His groan was so loud that he worried his victims would hear.

He made his way slowly through the woods, down a steep hill and breathed a sigh of relief when he spotted the Range Rover, parked behind the jeep. He quickly went to the entrance to the cave and took off his camouflaged mask and peered inside. He could barely see the shining beam of the flashlight farther ahead in the cave, beyond the streams of water dripping from the cave walls, leading to the shack.

Leroy smiled and rubbed the dirt from his clean-shaven face knowing that Melvin and Patty were close to exacting the family's revenge. And the added surprise of finding those two teenage bitches in there was a bonus. He knew they would laugh about that later, but now, he had to find that bastard father.

Worried that his part was still unfinished on this miserable night, he stumbled back to the jeep, wanting to leave the scene that had most definitely not played out in his favor. Getting in the jeep, he noticed the lights from an approaching vehicle, and he took off.

Not long after he was gone, Sam and Cara turned a bend and saw Ed's Range Rover parked on the side of the road. Sam pulled up about ten feet from it and stopped, choosing to approach cautiously, searching the area with a flashlight.

Sam looked into the open windows of the Range Rover and saw it was empty. Then Cara spotted the snapped branch and matted-down grass that looked as if someone had just passed through, making a path into the woods. "This way," she said, pointing.

Sam started to move but stopped. Thinking, he turned and stared at the Range Rover. "Hang on." Going to the front passenger side, he opened the door and lifted the seat knob. Watching the seat rise, knowing his brother's hiding spot, he reached under the seat and found Ed's gun. He pulled it out and unwrapped it from the towel, raising it to show Cara the weapon.

Cara was surprised. "Sam! How did you know he kept that there?"

"I know my brother." Sam checked the gun and joined Cara. "Stay close," he said.

Taking the path, they disappeared into the woods.

CHAPTER 56

P atty and Melvin neared the shack. Coming to the turnoff in the cave tunnel, Patty stopped and stood silently by the lone mining cart. She heard Melvin's gasps for breath behind her and hissed at him. Of course he wanted this to be over, she thought. But there was no way that a few broken ribs would stand in the way of victory.

She felt a smile cross her face as he marched up to the old back porch, crossing a large puddle that'd formed by the storm entering the cave from above. Although the shack's roof had caved in, Patty was unafraid.

She watched Melvin stand in front of the door and gave him the signal. Wincing as he put his arm around his ribs in an attempt to hold them in place, he kicked in the door, yelling, "Time to die!"

Patty moved into the shadows as Melvin entered. He shined his flashlight into the kitchen to see the lantern sitting on the counter. Setting the rifle down, he picked up the box of matches and noticed the counter was wet. Feeling the water from above drip down through the broken shack he picked up the cool lantern that was also wet and lit it.

He pulled his gun from his holster and marched down the hall to the main room to see Simon, still lying on the floor with the mask still covering his head.

Melvin laughed as he squatted down to roll Simon over, eyeing the partly eaten sandwich with blood on it.

"Time to die, gimp."

The sharp stick came from out of nowhere, thrust upward by the man wearing the hunter's mask, and straight into Melvin's chin, piercing his jaw.

The ranger jumped back and dropped the lantern into an old, rotted chair; flames began to lick the rotted fabric and spread. Blood squirted from his jawline as Ed Savage pulled the mask off and got to his feet.

Simon came out from the darkness and bashed the ranger's head with a shovel, barely allowing Melvin to squeeze off a shot that ripped into the wall as he fell to the floor, dropping the gun.

Stuffing the head covering into his back pocket, and glad he wet the lantern from the soaked curtains to cool it, Ed held his gun on the ranger. He then picked up the ranger's weapon as the flames quickly raced up the dry, wooden wall over the fallen man.

He grabbed Simon and ran down the small hallway. Opening the closet, he stared at Ava, who was holding her still-passed-out cousin. Ed picked up Heather and threw her body over his shoulder, and the group made their way out of the burning shack. Simon paused and turned around, making his way back to the room to grab the lighter fluid. He picked it up and splashed it back and forth toward the downed man.

"Burn, you bastard," he yelled, remembering the kick to the stomach and dropping the can.

He then hobbled to the kitchen, grabbed the rifle off the kitchen counter, and limped as best he could with his one crutch, following behind them to safety.

The rotted wood of the shack burned quickly inside the cave as Melvin tried to stand, and the flames were sent down a wall beside him. Melvin stood with his arm on fire, and he tripped, tumbling into the dining-room table, splintering it into the sideboard and rolling onto the floor.

As the flames moved up his arm, he saw the skeletons blacken in the increasing inferno. He got up and ran into the kitchen and fell into the door, yelling in pain.

Turning to look behind them, the group heard the ranger's desperate cries.

Ava turned to her father, trying to erase the horrifying scene. "Where does this lead?" she said, pointing down the tunnel.

"I don't know, but we're taking it," Ed said. "Simon, you okay to walk?"

"I'll make it. Let's go," he said catching up with them.

They moved forward just as Melvin got to his feet, batting the flames from his arm, which leaped to his chest, catching his beard on fire. He fell through the door and straight into the puddle outside.

Patty saw her brother and ran to him, taking off her coat to smother the flames.

The light from the burning shack helped the Savages see as they hurried. Ed spotted figures moving in the distance and felt a stab of fear in his gut. "Get down!" he demanded, forcing them to hide in a dark corner of the cave.

Just then, Heather came to and screamed bloody murder as she stared at the camouflaged hunter's mask sticking out of the man's back pocket...Her attacker had gotten her.

Ed dropped his gun. He put Heather down on the ground and tried to calm her. He knelt and grabbed her chin; he needed her to focus. "Stop screaming...stop thrashing," he said in as loud a voice as he could risk. "Heather, look at me. Look at me. It's me...Ed!"

Opening her eyes, she saw him—just as Sam fired the gun. Hearing his daughter's cries for help, panic had taken his heart.

The sound of the bullet echoed in the darkness.

Ed jumped back as the bullet grazed the left side of his neck. And as he hit his head on the cave wall from the shock, his teeth bit down hard on his tongue, and he yelled out. He felt the warm blood fill his mouth. Everyone screamed, throwing themselves to the ground for cover, and Simon's one good crutch snapped in half as he hit the ground.

Heather yelled, "Ed!"

"Dad! Dad! Please, God, no more!" Ava cried.

A cry was returned. "Ava! Is that you? Ava!"

Heather stopped yelling. Her heart filled with peace as she recognized the familiar voices. "Mom! Dad! Help!"

As they got closer, Sam dropped his gun, seeing the damage he had done. He realized he'd just shot his own brother, and emotion filled his soul as he dropped to the ground next to him.

Ed was alive, holding his neck with his left hand, but tears fell from Sam's eyes. "Ed! Oh my God! What have I done?"

Ed raised his right hand and grabbed on to Sam. "I'm all right. Get the girls the hell out of here!" he said, spitting blood.

Ava screamed out, "No, we're not leaving you, Daddy!"

Cara reached out and, with Heather's help, pulled Ava away from her father, as Sam looked into his wounded brother's eyes.

Ed nodded his head toward safety. "Go back the way you came. Take her," he begged.

"God, no! Ed!" Cara yelled, as she felt her own fire of anger and revenge ignite in her soul. "Where is that bitch?" she screamed; payback filled her voice.

As if responding to her plea, Patty moved from the shadows, raised the shotgun, and began to fire.

Simon felt the blast hit the side of his head, and he fell back to the ground.

Cara grabbed the girls. It took everything she and Heather had to get Ava to leave her father's side and run back to the entrance of the cave.

Sam remained.

"Go," Ed said, gargling blood.

Reluctantly, with tears falling from his eyes and a soul that was crushed by the weight of his guilt, Sam picked up Ed's gun and crawled away from his brother, taking one last look at Simon, who was now lying on the ground, immobile. Getting up, he ran after his wife. He would take care of them no matter what happened next. That was the only way left to honor his brother.

Patty reloaded her gun.

Ed lay on the ground. All of it—the wounds, the pain, the knowledge that his family was hurt, the blood seeping down his throat, watching a young man's brains burst from the back of his skull...All of it was too much. Delirium had set in. Sweat poured off his skin as if the storm were now inside him. His vision blurred, and he removed his hand from his wounded neck, dropping it to his side in the wet cave.

As he looked up at the stone ceiling, the shadows dancing from the flames brought the vision of his daughter Lisa, kissing him on the cheek and telling him she loved him. *Don't go, Daddy,* her voice pleaded in his head. The silly look on her face when she called him "Squidward." He refused to believe his little nugget was gone. He saw Ava, teasing him that his signature devilish grin didn't work on her in the garage by his Challenger. He could see his son, Tucker, on the aircraft carrier that last day. And Marlo, kissing her, loving her, marrying her…The images were all of the family he so loved.

Tears came running down his face, and he moved his hand to wipe them away. He smeared his face with blood and wet dirt, getting the mixture in his mouth and allowing the coolness of the earth to stop the pain inside. He forced his arm to his side, felt for the puddle near him, and made a fist in the mud. He was in pain; his neck stung like a hundred little stabbing needles were piercing his skin.

Taking a last look at a dying Simon, Ed felt himself give up. He had no more energy. Closing his eyes, he said a silent good-bye to the life he had so loved living. "Please protect them," he whispered.

As if answering a prayer, a response team was called for over the intercom at Pine Crest Hospital. Marlo Savage had just woken up from her coma.

CHAPTER 57

The flames on her brother were out.

Patty ran after the fleeing family. But as she passed by the two men on the ground, she stopped.

Simon stirred and opened his eyes. Feeling the anger, she kicked him in the skull.

Then, lowering the shotgun, she grinned. "Good. I wanted me to be the last thing you saw before going to hell." Shooting him twice, she laughed maniacally at the dead man, but she missed the body of Ed Savage flinching as she turned her head to the sound of the women screaming, farther away in the cave.

She started to follow and then stopped. Turning, she took a step closer to Ed, raised the weapon, and pulled the trigger. The click was audible, and her rage grew. She thought she had one more shot left. Grabbing the barrel of the gun, she swung it around herself, letting go. The butt of the gun slammed into Ed's jaw, and the last round fired, nearly hitting her. He didn't even try to fight back. He took the hit and kept still, allowing the monster to turn and run out of the cave.

"No more mysteries for you!" Patty laughed as she ran into the darkness.

Ed clung to the earth to keep from yelling out in pain. His military training was still at his core. Opening his eyes slowly, he turned his head. In his blurred vision, he saw a distorted image of a woman running away. Grabbing a handful of mud, he smeared it on his neck like a paste, stopping the blood and cooling the burn of his skin.

"Simon...I am so sorry." He sighed, as he stared at the dead body beside him.

No. This isn't ending this way. I'm not going to let these assholes win!

The thought raced through Ed's mind as he reached for the hunter's mask in his back pocket. Tearing it, he tied it around his neck to aid the mud and stop the bleeding. He ignored the slice in his tongue and spit the rest of the blood from his mouth.

Sitting up slowly and carefully, he spread his hands out on the ground to look for the missing guns. He found the one he'd procured from the store; then he crawled to the rifle Simon had dropped and used it as a crutch to help rise from the earth and make his way out of the cave.

Outside the cave, Sam, Cara, and the girls were free.

Ava saw her dad's Range Rover. "Our car," she said quietly; her mind was in a state of shock.

Grabbing her by the arm, Sam led her to the RV. "Come on!" he yelled.

He pushed her into the RV behind Cara and Heather. The girls stayed on the floor, and Ava looked to the back bedroom. Cara did not want her to see Nathan, and she called to her. "Ava, stay up here," she said.

Sam was quickly trying to get to the driver's seat and dropped the keys. Picking them up, he jammed the keys into the ignition and started the RV, gunning the engine. The RV came to life, and he floored the gas pedal, the tires spitting debris from behind.

CHAPTER 58

T he clouds parted, allowing the moon to shine brightly on this night-marish eve. Sheriff Arnie Mallard was standing at the bodies of the Rylands when a ranger's jeep approached with its high beams on.

Arnie moved away from the bodies, waving his arms. The jeep pulled up to a stop. Unable to see the driver, Arnie shielded his eyes.

As he lowered one hand to his gun, the door of the jeep opened, and the lights shut off.

At first glance, Arnie relaxed his hand from his gun and lowered his other hand from his eyes. "Jeez, Melvin, what's going on tonight? Where have you been? I need some help over here," he said. When Arnie turned to point at the bodies of the Rylands, he heard the distinctive sound of a hammer being pulled back.

Arnie whipped around. He leaned in closer, squinting his eyes. "*Leroy*? When did you…?"

Leroy pulled the trigger, shooting Arnie in the forehead and blowing the sheriff's hat off before he could finish what he was saying.

The lawman fell to the ground. Another dead body claimed in the night.

In pain, but able to drag Arnie to his jeep and get him in the driver's seat, he left Arnie slumped over the wheel and put it in drive, shoving Arnie's foot down on the gas pedal. The jeep started to move, and Leroy, holding the steering wheel with his right hand, turned it toward the side of the road.

Letting go, he watched the jeep head into the gully and smash into a tree. All that Leroy could see was the small glowing blue light of a cell phone illuminating the dead sheriff's face.

CHAPTER 59

The giant RV rocked as Sam sped down the bumpy road. He could almost feel the angry witch who had taken his brother from him following behind them in the night. The girls were hanging on to things and still down on the floor as Sam hit potholes in the road. When the door shot open in the back, Nathan's body fell from the bed, and Ava and Heather saw him and screamed.

Looking away from the road for just a moment, Sam missed the police cruiser that came speeding around the bend, and the two vehicles collided.

The cruiser turned to the left as the RV came up over it on its right. The cruiser was sent toward some large boulders near the side of the road, but Leroy opened the door and managed to jump before the cruiser hit. As his already wounded body hit the road, the red-and-blue lights standing for justice kept on spinning.

The RV hit the barriers on the opposite side of the road, and the driver's-side tires went over the edge. The RV landed on the driver's side and slid uncontrollably down a steep ravine at an angle, hitting a large boulder, spinning it around, and splitting it in half about three feet behind Sam.

The front of the RV, where Sam was sitting, came to rest farther down the mountain than the back. It smashed into the trees, and an old, rotted limb came crashing through the glass and pierced Sam in his right shoulder, pinning him to his seat. Sam slumped over onto the rotted limb and passed out.

The back of the RV slowed as the ground slope decreased, and it came to a stop against the trees. As the movement stopped, the screaming women were buried under debris and the body of Nathan Savage.

They were all scraped, scratched, and bleeding, but they got themselves up. Cara looked up and saw there was no longer a front to the RV, and she screamed out Sam's name. Seeing their grandfather dead and hearing her desperate mother's cries, Heather grabbed Ava to climb out and follow.

Cara stood on the earth, looking for her husband. She continued to scream out his name and started climbing the debris trail before her. When she got to the boulder that had split the RV in half, she looked down and saw him. She screamed for her man and made her way down to him. She stopped in fear to see Sam pinned by the tree. He was motionless; blood was running down his extended right arm. Cara screamed out, "Sam!" and began to cry.

Heather and Ava made their way to her, and they both stopped in shock. Something strange was happening with Cara. She had an odd look about her, and when she fixated on the gun lodged in the dashboard, she lunged for it. With the gun in her hand, she looked back at the girls. "Stay here," she ordered. Climbing past them and onto the boulders, she paused and looked back to Sam. "That bitch!"

Nothing was going to stop her.

Making it to the top of the hill, she saw the red-and-blue spinning lights from the cruiser. In the distance, headlights were getting near, and she recognized the Range Rover. She ran to the cruiser, screaming for help. "Officer, are you all right?" Getting to the open door of the cruiser, she saw that it was empty.

Down below, Heather and Ava were with Sam, and Heather lost it. She was crying, and she screamed out for her father. Sam opened his eyes and spit out blood, staring at his injured shoulder.

Heather screamed, "Daddy!"

Up at the top, Cara heard Heather's scream and turned just as Leroy made his move.

The man with the hunter's mask over his head ran out at her, yelling. Cara raised the gun and fired twice, hitting him only once.

Leroy didn't stop; he collided into her. She screamed as he knocked her against the cruiser.

Heather heard the gunshots. Turning from her father, she looked to Ava. "Come on!"

The Range Rover came fast. The driver honked the horn and Cara saw Leroy's bloody elbow and twisted it. Leroy screamed out, clutching his elbow and taking a few steps away from her. Cara saw the SUV and charged, pushing the man into the road. The Range Rover clipped Leroy, sending him past the other side of the road, where he rolled helplessly down the side. His face hit a rock at the edge of the ridge, breaking his nose, and he tumbled down into the water below.

The mist from the falls filled the air ahead of him as he struggled to keep from going over. The swift and cold water shocked him and sent him over, screaming. He fell backward, landing on a boulder sticking out from the mountain, snapping his back and crushing the back of his skull. Twisting and turning, the body fell out of sight into the waters below.

The Range Rover squealed to a stop, and Patty got out. She ran to the edge, screaming, "Leroy!"

Patty turned to see Cara right behind her. Her eyes locked on the woman, who raised Ed's gun in Patty's face and pulled the trigger. The gun's chamber was empty. She tried to squeeze off another shot, but there was nothing left. Patty reached up and started choking her.

Cara slammed the gun into the side of Patty's face with her right hand, grinding the metal into her temple. With her left, she grabbed at Patty's long, wild hair and pulled hard, dropping the gun and twisting Patty's head to the left. Patty screamed out, and the two women fell to the ground.

Climbing as fast as she could up the muddy hill, Ava slipped and slid. Heather grabbed her forearm, and the two kept climbing.

Patty and Cara were rolling over the road of rocks and mud tearing at each other when Patty slammed Cara's head against the ground. Able to free herself, she got up and ran to the Range Rover.

The bottle of Boone's Farm strawberry wine was there, and Patty grabbed it and threw it at Cara, missing her but giving herself enough time to go for the knife. It was caught under the gas pedal. She grabbed the knife and charged. As she held the sharp weapon over her head, the knife gleamed in the moonlight. Her long hair blew back behind her.

Cara rushed Patty and the two women collided as Patty brought down the knife on her, cutting her. Cara cried out and grabbed Patty's forearm, pushing her hand and the knife into Patty's side. Patty screamed and dropped the knife, grabbing for Cara's hair as they hit the ground. Cara rolled over onto Patty's back, digging her nails into her skull as she grabbed hands full of her wild hair and smashed her face into the ground, "Bloody Bitch!" She screamed out.

Heather screamed out for her mother causing Cara to turn toward her daughter giving Patty the chance to turn over and slap Cara across the face knocking her over.

Heather reached the top and saw Patty fling dirt into her mother's face to blind her. She then pulled Cara up from the ground by her hair, and with Cara bent over, she ran toward the bend on the side of the falls.

"I can't see!" Cara screamed as she stumbled, and Patty twisted her hands full of Cara's hair. Spinning Cara to face her, she let go and pushed her backward.

Cara reached out for Patty but missed, falling over and tumbling down the muddy slope not far from where Leroy had fallen, and into the water. She tried to swim away from the falls, but the current was too strong. Her scream filled the air as her body went over into the water.

Seeing her mother die, Heather screamed and charged. Patty turned and looked down at the knife, and they both went after it. Colliding, they fell to the ground. They were clawing and thrashing at each other and the knife got kicked away.

Able to stand, Patty pulled Heather down by her hair and kneed her in the stomach. Heather doubled over, and Patty pulled her by her hair to try to throw her over—attempting to send her down the same path as her mother had taken. Heather screamed, just as Ava made it to the top.

Ava saw them close to the edge and ran over, grabbing Patty by her hair and yanking back hard, pulling the woman off Heather.

Patty screamed as she let go of Heather's hair, but turned on Ava and slapped her across the face and pushed her to the ground. Heather fell to the ground, choking for air from taking the knee to her stomach.

Patty grabbed Ava and pulled her up and Ava saw Patty's cut side and clawed her nails into it. Patty screamed as Heather got to her feet and ran to them and pulled Patty's shoulder back and punched her in the face. The girls grabbed Patty's sides, dragged her to the cliff, and fell near its edge.

Ava grabbed the bottle of Boone's. "Remember this, bitch?" she screamed, swinging the bottle and hitting Patty on the side of her face. Patty's nose burst open, and blood spattered on everyone as Heather pushed her backward. She slipped and fell, grabbing Heather's ankle. Patty pulled on Heather to drag her down with her, and Heather kicked at Patty, stomping her foot into her face. The kick was too much even for the insane, and Patty let go, screaming as she fell down the steep hillside and into the water. "I'll get you," she screamed, disappearing over the edge, missing the rock that killed her brother and landing in deep water.

Ava pulled Heather up and away from the edge, and they held on to each other. Heather then pulled back from Ava in tears, as the shock hit her. "My mother!"

Ava saw the same hurt sadness in Heather's face and she could feel the panic inside her build. "We need to get back to your dad," she cried out wanting to calm her.

Moving slowly, they walked toward the Range Rover.

As they came around the side of the vehicle, the figure lunged from the woods.

The man was burned and bloody; a tourniquet was tied around his upper arm, and a syringe hung from his forearm. The girls screamed. He grabbed Heather's arm and pulled him to her. With the girls hanging on to each other, Ava's hand was caught, and she was pulled into him, too. He pulled Heather back, whipping her around him, and shoved Ava back down to the ground.

The sad excuse for a body advanced to where Ava was, dragging Heather with him. She was slapping at him when Ava looked up to see the giant ranger raise his foot and stomp on her leg, grinding all his weight down on her. She screamed out as Melvin swung Heather around, grabbing her with his other hand to choke her.

He raised Heather up to throw her over while increasing the weight on Ava's leg. Ava screamed out, able to sit up, she grabbed a rock and smashed it into his knee. Melvin raged, raising his foot in the air once again and almost losing his balance.

The bullet barely missed him as it hit the tree in front of him.

Melvin turned, dropping Heather on top of Ava, to see Ed Savage move from his spot at the tree line. Whether from adrenaline or shock, Ed charged and fired, hitting Melvin in the chest. When he fired again, the gun was out of bullets, and as the ranger arched backward near the edge, Ed ducked his head, hitting Melvin with his right shoulder. The ranger stepped back, nearly going over but managing to keep his balance. The syringe fell from the ranger's arm, and he screamed out, grabbing on to Ed.

The ranger dug his hand into the left side of Ed's neck, sending a jolt of pain like he'd never felt rushing through his body. The ranger's other hand reached up to choke him when Ed rammed both hands into the ranger's neck.

As they fell, Ed landed near Patty's knife, and he reached for it. The ranger advanced toward him, picking him up from the ground by his neck to throw him over, just as Ed brought the weapon up with both hands, stabbing him under his jaw, slicing his tongue, and lodging the knife in his gums.

The ranger screamed out, and Ed twisted the knife, breaking the handle off and leaving the blade lodged in the ranger's jaw. The ranger dropped him and leaned back. Ed hit the ground, groaning in pain, and got back to his feet. As the ranger stumbled, Ed punched him in the eye, knocking him over the edge. Melvin fell back over the girls and went down, tumbling into the water, his scream filling the air as he went over the falls, following his sister.

The moment the violence stopped, Ed's adrenaline ceased, and he fell to the ground. The torn mask from his neck had come off, and the girls crawled over to him, seeing his wound. Ava got up and ran to the Range Rover's open driver's door, and she released the back. She retrieved the first-aid kit and a towel; then she ran back over to Ed and wiped his neck. Heather pulled out the hydrogen peroxide, pouring it over the wound. It stung, and he yelled, as Ava held the towel, applying pressure to his skin.

Seeing that Ed seemed okay, Heather closed the kit and took it with her to the edge where her father lay below. She started making her way down as the sun finally began to produce a lighter shade in the sky, alerting everyone to the fact that the night from hell was finally coming to an end.

Ed lay on the ground against Ava. His neck was swollen, and he was bruised; blood and dirt covered his body.

She looked down while rocking him in her still-shaking arms. "My brave father, I love you," she said.

Ed opened his eyes to see his daughter looking back at him. Worry filled his thoughts for his daughter, and the only thing he could think of at that moment was to comfort her. He then smiled and gave his signature devilish grin. Ava laughed. "Okay, okay, your silly look works on me, too, you big goof!"

They both laughed, causing Ed pain. "It hurts to move," he said through gritted teeth.

Despite the pain and the horrible losses, father and daughter found some peace in the fact that they still had each other.

CHAPTER 60

Police and medical-emergency vehicles were everywhere. At the cave, Simon was being carried out on a stretcher to the ambulance. They slid the stretcher inside and covered his face with a sheet. Inside the cave, firefighters had extinguished the flames, and a gun was found and put into evidence.

Ed sat at the back of an ambulance, with Ava and Heather standing right outside where the emergency crew was pulling Sam up from below. They got him to the top, and Heather rushed to him. He raised his hand to her, and she took it as they moved past Ed and Ava to a second ambulance. After they loaded him in, Heather got in beside him.

"We can go now," Ed said to the crew waiting to load him and Ava. Ed got up and made it into the back himself, and Ava climbed in next to him.

An officer watching the ambulances leave turned and spotted the syringe and bagged it. Below him from the other side of the road, the searchers were looking in the water for any signs of life, and at the wrecked RV, rescue workers were pulling Nathan's body up the mountain.

Down at the lake below the falls, divers were pulling up a dead Leroy from the water. They laid him on the deck of the boat and covered him with a sheet. Cara was lying about three feet away from him on the deck of the boat. The search and rescue had become a search-and-recovery mission, as an agent placed a white sheet over Cara's now-peaceful face.

The discovery of their own sheriff Arnie Mallard, downed in the line of duty, was hard for all who knew him.

But the worst discovery were the Rylands—with the parents and the boy killed, the news had to be brought to the surviving child at home, a job no one wanted to do.

Down by the lake, along the shoreline, a wet hunter's mask lay in the mud, and small, wet footprints could be seen leading away from the water. A ranger badge was embedded in the sand.

The ambulances drove Ed, Ava, Sam, and Heather away from the area, leaving a police officer writing a report. He looked at the license plate of the Range Rover, 2SLA102, and wrote it down on the space on his form under the date of October 2. He read it out loud: "Two slay ten two." He took an uneasy step back from the vehicle, staring at it as if it were some kind of hidden message sent from hell.

CHAPTER 61

The auto accident on the overpass during the previous night's storm was bad. Now, in the light of day, crews were busy untangling the pickup truck from the old Ford Maverick. The owner of the pickup told them he'd blown a tire coming down the hill onto the overpass and had swerved into the Maverick, slamming into the side of the old and poorly maintained overpass. What they could not see due to the wreckage was that the axle of the Maverick had snapped and dug into the base of the overpass siding. With the pickup pulled away, they pulled the Maverick out, and the cement siding of the overpass came with it. Cracks appeared around the crash site, and the inspector closed the bridge.

CHAPTER 62

Two days later, Marlo had been moved from the ICU to a larger private room. With a bandage around her head, she was sitting up. Ed, who, after recovering himself, had been moved into his wife's room, was sitting beside her. She had her head on his chest, and she was weeping. The loss of her brother and probably her daughter weighed greatly on her already broken and battered mind, and she felt herself spiraling down.

Ed was always looking out for his girls, and not being able to fix this for his wife ate at him. He had his arm around her, trying to comfort her.

Ed was hurting both emotionally and physically. The surgery had gone well; the bullet had missed his carotid artery, and he was all stitched up. His jaw was bruised, and his bandages made him look like a sad partial mummy. He had scabs from scratches on his face, and he hurt all over.

Ava and Heather sat on a sofa under the window with a few scattered magazines between them. Ava's leg, where the ranger had stomped on her, was bandaged. "This waiting is getting to me," she said, tossing yet another magazine to the side.

Down the hall a nurse was pushing Sam in a wheelchair. They entered through the open door, and he pointed to the table. Noticing that Marlo's condition had not changed, she nodded to Ed and left the room.

Sam had the release papers on his lap. Being the family lawyer, not to mention one who frightened the hospital staff so much that they were not about to argue when it came to an early release—that and Ed's celebrity status—Sam spread the papers out on the table. He glanced over at Ed and saw Marlo crying. Ed shook his head, and Sam began looking the papers over and signing them one by one. Ed had arranged for a helicopter for his wife and had told the hospital that Niles was on his way for the others.

Sam's shirt was half buttoned; he had a bandage around his chest and over his shoulder. The loss of his wife was in the forefront of his mind, and everyone in the room could feel it. Quietly, Heather got up from the sofa and sat at the table with her father, taking his hand.

The nurse came back with a manila envelope tucked under her arm and a tray with pills and a cup of water for Marlo. Placing the envelope on the counter, she brought Marlo her pills and watched the vacant eyes stare back at her as Marlo took her pills and swallowed them without a word.

Ed watched Marlo hand the nurse the paper cup back, drop her arm, and cuddle into him. He watched the nurse turn to the counter, put down the tray, and pick up the manila envelope. "More papers to sign?" he said.

The nurse looked down at the envelope. "No, it's addressed to Marlo."

Marlo looked up. Studying the package, she accepted it from the nurse's hand. The envelope looked dirty, like the postman had dropped it in the mud-soaked streets after the terrible storm. Marlo ripped the top off, and a VCR tape fell out on her lap, along with an old newspaper article. She picked up the tape and looked at it, her face more than confused.

Ed picked up the newspaper clip and handed it back to her.

"What's all this?" she asked.

Ed shrugged as Marlo read the headline out loud: "Young Homeless Man Arrested for Dropping Rock over Expressway—Killing Two." She looked to Ed with questioning eyes and picked up the VCR tape.

Recalling the nurse as she was leaving, she asked, "Who sent this to me?"

The nurse turned and looked at the tape in Marlo's lap. "I don't know. It was at the nurses' station with the rest of the mail."

Marlo looked to the tape. "I need to see what's on this. Is there someplace here we can go watch this?"

The nurse smiled. "I'll do you one better. Down the hall in the conference room, we have a TV and VCR on a cart. I'll go get it," she said, leaving the room.

After she'd finished setting everything up, the nurse left to allow the family some privacy.

Marlo handed the tape to Ava, who pushed it into the slot and pressed play.

The tape was filled with static. It jumped a bit before going to a completely black screen, as a strange, female voice began to narrate.

"Nathan Savage, it was you who did this. You took my family; now I have taken yours. I'm only sorry that it took this long to take from you what you took from me all those years ago. The pain you have caused me has never left. Now it is you and your loved ones who will hurt. The newspapers are being advised of everything, and soon everyone will know what you did. You will never find me, because I am dead. I died a long time ago when the rock fell from your hands. But don't worry; I'll always be around watching...and laughing at *your* pain!"

The blank screen flickered; then an old house appeared. Through the front door, a man and a very pregnant woman came out. The Savages watched the video in silence.

The tape showed the family getting into the car and the little girl brushing what looked to be her mom's hair...the smiling face of the little girl in the backseat...the rock hitting the windshield...the horrific accident and the people running to help...

No one said a word as the tape continued to run, and the TV faded to black.

CHAPTER 63

From the blackness of a tunnel just a few miles away, the black limousine made its way up the mountainous road to the hospital. Niles Savage was alone in the back. With his reading glasses perched on his nose, he stared at the blueprints of the hotel that was nearing completion. With a rendering on the seat next to him, the housing-development plans sat at his feet.

Now that they were back in the beaming sunlight, an overpass came into view. Just as the limousine passed underneath, a large chunk of cement fell from the closed overpass, directly into the windshield.

The glass exploded. The driver was instantly killed. The limousine slammed into the guardrail, broke through it, and crashed down a small ravine. Niles was thrown forward against the limo's glass partition.

Cars stopped. People ran to the railing, and a woman climbed over, making her way down with a man following behind. Getting to the door, they stared inside at the man. Still breathing, his face was bleeding, and he reached out to the woman as 911 was called.

CHAPTER 64

Marlo was hysterical. Learning the reason her daughter had been ripped away from her sent her completely over the edge. She screamed at everyone, placing the blame on every Savage within her sight.

She glared at her husband. "*My* Lisa…*my* brother…both gone because of that bastard father of yours."

Ed was equally blinded with rage, but he was focused on Marlo's admonition.

Ava ran out to get the nurse as Ed and Heather held on to Marlo, keeping her in the bed and trying to calm her down, so she wouldn't cause harm to herself.

Two extra nurses took their places, one on each side of Marlo, pushing Ed and Heather away as the first nurse drew the needle. It was fast. The sedative worked pretty quickly, and Marlo started to ease.

Outside in the hallway, the trauma alert paged the staff, announcing that another MVA was headed in. ETA: six minutes. The staff left the room.

With Marlo zoning away to a quiet place, Ed sat next to her with Ava on her other side. Sam was feeling woozy himself as Heather ejected the tape and picked up the remote to turn the TV off. She hit the wrong button, and an entertainment gossip show appeared instead. And the news was all about Savage.

The segment was cut, haphazardly pieced together, and edited for optimal in-your-face sensationalism. It showed Ava slamming reporter

Wendy Storm against the police station and Ed getting the microphone shoved in his face and knocking the camera down, with a few provocative photos of Ellie Collins from her earlier modeling career.

The Savages all stared at the screen in shock. Even Marlo had her eyes on it, although not really understanding the colors and shapes as the drug took over.

The host on the show's set was beaming at this reporter's dream story with the video playing on the large screens behind her. It was Carly Tilton, a popular TV personality, who also had another hit daytime talk show. She was holding a magazine in her hand.

"Ed Savage is in trouble, folks, and he isn't the only one. Not only did his centerfold drop this week in *Cosmopolitan*, giving us an eyeful, but are charges of alleged murder now pending?" Carly opened the magazine to the centerfold, and her facial expression was overly exaggerated as the image hit the giant screen behind her.

The magazine had done an article on the classic actors in Hollywood and had chosen Ed Savage as its centerfold. And when they talked about recreating the Burt Reynolds bearskin-rug photo, Ed, being an animal lover, had come up with the idea of using a live bear cub, like the one in his shaving-cream commercial all those years ago. Ed posed on a faux-fur blanket; the cub was situated perfectly in front of him, to cover his rather hard-to-hide area, and a can of shaving cream was in front of the bear. It was a playful shoot, and everyone had a blast shooting it. They had no idea at the time what would be happening when it was released.

Carly grinned from ear to ear, knowing what kind of malicious spin she could inflect on this story, with naked photos to boot.

"You think this is something; we've got yellow journalism at its finest. And you can smell the lawsuits in the air. Check out what was captured yesterday."

The giant screen behind her went into the story.

Wendy Storm held her microphone, wearing a dress splattered with mud. "Reporting from Black Ridge: TV personality Ed Savage was jailed for trying to kill his wife. His daughter, who sources tell me could be an illegitimate child of one of his own brothers, could also be the source of contention in the family. The poor little girl went tragically missing after a horrendous recreational-vehicle accident, and she was left on the side of the road. While Ed Savage was recovering comfortably in custody, his daughter was left to the elements of a storm. Search teams had to give up looking for the girl due to the recent severe weather."

The video was patched together with shots of the burned-out RV as reporter Sandy Storm entered the story: "Ed Savage was later released from jail because—let's face it, viewers—his family is filthy rich. We found out his slimy brother, Sam Savage, who is the family's ambulance-chasing lawyer, sprang him from jail. Sources tell me Ed had a child with his former slutty costar, Ellie Collins, and the wife found out. Just how many more illegitimate kids are out there fathered by this murdering lunatic is anyone's guess." Sandy finished her report and walked over to her sister, and the two held up their microphones: "This is Wendy and Sandy Storm reporting from Black Ridge Falls."

Ed's mouth dropped open. He was speechless.

Sam looked at him. "What the hell was that?" he barked.

The gossip show continued with a reporter standing in front of Roman Savage's home. "We're outside the home of yet another brother of alleged murderer Ed Savage. The man's name is Roman Savage, and we're waiting for any comments he wishes to make about his family's upheaval at the hands of what most say is a diabolical killer."

The camera panned to Roman's African American wife, Gabby, and their daughter, Danni, as they pulled up into the driveway and got out of their Mercedes. Gabby Savage wore a beautiful Versace dress and was immediately mobbed. One reporter screamed, "Have you heard from your psycho brother-in-law?" and shoved a microphone in her face.

Gabby was scared, and she stumbled back against the car. She turned to see her beautiful daughter get blindsided by another reporter: "What's it like to go to school after your uncle most likely killed your cousin?"

Yet another reporter joined the attack. "Did you know your cousin was illegitimate? Could there be a secret regarding your birth as well?" The reporter blurted the accusations out while shoving her microphone in Danni's face.

Danni couldn't move. Scared, she looked to her mother. "Mom," she yelled.

Gabby was already halfway around the back of the car, pushing against bodies to get to her daughter, knocking a reporter back against the car. "Danielle, don't say one word," she ordered, pulling Danni and nearly tripping when the front door of the house opened and Roman appeared with their son, Chase.

A reporter ran directly at Roman and yelled, "What will happen with Savage Construction now that your brother will most likely be charged with attempted murder? Will you lose more business, like Donert Tower?" The reporter shoved the microphone at him as if it were a knife held by a true lunatic killer stabbing at his victim. Like Ed, Roman batted away the device and saw his wife stumble against the car in the crowd. His blood turned to fire—he had just found out she was pregnant—and he raced for his wife and daughter, reaching them in the chaos.

Gabby pushed through the reporters with Danni, as Chase got to his sister's side, pushing away a reporter. "Leave her alone," Chase yelled.

When they made it back to the house and slammed the door shut, the reporter turned back to the camera wearing a smug, self-important smile. "Stay tuned; we'll be back with more of this delicious story."

As they broke for a commercial, Ed raised his voice. "Heather!" he barked, reaching for his phone. "Turn that down." Heather muted the set, and Ed punched in Roman's phone number. He was infuriated beyond belief. Ed loved his wife and had *never* cheated on her. He had a special hatred for cheaters, and the thought of that horrible story being told live boiled his blood.

Ed looked at the evil envelope the VCR tape had arrived in as he listened to Roman's phone ring.

In another town far away, a postal truck moved down the street from house to house. Stopping outside an older, unassuming home, the mailman opened the mailbox and placed a manila envelope inside addressed to Stevie Galloway.

More mail was delivered.

The letter that some strange woman with long, wild hair had sent landed at the local newspaper. In it, she detailed her own mother's writings that she'd found hidden—taped under a dresser drawer, detailing the affair her mother had with one Nathan Savage.

PART 2
ED SAVAGE AND THE BLACK RIDGE CULT—SURVIVING SAVAGES

CHAPTER 65

The first week after they returned home was hectic. One of the things on the long Savage to-do list was trading in the Range Rover. Driving it home—and the thoughts of what had happened—kept the fear in everyone.

Upon landing on Berman Medical Center's rooftop in Port Roberts, New York, Marlo was checked in for more tests. Her doctor wanted to go over everything that his patient had been through. The nights she would spend there were good for many reasons as well, including her mental state. The loss was so huge, and the hope of finding Lisa was diminishing—and the mind-numbing facts of why all this had happened made everything worse. The medications Marlo was on were helping; she was calmer, and the arguing seemed unending.

Ed was with her at the hospital and needed to get to the dealership before they closed. "Marlo, are you sure you don't want me to stay? I can deal with the car tomorrow," he said.

Sitting in her bed, Marlo adjusted her pillow and looked to her husband. "No, I'm fine. Actually, I feel like I could sleep for a week. You go ahead."

Rising from his chair, Ed kissed his wife good-bye. "So, I'm thinking of getting a black one; what do you think?"

Marlo paused for a moment. "I love the blue color of your car; get a navy one."

Ed forced a smile. "Okay, navy it is."

Ed left his wife's room. On the way to the elevator, he was reminded of the fights they'd been having prior to this whole Black Ridge hell, not to mention this new round of misery. If a navy Range Rover was what she wanted, he was tired of fighting.

At the dealership he saw the perfect color, Mariana black, which looked navy and black at the same time. "I'll take this one," he said to the salesman.

Leaving the dealership, Ed stopped at this favorite pub and ate quietly. He needed the peace above all else right now.

It was late when Ed got home; the house was dark and quiet. He checked on the girls and then went into his master walk-in closet and changed, putting on his pajama pants and a T-shirt; he then went downstairs to pour himself a nightcap and headed to bed.

The sound of breaking glass in the distance woke him. Ed opened his eyes and sat up straight, feeling the terror that hadn't subsided since their return home.

Ed's floor plan was large, with a guesthouse in the backyard on the other side of the swimming pool. The guesthouse was empty due to the remodel Marlo had underway. But when Ed moved to the window of their bedroom, he saw that the guesthouse door was open.

Swallowing the shot of panic, he went to the sliding glass doors, flipped on the outside lights, including the pool light, and opened the sliding door, quietly stepping onto the balcony. It was cold, and he could see his breath. He closed the sliding door and looked over the railing to the small building and saw that all was quiet. Taking the outside stairs down from the balcony, he went around the pool to the open door. There, he saw broken glass that had come from the narrow window next to the door.

He pushed the door open wider and peered inside, reaching for the light switch. The light bulb in the ceiling popped when the electricity made contact, and the broken bulb shattered inside the light fixture, hidden by the plastic covering it.

The plastic left hanging in the windows by the painters had fallen in places; painting supplies were scattered about, and two ladders as well as the kitchen appliances made barricades for Ed to walk around. The door to the bedroom was ajar, and a strange light was on.

Ed moved to the bedroom and pushed the door open. There he saw the flashlight, alone, lying on the floor, its beam shooting toward him across the floor. He went over and picked it up, causing it to shut off. In the dark he tried shaking it. The top portion was loose and came off, falling to the floor. He picked it up and screwed it back on, and the flashlight once again illuminated the room.

He heard the voice: "Remember this little trick?"

Ed turned immediately as the crazy woman from Black Ridge Falls stepped from the closet and swung the shovel, hitting him in the face. Ed took the hit and fell to the ground, motionless, dropping the flashlight, which rolled a few feet away.

Patty laughed maniacally, dropping the shovel and moving from the bedroom to the kitchen to grab a knife. Returning to Ed, who was coming out of his daze, she knelt down to him and grabbed his face with her clawlike hand. "Wake up, sweetie," she cackled.

Ed opened his eyes as Patty brought down the knife into his chest—stabbing over and over as his blood splattered on her arms while she sent him to follow the loved ones who'd gone before.

Patty got up laughing, her dress covered in Ed Savage's blood.

As Patty left the guesthouse, she created a trail of blood as she moved around the pool and ascended the outside stairs to the balcony.

Down the hall from Ed's bedroom came the sound.

"No!"

Ava woke from the bloody dream—the same dream she'd been having since they'd come home. She reached for her bottle of water—empty. Getting up, she left Heather alone, asleep sleeping in her bed across the same guestroom.

Ava went down the inside stairs to the kitchen and retrieved more water. The light from the refrigerator hurt her eyes. Shutting the door, she stared out at the pool, wondering why it was lit up at this hour.

Upstairs, Patty's almost demonic reflection stared back at her from the sliding glass door as she moved it carefully on its glider and entered the bedroom.

Silently, Patty moved down the hall to the open door where Heather was sleeping. She moved next to the bed without a noise and raised the knife. The man's blood dripped down on Heather's face, and Patty smiled wide when Heather's eyes opened and widened with fear. Without a word, Patty slammed her hand over her mouth and brought down the weapon, stabbing until the girl ceased to fight and her arms fell lifelessly to her sides. Patty stopped to admire what she had done, putting the finishing touch to the girl's corpse as she slit her throat with a flourish.

Patty then went to the window and opened it. The cold breeze filled the bedroom, and blood dripped onto the windowsill. She started to climb out. Stopping, she looked back toward the open bedroom door.

As she made a small noise, Patty listened carefully to the footsteps that now raced to the stairs, directly into death's grip.

The guest bedroom window was open; it was so cold.

Ava could see her breath and trembled. With a small sigh of relief, she stared at Heather lying covered in the bed, still sleeping. Her back was to her. Walking carefully across the floor in order to not bring even more panic to both of them, she nudged Heather's shoulder to wake her.

"Heather, Heather, wake…" Ava stopped, rolling her body over.

The shock overcame her as she stared at Heather's cut throat, the stab wounds, the blood everywhere. Heather's lifeless body stared at her from her bed, and Ava screamed. Noticing the blood on the windowsill, she turned to escape the bedroom, running directly into the crazy woman's arms.

Patty's eyes shone green from the moonlight, between her yellow teeth and her witchlike hair; she wore that ugly dress from that horrible night in the mountains. "Thought you could get away from me, did you?" Patty cackled and raised the knife, charging Ava, laughing insanely.

Ava raised her hands and tried to stop Patty's arm from coming down with the knife. She pushed and pushed hard. Patty fell back, giving Ava a chance to escape. Ava ran to the hall, but Patty jumped forward, catching her feet and tackling her to the floor. With her long, clawlike hands, she pulled herself up, turning Ava over and looking directly into the frightened girl's eyes. "Miss me, sweetie?" She laughed in Ava's face.

Ava grabbed at Patty's skin, digging her nails into the flesh of her face and rolling her over to get to her feet. Patty reached up and grabbed Ava's long hair. Pulling her back, turning her body as she rose, Patty pushed Ava backward into the upstairs railing.

When the wood splintered, Ava screamed out, twisting and falling from the second floor and landing on the glass table below. It cracked, and Ava's side was impaled.

Near death, Ava tried to move but only succeeded in cutting herself more. She opened her eyes to see Patty creeping to the ledge and looking down at her. Patty's hair hung down, and she screamed out, "You're mine now." Leaping from the edge, knife pointed at Ava, she fell through the air, landing on top of her bleeding body.

Ava issued a bloodcurdling scream—waking a very much alive Heather, who was now sitting beside her, and a healthy, breathing father, who came running down the hall in his pajama pants and T-shirt.

Ava was still caught in the murderous nightmare, and he shook her hard to bring her back into reality. "Ava, Ava, wake up! I'm here, baby! You're safe," he yelled to her.

Ava finally woke from her nightmares and clung to her father for life. Heather held her hand.

"Ava, I'm here, baby. Heather is too. I love you, and we're here." Ed kept repeating this mantra to his daughter until, together, Ed and Heather stopped her hysterical crying.

CHAPTER 66

The partial bridge collapse was ruled an accident. A "coincidence" was the explanation given for the piece of cement that came loose from and fell onto the limousine at that exact moment. Coincidences be damned; Ed Savage wasn't buying it.

Back home, the Savages were preparing for funerals. The idea of preparing for any funeral was taxing enough on the emotions, and the Savages had to deal with four. Nathan and Cara Vanderran Savage would be interred. Simon Winchester was to be cremated. Marlo had accepted her daughter's death and was planning an empty-casket memorial, which Ed was dead set against. He would not accept the loss, and he vowed to find her.

Ed's son, Tucker, and Sam and Cara's son, Chet, were deployed in the navy on an aircraft carrier currently resting in the Atlantic on maneuvers, and they would not be making it home. The same went for Roman and Gabby's daughter, Lana, and Logan and Maura's daughter, Kate—they were in the middle of a crucial time at West Point, and as hard as it was on them, they would be paying their respects at a later time.

The reading of the wills would follow, and big money was up for grabs. With Ed's insane schedule and the busy lives of his brothers, it had been years since they were all together in the same room. Things were about to change.

Ed Savage was thrown in too many directions when he got home. With everyone else out of harm's way, he could focus on finding Lisa.

The reward flyers hadn't produced any serious leads, and he'd contacted everyone he could think of for help—including reaching out to his past.

Marlo's mood changed from sadness and crying over her loss to anger and constant fighting over why it had all happened in the first place. Worse, Marlo did not even have her parents to turn to, since they'd been killed in an auto accident six years ago, leaving just the three children—Maggie, Marlo, and Simon—to fend for themselves. Now Marlo was questioning everything.

Even way back, when Ed didn't exactly explain the family business, it was secrets and lies everywhere she looked, and she screamed about them, too. Marlo was losing it at times, but her sister, Maggie, could be counted on to come to the rescue. She could calm Marlo down. And Ed booked a plane to get her there as soon as possible.

Ava had pulled into herself a little more. Ed would often find her in Lisa's room looking at her things, but she was never totally withdrawn. Maybe it was seeing her mother and the fits she was having that kept Ava in check. Whatever it was, Ed was certain Ava would somehow come through all the pain.

He worried about Sam, dealing with Cara's death. He had a sense that Ava's strength would help out Heather, whom he was also concerned for, but still the thoughts of his daughter Lisa weighed on him like bricks.

Ed's career, however, was in jeopardy. One of the shows he was preparing for, which was due to start production, came to a screeching halt when the powers that be met behind closed doors to decide Ed's fate: either push on or drop him immediately.

Ed had two others airing; one was coming to an end, and the other had just started. A third was due to premier soon. More private meetings were taking place, and Ed was stressed.

Then, there was the news. The letter a crazy woman had sent to a newspaper had started a firestorm. The old case delving into her parents' auto accident got the talking heads on television yammering about the Savage family once again. Lawyers were being brought in. The homeless person jailed all those years ago could be innocent, but what exactly was the truth? It was going to be hard to find with Nathan being deceased, and Niles wasn't happy about it.

For what the family went through, Niles got off easy. Sam had told Ed what had happened when Nathan died, and together the confidants decided to keep that to themselves, for the time being. Niles stayed absent from the office while he recovered from his minor injuries.

The story of what had just happened and the deranged reasons behind it was bad enough. Dealing with the truth of this insanity—the facts—Ed could handle, explaining as best as he could. What could go wrong?

The two stupid and completely foolish Storm sisters were what had gone wrong. Everything they'd said was a lie, and in their desperate attempt to attain fame, they, in one newscast, had nearly destroyed him.

The news station immediately put out a statement regretting the airing of the story, apologizing for the untruths. The Storm sisters were immediately terminated from the station, and the executives were sweating, waiting for the lawsuits that were sure to come. Then the other news outlets weighed in, damning the Storm sisters and laughing at their stupidity.

The on-air apology didn't matter; the damage was done, and people were talking. Add the true story and the lies together, and the lines became blurred for the Savages; the interviews coming would be brutal.

The upside in this hell-go-round that Ed could not escape was the encouragement from his fans. The Internet exploded with support for their hero. Ed's fans even started a petition to keep his shows on air. This was one of the few positive things in Ed's life right now.

But Marlo...Marlo had him scared.

One night in a fit of rage, she threatened him with a divorce, not believing him when he told her he knew nothing about his father's past antics. Added with the fight she'd picked with him a week before leaving for Black Ridge Falls, all of it was still at the center of his mind.

Getting lucky enough to be given a Stephen Bay script had been amazing for him, until the doozy of a fight diminished his happy thoughts. The timing was just so off; the movie was the talk of the entertainment gossip shows, and Marlo had just blown it at a small-role audition. The part was big, and Ed liked the character, but Marlo's career envy had spiked, and the added guilt of taking the role seemed impossible. The time alone without her husband was wearing on her, and although she had valid points in her argument, she would always throw in his face her lost career…What could he do?

Then came the new RVs and the trip to hell and back.

The sick, sorry, and sad part was that Ed had hated his father long before everything had occurred, but he had pushed back the memories for the sake of raising his family. Now, well, what could he do but try to fix everything once again? The problem was that he was hurting, too.

Ed was called to the studio; a board meeting was taking place, and they demanded his presence. The secretary led him into a private waiting room where all the current tabloids were spread out on the table for him to see. She asked him if she could get him anything; the answer was no.

Ed picked up one of the brightly colored tabloids with "Savage" splashed across it. One featured a photo of Ed's old costar, Ellie; the words "Slutty Ex-Costar" were written in giant, red letters across the cover. He opened it and read what everyone in the board meeting must have had in front of them right now.

The door to the private waiting room opened, and a beautiful woman appeared carrying two coffees. He didn't hear her until she placed one of the cups down in front of him. "Can your slutty ex-costar buy you a coffee?" Ellie Collins asked.

Ed smiled at last, getting up from his chair. "Ellie!" he said.

The two friends hugged, and Ellie put down her cup, as Ed pulled out the chair for her. "How's the new baby?" he asked.

"The baby's fine; his older sister thinks he's hers! My cute little man, Alice, is with them," she said.

Ed smiled and thought of his little nugget…His smile faded. "Ellie, what are you doing here?"

"I heard about you getting called in here, so I'm here to help. What can I do?" she said.

Ed sighed. "I wish I knew. I'm at a loss."

Ellie looked at him hard; she could see the stress was getting to him. "So what's your plan when they call you in there?"

Ed put up his hands. "I got nothing. I figure I'll listen and take it from there," he said, more than a little defeated.

Ellie looked surprised. "What? Ed Savage doesn't have a plan? You're the guy who had security eating out of your hand when we got caught going down in the bobsled filming at the track for the Olympics! Remember that episode?" she said, smiling.

Ed smiled back, remembering. "Yeah, that was a fun day. You know, I was thinking of…never mind. It's nothing."

Ellie prodded him to get him to speak. "Nothing? If I know you, and I do, you were planning on getting a crew together and ripping this story apart, starting with that insane witch!"

Ed pushed away the papers in front of him. "Well, yeah, my first rational thought was to do just that. But Marlo…she's…She's having a hard time adjusting." He paused. "Maybe after her sister gets here today…maybe after."

The secretary opened the door. "Mr. Savage, they're ready for you."

Ed held up his hand. "Be right there," he said. Nodding, the secretary closed the door and disappeared down the hall.

Ed started to get up, but Ellie placed her hand on his shoulder, keeping him in his seat. "Ed, listen to me. Go in there and demand a crew. Tell them if they don't give you one, you can get one yourself. Hell, you have crews all over the world that want to work with you. But tell them you're willing to keep this in-house. You take charge in there. Tell them you're going up there to Black Ridge Falls, and you're going to rip this thing wide open. And then present them with the story that will blow their ratings sky-high! You can do this. You've been with them a long time. Your fans are behind you, and the Internet is surging with support!" Ellie said. She looked to the papers and saw the one with Sandy Storm and her quote about the slutty costar. She picked it up. "Just leave this little bitch reporter that said I was slutty to me!" Ellie said, making a funny smirk.

The fire in Ed's belly returned. He looked to her smiling face and gave her his signature devilish grin.

Ellie leaned back in her chair and smiled. "My work is done. Now go get 'em."

The blood flowed hot in Ed's veins. All he needed was support, and he had it.

He stood with Ellie and hugged her again. "Thank you. Really—you're right. And I'm doing this with or without the studio."

Ellie picked up another paper. "Of course I'm right, and what's with their names, anyway? Wendy and Sandy Storm? Their parents were real assholes," she said with a grin.

Ed laughed. "Yeah, seems they have a sister named Halle, too. I had to dig a little, but I found her—maybe you've heard of her? She broke the story on the sorority murders in Connecticut a while back."

"Nope, can't say that I have," Ellie said, looking at the paper. "Keep me up on these assholes; my lawyer is getting ready on my end with a serious defamation suit."

Ed took the paper from her. "Yeah, Sam is working on that, too." He tossed the paper on the table. "I'd better get going."

Ed hugged her once more, placed a peck on her cheek, and headed to the door.

"Ed, wait." Ellie dug in her bag and pulled out a business card. "Here. Aisha Thomas—she's good. I've talked with her, and she's already on it. I would do this myself, but with the kids it's impossible."

Glancing at the card, Ed stuffed it in his shirt pocket. "Will do." Winking at her, he left the room.

Ellie looked at the table, picked up the tabloids, and threw them in the trash. Exactly where they belonged.

CHAPTER 67

At Savage Tower, Sam Savage was in his office busily preparing the defamation-of-character lawsuit that would be brought against the Storm sisters and the stations that'd aired the damning and completely false story. The anger from his loss was fueling his work. Sam was not missing a thing. Still, as he neared the lawsuit's completion, the heaviness of losing his wife was smothering him. He took a deep breath. Coping with his loss right now would have to wait, but he was not looking forward to the coming crash he knew was inevitable.

The Savage brothers were busy. Roman Savage had lost a few clients because of the headlines. In his real-estate office a few floors down from Sam, he was on his phone with a client of another high-rise with multiple units he had been selling. Across from his desk near the window were the renderings of the hotel Niles had had in the limousine. One had the name Hotel Savage on it; another, Hotel Vanderran; and the last one was named Vander Place Hotel.

"Jack, Jack, listen to me. I still have buyers. I have showings before the funerals, so don't worry; I'll get these sold for you," Roman said, turning in his chair. "Look, the hotel is basically finished, and the first phase of the family housing development is complete. We're starting on the second now. Sales have not stopped one bit, and that's *all* Savage. Ignore the headlines for now. The lawsuits are coming, and so will the buyers."

Across the Atlantic, the youngest Savage brother, Logan, had been happy. Maura was on her way to him…until this had happened. Living in London, far away from his father, Logan's life was perfect. It was only when he had to visit the States for business with Roman that the memories returned, but now they were in the headlines right in front of him.

Maybe going for Nathan's funeral would be different. He kept telling himself that, but the knots in his stomach told him otherwise.

The headlines in London of Cara Vanderran's murder were sensationalized. Her other sister, Zolie Vanderran, stopped her book tour and cancelled her wrap party. Distraught, now at home in her mansion, she was upstairs packing for the trip to the States.

Zolie held up a couple of expensive dresses and tossed them on an oversized chair. She then reached for her drink to find it empty; nothing but ice cubes and a squeeze of lime was left to calm her nerves. The clock on the dresser read 10:00 a.m. She had her priorities on this dreadful day.

She looked to the bedroom from the closet, and a pained feeling came over her heart. She marched from her bedroom to the hallway at the top of the stairs and grabbed the handrail. Looking over, she screamed, "Bring me my gin!"

She then went back inside her bedroom, into the palace-sized walk-in closet, and picked up the two dresses. Holding them, she looked to the photo of her and her sisters. It was the same one used in the paper: "Vanderran Sister Takes Crown." She dropped the dresses to the floor and picked up the framed photo. Tears came swiftly as she thought about her beloved sister being gone, and she collapsed onto the chair. "Cara," she whispered, "I miss you so."

Outside, instead of preparing another gin and tonic, Cecile, the live-in maid, was attending to the luggage of Zolie's daughter, Amanda Kenowith, who'd just cut her Paris trip short with her girlfriends due to the sorry mess in the States.

Amanda was twenty-six. Her girlfriend and business partner, Jacqueline Holt, had a ladies' shoe line, and they were looking into merging Amanda's new clothing line with hers.

Waving good-bye to the limo that was dropping her off, Amanda turned and smiled at Cecile attending to the bags, and she picked one up herself. Inside the house she had started to go to her mother's study when she heard crying coming from upstairs. She dropped her bag and ran up the stairs, entering the closet and putting her arms around her heartbroken mother.

Zolie looked at her daughter. "Oh, Mandy...What are we ever going to do?"

Amanda sat next to her mother and held her. "I'm so sorry. I'm here now...I'm here," she said, trying to comfort her mother as Zolie cried in her arms.

CHAPTER 68

Patty's cabin was a mess the morning after that insane night in the mountains. They had to move fast, and they had to be gone. And they had help.

There was blood and used bandages everywhere. The furniture had been pushed away, and a mattress now stained with blood had been placed on the floor near the cellar door. There were sterile wrappings, scraps of bandages, discarded squeezed out tubes of antibiotic ointment, and bloody instruments in a metal bowl on a small table next to it. In the kitchen on the counter, a black doctor's bag was sitting next to a man drying his hands at the sink. The silver-haired man from the pharmacy had done what he could. Picking up his bag, he left out the back kitchen door.

A blood path actually led from the front door to the mattress on the floor near the cellar door, which was open, with a light on at the bottom of the stairs.

On the floor in the cellar, Melvin Galloway lay in the center of a pentagram wearing a black robe with strange satanic symbols on it, tied at the waist and open at the chest. The robe's sleeve was torn off for his arm, which was burned and covered in a triple antibiotic ointment, and his face was slightly disfigured, with the hairs of his beard singed into his skin under his swollen face. He had bandages on his chest, neck, and jaw where Ed had wounded him.

Next to him was a white bowl with a bloody bullet in it, along with a bloodstained pair of needle-nose pliers with the blade of a knife clenched between them. A black candle was sitting in the center of the bowl with small bones arranged in a peculiar pattern.

In a room in the back of the cellar, Patty slipped on a black robe with the same frightening images and removed a jar that played home to slimy, black leeches in a strange green mixture. She took it to the dresser where the bowl and muddler were still sitting and slopped the potion into the bowl. She then lit a match and dropped it into the bowl. The fire popped, but as she added the final powder, the fire inside the bowl extinguished. The leeches were smoking and moving in the singed sludge.

Closing her eyes, Patty started to speak in her ancient language, rolling her head back as the words grew louder. She was scraped up and bruised, but she could feel nothing as she took the bowl to the back room. She placed it on the altar set atop an inverted deer's head, its throat freshly slit and its antlers making the perfect stand; black candles were illuminating the open book made of skin. She read from it, intoning her spell with great gusto from her altered state.

While Patty was busy in her madness, the door under the cellar stairs opened slowly, and a bearded man appeared. He was dressed in a black, hooded robe and cowl. He looked past Melvin to Patty. Seeing that she was busy doing what he'd instructed her to do earlier, he quietly moved to Melvin and pulled out a syringe from the folds of his robe, injecting it into Melvin's neck. He then produced a small, plastic baggie filled with a fine, white powder, and he reached down and forced Melvin's mouth open, pouring the powder in. He then moved back and opened the door under the stairs that led to a tunnel, closing it quietly behind him.

After Patty finished her incantation, she picked up the bowl and carried it over to her brother, pouring it over his chest. She threw the bowl behind her toward the dresser, and the muddler fell, slamming to the floor. The sound not waking her, Patty got on her knees and rubbed the disgusting mixture all over her brother's swollen, wounded body, chanting.

The ranger opened his eyes.

CHAPTER 69

A t Titan Studios, the secretary led Ed into the conference room. He was surprised to see all the work his agent, Rachel Shepherd, had done to prepare for the meeting.

Rachel had brought in giant, freestanding display boards of all Ed's shows and placed them around a TV monitor, which was showing Ed's promos. Although muted, the effect was strong.

Ed paused and took in his TV-acting life as he stared at the life-sized posters of the first shows and specials he'd ever done: *Badges, Phantom Finders, Savage Strength, Archive Raiders, Savage Mysteries, Savage Life, Savage Cases,* and finally, *Savage Past*—the newest, four-episode Halloween special for next October, which was set to start shooting in three months.

The episodes for *Savage Past* were written in the style of Hollywood's vintage horror movies. Although Ed had a passion for law, he had wanted to get back into character acting like his *Badges* days, and when his buddy from college resurfaced into his life with new material he'd written, it was meant to be.

The mock-up had a picture of Ed standing in the ruins of an old sanatorium dressed as a 1930s surgeon; he was holding a glass syringe to a patient tied to a gurney amid the broken-down, paint-peeling, dusty remains of an exam room. An open, padded door with a small window for viewing the damned revealed rust-colored scratches made by bloodied human nails. The words "Let Me Out!" were scratched on the inside of the door.

Ed looked around the room at his past, present, and future in a profession he absolutely loved. He wondered if it would continue.

He had not seen the new artwork for *Savage Past*, and he moved over to it and stared. He could tell it was a rush job, not as polished as the others, but he knew it had to have been rushed for this meeting. He took a moment to admire it and then turned, standing next to his image on the life-sized cardboard cutout, and looked to his agent. All eyes were on Ed.

"Well done, Rachel; I like it. Someone's been busy over the last few days."

Rachel Shepherd had been with Ed since she got him his shaving-cream commercial—the one that lead to *Badges*, and later to a series being shot near the Winter Olympics titled, *Savage Strength*. The lead had broken his leg in a skiing accident, and Ed was recast in the role. The series didn't last much longer, but Ed's name caught on with viewers for future shows.

The cable channel, KBEX-CABLE, had been like a second family to Ed, and Rachel was always there looking out for him. She protected him and had his best interests at heart. Their relationship was more than actor/manager. They actually cared for each other and had become true friends for life, a rarity in Hollywood.

Ed took a seat, noticing all the tabloids on the table. Rachel picked up her notes in front of her and smiled at him. "It's been quite the morning. I was just telling them that the ratings for your shows have jumped, according to the latest numbers. The Internet is buzzing with stories of support for you and your family, and your fans are voicing their opinions," she said.

Sitting at the table was Milton O'Malley, CEO of the studio where Ed shot parts of his shows. The executives from the cable channel were also there: Sally Hayes, Tim Richardson, and Carol Simmons.

"Before we get started here, Ed, we want you to know we're here for you. And I hate what's on the table here," Milton said. The others nodded in agreement, as if knowing that what was coming next was unpleasant. "But this is business, and not everyone's a fan out there!" Milton said, patting the stack of papers and tabloids in front of him, each one with headlines uglier than the last. "Ed, what the hell happened up there? The church groups are all over this!" He smacked the stack of papers again and pushed them toward Ed. "And what's with the spooky symbols?"

Ed glanced at the papers, recognizing the one on top from the other room. He looked down in thought, furrowed his brows, and looked back to Milton. "What are you talking about? What symbols?"

Milton reached for the papers, digging through them and pulling one out. He glanced at it and tossed it toward Ed.

Picking it up, Ed was surprised. The photo was of the burned-out RV still sitting up at Black Ridge Falls. A large pentagram had been drawn around the RV using some kind of black, clumpy mixture containing what looked to be pieces of crows or ravens. Strange symbols depicting evil were drawn on the RV and the debris all around it. There were bones of who knew what hanging from the twisted metal and stacked near the door and every broken window. Mutilated dead animals had been attached to different animals: a rabbit with the wings of a crow, with large veins from a deer, elk, or bigger animal, was front and center.

Ed had studied and starred in movies about lost civilizations, burial chambers, and places thought to be the stomping grounds of serial killers, including the Zodiac killer, but in all his travels, he had never seen or heard of anything involving a spectacle quite like this.

He was confused. "I've not seen this...when did...?" He stopped himself, looking at the date of the paper. "Oh, this is the latest onslaught. I haven't seen today's anything! I don't know what this is. It wasn't like that when we left," Ed said, tossing the paper back on the table.

Milton kept his gaze on Ed. "This is what the church is going on about. The board is beside themselves. Yes, your numbers are good, and your fans are with you, but the religious loonies are calling you all sorts of things, and the press is eating it up!" Milton said.

Milton patted his portfolio of newspaper clippings. "Ed, are you all right?" he asked. "Maybe some time off would be good for you," he said.

Ed looked at him and then at his posters. He glanced at the muted monitor showing his promos. "No. I'm not all right," he barked.

The executives glanced at each other, but Milton kept hold of the reins. "Ed, given the situation, the studio knows you had nothing directly to do with the actions of...others, so long ago. However, until things settle down, we're pulling all your shows. Just for now."

The moment Milton said the words, Rachel Shepherd looked right at him with complete shock and anger. She glanced down at her recorder on the table, which was front and center and on, smiling with her eyes.

Whatever it was that Rachel caught went right over Ed's head. He was thinking of Ellie Collins, and the fire in his belly was increasing. He shifted in his chair. "Milton, I understand you having to do what you think is best, but what about *Savage Life*? There are still three more episodes left to air."

"Sorry." Milton paused, lowering his head. "Damn it, Ed, you know this isn't personal. My kids love your shows, and if I could, I would leave your shows running. But there are church groups out there demanding your head. The messed-up stories by the idiot Storm sisters, added together with this voodoo or whatever it is, have caused unwanted attention on the studio from the zealots. It was all I could do to keep your current shows on hold with the board. They wanted to sever all ties."

The rage in Ed's belly burned hotter. He'd known Milton for years and met his kids at a Comic Con once. But he also knew Milton always covered his ass with the board.

Ed turned to the cable executives. "And you?" he asked.

Sally Hayes, the CEO of the cable channel, looked down at her notes and closed her portfolio, pushing it forward. "Ed, you've been with us a long time." She waved at the posters. "Looking at the work you've done for us and the ratings your shows earn, we're staying behind you. We're not stopping. But the studio does have some pull on the airing of your shows, and we're still a ways from coming to an agreement to get a release. Until then, I'm sorry, but all current and upcoming series and specials are on hold."

"What about the new one? We were to finalize that one next month," Ed asked.

Tim Richardson took his glasses off and put them on the table. "Ed, the contracts have not gone to the studio yet; we can shop that one around," he said.

Ed glanced over at Rachel; the odd smile was still on her face, and she winked at him.

Completely confused, Ed sat back in his chair and looked at the posters. The monitor near one of them caught his attention. It was the older episode shot last year in Australia, Lisa's favorite: Ed was holding a koala near a lighthouse. The muted monitor showed Lisa asking to pet the animal. Ed watched in silence as Lisa smiled wide and hugged the koala. The fire in his belly erupted.

Everyone in the meeting saw what Ed was looking at; it was Rachel who grabbed the remote and turned off the monitor as fast as possible. "Oh, God, Ed, I'm so sorry. I didn't get a chance to edit this; they said it was ready."

Ed glanced to her. "It's fine." He turned a glare on Milton. "What's it going to be? Are you going to stay a jerk, or will you release my shows, so they can be aired? And don't lie to me and tell me you have to wait for the board. The final word is yours, so what's it going to be?"

The heat was on, and Milton turned a shade of red. It was obvious that he knew Ed was right, but he also knew what the board had made quite clear. "Sorry, Ed, I can't answer that right now. 'On hold' is the best I can give you."

Ed leaned across the table and looked at Milton, his eyes piercing his soul like a sharpshooter. "Have it your way," he said. He then looked to Tim Richardson. "Tim, *Savage Past* starts shooting in three months; we still on?"

Tim nodded. "Yes, funding's in place, locations are booked, the crews are hired in the different locations—there's no problem on our end. Like I said, studio contracts were to go out soon."

Ed glanced back to the monitor that had his daughter on it only moments ago; the fire inside raged on. "Hold the contracts; shop them around. Hard!" He looked to Sally. "And I'm going to need a local crew. There are still unanswered questions up at that damn mountain, and I'm going to find the answers. Starting with that woman!"

Carol Simmons looked uncomfortable. "Ed, from a liability side, we have to do this right. We can't send staff up there yet. They haven't found that woman or her brother, that ranger you spoke of. I'm not sure we can get people. I'll do what I can and get back to you," she said.

Ed looked down and noticed the card in his shirt pocket. "I'm going to need them on board by tonight. I'm leaving first thing tomorrow. Call me by five," Ed said as he got up from the table. "We're done here. I'm going to be late."

Ed thanked the cable executives and his agent and left without a word to Milton.

The reading of Nathan Savage's last will and testament was the next meeting he had to get to, and he was definitely going to be late.

As the meeting broke up and the cable executives sent glares in Milton's direction, Rachel placed the recorder into her bag and walked away. She wore a satisfied grin that would've made the Cheshire Cat truly proud.

CHAPTER 70

Nathan's will stipulated that it had to be read immediately following his death.

The board of directors of the family construction business was nothing less than a pit filled with vipers ready to strike, and Nathan Savage had known that very well. He didn't want to allow any of them time to maneuver or form any scheme against the family, so the will had to be read. With the funerals only days away, nothing was going to stop the reading, not even Logan Savage's absence.

The elevator doors opened onto the fifty-third floor. Sam and Maura Savage, dressed in raincoats and carrying wet umbrellas, entered the offices of Parnell F. Bancroft and Associates. The receptionist was waiting for them, a nice woman who took their coats and escorted them to a lavish boardroom. The view outside matched the pain and sadness within the room. The entire city seemed to have gone dark, weeping over the loss of the Savages.

At one end of the room was a spread of finger sandwiches, hors d'oeuvres, and a bar. The receptionist offered drinks, which were politely refused, but just for now. Nathan apparently had a wicked sense that after the reading of his last words, more than a few would be headed straight to the bar for some much-needed alcohol—such a thoughtful father.

Below, in the lobby of the high-rise tower, Marlo and her sister, Maggie, were waiting for Ed to arrive. Marlo looked at her watch as she stood at the doors leading into the lobby near the garage elevators. She looked agitated. "He should be here by now," she said.

The main doors opened, and Maggie looked on as strangers entered the building, "Who knows how long his meeting will last? I'm sure he's on his way," Maggie told her.

Marlo was preoccupied in thought and checked her cell phone when the garage elevator doors opened, and Roman and Gabby Savage entered the lobby. Marlo looked up; seeing them, she shot a look to her sister. "Not a word," she said.

Roman Savage was the third son in the family, graced with the same dark features that all the brothers had inherited. He was fastening the umbrella while his wife, Gabriella "Gabby" Savage, untied her trench coat. She was a woman who lit up a room just by entering it, even on the rainiest of days, and she was as sweet as she was beautiful. Seeing Marlo, she immediately went to her.

Reaching out with both hands, she greeted Marlo with a hug and a genuine look of concern. "I can't wrap my mind around any of this. How are you holding up?"

Marlo pulled back and looked Gabby in the eyes; the hurt was apparent on her face. "As well as can be expected, I guess. You remember my sister, Maggie?"

Gabby looked at Maggie. "Of course, good to see you," she said. They hugged, and Roman came up beside them. Hugging Marlo, his voice was nothing but concerned. "Hey, honey, anything you need, just say it, all right?"

The elevator chimed and opened. Roman, with his hand on the small of his wife's back, led her to it. They stopped, looking back to Marlo and Maggie. "Aren't you coming?" Roman asked.

"We were waiting for Ed," Marlo said, looking back to the lobby doors. "You know what? He can meet us upstairs." With that, the four boarded the elevator.

As the elevator took them to the fifty-third floor, Ed, running late in his Jaguar, was not far from the building, stuck at a red light. He punched Aisha's number into his phone, connected to his car audio; the line rang twice, and Aisha picked up.

"Hello."

"Aisha Thomas?"

"Yes."

"Ed Savage. Ellie Collins gave me your card."

"Yes. Hello, Ed. Good to hear from you," she replied.

Ed smiled, hearing her voice coming from the dashboard speakers. The light changed, and Ed moved with the traffic. "Ellie tells me you've been working with her."

"Yes, we've worked a few stories over the years. Ellie filled me in on yours, and I've been digging around on this Patty Galloway woman's family. I think we should meet," she said.

"My thoughts as well. I'm on my way to a meeting and then leaving for Black Ridge Falls tomorrow morning. Can we meet tonight?"

"No, tonight won't work. Pick me up in the morning. I was planning on going up there myself. Now I'll just go with you."

Ed was surprised but somehow comforted by the fact that he would not have to go alone into that nightmare again. "I'll call you early in the morning. See you then."

The conference room on the fifty-third floor was filled with quiet hellos as they waited for the man himself. Parnell F. Bancroft had been with Nathan for years. Good old Parnell would handle the cases Nathan wanted kept away from Sam and the rest of the family. The two went way back, and Parnell now welcomed the Savages into his conference room.

The table was huge, but only ten chairs were set around it; the others had been removed from the room. Not one to mince words, Parnell immediately went to the head of the table and sat down, opening his portfolio. "Shall we begin?"

The Savages took their seats. On Parnell's right sat Niles and his wife, Charlotte, and then Roman and Gabby. To his left were Sam and Maura and then Maggie and Marlo, leaving the empty chair at the end for Ed.

Parnell looked at his portfolio and pulled out a sealed document containing the last will and testament of Nathan Savage. He placed it neatly in front of him and looked to his guests. The empty chair at the end of the table stood like a beacon of blight that angered him. Lateness was a form of disrespect.

As Parnell removed his glasses to say something, the doors to the conference room opened, and Ed entered. "Just in time, I see."

Ed could see that old Parnell was miffed, but he didn't care. He took his seat and looked to his wife. Reaching for her hand, he held it and smiled at her.

Parnell pulled the solid-gold letter opener from his portfolio and, with a dramatic sweep of his wrist, opened the envelope. This was his show, and no late arrivals were going to take away from it. He then pulled out the surprisingly thin documents from the envelope and placed them in front of him.

The room was dead silent; all eyes were on the documents. Everyone could see how much Parnell loved this, acting like the designated ringmaster under the big top as he cleared his throat.

"Nathan and I knew each other for a long time," he said. "It pains me that my friend is gone, and I am truly sorry for your losses in this tragic affair. Nathan came to me after Marcie died and directed that this last will and testament be amended."

Parnell then lifted his hand and held up the papers, pulling the top one off and placing it on the table facedown.

"Nathan divided the will into shares of the company and cash, which will be disbursed as follows. To my brother, Niles Savage, already owning fifteen percent of Savage Construction, I leave nothing: zero additional shares and the sum of one"—Parnell paused and looked at Niles before continuing—"dollar, for reasons he knows all too well."

Gasps were heard around the table, and Niles sank in his chair. His wife, Charlotte, smiled dryly and pulled her large purse onto her lap, as if Nathan had the power to come back from the dead and steal what they had left for spite.

"To my son, Logan Savage..." Parnell paused to look at Logan's wife. "Maura, my deepest condolences for the loss of your sister."

Maura forced a polite smile.

Parnell turned back to the documents. "To my son, Logan Savage, I leave the sum of nine percent of Savage Construction and ten million dollars in cash."

Eyes shot from Maura to Niles, yet the room stayed silent.

"To my son, Roman Savage, I leave the sum of nine percent of Savage Construction and ten million dollars in cash," Parnell said.

Everyone in the room was quietly adding up the score in their heads. With 33 percent of the company gone, 67 remained. Gabby took her husband's hand in hers and smiled at him.

"To my son, Samuel Savage…" Parnell paused and looked at Sam. "I'm so sorry, again, for your loss in this matter," he said.

Sam nodded stoically, and Parnell continued, "I leave the sum of sixteen percent of Savage Construction and twenty-five million dollars in cash."

Everyone in the room recalculated; 51 percent was left, and an estimated several hundred million remained.

Before continuing, Parnell rested his hands on the table with the document and sighed. "Ed, Marlo, I pray they somehow find her safe."

Marlo stiffened up, and Ed tightened his hand on hers as Parnell continued.

"To my son, Edward Savage, I leave the sum of fifty-one percent of Savage Construction and all remaining assets, which include four hundred fifty-three million dollars in cash, as well as all stocks, bonds, shares, and properties. My son, you may have all of it. I want it to be your headache now."

Nathan Savage had lived frugally. No one ever knew exactly how much he had. They had guessed over the years but never imagined it was this much. Gabby noticed Marlo smile and glance at her husband, offering a side grin to her sister.

Parnell continued, "Ed, you were the only son to stand up to me that day in the garage, and you wanted nothing to do with the company."

All eyes shot to Ed. No one but Sam had ever been privy to what had happened in some garage long ago or to Ed standing up to Nathan. To Marlo, it was another lie, another nondisclosure of things she should have known.

The simple truth was that Ed was ashamed of having had to confront his father in the first place. The sad fact of having to do it was nothing Ed wanted to rehash over the years—with anyone. Wanting to protect his family in any way he could from any embarrassment that could come from the antics of their grandfather, Ed had remained silent. And seeing Nathan smack Ava with the paper that day had brought back memories of visiting his brothers in the hospital after one of Nathan's "special" punishments had been wielded, and that was why he *had* to do something back then.

Ed sat back in his chair and sighed. The weight of what had just happened added to his earlier meeting at the studio and his plans of returning to Black Ridge Falls—life was becoming far too much to deal with.

He also felt bad for Sam, who had been with the business his whole life. Part time or not, Sam knew it inside and out.

Sam sighed and looked at Ed. "So much for running the company," he said.

Ed attempted a smile. "Well, you did shoot me with my own gun," he said, and then he went into his devilish grin. Sam started laughing along with everyone else, lifting the mood for a moment...if only for a moment.

Sam always wondered about his big brother's wicked sense of humor.

Ed looked over to the bar. "You know what, Sam? You can run the company. I don't want it—never did. I'll give you my damn shares. I just don't care anymore. Now, I can use a drink."

Marlo was not happy with Ed giving away anything, and she exchanged another look with her sister.

This was the moment Parnell F. Bancroft was waiting for. Having known the contents of the will, he was eager to deliver Nathan's final instructions. "Not so fast with the drinks, Ed," he said, grinning. "There's more."

Parnell again lifted a page from the will and turned it over facedown on the stack. He lifted the next and looked to his audience. "This is exactly how Nathan prepared this part of his will," he said.

Parnell looked to the papers: "Ed, the entire disposition of my holdings in my last will and testament just read to you shall not be changed or altered in any way by you, or anyone, for the next ten years. You left our family to act. Now it's my turn. Failure to comply with the terms set forth will result in a total revocation of all disbursed assets to *all* parties. All assets will be returned to the trust, and you and your brothers receive nothing. My will stipulates that my firstborn son, Edward Theodore Savage, will be in charge of Savage Construction for the next ten years. After that, do with your life as you wish—that is, if you can make it ten years. You proved yourself at West Point that first year; now I'm multiplying that by ten. Did you really think I was going to let that slide? As for your little shows you love doing so much, have fun getting out of your contracts, and I'm sure you can find the time to keep at least one of them going."

Parnell finished and looked up at the group. He then placed the paper on the stack, facedown like the others. "That's it," he announced.

To the outside world, growing up Savage looked very much like winning the lottery. But behind closed doors, things were far different. Living the privileged life had a price, which came from living under the thumb of dear, old Dad.

Ed thought of all the rules over the years.

His father had made colonel in the air force and ran his home like a boot camp. Growing up, the boys had rules, rules they would follow or face Nathan's wrath.

West Point was one of those rules. Nathan was a graduate, like his father. And Nathan had known that he couldn't control his sons' futures, but he laid down the law with education. His sons had a choice: either get accepted into West Point from high school or get cut off from the family money right then and there. If, after completing their first year at West Point at the top of their class, they still did not want to continue there, then Nathan would honor their wishes. That they proved they were men, at least for one year, was enough. And he would pay for the remainder of their college in any institution of their choice. He figured no one could possibly leave one of the most prestigious institutions in the country. It ate at him that he was wrong.

Ed and Sam had opted out after their first year, finishing top of their class, beating Dad at his own game, and had gone on to Cambridge. It was Roman and Logan who'd stayed, even though they were at top of their class. Perhaps it was the time spent in the hospital after a Nathan-style punishment in their youth that kept them there all those years. If it was, they never spoke of it.

Ed was depressed. Everyone knew he wanted nothing to do with the company. Now there was no way out. Ed looked back over to the bar. "I can use that drink now."

The news of Ed's windfall made Marlo happy. Even her sister was pleased, showing it with the relieved and greedy looks they exchanged on the way to the bar.

Gabby, who witnessed the looks, quietly questioned what the two were up to.

Niles's wife, Charlotte, also got up from the table and went to the bar. She grabbed a bottle of Armagnac and a glass and brought it to the table, setting them down in front of Niles. "Let this kind gesture be my last," she said.

Everyone in the room heard her but didn't know what to make of her comment. Charlotte then opened her purse and pulled out an envelope, dropping it in front of her husband. "I'm divorcing you, Niles, *and* this family."

Charlotte Savage had had enough. Though they'd had marital problems prior to learning of this mess in the mountains, the ugly truth was something she wanted no part of.

Charlotte then turned away from the table and walked to the door. Opening it, she paused and turned back to take one last look at her extended family. "I love you all, but I don't want to be with you," she said. With that, she left the room.

Niles was dumbfounded. He just stared at the closed door, not saying a word. It was Parnell who lifted the Armagnac and poured Niles a glass.

Niles looked from the door to the envelope and passed it over to Parnell. "Get back to me on this," he said.

At the bar, Marlo and Maggie whispered something to each other while selecting a bottle of champagne. Gabby overhead the strange ending comment from Maggie: "Beat you to it."

"Beat you to what?" Gabby asked.

Marlo and Maggie looked like five-year-olds caught with their hands in a cookie jar, and quickly Marlo smiled, holding up Ed's favorite bottle of Jim Beam's Devil's Cut Bourbon Whiskey. "This, silly," Marlo said. Laughing, she put the bottle down and grabbed some glasses. She iced hers and left his empty; Ed preferred his whiskey neat. Gabby didn't buy it.

When Marlo finished pouring Ed's whiskey, she brought it to him, placing it in front of him and Gabby poured one for Roman.

Looking at Maura sitting without her husband, Roman could see she wished Logan was there. "Maura, when will Logan and the kids' flight arrive?" he asked, taking his drink from Gabby.

"They're due in the morning; eight thirty, I think," she told him.

"How about I pick you up and we drive to the airport together to get them?" he asked.

Maura smiled. "Thank you, I would like that."

Everyone could see that Maura had a lot on her mind, and she needed her husband. She so wished her sister, Zolie, was beside her.

Earlier that same day, she and Sam had gone over Cara Vanderran Savage's will, which left everything to Sam and their two children, Chet and Heather. And surprisingly, Marlo Savage was mentioned in a business contract of a future restaurant the two had been planning.

Beat you to it. That stuck in Gabby's mind as she watched Marlo rub Ed's shoulders from behind his chair.

Ed could feel the tension lifting from his soul. He looked up to his wife and was reminded of the moment in the RV when she was rubbing his shoulders, and he winced the thoughts away.

He grabbed his glass and looked at his wife, telling her he loved her.

Marlo smiled back to her man; the thoughts in her head were overwhelming.

Ed looked outside. The rain had let up some, but a storm was coming.

CHAPTER 71

abby Jones was a successful businesswoman when she'd met Roman Savage. She owned her own jazz club on Restaurant Row, in the fun part of town away from the towers of downtown, where the Savage Construction Company sat.

One night, after selling several units in an apartment tower, Logan had taken his brother Roman out to celebrate. They'd stopped for drinks at Gabby's jazz club on a night her singer had called in last minute with a sick child she needed to take to the hospital.

Gabby, a singer herself, although she hadn't performed in years because she didn't feel the need, went on stage and made the announcement. Not wanting to disappoint her customers, she told them that if they didn't mind, she would give it a try. Everyone applauded.

Gabby started with Phyllis Hyman's "Pride of My Life" and followed up with Tina Turner's "Private Dancer," and everyone loved it, including Roman. The next night Roman went back for a drink alone and sat at the bar, listening to her as she sang some Eartha Kitt songs, "Where Is My Man?" and "Whatever Lola Wants." One thing led to another, and a year and a half later, they were married.

Roman and Gabby's kids intermingled with the rest of the family. Their oldest, Lana Savage, was inseparable from Maura and Logan's daughter, Kate, and when they moved to London, Lana went to visit often. Their son, Chase Savage, was also close with Logan and Maura's son Ty, and they were in sports leagues with Jake, Nash, and Noah. Their daughter, Daniela "Danni" Savage, was in the same grade as Ava and

Heather. Danni and Chase had wanted to go to Black Ridge Falls with the others, but a trip to see Gabby's parents had been planned for that week, so they didn't go, much to the happiness of Gabby and Roman.

In the car, after the reading of Nathan's will, Gabby turned to her husband. "Roman, was Marlo acting off tonight?" she asked.

Watching the road in the slippery coat of light rain, Roman barely glanced at his wife. "I don't know. She's been through a lot," he said.

Gabby thought of what Maggie had said earlier. "I know, but it's Ed I'm more worried about. He got real quiet tonight…after all that was said."

The light turned red, and Roman slowed to a stop. "I noticed that, too. I don't know what to believe anymore. In the last few days, everything went to hell. I'm going to call him in the morning," he said, taking Gabby's hand.

"I hate this," she said, looking at him.

"Me, too. But think of it this way. At least it can't get worse." The light changed to green, and they moved through the intersection.

Not long after getting home, Ed took a shower to wash the day off. He then went to his office, glanced at the landline, saw no messages, and picked up his cell phone to check, hoping to hear from Carol Simmons about a crew for tomorrow's trip. The message was not good, although he kind of thought that would be the case. The liabilities of sending someone into harm's way were impossible to cross, but he did have friends.

Ed called Tanner Ronson, a cameraman who had worked with him on and off over the years. He answered on the third ring.

"Hello."

"Hey, Tanner, Ed Savage. Long time, how are you?"

"Ed, no shit! How the hell are you, buddy? You all right?"

"It's been a rough few days to say the least," Ed said.

"I've seen the news. Ed, I'm so sorry."

"Thank you, Tanner. Listen, I have a favor to ask."

"Anything, what do you need?"

"Well, you can say no to this; trust me, it's a big favor."

"Okay, what is it?"

"I'm in a bind. I need a cameraman for tomorrow. I'm going back up to Black Ridge Falls to get some answers. Now, I know it's a big favor to ask, and I'll certainly understand if you don't want to go up there. Hell, I don't even want to go back up there, but I have to." There was a long pause on the line. "Tanner, you there?" Ed said.

"Yeah, I'm here; count me in. What time are we leaving?"

"I want to get there early. I'll pick you up at seven."

"I'll be ready."

"Thanks." Ed hung up the phone and looked up to see Marlo standing in the doorway. Looking in her eyes, he felt as if a new storm had arrived.

"You're not going up there," Marlo stated. "You can't."

"I have to. I'll be back before the funerals. There are things unanswered," Ed said as he tried to move past her, but she raised her arm and leaned into the doorway.

"No. Not this time. I won't have it," she said with a cold, determined look.

Ed stopped and took a few steps back. "Look, I've made up my mind. I'm going. You have Maggie here, Ava needs you, and I'll be back soon."

"Damn it, Ed!" Marlo yelled. "This isn't one of your goddamn shows! Something could happen…again. You know there's still evil up there, and we need you *here.*"

"Nothing is going to happen. They're dead, Marlo. They're in the lake," he said, trying to reason with her.

"We don't know that. They haven't found them yet. They could have lived. You're crazy to go back up there! Look, we've had an insane day today. Let's just leave, pack some bags and just leave," Marlo said, sounding desperate.

Ed could see something different in her. Not sure what was lying just under the surface, he tried to comfort her. "Marlo, really, everything will be fine. I'll be home before the funerals. You need to trust me. I feel I need to do this."

"You feel you need to do this?" Marlo repeated sarcastically. "How many times have I heard that before? How many times, Ed?" Marlo screamed. "No, you're not going, and that's final."

"I'm going, and you need to back off a bit and look at this another way. I have to find out about this family that came after us. I *have* to, Marlo, to protect you and Ava!"

"Protect us!" Marlo spat at him. "Like you did up there? Lisa is dead! Dead! Where the hell were you when I was being attacked? Protect us *now*? You bastard!" she screamed.

"You've given up on Lisa. I haven't," Ed yelled back.

"How dare you!" Marlo screamed as she raised her hand to slap him.

Ed caught her hand and held it, and with his other hand, he grabbed her other shoulder. "Marlo, stop," Ed shouted at her.

"Let go of me," Marlo screamed, and she pulled away from him. "They found her blood, Ed. Her blood!"

Seeing Marlo becoming unhinged even more scared him. She knew where he'd been when the nightmare of losing their daughter had occurred, and her words were like knives shoved into his heart. "Marlo, calm down; where are your pills?" he shouted back in anger.

"Calm down?" Marlo screamed, eyes wide and frantic. "Your words are angering me, and I'm allowed to be angry with you, Ed Savage. Fuck you!" she screamed in his face. "You think I need pills? I'll tell you what I need. I want a divorce!"

Apparently their anger was loud enough for the whole house to hear, as Ava ran into the office. "No, stop it, both of you. Please," she said, and she started to cry. It was Ed who went to hug her.

Marlo stared at them with a cold look. "She's always been *your* daughter. Go ahead. Go. See if I care," she screamed. "I'm going to the Four Seasons." Turning, she left the room to grab Maggie in the kitchen.

"Come on, we're packing."

Ed was in shock. "Go on upstairs," he said to Ava.

Ava had seen the arguments before and left without a word.

Ed stood there for a moment, seething in the loudness of the quiet room as her words ran through his head. Had she finally come to terms with what the doctor told her? His thoughts went back to her doctor's office after getting home. *Is that why she's lashing out?* He was tired of taking it from her, but he had been told to wait *and let her tell him.*

Ed went back to his desk, picked up his cell phone, and made one more call…back to his past.

The call was picked up quickly, and Ed looked to the doorway. "Tallulah, it's been too long."

CHAPTER 72

Nathan wasn't finished with his bag of tricks. He had instructed Parnell F. Bancroft to leak the story to the newspapers immediately following the reading of the will, and the next morning the story broke.

Ed got up early the next day, and, after dropping off Ava at Sam's to stay with him and Heather since Marlo had gone to a hotel, he picked up Tanner and drove to Aisha's building. He parked the new Range Rover outside and waited for her appearance.

Inside, headed down in the elevator, Aisha had the morning paper folded in her shoulder bag and was with her fiancé, Danny. "How long do you think you'll be gone?" he asked.

Aisha looked from the glowing floor buttons above the elevator car doors to him. "A day or two at the most," she said. The elevator opened on the lobby.

Walking outside, Aisha looked for a Range Rover and saw the man who was king of the media gossip standing beside one. He walked forward.

"Ed Savage, it's nice to finally meet you," Aisha said, reaching out her hand to him.

Ed took it, trying not to stare too long at the stunning African American woman who looked better than he'd imagined from the voice in his dashboard. "Hello, Aisha, pleasure's all mine."

"This is my fiancé, Danny McIntyre; Danny, Ed Savage," she said.

Ed reached out to shake his hand. Danny paused just a moment and then extended his in greeting. "Savage? This morning's paper Savage?" he asked.

They shook, and Danny looked at Aisha. "You didn't tell me this was the story you were working on," he said.

Ed had not seen the morning paper and was at a loss. "I'm sorry. What story?" he asked.

Aisha pulled it from her shoulder bag. "I'm very sorry, Ed. I thought you knew."

The headline read: "Savage Brothers Rake in Millions."

Ed took one look at the headline and cringed. "Nope, haven't seen today's paper. I've had enough news lately." Taking the paper from Aisha, he read the first line or two and then folded it up and handed it back to her. "I'll deal with this later; we need to get going," he said.

Danny got visibly upset. "Excuse us, Ed. Aisha, can I have a word?" Danny placed her bag on the sidewalk and walked Aisha a few feet away.

"What are you doing? That story at Black Ridge was messed up. I don't want you going there," Danny said with concern, seeing Ed load her bag in the back.

Aisha looked him directly in the eyes. "Danny, I got this. I've been working with Ellie, and this is my chance. If I'm right, this will be perfect for my career."

Danny was upset. "You're a reporter, a TV-film writer. You're not a cop. This could be dangerous," he said. He saw in her eyes he was not going to change her mind. "You and your stories." He looked over at Ed, who was now in the driver's seat of the Range Rover. "Yeah…I can't fight you and win when it comes to that job of yours, but you have to promise to call me every ten minutes!" he said.

Aisha pulled him close and kissed him. "Everything will be just fine."

CHAPTER 73

olie Vanderran had her driver stop at Wallingford's Jewelers Boutique to see Catherine Wallingford before driving to the airport. She needed to pick up the jewelry Cara had left to be made into gifts for her daughter, Amanda, and the girls from the States. "I won't be a moment," Zolie said to Amanda and her husband, Tom Kenowith, getting out from the limousine.

The appearance of Zolie Vanderran entering the boutique had Catherine's employees jumping to attention. One sales associate immediately picked up a phone and alerted Catherine in her office upstairs of Zolie's arrival.

Another greeted her. "Ms. Vanderran, this is an unexpected pleasure. How can we be of service?"

Zolie heard the footsteps on the stairs from Catherine rushing down them. "Zolie! What a nice surprise," Catherine said.

"Oh, it won't be, darling. Sorry to drop in without calling, but the bracelets—by chance, are they in early?" she asked.

Cara had been in London a few weeks before flying back home and making that ill-fated trip to the mountains. She had dropped off some older necklaces that had been in the family for years, wanting them made into bracelets for the girls. They were sent to a specialist, who was working on them per Cara's meticulous instructions.

Catherine knew all about them, but they were not finished. "I'm so sorry. I had no idea you wanted them sooner than we discussed. And, Zolie, I'm so sorry; the news is…dreadful," she said.

"Thank you, Catherine. Well, I tell you what. Can you forward them to me in the States at once? We're leaving today for the funerals, and it would be magnificent to give them to the girls while we are there."

"Of course. I have your home address, and I'll see to it myself," she said.

"Thank you, Catherine. Although I'll also be staying at the new hotel. Call my assistant for the address I'd prefer they be sent to. Now I really must be going," Zolie said.

"Not a problem," Catherine said, almost curtseying to the famous Vanderran as she escorted Zolie out of the store.

CHAPTER 74

fter stopping at the Black Ridge sheriff's station to see if any further leads on Lisa's whereabouts had been reported, they drove to the crash site with the disappointing news.

Ed, Aisha, and Tanner stood staring at the burned-out RV; things had certainly changed since Ed was last there. They could see the large pentagram around the RV, and Tanner had the camera trained on Ed as he moved around the area. "I pulled up to about here and ran down to this area," Ed said, attempting to recreate the path of that ugly night. "I had fallen, and when I got up, I could see Marlo standing on the side of the RV when it exploded. Then I was hit from behind." Ed moved a few feet to where he was found. "I landed around this area," he said, pointing. "Then I woke when the medics found me." He waved his hand across his neck in a "cut" motion, and Tanner shut off the camera. He then looked at the RV and sighed, as they started making their way down the embankment. Getting closer to the RV, they saw the strange symbols and smaller pentagrams, and they winced at the horrific sight of the combined animal carcasses, which had been torn into from other animals. "I came back here just before we left. None of these markings were here," Ed said. He waved Tanner to film where he was headed, to the front of the RV where the driver's side was crushed into the ground, and the windshield was a charred spider's web of cracks.

There, drawn with a black, tarlike substance, were inverted numbers, letters, and shapes etched in circles with a line drawn through them all. Above were numbers in white with a dash after them. Ed stopped and took a step back. "RPMs! I've seen these before, except… Something's different," Ed said, looking directly to the camera. "That movie I did years ago…*The King, The Witch, and the Maiden.* I did it on location at the Carman Castle of Scotland." Ed pointed to the white numbers. "These are RPMs, 'ritual protection marks,' from around the sixteenth century. I was shown these exact symbols, which had been drawn by actual witches in ancient caves. But these—" Ed pointed to the black, inverted ones. "These symbols are black magic. Someone's protecting the black magic at work here with some truly powerful white magic," he said.

Both Aisha and Tanner took a step back. Then Ed and Aisha pulled out their phones and started taking pictures of the markings, while Tanner filmed them.

Ed moved around to the undercarriage of the RV and looked up to where the door was blown out, hanging down in a twisted heap. There were more markings, along with a dead buck propped up against the wrecked vehicle. Someone had slit the buck's throat and attached wings from a hawk to its sides, using veins as the ties. There was a dead bat in the buck's mouth and a snake around the buck's neck. Aisha took one look and turned her head away. "Ed, I can't," she said and walked away.

She got a few feet from him and stopped. There she saw the makeshift grave mound with the personalized mud flap, "SAVAGE 1," slightly bent over the ice chest lid used as the marker.

Ed saw it too and panicked. He raced to it and dropped to his knees and started pushing the dirt aside until he found it—the doll with the cracked porcelain face that had belonged to his daughter. He cried out and continued to push away the dirt until he came to the hard stone surface they were standing on.

Ed picked up the doll and his face broke up. He clutched the doll to his chest, and the emotion poured from him. He got choked up, and Aisha bent down next to him and hugged him.

The emotion in Ed turned to anger, and he remembered his training. This type of psychological mind fucking was a game, a sick one at that, but Ed knew the rules and played to win. He spit on the grave and stood. Grabbing the mud flap, he turned to the others. "If it's a war they want, it's a war they're gonna get."

He turned back toward the Range Rover and swung the mud flap over his shoulder as he made is way away from the RV carrying the porcelain doll.

Aisha followed him, while Tanner stayed behind filming the buck and the disturbed makeshift grave. He then turned the camera on Aisha as she caught up with Ed, putting her hand on his shoulder. She said something to him that Tanner couldn't hear, and they kept walking back to the ridge where the Range Rover was parked.

Loading the mud flap, doll, and camera in the rear of the SUV, the three of them were spooked. "Did you find anything out about the family that's tied to this?" Ed asked Aisha.

Aisha took a bottle of water from a cooler. "Nothing at all like this! I found the birth certificates and the accident report from the paper long ago. You told me about Patty and the twins, and I did find an article about the boys being hospitalized when they were young, but nothing about witchcraft. But then again, I wasn't looking for anything related to this kind of…stuff. I'm sorry; I didn't get to see yesterday's paper with the markings until this morning."

Ed looked at this woman and remembered the good times he used to have with Marlo. "You have nothing to be sorry for," he said.

Aisha winced. "Still, I should have caught it…Oh, the only other things I found were that after the accident, the kids were bounced around a bit; different coal-miner families took them in. And that older sister I told you about? Stevie Galloway? She just disappeared from here, never to be seen again. So she's a dead end."

CHAPTER 75

T he Hotel Savage had a last-minute name change due to all the gale-force drama being splashed across the tabloids and TV screens from the gossip shows and reporters.

Niles was out front of the hotel directing the large truck with a crane to lift letters from the already-in-place sign off the side of the building. The new letters were on the truck waiting to replace them.

A table was set up under the porte cochere, and on it were the renderings from Roman's office. The one with the Vander Place Hotel was on top of the older Hotel Savage rendering. Niles thought Zolie just might pass on the gin and tonic and go right to the champagne when she arrived.

The property was beautiful; the hotel sat on a private ocean inlet to the north in Port Roberts on the East Coast. Behind the hotel, at the dock, was a 180-foot-long dining yacht named *Vanderran*. This had been a joint project of the Vanderran sisters to offer dining at sea for their guests.

The housing project was well under way next to the hotel. The closer homes were completed, and another division had just started; the lot separations in the next adjoining parcels of land were being dug.

On the other side of the hotel, the land raised up about eight feet to a bluff with tall grass that stretched for quite some way. At the far end away from the cliffs sat an old theater built in the 1920s. The Mystic Theater, once a home to mostly B movies and serials, had eventually gone bankrupt. But the inside was truly amazing. The old, ornate theater still had the original metal-and-glass chandeliers, and the seat boxes on the side reminded one of theaters frequented by ladies in gowns. The moldings were brilliant, found amid the peeling paint of decades past—so brilliant and with so much history that Ed had actually planned on shooting a segment for his new series within its walls.

Nathan and Niles had wanted to tear the theater down to make room for more houses, but Zolie Vanderran had put her foot down. She'd imagined a complete restoration, and with her tycoon husband, Tom Kenowith, and his construction company working jointly with Savage Construction, Zolie was going to have her way.

Below the Mystic on the beach was a raised stretch of land that jutted out in a triangular point into the water, directly to where an old lighthouse still stood. No longer needed, it had fallen into disrepair and wasn't safe to climb, just like the old stairs leading down from the cliff to the lighthouse. This had history as well, and the Savages couldn't tear it down even if they wanted to. So it was decided that the lighthouse would be restored along with the theater and the stairs.

Quietly and ominously, the theater stayed sitting far from the cliffs with the haunting, windblown trees forever reaching toward it like grasping claws to the sound of the wind racing across the field. The road to the theater was blocked off with a barrier, and a tightly locked fence ran around the property to keep people out. However, from the recent storms, part of the fence had blown down—just something else for Niles to attend to.

CHAPTER 76

Catherine Wallingford was surprised to find out the bracelets were indeed ready when she called to check on their status. It would take her staff over an hour to go and get them, but not wanting to disappoint Zolie Vanderran any further, she went to pick them up herself. They were exquisite and expensive, and the thought of something happening to them in transit was something she was simply not going to deal with.

After picking them up, since she wasn't far from her home, she stopped there and phoned Zolie's assistant to check on the time of her flight out. Thinking that if she couldn't catch her at the airport, she would deliver them herself, she packed a bag and called her office to have them book her a ticket. It was too late to catch her, but Catherine would make sure the expensive, stunning pieces went directly from her hand to Zolie's.

CHAPTER 77

E d, Aisha, and Tanner stood out front of Patty's cabin; they could see the yellow police tape from where they'd parked. Ed walked up to the door by himself and saw that the seal had been broken. He looked in through a window and saw that the place was a mess—bloodstains were on a mattress and on the floor, along with a few soiled bandages scattered about. The place also looked quiet, so he knocked on the door. When no one answered, he pulled a medical glove from his pocket, put it on, and tried the handle; it was locked. He then waved Aisha and Tanner to follow him and led them around the back, passing between the garage and the kitchen.

Arriving at the backdoor of the cabin, Ed saw that the police tape there had also been torn. He looked inside the back kitchen window and saw the overflowing garbage with bloody bandages and yellow, balled-up police tape there and on the floor. Still gloved, he tried the backdoor—locked. "Really! Is nothing going to be easy?" he said. He took a quick look around and then raised his foot and kicked the door in. It swung inside, smacking the interior wall. He then pulled the door closed, peeled the remaining police tape off the door and the doorjamb, and balled it up in his hand, tossing it by an overflowing trash can next to the steps. He then took off the glove and nodded to Tanner, and he turned the camera back on. The light came on, and Ed looked directly into it. "Inside this cabin are the answers to the madness that's surrounded my family. It's personal, and nothing on this earth is going to stop me from finding out what those answers are." He then easily opened the door on camera.

Ed then motioned Tanner to cut the tape. He pulled more gloves out and handed a pair to each of his cohorts. They put them on and entered the cabin's kitchen.

It was in a state of chaos. There were bloody prints of different sized shoes leading from the main room to the kitchen sink. Blood had spattered on the counter, on the faucet, and in the sink. There was an empty, torn forensic-evidence bag on the floor near the garbage.

"They're still alive," Ed said as he moved deeper into the cabin.

"This isn't right. I can't believe the police left all this," Aisha said.

"You haven't met Officer Rumple," Ed said with a smirk. "Maybe they got what they needed, and some of this happened after. Don't touch anything without your gloves."

The dining-room table was knocked over. There were broken plates and old remnants of stew spilled on the floor; delighted roaches were investigating the area.

Aisha found a pile of mail on the counter, and she waved Tanner over to film as she sifted through it.

Ed saw the TV, the two VCRs, and a stack of new blank tapes on top knocked over like dominoes. The sealed cellophane on the new tapes had yellowed. Dust covered everything, except a smear across the top corner of the VCR. Behind it was another VCR tape with a label. He reached down and pulled it free, reading its title: "Day Momma and Daddy Died."

Ed looked over his shoulder to see Tanner with his back to him, filming Aisha as she looked at the family photos on the wall. Ed quietly placed the tape in his inside jacket pocket, quietly thanking the stupidity of one Officer Jackass Carl Rumple.

With the tape concealed, he looked at the blood path from the front door, which led to the cellar. A huge bloodstain, like something was dropped and dragged to a door off the main room, was evident. "Tanner, get this," Ed said, pointing to the blood trail.

Tanner filmed to where Ed was standing next to the slightly open cellar door. Ed looked into the camera. "Not really wanting to go in here," he said, looking at the blood on the doorknob.

Ed kicked open the creaky wood door and stared down the cellar stairs. The wretched smell hit them immediately.

"Oh God, what is that?" Aisha said, making a face and putting the back of her gloved hand to her nose.

"Smells like something died down there," Ed said, pulling on the light string to see the one low-watt bulb attempting to light their way. The light from the camera was brighter, and Tanner moved in front of Aisha, giving off more illumination to the others as they descended the stairs.

The cellar ran the whole width and most of the length of the cabin; the room was large, with a second, smaller room in the back. Ed moved farther in and noticed the large pentagram on the floor. The blood path led to the center and stopped. There were strange symbols drawn around an outline of a man, and bones of different animals had been left there in various piles. The smell of death was almost choking. Squatting down for a better look, Ed studied the symbols. He then looked to the camera. "Witchcraft. I've seen symbols like these before."

Aisha moved from the pentagram to the dresser, seeing the stack of strange books. She took a picture of the titles with her phone. "Ed, over here," she said.

Ed rose from the floor and saw the bowl with the remains of rotted creatures mixed with the same slimy substance that coated the floor. It was tilted against the dresser where it had been thrown and had invited the roaches to come and enjoy.

Aisha picked up a book and flipped through it; then she put it down and sorted through the rest. She picked up the one made of skin and opened it. More strange symbols and a language she recognized as some form of Latin met her gaze. "Hey, Ed. *Cantus Mortuus?*"

Ed looked at the open book and saw the words and strange symbols. "*Mortuus*—it means 'dead.'"

"*Cantar* in Spanish means 'sing.' *Cantus* may mean 'incantation' or 'spell,'" she guessed.

"Spells of the dead?" he said, looking at her in disbelief.

Aisha flipped a few pages; more strange symbols filled the pages.

"That's coming with us," Ed said, as he opened the drawer to find the remains of more dead creatures covered with insects stored inside.

The smell hit them harder, if that was even possible. He closed it quickly and opened a second drawer below, which had a stack of tablets inside.

Ed pulled out his mini flashlight and pulled the tablets from the drawer, scraping them against the bottom of the drawer above them, knocking the pages of another tablet caught up underneath. He dropped the tablets and pulled the hidden one free.

On the pages were word puzzles of sorts. But they weren't exactly the type of word puzzles found in the Sunday paper. These looked like an attempt to mimic the Zodiac. He'd studied those puzzles when he had once tracked a copycat killer for his show *Savage Cases*. He flipped through the pages of the tablet and saw a hand-drawn key to the puzzles. Someone *was* attempting to recreate the infamous puzzles of the Zodiac killer. He then moved back to the floor and looked at the symbols again, turning to Tanner with a grin. "Make that *attempted* witchcraft."

The creaking of the door to the other room spooked them. They all secretly hoped that a window was open in the old basement and a draft had caused it to move, yet Tanner moved the camera away from Ed and Aisha and aimed it at the door. Ed put down the tablet and slowly approached the door, bending to pick up a large muddler he spotted, raising it in front of him.

Slowly, he opened the door and shined his flashlight inside. There, in the smaller room, was an altar of some sort with tapestries hanging behind it. They entered and saw the altar was stained, as if it had been recently used for a sacrifice. There was a rat eating from the inverted buck's head, black candles, a dead blackbird in a bowl, and blood that had been poured down the altar cloth. On the floor were the remains of different animals and what looked to be veins spooled up in a bowl like spaghetti.

"What the hell did they do in here?" Aisha asked in disgust.

"I think it's their sewing room," Ed said, eyeing the strange symbols on the tapestries. He then felt something touching his hand and saw a leech trying to attach itself to him from the muddler. He dropped it in the corner near the altar. At the sound, several ravens that had perched behind the tapestries flew out in a rage, scaring the hell out of them.

Ed and Aisha raised their hands to keep the birds away. She screamed, putting her hands up and falling into his chest just as Ed put his arms down around her. Aisha lifted her head, and they looked into each other's eyes. And for a brief second, Ed was stunned to feel the quick moment of attraction during a time that should have been only about utter fear.

Tanner, being the expert cameraman he was, kept the camera on the ravens and followed them as they flew out into the next room and up the cellar stairs.

Ed and Aisha's stare was longer than expected, and they both forced themselves to pull away and look toward the birds, when Tanner turned back, laughing. "That's going to make a great shot!" he said. "You should have seen you two."

Ed tried not to think about what had just happened.

Moving back to the dresser, he looked at the books on witchcraft, voodoo, and other fun children's titles for the demented. Noticing the newspaper article sticking out from the skin-covered book, he opened it to a page depicting a strange-looking pregnant woman. The article that had been in the package delivered to Marlo back at the hospital was marking the page. He glanced over at Aisha and Tanner, who were filming the altar, and placed it in his pocket. He then thumbed through the book's pages.

Tanner and Aisha moved to the pentagram on the floor, and she squatted down to stare at the huge bloodstain in the middle. "Someone bled out here."

Ed grabbed the tablet with the skin-covered book. "I think we've got what we came for. Come on," he said, feeling the tape safely hidden under his jacket.

Tanner helped Aisha up, and they followed Ed, moving toward the stairs. But as Ed took the first step up, he noticed something was behind them. He could see between the wooden steps that yet another tapestry hung behind the staircase. Stopping, he walked around and looked beneath the stairs. The tapestry was against the wall, but something was off. Reaching out, he pulled it back and found a hidden door. The three looked at each other as Ed took a deep breath and reached out to open it.

Aisha grabbed his arm. "Are you sure?"

Ed nodded, and Tanner aimed the camera.

As he pulled back the tapestry even further, it fell from the wall above the door. Throwing it aside, Ed opened the door to see a tunnel. The darkness of the tunnel was absolute. He pulled his flashlight and stepped inside.

Aisha and Tanner followed Ed about fifty feet to find another locked door. Ed tried to break it open but couldn't. "Sorry. Thought this might lead to the shack we found Simon in," he said. "Come on. We'll go back."

The trio moved back down the tunnel to the cellar and made their way up the stairs.

Ed led them down the hallway to search the rest of the cabin, and they moved into the bedroom. On Patty's dresser sat even more photos of what looked to be her as a child, back before her parents died. One photo showed a thin but happy little girl, with an older girl standing beside her. Aisha pointed to the photo. "Ed, meet Stevie Galloway. This must be the sister I was telling you about."

Ed took out his phone and snapped a picture of it. "*Any* clue what happened to her?"

Aisha had moved to the closet and was looking at the ugly clothes hanging inside. "Nope, all I could find were the birth records: no marriage or death certificates, nothing. But I must say Patty here had some hideous taste in clothes."

"Maybe she married a cousin in the woods or something," Tanner joked.

Walking back up the hall to the bathroom, they spotted even more bloody bandages on the floor and dirty clothes thrown into the tub. Ed looked at the mirror and read the words, "Stop it," which had been written repeatedly by bloody fingers. There was an open pill bottle in the sink. Ed picked it up, and Aisha photographed it. The prescription was for Patty Galloway. "Risperidone," Ed mumbled. "Any idea what these are for?"

Aisha shook her head and reached up, opening the medicine cabinet. There were many other drugs in there, including Olanzapine,

Quetiapine, and everyone's favorite, Xanax. They took photographs to research the drugs later on.

Back near the kitchen, Aisha opened the sideboard drawer and found syringes, tourniquets, and even more pill bottles. "A regular pharmacy in here. What were they doing?" she said, as Tanner filmed.

Moving to the garage, they were surprised to find the doors unlocked. Ed opened them and stood still, looking in. It was empty, except for stacks of boxes and junk piled high along the walls. He moved to the back, where there was a second room hidden behind a partition.

Aisha and Tanner followed Ed to find yet another set of stairs leading down to a small landing. There was a door with a board jammed up against the knob, keeping it closed. Ed looked to the others. "This just keeps getting stranger and stranger. Wait here," he said.

Ed moved down the stairs and kicked the board aside, unlocking the latch and opening the door. It led to the tunnel they'd just investigated inside the house.

Aisha called down to him, "This is just all kinds of wrong."

Ed looked up into her worried eyes, making his way back up. "Who *are* these people?"

They moved out from the garage, and Ed closed the two barn doors.

At the Range Rover, Ed took off his gloves, reached inside, and picked up a plastic bag from the store. He dumped the contents of gum and protein bars into the back cargo area and placed their gloves inside the bag. He then pulled his phone out and punched in Ellie Collins's number. She answered in two rings.

"Hey, Ed, how's it going?"

"It's going," he replied. "Found some stuff, but I need my laptop to research. I should have brought it, but, of course, I forgot. I need the files on the Zodiac killer story that I did; remember it?" Ed said.

"Yeah, not one of my favorite stories, but whatever I can do to help."

"Can you go over to my house? No one is there. The gate code is five-six-four. Go around the house to the fountain, and under the stone frog is a key to the French door off the kitchen."

He paused so Ellie could write down the information. "Got it: five-six-four...frog," she repeated back to him.

"Inside my office, or up in my bedroom, is my laptop with the files from *Savage Cases*," Ed said. "Can you send the Zodiac files to my cell?"

He heard her child cry out as Ellie finally spoke. "Sure thing, Ed. I can go over right now. We just finished an early dinner, but Alice isn't going to be too happy about this."

"Thanks, Ellie. I found something I want to study on the way back home. We'll be driving all night and there's no password to worry about," Ed said.

"I better get going, so I can get back. You know, 'happy wife, happy life,' and all," she said.

Ed smiled into the phone. "Boy, do I."

Ed hung up the phone and looked to Tanner. "You mind?" he asked tossing him the keys.

"Not at all," Tanner said catching them.

Ed then called Sam and got his voice mail. "Sam, we're on our way back home, and it looks like they're still alive. Keep an eye on everyone, and I'll be home soon."

As the trio of researchers settled inside the Range Rover and drove away from the mysterious cabin, a bearded hunter moved from the woods. Dragging a dead pig, he waited until they were out of sight. And as others appeared behind him, he dropped the animal and ran to the cabin, running down the stairs and screaming at the top of his lungs.

The book...the tablet...They were gone.

CHAPTER 78

By the time Ellie had calmed down her partner and arrived at Ed's home, it was completely dark. Heading down the street, avoiding the old, tan van that looked abandoned on the side of the road, Ellie slowed the car and turned into Ed's driveway. The outside lights were on, and the home looked truly inviting.

Ellie parked. Leaving her purse and phone behind, she made her way to the gate. Entering the code, she entered the backyard, which was beautifully lit and landscaped. At the far end of the pool, she spotted the fountain with the little frog statue beside it. She lifted it up, retrieved the key, and went to the backdoor and unlocked it. The sound of the pool bubbles startled her, and she turned around to see the electronic pool cleaner moving across the darkened pool, doing its job.

Opening the back door Ellie turned on all the light switches, noticing the pool's light illuminate the backyard. Ed's office was near the kitchen. She had been there many times and went right to it. Flipping on the light, she went to his desk. "So, where's the laptop?" she said to herself.

She sat at his desk and opened the drawers. Bumping the track pad of the larger computer, she caused the computer to come on. She did a quick search and came up with nothing. "So much for storing it in the cloud," she said, as she searched the credenza behind the desk. Not finding the laptop anywhere, she made her way upstairs.

In the bedroom she turned on the light. On the table, between the chairs near the balcony, was the laptop. She sat down. When she turned it on, the glow from the computer lit her face. She found the files and sent them to Ed. Watching the documents being sent, she sat back in the chair and sighed...just as the lights went out.

The computer's battery kept the laptop glowing, and she saw the files had been sent. Alone in the dark, she stood and heard the water in the pool.

Ellie sat the laptop on the table and moved to the sliding glass door, opened it, and looked down into the backyard. The lights in the pool and backyard were still on and water was moving in small waves, like someone had just been swimming in it. She looked from the deep end to the shallow end and saw wet footprints leading from the pool toward the house.

Scared, she looked to the stairs leading to the pool, and on the railing wall was a large, shadowy figure. Without thinking, she turned and ran into the bedroom slamming the sliding glass doors closed and locking them. She then ran out of the bedroom, down the hall to the stairs.

Ellie started down the stairs but stopped dead, eyeing the wet, dripping ranger's hat that hung on the post of the railing. She screamed. Running back to the safety of Ed's room, Ellie closed the double doors and locked them. She reached into her pocket for her phone, remembered she'd left it in the car, and looked to the portable landline on the nightstand for help. She rushed to it, scared out of her mind and not even thinking it wouldn't work without power, grabbing it just as the double doors were kicked in.

Ellie screamed and dropped the phone when she saw the grotesque man dressed like a forest ranger. He was dripping wet; his face was a maze of scars and burns. His upper lip had seared into his gums. He had stitches under his jaw and neck, and his odd-looking uniform was tattered, as if he had crawled from his grave to get to her.

The ranger lunged, and Ellie tried to open the sliding glass door. He grabbed her, lifting her up and throwing her into the mirror of the dresser, which shattered, cutting her skin, as she fell on the perfume bottles and then onto the floor, screaming. One of the perfume bottles opened, and Ellie grabbed it as the ranger caught her with one hand and pulled out a knife with the other. She tossed the perfume in his eyes, and he issued the most horrible sound. Dropping her, he brought his hands up to wipe the stinging chemical from his eyes.

Ellie got up and ran for it. But her heart literally stopped. There, running toward her in an old dress with witchlike hair flying all around her head, was the woman that she knew Ed had been speaking about.

Screaming like a banshee, the woman named Patty dove at her, tackling Ellie and bringing her down to the ground. They tumbled into the bedroom and crashed against the chairs, smashing them against the sliding glass door sending cracks throughout the glass.

The ranger intruded. He grabbed Ellie once again and picked her up, stabbing her repeatedly with the giant knife. He then threw her straight through the cracked sliding glass door, where she smacked her head on the cement post of the balcony. Ellie stirred and tried to move away, but the ranger kicked through the remaining glass and stomped on her back, cracking her spine. She screamed out as he reached down, picked her up, and threw her from the balcony.

Ellie screamed as she hit the water in the pool. Blood changed the blue water to red from the pool light, and the ranger looked over to see her surface for air. He then climbed to the railing and jumped, feetfirst, sending the now-broken woman to the bottom of the pool.

The final sight for Ellie came in the form of a distorted view of a woman from hell smiling down at her. As the water filled her lungs, Ellie wished to God that she had listened to the love of her life...and stayed as far away from the Savage home as possible.

CHAPTER 79

T he accident on the freeway was bad. Several vehicles were involved when the bread-truck driver, Lyle Peepers, reached for a jelly doughnut he had dropped on the floor just as the cars in front of him slowed. By the time they cleared one lane for traffic, hours had passed. Ed was going to be late for the funerals, but just how late, he had no idea.

Sitting in traffic in the backseat for a change, Ed looked at the photos he had taken on his phone of the pill bottles in the cabin. He included them in an e-mail as he tapped out a message addressed to a woman named Tallulah.

The weather matched this day of mourning; dismal, dark-gray clouds hung in the sky, promising yet another round of rain.

By the time Ed dropped off Aisha and Tanner, he got home as quickly as he could. Driving down his street, he was surprised to see Ellie's car. Thinking she may have had car trouble, he parked next to her and got out.

Glancing in Ellie's car, he noticed her purse and her cell phone sitting on the console. The message light was flashing on her phone.

Ed looked to his house. Everything seemed all right from the outside, but he immediately felt a chill. Running to the front door, he unlocked it and stepped inside, yelling for Ellie. When he took that first step over the threshold, he nearly slipped on the water covering the entryway floor. He noticed that the carpet on the stairs was dirty and wet in places, and the footsteps going up were huge, as if a giant had used his home last night as a hideout.

Ed looked up the stairs and yelled for Ellie as he ran, looking in the bedrooms as he made his way down the hall. He stopped when he saw the kicked-in bedroom doors. Moving cautiously into the room, his heart fell when he saw the broken sliding glass doors...and the blood.

The blood spatter could be seen on Marlo's shattered mirror, and the contents from the top of the dresser were scattered across the floor. He looked to the patio and saw even more blood.

He didn't want to go any farther, afraid of what he would see, but moving to the railing out of need and the hope that there would be nothing horrid to meet his eyes, he looked over.

Hope was officially gone. Ellie was floating in the pool; the water was dyed red with her blood. Ed staggered back, digging out his phone. As he leaned against the house, he called 911.

CHAPTER 80

The dark clouds hung in the sky; had Sam driven past Ed's home for the service, they would have seen Ellie's car. His mood was dark with the loss of his wife, and he didn't see Ed's message until he was on his way. Being the first to arrive, he excused himself from Heather and Ava and called Roman and Logan.

The dreary service at the cemetery ended with no sign of Ed. Marlo was angry. Talking to Maggie, she was adamant, saying how she would never forgive Ed for missing their own beautiful daughter's memorial, let alone everyone else's. It was just one more thing to add in her divorce petition. She was so angry, in fact, that when she was leaving with Maggie, a reporter stopped her and asked her a few questions—questions she was now more than happy to answer.

CHAPTER 81

E d Savage's home was a circus. The police and medics were one thing, but the reporters were another. And the familiar faces of Wendy and Sandy Storm were there, adorned with self-satisfied grins. Now working on their own, they were not going to give their older sister the satisfaction of saying, "I told you so." They stayed as far away as they could until Ed left for the funerals. That was when they pushed up front with a camera and barged inside, filming away.

Ed had rushed to the cemetery, arriving long after everyone had gone. He wished it had started later and that everyone would be there. He was panicked at the thought of Ellie, and he needed someone, *anyone*, to help. He didn't think Marlo would be sympathetic from the last message she'd sent him. With all the chaos at his home, his phone was ringing nonstop. But he'd silenced his phone to deal with the authorities; and anyway, if he'd had picked up, he wouldn't have known what to say; he was in shock.

Marlo's last message was nasty; she'd ripped him a new one. Repeating all the horrible things she had thrown in his face the other evening, she added even more cruel things about missing their baby daughter's service. More hell would be paid.

Knowing he would miss the service, Ed hadn't bothered with the black suit; instead, after a quick shower in the guest bedroom, he dressed casual and grabbed a jacket. Parking at the cemetery, he glanced in the rearview mirror and noticed he'd forgotten to shave, but scruffy Ed would have to do.

Walking up to the three Savage graves was hard. He was thinking it was his fault Ellie had been murdered, and it was a wonder Ed was functioning at all. Seeing Lisa's name on a headstone finally broke him in two. His hope of his little nugget being found safe was all but a memory. Ed choked up, and the emotions flowed. He fell to his knees crying. He patted the earth above his innocent child's empty casket, picked up the stuffed koala that someone had placed on top of her grave, and clutched it against his chest. It was over. The breakdown had arrived.

CHAPTER 82

The same tan van that had been parked outside the pharmacy when Sam and Cara had posted the flyers and down Ed Savage's street the night of Ellie Collins's murder sat covered in dust.

The farmhouse looked innocent enough from a distance. But up close, the window coverings were all shut tight. Behind it, the tall, wooden fence blocked the miniature tent city completely from view. There, a little girl named Becky, red haired and freckled, about eleven years old, was busy with her chores—chores she had no choice but to do.

She could hear the crying from inside the basement but knew she couldn't help. She remembered when it was her who was crying in that very same room.

Lorna Smutty brought the tray down the creaky stairs to the basement and unlocked the door. When she opened it, Lisa Savage sat on a dirty mattress in a room with small windows up near the ceiling in the back corner of the home. The white prescription bag for her asthma medicine was torn open; it lay near her with her inhaler neatly sitting on top of the only clean space in the room.

"I want to go home," Lisa cried.

"This is your home now, Lisa," the fat woman said.

"No. I want my daddy," Lisa said, deathly afraid of the mean woman.

"We told you, honey; your parents are dead. They died in the accident, sweetie, remember? We're your family now."

Lisa stopped crying and was confused. "I want Ava and Tucker."

The woman slammed down the tray, knocking over its contents and spilling the juice box. "They don't want you!" the woman screamed at the frightened little girl.

Lisa burst into tears and hid her face on the dirty mattress.

"You'll come around; they always do," the woman said, slamming the door shut behind her.

CHAPTER 83

Jillian York, the first Mrs. Edward Savage, was a real piece of work. Sitting in her penthouse with the news muted, she read the morning paper, making the Savage funerals a "top priority." But sitting on her table was an older headline: "Savage Brothers Rake in Millions." The woman was plotting.

But it certainly wasn't the first time. Jillian had married Ed for his money, plain and simple. The thought of Savage Construction and the lavish offices at Savage Tower, the big homes and fancy cars—everything had thrilled her. The problem for Jillian had been Nathan. He'd had a tight grip on the company money—and he had her pegged as a money-grubbing, social-climbing little tramp who had Ed fooled. Ed's salary at the company was in the six-figure range at the time. More than enough for most. But with dreams of country clubs and unending vacations in the future, it was simply not enough for Jillian.

She didn't know anything about Ed when they'd first met, and she was definitely attracted to the tall, dark, and handsome stranger. Her girlfriend had pointed out the over-six-foot-tall stud at the bar of the country club's Christmas party, and she'd made her move.

That was another thing that got her. Ed hated the stuffy country clubs his family forced him to go to. He would rather be outside doing anything else, like hiking a trail and getting exercise, riding horses at the arena and practicing polo, or water skiing and playing a round of golf. Then there was his teenage joy that never left him, his love of photography. Ed would sometimes wonder off with his camera bag and be gone for hours, seemingly ignoring her.

Then he would go walking. He loved finding new things to explore and places to eat—not lounging around a pool and being waited on. But Jillian believed that with hard work she'd change all that.

The only time Jillian forgot about the country clubs, money, and other social nonsense was in bed. The sex was great, and if there was one impressive thing the Savage men inherited from their father, it was being able to fulfill a woman in bed. Ed was gentle with her when she wanted him to be, but she liked his savage side the best. Ed was a true wild man in bed, and that was what she preferred; the guy lived up to his name.

One evening, Ed was emptying his pockets on the dresser, and a business card fell behind it. Needing the card, he moved the dresser away from the wall to get at it, and that was when he noticed the hotel-room key card in the little envelope next to his wife's things.

He picked it up; the room number was written across the envelope in Jillian's handwriting. On top of the dresser was Jillian's purse, which she had thrown against their wedding photo, spilling some of its contents. A trollop-red lipstick had rolled out.

Ed had heard Jillian enjoying her bubble bath before dinner in the master suite, and he picked up the phone. The automated system routed the call to the hotel room, and when the man answered in his usual pompous flair, "Jeremy Bigelow," Ed hung up the phone.

Jillian had known that of all the people for her to cheat on him with, Jeremy was the worst. His father, Jacob Bigelow, owned Bigelow Construction, Savage's biggest rival, and they played dirty at everything. Ed had known Jeremy for years, and it was never friendly.

Not surprisingly, Ed was crushed. He didn't see the affair coming, and he was in love with her. When she'd exited the bathroom, Jillian still remembered that stunning man, sitting on the bed, holding the hotel-room key card in his hands. She had gasped, searching for some excuse. The lie she invented didn't work, and in the end, it was no use. She had made a huge mistake. Jillian York clearly saw she had broken Ed Savage's heart, and she would never be offered another chance.

Now, Mrs. Jillian York Savage Bigelow was having fun reading about the millions Ed was inheriting, and she was rethinking the way the past had played out. The TV flicked to one of Ed's promos, and she turned up the volume. There he was, looking at her in her penthouse from the screen, and Jillian smiled wide. She certainly had a secret...and Marlo Savage wasn't going to like it.

CHAPTER 84

isha Thomas was at home at her desk with the books from the store in front of her. Her home computer was open to a page about cults, while her laptop sitting beside it had pulled up a page that converted Latin to English. Aisha picked up the creepy, skin-covered book of spells carefully and noticed something was stuck inside the spine.

The old, faded piece of paper had been folded and shoved up inside the binding. Opening it, she read the words: *Familiarum fit unum quia vindicta iamdudum aetherias.* Although she knew some, understanding just a bit of the phrase, she tried to comprehend: "Families for one, then…something," she whispered to herself. "Vindictive or revenge… maybe…then…no clue at all."

She began entering the words into the computer; the information superhighway threw back the answer in seconds: *The family comes together for punishment nears.* Looking at what she wrote, Aisha looked up to her computer at the article she had found on cults operating in the area of Black Ridge Falls. "The family?"

She began reading the article and paged down to photographs taken of a group of Satanists, seeing the crazy woman referred to as Patty Galloway standing next to a man she did not know. "Oh my God, there's more of them!" she said out loud. She read further and saw the headline focusing on a bloody animal ritual that took place on someone's farm. She found another picture of the man who'd been with Patty, a man by the name of Marcus Bowers.

On her yellow legal pad, Aisha had the names of the prescriptions they'd found in the cabin and learned why they were prescribed. A psychotic break—the pills were antipsychotic drugs used to treat the mentally ill.

Aisha picked up her cell phone and called Ed; it went to voice mail. "Ed, call me back; I found something. I'm sending you the article. Scroll down to the photograph below it. Patty is with others, a cult of some sort. Self-proclaimed Satanists and some other weird stuff. She's not alone, Ed. The man she's photographed with is named Marcus Bowers. Turns out he was jailed once for some animal ritual that was done on a farm when the guy was on an LSD trip. He's bad news. Read the article; you'll see what I'm talking about. And the drugs she's on? All scream big-time mental patient, so be careful! Call me when you get this!" Aisha hung up her cell and sent Ed an e-mail, copying the link to the page from her computer. She then found the page on her phone and took a screenshot of the man with Patty.

Shutting her laptop, she placed it in her bag with the rest of the books. Grabbing her coat, purse, and keys, she rushed from her apartment.

CHAPTER 85

Vander Place Hotel was not open yet. However, even with the light staff they had, there were enough to get things in order for the arrival of the family. The gates leading to the property stood open right now, waiting for their guests.

Zolie Vanderran stepped from the car, looked up at the name, and smiled. Amanda closed the car door and stood next to her, as Tom looked to the sign. Zolie's smile faded. "Such a proud moment on such an unbelievably depressing day," she said.

There was a florist's delivery truck parked out front, and they watched the deliveryman exit the hotel, open the driver's door, and finish filling out a delivery report. Knowing the hotel was not open yet, the three entered, passing the man, who offered up a big smile. Zolie stopped to tell him that in the future, no deliveries should ever be allowed through the front entrance, and then she walked into the building.

The lobby was impressive. The furnishings were perfect.

On the wall behind the desk was the announcement, yet again—Vander Place Hotel, the name Zolie loved. Empty vases stood on each end of the back counter behind the front desk, and a blonde woman arranged flowers with her back to them. As they approached, the woman turned and introduced herself as Eve Blakely, the newly hired front desk manager, whose smile was beyond welcoming. "Mrs. Vanderran Kenowith, Mr. Kenowith, Ms. Kenowith, welcome to Vander Place Hotel. We've been expecting you," Eve said.

Zolie was impressed; this woman was not only charming but also beautiful, a perfect choice for a guest's first impression. "Thank you, Eve. A little late in the day for flowers, isn't it?" she said, smiling and testing the manager.

Eve was slightly embarrassed, and she smiled. "Yes, they should have been here much earlier. Won't happen once we're open," she said.

Knowing her mother was a perfectionist, Amanda was enjoying the moment. "Better not," she added with a wink.

Eve immediately pulled an envelope from the drawer behind the desk. "Here are your room keys. The presidential suite is, of course, yours, and we opened the adjoining room for your convenience."

Looking around the empty lobby, Tom wondered if there was someone to get the luggage from the car, just as a bellhop appeared from the back room behind the front desk. "Ah, there you are," he said, tossing him the keys. "It's right out front."

The bellhop caught the keys, embarrassed for not being ready and out front when the most important guests arrived, and ran to get the luggage cart near the front of the lobby.

Handing the room keys to Zolie, Eve told her she had a message. "Mrs. Marlo Savage wanted me to tell you to get settled and to meet them at the yacht upon your arrival," she said.

Zolie thanked her, and they moved to the elevators.

Entering the presidential suite, Amanda went right to the window, looking down at the beautifully lit yacht. "No half measures here, Mother. Dad, come look; it's charming," she said.

The first thing Tom noticed was the turbulence of the sea. Zolie noticed it, too, and side-eyed Tom. She smiled, and he nodded. They knew they weren't going.

"It's larger than I pictured," Amanda said, excited about going out.

"Maybe tomorrow," Tom announced. "It's too rough out there tonight. I'd be sick before we left the bloody dock."

Amanda looked to her parents.

"I'm going to stay in, too," Zolie added. "I've had enough of Marlo for one day."

Earlier, at the funeral, Marlo had made it a priority to tell each and every one of them how angry she was at Ed for missing their daughter's service. It didn't matter if anyone else was upset Ed was not there. It was all about Marlo, and she trashed him to everyone.

"Oh, she's going to be stomping mad!" Amanda said with a laugh.

Zolie turned away from the window with a grin of her own. "Oh, I know."

CHAPTER 86

I t was a known fact that Simon had wanted his ashes buried at sea, and Marlo made sure that her poor brother would get his last wish from aboard the fancy yacht. The sea was a little choppy, and the dining vessel bounced a bit at the dock. The Vanderran superyacht was all lit up.

Niles's two sons, Chance and Landon Savage, and their wives had been in charge of hiring the staff for the hotel. They had been working hard for months. They each purchased new homes in the development next to the hotel, so they would be close by at all times. When the hotel construction was near finished and the decorating and furnishing were complete, Niles had sent them and their families on a cruise as a thank-you for all they had done.

Niles hadn't spoken to them about the enormity or brutality of the disaster at Black Ridge Falls, but he knew they would be finding out from the tabloids. He later told them not to rush home; the funerals were going to happen, and there was no way they could get home in time anyway. But they did send their condolences.

The staff on the yacht was told that every table had to be set for dinner with the exception of one, which was near the windows of the second-floor dining room. That table was reserved for Marlo, who had set up the photograph of Simon and placed his urn next to it.

Everyone who boarded the dining superyacht was impressed; it was beautifully appointed. Each set table had a candle in the center of it, although unlit for safety reasons due to the shortage of staff.

The only ones missing were Zolie, Tom, and Amanda, and even though Ed was not there, he was expected. Marlo wasn't counting on it.

The adults were on the first level in the largest dining room. Drinks were being served, and hors d'oeuvres were being passed out, when Amanda walked up to the yacht alone. She could see Logan and Maura's daughter, Macy Savage, and the rest of the younger Savage members on the upper deck, and she waved up to them as she boarded.

This was Marlo's event, and Amanda could see that she was more than a little miffed that her mother and father were not beside her. The look on her face could have sunk the ship. "Amanda, hello there, darling; where are your parents?"

Amanda immediately eyed Maura for support. "I'm sorry, but my father doesn't have the sea legs he used to, and he's afraid the waves are too rough for him. Mother is staying with him."

Marlo was pissed but forced a smile. "I'm sorry they can't make it," she said.

Wanting to get this out of the way, Maura suggested to Amanda that the others were upstairs waiting on her. Amanda was glad for the life preserver and excused herself, running away from Marlo.

Sam joined Roman and Logan on the far side first-floor deck and was glad they were alone. He hadn't gotten Ed's message until this morning, and he'd tried calling him but couldn't get through. After calling his brothers to tell them Ed's suspicions of the Galloways' surviving, they'd decided to keep it quiet until after the service. "Any word?"

"Nothing," Logan said.

"We need to say something," Roman suggested.

"Not yet, let's give Marlo her time," Logan added.

"Agreed," Sam said, "we're all safe here."

"Guys, here she comes," Roman whispered, seeing Marlo moving toward them.

Coming through the doors and seeing them without Ed hurt her, and for a moment she was her old self again. "Hey, guys, we better get going," she said.

Logan smiled. "Oh good, Ed's here." The youngest Savage brother was excited to see his older brother. It had been too long.

"No, I still haven't heard a word from him. But it's getting late, and the day is getting away from us," Marlo said, watching Sam and Roman check their phones. Not seeing any messages and not having a clear signal, they sadly agreed.

"Would one of you tell Niles we can be going now?" Marlo asked.

Roman put down his glass. "I'll tell him," he said and moved in the direction of the bridge, pausing at his wife's side.

"How's my beautiful new mother-to-be?"

"Shush," Gabby said, looking around like they could be caught passing notes in school.

Roman laughed. "This is why I love you," he said as he kissed her.

Reaching the top deck, Amanda was greeted warmly by her cousins. Macy was there to meet her with a hug. "You took forever getting here. What took so long?" Macy asked.

Amanda looked to her and the others. "I know, and I'm so sorry. After the funerals, it just took forever to be on our way."

Ava was next to hug Amanda. "Did my mom give you the third degree?"

"It was abundantly clear she wasn't pleased that my mom and dad passed on coming tonight," Amanda said, moving to Danni for a hug.

"I don't think my mom wanted to come on this either," Danni said.

Amanda pulled back. "Why is that? It's beautiful."

"I don't know, just a hunch," Danni told her.

Heather was last to greet her. "Well, I'm glad you're here! Come on; have a drink with us," Heather said, leading her to a table.

Macy's brother, Ty, and Danni's brother, Chase, were enjoying a cold drink at the table, and Amanda spotted the bottle of vodka immediately. "Are everyone's parents okay with the drinking?" she asked, eyeing the booze.

Chase took a drink from his glass. "Who's drinking? This is diet soda," he said, laughing.

Ty raised his glass to toast him. "Yeah, diet soda!"

"I'm sure they may expect we're doing it, but they aren't saying anything," Macy said, adding more soda to her drink.

Amanda remembered the days of babysitting her cousins and decided it was best not to partake in the drinking. She moved behind the bar and iced a glass for herself, pouring a sparkling Perrier and adding a squeeze of lime.

Amanda took a sip and looked toward the dock to see someone she did not know. "Who's that?"

All eyes turned and looked to see Lucy stepping onto the dock. Excited to see their friend, Danni jumped up and rushed to the railing. "Lucy, what are you doing here? Come on up," she yelled down.

Heather and Ava were equally surprised. "Did you know she was coming?" Heather asked.

Ava tucked her hair from her face. "No, but I'm glad she's here."

Danni put her glass down and ran to the stairs. "I'm going to meet her," she said.

When Lucy boarded the yacht, she saw him, the youngest Savage brother; Logan Savage was to her the one who should be the star, not Ed, who to her was too old and past his leading-man days. To be fair, Ed looked a lot like Logan in his earlier films, but that was another double-feature fantasy she sometimes dreamed about. Of course, she wouldn't turn down any of the Savage men if given the opportunity.

She had a thing for older men, like her teacher Mr. Wilder; she fantasized they were more experienced and could appreciate her young body. Staring at Logan, she figured it would be a treat for the strapping hunk, since his ex-beauty-queen wife was to her nothing but an old cougar. Standing there practically drooling, she almost didn't see Danni coming toward her.

"What are you doing here?" Danni said, waving her to the stairs.

Lucy paused, glancing at the water, tossing over the fantasy of pushing Maura off the boat and being under Logan. "I had to come; it's too weird back home…with Mia gone," she added for flair. "I know she and I weren't as close as…we could have been, but I just wanted to be with you guys," the lying little troublemaker said with conviction.

Danni put her arm around her. "Well, I'm glad you're here, then. Come on up; the others will be happy to see you."

Roman got to the bridge to find Niles and the freshly shaved captain going over a map. "Hey, Niles, Marlo wants to get going," he said.

Niles looked surprised. "I didn't see Ed board. Is he here?"

Roman sighed. "No, no one has heard anything, and I'm worried. This is not like him at all!"

Niles looked to the captain. "Well, you heard him. Take her out," he ordered.

The captain increased the throttle, and the engines roared. Niles and Roman left the bridge and made their way back to the others just as the captain sounded the horn.

The food server and the bartender, who were also serving as deckhands, excused themselves from the guests and untied the ropes for the journey, tossing them to the workers on the dock. Just as the yacht started to move, running footsteps could be heard behind them.

"Hold up, hold up!" Ed yelled, running to the end of the dock. The captain saw him and slowed the engine. The yacht bounced a bit, but Ed made it just in time.

The captain then stepped from the bridge and watched Ed leap onto the yacht. He looked to the deckhands, and one of them looked back, offering a silent nod. The captain then looked down the side of the ship at the two waiters dressed in black and white. They saw him and jumped off the yacht at the last minute. The captain turned back to the bridge and smiled, remembering the last time he'd seen Ed Savage...inside Patty's cabin.

CHAPTER 87

Zolie, now changed into slacks, exited the elevator with Tom in the lobby. Eve Blakely was not there, and even though the place was lit and beautiful, there was a haunting feeling of somehow being all alone.

Zolie went behind the front desk and opened a drawer, pulled out hotel stationery, and wrote a note: "Amanda, we're going for a walk to the Mystic Theater. Tried to leave a message on your cell; see you after your voyage."

Leaving the note on the front desk, they then went to the doors, to find them locked. Tom called out for Ms. Blakely, but she did not answer. Instead, he moved to the side door and opened it. "Here, we'll leave this unlocked to get back in," he said.

Walking outside and up to the bluff on the far end of the hotel, they could see the lit yacht in the distance as they navigated the wind-blown fence and walked toward the old theater.

The windows at the Mystic Theater were old and dusty, and some were broken. Tom could have sworn he saw a movement in one of the windows.

The neglected and decaying building instilled that all-out creepy feeling into a person's soul. Zolie and Tom may have felt a little spooked being alone in the hotel lobby, but here the quiet really spooked them. The old place certainly brought with it a higher dose of fright.

Stepping inside, Tom was apprehensive about going farther, but not Zolie. She had been there a few times and actually loved the old building. She had told him about this place several times, and now she was able to show him in her excitement what it was exactly she wanted to save.

The lights were working, thankfully, and once inside, Tom fed off Zolie's excitement, causing his uneasy feeling to slowly evaporate as they walked farther inside the old theater.

Unfortunate, really, seeing as Tom's fear was warranted. Someone was in the Mystic watching, just waiting for his next chance to please his captain.

CHAPTER 88

E d made his way inside, and it was Logan who saw him first. He raised his hands, yelling, "Hey, there he is!" He moved to Ed, and they shared a hug.

Roman and Niles arrived from the other direction, both smiling and relieved that Ed had made it, as Sam came from the stern. It was the first time the four brothers had seen each other in years. Even with the sad reason why they were all here, it was also a happy reunion. The cheer was contagious, and everyone seemed to forget for a moment all the pain the family was sharing.

Ed was happy to be with his family. Too much hurt and loss had built around his heart, and he needed the support himself. He had to tell them the news of Ellie Collins, and he tried to pull them aside to do just that, but the teenagers ran down the stairs and joined them.

Ava ran right to her father and hugged him. As much as Ed wanted to tell them the horrible news, this exact moment was not the time. He held it back…and Marlo appeared. The stress of the day had worn her down. She was obviously worried something had happened to him, and he knew she was also mad as hell. But as he looked into her eyes, seeing the anger melt and relief set as she saw that he was in fact safe, he pulled her into his arms and hugged her.

As the yacht moved away from shore, everyone came together on the second floor, mostly enjoying the cruise out to sea and catching up. Roman and Gabby had brought a DVD of one of the last events that everyone was together. It was one of the better film's they had that showed all three of the now-deceased family members and the lost soul of Lisa alive and well, as the memories played out on the large flat-screen in front of a sitting area.

A videographer had been hired for the event, which had been a polo match the four brothers played in years ago. At the time, the Savage brothers were a formidable team to beat. Everyone was there; the Vanderran twins, Cara and Maura, were seen together stomping the divots with their sister, Zolie, in fancy hats and holding champagne flutes. The Savage women were all laughing with them: Gabby, Marlo, and the younger girls, too, Ava, Heather, Danni, and Macy, in their pretty hats and having a ball. Simon was out there as well, holding little Lisa's hand while she ran from divot to divot stomping them down.

Tuc and Chet were at West Point then, and Lana and Kate had passed on the event to be at their friend's wedding.

But then, there were the men, with the name on Savage Tower, money, stardom, and definitely something to look at; the one thing the young polo tarts who would walk by with their alluring hellos in search of a rich man to snag didn't count on was the Savage men's loyalty to their wives. The Savage women knew this trait well, yet they always had an insult for the pushy little bitches who needed that verbal slap to the face—a volley they loved returning...

Nathan was out there holding a camera on his four boys as they walked their horses out to the field for a photograph—the same photograph Ed had enlarged for his office. Chase and Ty were with Nathan, holding his camera equipment and helping take photos.

The DVD went on to show the game, with the guys on horses playing and rallying after the opposing team shot the ball downfield. It was Ed who'd saved it with a back shot to Logan, who'd hit it farther up the field to Roman. Another player intervened and stole it, but Sam was able to ride the other player off, hitting it back to Roman, who then scored the winning point.

Ed watched the DVD and remembered that perfect day for the family, long before any marital problems and long before this nightmare.

When the time came and Marlo wanted to start the service, she paused the DVD and had Niles tell the captain to slow the yacht down. Once the engines stopped, the service began.

Marlo stood up front and looked out at her family. "I'm not going to make this long and drawn out. It's been...*rough* seems far too small of a word...But we're all hurting. Seeing all of you helps me. Now it's just my sister, Maggie, with me as far as roots are concerned. You Savages are so lucky to be so many. Simon saved my life when we were young, and he paid a heavy price for it. Now he is finally free and with our family. So with that, I raise my glass to my brother, Simon. I salute you."

Everyone raised their glass with Marlo, and Maura noticed that Gabby was drinking water.

Marlo then picked up the urn and carried it down the stairs to the main deck.

With everyone following her, Maura whispered to Gabby and Roman, "Why are you drinking water?"

The look Gabby returned was a dead giveaway, and Maura was overcome with joy on this miserable day.

"Shush. Don't say anything about this. Not today," Gabby whispered back with a face filled with love as she looked from Maura to Roman.

Maura smiled and looked to Roman, who nodded, his face proud as a new father could be.

Seeing the others ahead of them down the stairs, the three followed and joined them at the bow of the yacht.

Marlo moved to the far end of the bow as the clouds parted and the sun shined down, bringing with it a calm. Even the sea seemed to stand silent, as if God Himself had silenced the waters for this moment. Everyone watched as Marlo sighed; then she opened the urn and released its contents to the sea. "Good-bye, my brother," she whispered. "I love you." The ashes blew in the wind, giving Simon the peace he had so long deserved.

Marlo just stood there, watching. Ed came up behind her, putting his arms around her and holding her against him. In this moment, this exact moment, feeling the warmth of the sun, Marlo melted into her husband's arms. Feeling his strength and wishing they could stay like this forever, she knew it was impossible. The hurt was everywhere, deeply ingrained now, and she really didn't know what to think. Was she changing her mind about the divorce?

With everyone outside on the lower deck, alone in the second-deck dining area, the captain entered and stopped the DVD, ejecting it. He hit the switch on the DVD player to the local TV station, and the yacht's satellite went to work.

As they got back into the main dining room, they could hear the television from the second deck speaking loudly. Gabby and Roman were near the stairs and went up to turn it off; a few others followed. The DVD had been ejected. It sat in the tray innocently, but what was on TV was not so innocent.

The evening news was showing a scene at Ed Savage's home, and the footage was of police tape and news vans. Seeing this, Gabby dropped her glass of sparkling water, and it shattered on the floor. She gasped, "Oh God, what now?"

Downstairs the others heard her and rushed up, crowding into the second-floor dining area to see what was happening.

If the timing of the magazine centerfold was bad, the timing of *this* story could not have been worse, considering Ed had not yet told anyone what had happened. Sure, he could have interrupted the trip down memory lane, but they were all together and safe, and after the service they were all headed to the hotel. Ed knew he had to tell everyone about Ellie in person, so he'd chosen to wait. There was also the fact that he was in shock and had broken down at the cemetery over the probable loss of his precious daughter. His thoughts were scattered, and he didn't know what—or how—he was going to tell them.

The other reason the timing was bad was that an episode on TV that Ed had guest starred in had aired just last night. Ed had shot a series of guest spots on the hottest police drama on TV, called *Precinct Wars*. The show was about two female cops who were sisters, working in neighboring precincts in the heart of the city. Their cases would always seem to get intertwined. The studio behind the match of the lead, raven-haired women was brilliant, taking Angela Hammond and Julie Hennelly, from previous *Law Wars* shows, and matching them together for a powerhouse series.

The ratings were high, commanding huge advertising dollars, and the studio wanted more. That was when the writers wrote in the cops' brother, an attorney who, after a divorce, moved back home and joined a firm between the precincts. The search was on for a handsome, dark-haired leading man, and Ed got the part. The ratings jumped with the help from fans from his shows.

Ed's character was thrown into a case with his sisters involving a dirty cop and an even dirtier internal-affairs lawyer.

The producers of the show had talked to Ed about a spinoff series, and he was excited to look into it. The several-episode story arc ended with one of the sisters in danger and the other, with her brother, Ed's character, in pursuit. The climactic chase scene at the end had Ed's character shooting the in-uniform dirty cop, and that particular episode just happened to air last night.

The Savages who congregated in the second-floor dining room were in shock. The news story was quickly drowning all their hope and bringing each and every one of them to a bad place. On-screen the news was reporting that one Ellie Collins was murdered in Ed Savage's home, and they even pasted in clips of the series that Ed had guest starred in, where he was shooting a police officer, as if the media needed *more* to make him look like a repulsive killer. This was a story for the *National Invader,* a slimy tabloid dream story. Ed's agent, Rachel Shepherd's, workload had just passed impossible.

The Savages were scared. Marlo and Ed were last coming up the stairs to see the news report. They were in the back of the crowd, and Marlo pushed her way to the front. The anger returned to her in a flash, and she panicked. "It's not over? It's not over!" she said, stepping back from Ed and raising her voice to him. "You *knew* this! You knew this and didn't tell us," she screamed.

All eyes were on Ed as Marlo raised her hand and slapped him hard across the face. She pulled her hand back to slap him again, and he grabbed her arms, allowing her the first one because somehow he felt he deserved it. He then turned her to hold her still against him. "Marlo, stop. I didn't want to ruin your time with Simon. I'm sorry," he said.

Everyone saw Marlo slap Ed, and they looked away. Marlo then started crying and became hysterical. "Don't touch me. Let go of me!" she said, pulling away from him. "How could you not tell me?"

Maura and Maggie got between them, and Maggie held on to Marlo, looking at Ed as if he was guilty of something, just like everyone else.

Ed felt alone. No matter what he tried to do, everything seemed to backfire. How did the TV get turned to the exact channel at this exact time when the DVD was left there for their return? It was as if something or someone out there was plotting against him every second of the day.

The barrage of questions started. He held up his hands and yelled at everyone to stop. He looked around—even Ava's eyes were filled with confusion and hurt. As were his brothers'. He was going to make this right.

"Okay, I'm sorry. I'm sorry I didn't tell you sooner. This is why I was not at the funeral," he said, moving away from everyone and turning back to face them all alone. "We were late driving back due to an accident on the freeway. I had called Ellie the night before to go to the house and send me a file from my computer. Ellie went there and sent it to me. That's the last thing I know. When I got there this morning to change, her car was there. I found her." His eyes welled up. "Because of my asking her to go to my home, she's dead. She's a mother with a baby, and she's dead, and it's all my fault."

Ed was losing it. *Don't go, Daddy,* his daughter's voice in his head and the weight of his lost little girl was crushing him…now Ellie…The loss and pain were killing him.

Marlo only saw red. "*I'm* a mother, and I lost *my* baby and had to bury her empty coffin *alone* today, Ed!" she screamed.

Maura pushed away from Logan and went to Ed. She looked at Marlo and screamed, "Oh, shut up, Marlo! We've heard enough!" She put her hands on Ed's shoulders. "None of this is your fault, none of it," she said. She hugged him, looking back to everyone for added support.

There were times when Sam would look at his wife's twin and see her—how could he not? This was one of those times. "She's right, Ed. You can't blame yourself."

Heather looked to Ava in fright. "That could have been you…or your mom," she said.

Marlo heard her and yelled, "Had we been in that house, that *would* have been us! Oh my God," she screamed, "I told you to stay home… that we should just go!" Her screaming became frightening. Everyone on the yacht was scared.

Except one.

The captain of the Vanderran dining yacht turned the vessel back to shore and increased the speed.

CHAPTER 89

Catherine Wallingford arrived with the bracelets in hand. Happily, she picked up the beautifully wrapped package in the boutique bag and went to the hotel. When she found the doors locked, she peered inside. Seeing no one about, she tried the side door and found it unlocked. Entering the lobby, she went to the front desk and found Zolie's note to Amanda.

Catherine left the note and went back to her car. Grabbing her sweater and leaving the package, she went looking for her most important client, walking in the waning daylight toward an old, majestic building that somehow reminded her of a horror movie.

CHAPTER 90

As the sun was near setting and twilight was near, the captain removed his hat and threw it to the floor. Squatting down to open a drawer, he pulled out a rope. Locking the port door, he secured it with one end and ran the other end of the rope to a pipe running down into the deck of the bridge.

He turned the key and locked the coordinates into the yacht's steering box, breaking the key off to keep anyone from changing the path. The captain was busy as he then opened the starboard door and went out, locking it behind him. Tossing the key overboard, he moved down the side of the speeding yacht to the stern, just as it was approaching land.

Marcus Bowers found his hiding place to jump off the yacht at the right moment and smiled wide. He couldn't wait to see Patty again.

CHAPTER 91

On the other side of the hotel from the Mystic Theater, Wendy and Sandy Storm parked their car in one of the driveways belonging to a new home in the development, and they made their way down wooden, rickety stairs to the beach.

Hurrying, Sandy slipped, catching her big cardigan sweater on the railing. When she grabbed on to balance herself, she dropped the camera over the side. It hit a large rock and shattered, knocking the lens off.

Wendy turned and screamed at her sister, "You stupid bitch!" She reached for the camera and tried to see if it still worked, but it was hopeless. She glared at Sandy. "You better remember every detail down there," she said.

Wendy then pulled out a small recording device from her front pocket. "I'll get every word, but you *better* remember every detail you see, or we'll never work again." She then shoved the camera into her sister's hands and continued down the stairs, when she heard it drop to the ground near a garbage can and break further. "Fuck! I borrowed that. You'll pick this up on our way back."

Sandy shot her a dirty look.

CHAPTER 92

In the dining room, the questions and screaming continued, and Chase and Ty were over it. They motioned to the others to go back upstairs, but the girls wanted to stay. Happy to leave the drama with the girls, the two cousins went up the stairs to get another drink. The wind hit them immediately, seeing how close they were to land—reality struck the boys at the same time. The speed of the yacht was too fast... They were going to crash. Panicking, they ran back down the stairs.

Yelling as they ran into the dining room, they got everyone's attention. "Stop fighting, you guys; we're in trouble!" Ty yelled.

"We're going too fast. We're going to hit the dock!" Chase yelled, pointing to the windows.

The screaming stopped immediately as the adults ran to look. Ed and Roman went out starboard, while Logan and Sam ran to the port side. They could see the shore fast approaching, and they raced to the bridge, but before Roman followed Ed, he stepped back inside the dining room and yelled to the others to brace themselves. The look on his face said it all to Gabby.

Gabby grabbed Danni, and the two of them ran for life jackets. Below the padded seat cushions, Gabby started grabbing life preservers and handing them to Danni, yelling to the others to take them. Everyone found a safety device and then ran to find something to hang on to, anything they could find.

On the bridge, Ed got to the starboard door and tried to open it, while Logan and Sam arrived at the portside door. The doors were locked, and they could see the rope inside tied off. Logan and Sam tried to open the windows on their side. They could see Ed when Roman arrived frantically trying to open the door. Not getting the windows to open, Logan and Sam moved around to Ed and Roman to help them.

The yacht was getting closer and closer to the dock, where Zolie and Tom were now walking. They had left the Mystic and chosen to walk the beach to see the beautiful sunset disappear beyond the cliffs behind them, and to greet the voyagers after all.

Tom noticed the yacht coming in far too fast. "Good God, they're going to bloody hit."

Tom and Zolie stood frozen with fright. He grabbed her, and they turned, running back down the dock and trying to get to the safety of the shore.

With the wind blowing and the yacht getting closer to the dock, Logan waved his arms to the others. "Back inside! We're going to hit!" he yelled.

Sam, Roman, and Ed looked to the dock, and they all turned to run back to the dining room with the others.

By the time the Savage men got back from the bridge, everyone was holding on to something. Marlo and Maggie were together, frantically trying to put on their life preservers and hold on to the handrail. Niles and Maura were two tables away. Ava and Amanda were at a serving counter on the port side, with Heather and Lucy a few feet away at the railing. Ty, Chase, and Macy were holding on to the railing of the third-floor staircase, and Gabby and Danni were holding on to a pillar in the center of the dining room.

Just as the men saw where everyone was, the yacht smashed into the dock at a full speed of seventeen knots. The speed of the yacht pushed it up onto the ramp that led to the water level. The vibration of the yacht hitting the dock knocked Zolie and Tom to the ground as they ran to the shore. The yacht tilted starboard, and the screaming began.

The yacht groaned. Everyone saw the water coming closer to the starboard windows as the yacht continued to tilt. The collision and upward movement knocked the Savage brothers into the now-moving tables and chairs.

Marlo and Maggie tried to move away from the windows, up the slanting floor between the tumbling tables, moving debris to keep from hitting the windows nearing the water. Niles pushed Maura from behind, and they both fell forward as all the china, furniture, and anything not secured came toward them.

As the yacht tilted farther, Gabby and Danni, at the pillar, lost their grip when a table smashed into them. They both fell to the slanting floor and into Marlo and Maggie, pushing them in one direction while Gabby and Danni went in another.

Ava and Amanda at the service counter tried to stay on the port side as the yacht tilted. Amanda grabbed at the edge as the drawer opened. She managed to hang on, but the edge of the drawer came loose, and she fell backward, pulling the drawer full of knives with her. She fell onto the floor and under a table as it tipped toward her, and the knives hit the underside of the tabletop she was under. When the drawer dislodged from the counter, it split the side where it was secured to the floor, weakening it. With the yacht tilting farther, the floor beneath the counter split, and the counter came loose, sending Ava starboard.

The handrail that Ty, Chase, and Macy were holding splintered from the wall scaring Macy, and she was thrown from the stairway. Chase tried to grab her but missed. She screamed as she fell, landing on a tipped-over table and hitting the base hard enough to knock the wind out of her.

Lucy panicked and grabbed on to Heather, who tried to hang on, but it was too much for both girls, and they fell to starboard.

With the wall splintering and the handrail loose, Ty and Chase moved up the third-floor staircase to the top dining and bar area. But it was a bad move. When they got to the top, the yacht came crashing down into the water, throwing them hard into the corner of the bar. Chase hit his head; the pain exploded behind his eye, and blood filled his sight as his nose hemorrhaged. Ty hit the edge of the bar on his side, cracking ribs and sending him behind the bar, with bar furniture hitting them square on and glassware exploding above.

The table where Simon's photograph sat had caught fire when the yacht hit—the candles Marlo had demanded to be lit were knocked over, catching the tablecloth as they fell to the floor.

The glass windows on the starboard side exploded inward, and the water rushed in as the yacht beached itself, partly on the dock and sand. The glass showered everyone as they frantically moved in the opposite direction, not knowing how close they were to the beach.

The yacht had hit so fast that no one knew were anyone ended up, and with the yacht finally stopped, the dining area was only partly submerged, allowing the fire to spread.

The witnesses on the beach were stunned. Zolie and Tom picked themselves up and ran to the stricken yacht, coming as close as they could on the damaged dock. They were yelling for their family, looking for a way in.

On the other side of the dock, the captain, Marcus Bowers, emerged from the water and ran under the dock beneath Zolie and Tom, who were frantic up above.

The Storm sisters were shocked by what they'd just witnessed and pissed they didn't have the news camera to film it all. Their phones were useless being so far away. They then made their way to a garage on the beach when they witnessed a very wet man, dressed as a captain, running away from the scene.

In the front of the hotel, just as Aisha pulled her car into the hotel parking lot, she heard the loud collision and got out of her car. Seeing a lookout on the side of the hotel, she ran to it—a fancy yacht had just been turned into kindling. "Ed?"

CHAPTER 93

C atherine Wallingford loved her client; that was a given. But standing inside the Mystic Theater was making her second-guess her decision to come to the States. When she heard the loud explosion outside, she ran back to the door she'd entered to find it was now locked. She banged on the door and yelled, but no one came to open it. The sound of chains behind her added to her fear, but when she turned around, she saw nothing but a silent lobby.

She remembered passing another door inside the theater, and she ran to it. Running down the aisle to the side exit, she pulled back the musty velvet curtains and pushed on the door, but it was also locked. She screamed while pushing and pounding on the useless door. Giving up, she turned to find another way out.

At the top of the aisle, a woman was standing as still as a mouse. At first, Catherine was startled; then she called out to the pretty, blonde woman as she moved toward her. "Oh, thank God. I was locked in," she said, trying to find a smile.

But the look on the pretty woman's face was cold. Catherine stopped speaking, and her feelings turned back to fear. She froze, noticing the other exit on the far side of the theater. She looked back to the stranger and noticed the name tag that read "Eve Blakely" pinned to her jacket, and she watched her smile. It wasn't friendly.

Catherine Wallingford was no pushover. While she was most definitely proud of being British—that is, reserved, polite, and never one to become a screaming fishwife in public—she was also a fighter.

Catherine backed away down the aisle and ran across the theater toward the other exit. She was about ten feet from it when she heard the chains again, and out from the darkness, a man dressed like some sort of ranger stepped forth, pulling back the heavy velvet drapes and holding the chains in his hand.

Catherine screamed, seeing the grotesque giant of a man standing before her. Throwing her weight backward, she fell to the floor. The ranger moved toward her swinging the chains, which broke the rotted theater seats they hit but missed her.

Catherine got up and ran up the aisle, straight at the pretty stranger, who was suddenly wide-eyed with fear. When Catherine got a few steps from her, the woman put up her hands and yelled, "Wait!"

But Catherine screamed as she said it, and being a pissed-off and royally scared Brit, she slammed into her, pushing her back into the lobby and against the far wall. As she pulled away, the woman swung her fist, clipping Catherine in the chin. Catherine's head turned to the right, but to her attacker's apparent surprise, Catherine's left hand reached up and grabbed her forearm. With her right, she punched the woman in the face.

Stumbling back, Catherine turned to her right and saw an alcove. She ran to it, finding the stairs up to the balcony. Up she went. The curtains were closed. She ran, pushing into them, and stumbled onto the balcony.

From down below came the scream. Peeking over the balcony, Catherine watched the woman who was now down the aisle, seeing the ranger making his way toward her. The light caught the hideous man's face, and she saw it. Screaming, she bolted up the stairs after Catherine. Eve burst through the curtains, and Catherine was ready.

She grabbed the woman and swung her around, trying to throw her out of her way, but Eve held on, and both women went tumbling toward the aisle.

They were both able to get up, but Catherine grabbed Eve by the throat and started choking her. Eve was trying to speak but losing air. All she could do was punch Catherine in the stomach. Catherine let go of Eve and doubled over as Eve grabbed her by the hair and yanked her head back. She slapped her in the face as she choked for air, wanting Catherine to stop.

Catherine fell backward but grabbed Eve's clothes, pulling her with her and tumbling to the ground, hair flying as they hit the balcony railing.

They both got up. Eve was trying to scream, "Stop! Stop! This isn't…"

Catherine went for her throat again. She saw that her attacker was losing consciousness, and as Eve's strength left her, she started falling to the ground. Then, with all her might, she pushed with her legs and sent Catherine against the railing.

Then the giant hand of the ranger appeared over the railing, slamming into Catherine's back. Startled, she let go of Eve, dropping her to the ground, and the ranger pulled her backward over the railing. Catherine screamed, and the ranger let go, sending her into the air, flying, landing on the rotted wooden seats. The seat backs splintered, impaling Catherine in her abdomen and snapping her neck.

As Catherine waited for death, she saw the people dressed in black-and-white uniforms, a bellhop, and a dockhand, all just standing there. She had no idea why such a strange audience filled the old theater, standing silently, watching her deathly performance.

CHAPTER 94

The yacht tilted to starboard; the bow lodged into the dock about thirty feet from shore, and the satellite had snapped off and was underwater. Inside, the smoke from the fire started to spread as everyone attempted to get up, get out, and assess the damage done.

Maura pushed a chair off her, trying to stand. Logan was a few feet away and got up, removing a table between them, and went to help her. Niles was behind her getting to his feet. When Maura grabbed on to Logan and looked over his shoulder, she saw Macy lying amid the debris. Her breathing was labored, and she was looking to her parents. The color from her face was gone, and she was scared.

Maura screamed out, "Macy!" and lunged toward her daughter, slipping in Logan's arms as she moved.

Roman was getting himself up by putting all his weight on a table edge. He slipped and fell, grabbing the table for support.

Ed yelled from under the large table, gasping for breath. Roman looked at what he was leaning on and pushed it away to see Ed below him. He extended his hand and helped him up. "Sorry, you all right?" he said.

Ed got up, holding his side where the edge of the table had jammed into his ribs. He looked to his brother and the fire behind him. "Yeah, now help me get that out, and remind me to kick your ass later."

Roman turned to see Sam get up. They grabbed tablecloths and started smothering the fire. Ed saw a fire extinguisher next to the broken railing to the third-floor stairs and climbed up to it, grabbing it.

Balancing as he came back down, Ed aimed and fired the extinguisher. Between him and his brothers, they were able to quickly put it out.

They could hear Tom and Zolie yelling for them, and from the angle of the yacht, he could see the piling signage on the dock. Ed yelled back, "Tom, get to the bow! We'll get everyone out that way!"

After a moment, Tom yelled back, "The bow is clear!"

The white smoke from the extinguisher started to dissipate, and Danni struggled to free her mother from the piled-up furniture. Ava had gotten herself up and was helping her, and Roman made his way to them. After he pulled his panicked wife free, Gabby hugged her husband and daughter as the adrenaline flashed through her body. She then pulled back, raising her voice in fright. "Where's Chase?" she screamed, ignoring her own pain.

Roman grabbed her and looked right into her eyes. "The baby… Are you all right?"

Danni heard her father and learned the news that very day as she watched a tear come from her mother's worried face.

When the windows had exploded inward, Marlo and Maggie had gotten the worst of it. They each suffered cuts to their faces and forearms when they put up their hands to brace themselves, but they were able to turn away when Gabby and Danni fell into them. They fell between the tables to the floor. Much of the debris on top of them was not pressing down. Luckily, they were protected in a small space.

Heather and Amanda were pulling things off them. Ed and Sam saw them lifting a heavy table, and they intervened. From under the water near the broken windows, Lucy came up for air, gasping, "Help!"

She grabbed on to the window ledge and managed to pull herself toward the others. Logan got up from Macy and watched Niles step into the water, pulling her up the slanted floor, right into Logan's arms. Lucy clung to Logan for life, but the attraction on her face was clear as she buried her face into his chest, and Maura recognized the little polo tarts' novice move at once.

"Chase!" Gabby screamed through her tears. "Has anyone seen Chase?" she said, looking in the wreckage.

"Ty!" Maura screamed. "Where's Ty?"

Logan pulled away from Lucy and went to be at Maura's side, holding their daughter up as her breathing became more and more labored.

Macy looked from her parents to the staircase where Ed had retrieved the fire extinguisher, and Logan and Maura followed her gaze. "Upstairs!" Logan yelled. Logan and Roman made their way to the stairs and climbed up them.

At the top, they saw Chase against the bar just above the waterline, looking panicked. His hands were cut and bleeding and he was using his shirttail to wipe the blood and glass fragments from his face. They saw Ty's legs from behind the bar, and their fathers' fear spiked.

Roman knelt down to his son. He could see the blood behind his eyes. Chase tried to talk. "No, son, don't speak. I'm here," Roman told him.

Logan cornered the bar to see his son buried under bar debris; he was holding his side and also had the wind knocked out of him. He got to him, pushing away bottles, and pulled him into his arms as his breathing started to return. The pain in his side shot though him, and he curled into his father's arms, gasping for air. "Dad! Dad! It hurts to breathe," he said.

Logan looked around and could see that getting to the dock from there was not an option. He helped his son around the bar and told him to stay there with Roman, and he would get Ed and Sam to help them all down.

Downstairs, Ed and Sam were pulling Marlo and Maggie up from the floor when Logan made it back to them. "The boys!" he yelled. "Upstairs! Ed, Sam, I need your help."

Gabby screamed out, "No! Not my baby!"

A feeling of dread shot though Maura as she held on tight to Macy. When Gabby passed Logan, Maura saw the look on his face, and she knew it wasn't good.

With Marlo and Maggie up, Ed pointed to the front of the dining area above the water. "We're going out through there. Everyone, move that way," he said.

Ed and Sam then made their way to Logan and stopped to check on Macy. Maura looked up at them. "We need to get her to a hospital," she cried.

The sound of the bottle being kicked from the stairway got everyone to see Ty as he stumbled, tripping and yelling out on the last few stairs to the floor.

Knowing his son was hurt, Logan moved to him. "I told you to stay put!" Logan yelled, worry in his voice as he helped him to his mother and sister.

"Dad, my ankle hurts bad." Ty moaned.

Gabby, seeing her son bleeding in Roman's arms, screamed out and made her way to him.

Everyone below heard Gabby and looked to each other with fear. "Get them out of here, Sam," Ed said, and he raced back to the stairs to make his way up to the third deck.

Gabby was at her son's side with Roman. Ed could see the blood from Chase on Roman's and Gabby's clothes.

"We've got to move. We've got to move now!" Roman shouted.

"He needs an ambulance," Gabby cried.

As Sam made his way to the bow, Wendy and Sandy Storm had run up the dock toward a frantic Zolie and Tom. "What can we do to help?" Sandy shouted.

The glass shattering from a window at the bow above the waterline startled them. Sam was climbing out.

"Sam!" Tom shouted, waving his arms. "Sam, you can get to the dock over here."

"Okay, we're coming out this way," Sam yelled back, just as Wendy and Sandy moved into view. Sam stopped and stared at them. "You two!" Sam's voice was enraged. "Tom, Zolie, they're the reporters from Black Ridge Falls," he shouted.

Zolie and Tom looked to them with wonder.

"But we're here to help. Really!" Wendy shouted back.

Behind Sam, Heather climbed out. He reached down, pulling her up to Tom, who helped her onto the undamaged part of the dock. Behind Heather came a wet Lucy and then Amanda.

Zolie practically pulled Amanda up all on her own to the dock. "Oh, Mandy, Mandy, thank God you're all right," Zolie cried.

Amanda grabbed on to her mother, and the tears began.

Seeing Lucy wet and cold, Sandy took off her big cardigan and wrapped it around her.

Maggie was next to exit the stricken yacht, followed by Marlo; getting her blouse caught and ripping part of of it, and glad she wore the tank top underneath it.

Sam then called to Tom to help him with the others. Zolie knew something horrible had happened and clung to her child.

CHAPTER 95

At the base of the lighthouse, Marcus Bowers entered and took off his wet shirt. There was a duffel bag there with clothes in it, waiting for him. He pulled out pants and a shirt and tossed them on a small bed. Stripping off the rest of his wet clothes, he opened a closet and saw the corpse of the real yacht captain he'd murdered. Blood from the gunshot wounds covered his chest, and he threw his wet clothes in on top of him.

On the table near him were the forged documents with the Savage brothers' names on them. Next to it was a tablet, where he'd been practicing their signatures. His identity-theft scheme would have to be quick, and Ed was next on his list. With Ed being a celebrity, he would have to move fast, but the others, after succeeding with one Savage family, he could take a little more time with in sending their money offshore.

The lighthouse door shot inward, and Eve Blakely marched in and straight at the man, slamming the door behind her.

Now with dry pants on and slipping a shirt over his head, he shouted, "Quiet, they'll hear us!"

Eve was scared. Her face was bruised, and her body felt like it had been crashed against the rocks in a tumultuous sea.

Seeing this, he smiled. "What happened, Stevie?" he asked, moving to block her view to the table with the fake documents.

Stevie Galloway threw the fake name tag across the room. Eve Blakely was the identity he'd given her to apply for work at the hotel, and after getting a job, she had supplied information back to her younger sister, Patty, and to Marcus. The only problem was that Stevie was not like Patty at all.

"Marcus!" she screamed. "That thing in the theater! My God! What have you done to Melvin?"

Marcus looked at Stevie and realized his puppet-master scheme with this particular Galloway was failing.

Not getting a word from him, Stevie continued, "This ends now! I don't know what I've gotten myself into, but this is not something I want anything to do with. Now, where is my sister?" she said.

Marcus Bowers was quite the magician, an orchestral maestro used to getting his way. He had many followers, and he used them to lead him to people with money. He'd met Patty at an Alcoholics Anonymous meeting years prior and loved the stories she would tell of the accident that'd killed her parents. Marcus had moved out near Black Ridge after being released from jail, where he'd been for scaring a poor woman half to death with his lies of the occult and bilking her out of her savings.

Patty had been then, and still was, easy prey, and it wasn't long before he had her hooked on antipsychotic drugs. He manipulated her into believing he had powers. Patty, being weak to begin with, believed everything he told her. In Patty's mind she was becoming a witch, with powers like Marcus, and would soon be cured from the pain of losing her parents.

The twins, Melvin and Leroy, had taken a little more time. But by introducing heroin, LSD, and crystal meth into their lives, Marcus soon had them believing he was their savior.

Stevie was not as easily fooled. It took a lot of persuading to tell her to take the job at the hotel and to give them information, all to help her sister, Patty. But she did it out of guilt, from running away after the accident and leaving Patty and the twins in that godforsaken mountain town. "She's dead," Stevie screamed. "That woman at the theater. Melvin killed her. You said to keep her there. You said to just keep her there. That Patty needed to speak with her. Now, where is she?" she demanded.

"What woman?" he asked, looking directly at her.

"I don't know. That British woman, blonde; I didn't get her name before Melvin threw her from the balcony," she said, full of anger.

Marcus looked thoughtful. "I have no idea who you're talking about." He had instructed her to keep Zolie at the theater, but he had seen her with Tom on the dock, and she was a brunette.

Stevie was boiling under her skin at not getting any answers from him. "Where's Patty?" she screamed.

Marcus was growing tired of Stevie, and he grabbed her by her throat and pushed her against the wall. "You would do best to shut your mouth, little missy." He then pulled her toward him and slammed her back against the wall.

She hit her head and fell to the floor, passing out. Marcus then hid the papers in his duffel bag, grabbed his jacket, and left the lighthouse, wondering just who this other British woman was. This was someone not planned on, and Marcus didn't like surprises.

But Stevie had served her purpose, overhearing Sam talking to Roman about buying the RVs that day she interviewed. He was pleased with his luck that they'd chosen his brochures, and that stamp he bought was bringing him a fortune.

After all this time, work, and energy, nothing was going to keep him from the Savage money.

CHAPTER 96

D ark clouds were coming in from the water, promising that the sky was going to turn ugly, and the sea was becoming violent as the sun finally set in the west. The second part of the storm that came in earlier while they were in the mountains had arrived.

With almost everyone on the dock, Logan was helping Ava out from the broken window, and Ed was right behind her. She turned to help her father up. Standing in his arms and seeing Wendy and Sandy Storm, she freaked out. "What are *they* doing here?" she yelled.

Ava took a step, almost falling, and Ed caught her. "It's okay; ease up," he told her.

"Ava," Wendy shouted from the dock. "We're sorry! We want to help."

Ava looked to her father. "Dad! You can't believe them," she begged.

Ed glanced at the gruesome twosome who had so far done their best to make his life miserable. He then guided Ava to Logan. "Don't worry, honey; I'm not buying their crap," he said.

Ed and Logan helped Ava to Sam, who was waiting at the dock. "I've got her," Sam assured his brothers. He then helped his brothers up to the dock.

"Where is he? Where is the captain? This is all his fault!" Niles yelled.

Sandy and Wendy looked to each other, and they both spoke up at the same time. "We saw him!"

Everyone looked to them, and Wendy stepped forward. "We were by that building over there," she said, pointing to the garage with the sign, "Savage Beach Tours," above it. "He came out from under the dock when you two ran down it." She pointed to Zolie and Tom.

"He was soaking wet, too!" Sandy added.

Logan looked to his uncle. "Who is that man, Niles?"

Niles was just as confused as everyone else. "How do I know? I just met the guy today on the yacht," he said.

Roman was angry. "What do you mean you *just* met the guy? Who the hell hired him?" he barked.

"You don't understand," Niles replied. "Chance and Audra hired the guy, and Landon and Roxie told me the guy knew what he was doing, and his references were impeccable," he said.

Ava moved over to the Storm sisters. "You say you want to help. Where did he go?" she demanded.

Both pointed toward the lighthouse down the beach. "He ran down in that direction," Sandy said.

"We really did come here to help," Wendy added.

Ed was furious with these women, but for now he needed to get Chase, Macy, and Ty to a hospital. "You came here to help yourselves." The Storm sisters looked guilty as hell and recoiled at his words. "I'll deal with you two bitch sisters later, but for now we need to get to the hospital. And for the record, I love my wife and have never, and will never, be with another. My marriage vows are sacred! Print that!" Ed growled.

Ed moved past the Storms toward the beach to get a better view of the lighthouse just when Aisha Thomas appeared. Everyone was surprised when she came running up, and Wendy double-checked to make sure her recording device was still on.

"Ed!" Aisha shouted. She ran to him as Marlo walked toward them. "Is everyone all right?" Aisha asked, looking to him and everyone else. She could see Chase and Macy. "I'm so sorry," she said.

"Who's this?" Marlo shouted as she pushed back her hair from the wind.

Ed turned to Marlo and introduced her to Aisha. He mentioned that she had gone with him to Black Ridge Falls—a big mistake.

"Oh, so while I'm burying our child, you're running around with this!" Marlo shot out, looking Aisha up and down.

"Marlo, if I have to get up from my son, I swear I'm going to hurt you. Now, shut up!" Gabby screamed.

But whatever ice had melted from Marlo's heart, back on the yacht before the crash, it was back, and she wasn't having it. "Mind your own marriage Gabby!" Marlo shot back.

Aisha wanted to throw some shade herself but let it go; there were other things happening. Ignoring her, Aisha looked at Ed. "Did you get my message? Did you see the article?" she asked.

Ed shook his head. "No," he said, reaching for his phone in his jeans pocket. "I don't have any service out here; what was it?"

"You won't have service out here for a few more days; the storm last week damaged part of the power plant, and they had to shut down certain areas until the repairs can be finished. The cell towers are still offline," Niles said, pointing to the cell tower with the surveillance camera on it.

"What was it?" Ed asked Aisha.

"She's not alone," Aisha told them. "She's mixed up with a guy named Marcus Bowers, a sick, so-called Satanist who was released from jail. The pills we found were all antipsychotic drugs. Patty is one sick woman, and this Marcus guy is dangerous! He hides behind a cult. He has people, followers. Here, I'll show you; service or not, I took a screenshot of that page," Aisha said, fishing out her phone from her pocket and finding the photograph of Patty and Marcus from the article, showing it to Ed.

"Let me see that," Niles said, reaching for the phone. "Jesus...Ed, that's the guy. That's the man from the bridge," he said.

Ed's brothers had also seen the captain earlier, and Roman got up from Gabby and Chase to take the phone from Niles. Nodding, he handed it to Sam and Logan. "Aisha, what does this man want with our families? Why is he here?" Roman asked.

"I don't know, but I'd take a guess and say it's money. He was jailed for stealing from a gullible woman by getting her to believe he had powers. Powers he attained from animal rituals. The only other thing I found was on the twins. They may look alike, but one of them had a medical condition called dextrocardia—a condition where the heart is on the opposite side of the chest," she said.

Ed remembered shooting Melvin in the chest. "That explains how he could have lived, my putting a bullet in his heart," he said.

"It certainly does," Aisha agreed. "I then got in my car and drove here as fast as I could. I didn't have time to keep digging," she said.

"Animal rituals! Satanists!" Lucy screamed. "What the hell is going on here? I don't know about the rest of you, but I'm getting out of here right now!"

"We're all getting out of here now!" Sam yelled. "Niles, how far down are Landon's and Chance's homes?" Sam asked.

Niles looked from Sam down the beach past the garage to where Sandy and Wendy said they had come from. "About half a mile, but Landon's home isn't ready yet; they're staying in the hotel and with Chance. The beach runners are in the garage."

"Beach runners?" Sam eyed the garage.

"Oh yeah," Niles said and smiled, "Landon's customized babies."

Sam was moving down the dock to the garage where Niles was pointing; Ed followed. He stopped and turned back to tell the kids to stay put.

Roman moved over and grabbed Niles. "Come on; you're coming, too," he said.

Sam opened the double garage door to find the pair of classic Land Rover Defenders; the four-door customized ragtops had been outfitted for beach exploration and picnics. The last row of folding seats of the eight-seat Defenders had been taken out, and refrigeration units had been installed, with a padded seat cushion on top. The paint job was shiny new: "Savage Beach Tours" was painted on the side of the vehicles. One a vibrant blue, the other, red—they sat with their tops open and ready for adventure.

Sam went to the red one and looked in the glove box for the key. Ed went to the blue one and pulled down the sun visor, also looking for keys, with no luck.

"Where are the keys?" Sam asked when Roman and Niles arrived.

"Hang on. The garage-door openers to their homes should be in there, we still need to change the codes before we open," Niles said as he went behind a counter and grabbed the keys from beneath it. "Here you go," he continued, tossing them to the guys.

Both Ed and Sam caught the keys and found the garage-door openers. As they started the engines, Roman and Niles got in, and they drove out of the garage to the end of the dock, turning in the direction of the housing development.

As the men got out of the Defenders, Maura noticed the pained look on Gabby's face.

CHAPTER 97

At the Mystic Theater, Marcus looked at the corpse of the Brit who'd gotten in his way. "Too bad. Such a pretty little thing," he said with a smile. As if taking the final bow of his performance, he leaned over and kissed her, placing his hand on her breast.

Hearing a movement behind him, he rose and pulled a syringe from his jacket pocket. Melvin was slumped against the stage, going through withdrawal.

He moved to Melvin and showed him the needle. "All your pain will soon go away, Melvin. Just remember to do what I ask." Kneeling down, he injected Melvin with the syringe. "That's it, Melvin; let nature take its course," he said, laughing as he watched Melvin's eyes roll back in his head.

CHAPTER 98

After carrying Macy, with Ed's help, Logan secured her in the back-seat of the red Defender. Maura got in next to her, and Logan told Ty, with his broken ribs, to get in the front passenger seat.

Ed looked at the blue Defender, where Roman and Sam had placed Chase in the backseat next to Gabby. "Niles, Chance and Landon still have their hunting guns?" Ed asked.

Niles was opening the door for Ty, and helping him in with his sprained ankle. "Yeah, Chance does at his house. But we have some here, too. Skeet shotguns up at the hotel."

Marlo stood between Ed and Niles. "I didn't see any place to shoot skeet here. Where's that at?" she asked.

"It's not built yet. The stairs up to the bluff at the far end of the hotel lead to an unfinished shooting area. That's going to be where it ends up, but the shotguns are here in the hotel," he said.

Ed leaned against the red Defender, deep in thought, and then looked to everyone. "We need a plan here. Roman, you and Logan drive down to Chance's home. Call the police and find the guns. We'll get the shotguns from the hotel. Niles, you'll have to go with them and show them where they live, so tell me where the guns are," he said.

"I know where they are. In that storage area off the kitchen," Sam said, looking to Niles. "Right?"

Ed looked at Sam.

"When we got here, I looked around. I wandered in there and saw them," he said.

"He's right," Niles said, closing the door after Ty got seated.

"All right then. When you all get there, leave. We all won't fit in the cars. Get in and drive out of here. Get as far away as you can. We'll get the shotguns and get in my car and just leave. Let the police deal with this," he said, wishing he was alone, so he could handle this himself.

Everyone was nodding in agreement and looking at the remaining open seats. Ed realized they were waiting to see who would go first. "Zolie, you and Amanda ride with Maura. Logan, you're driving," he said.

Ed then looked at the empty seats in the other Defender and at Lucy, shivering from being cold, wet, and scared. "Lucy, get in. Chance's daughter is about your age. She'll have something for you to change into. Danni, you too, get in," he said.

After Zolie and Amanda got in, they noticed the padded seat on top of the refrigeration unit. Zolie waved to her husband. "Tom, there's room; come on. You girls," she said, patting the cushioned seat behind her and pointing to Ava and Heather, "on top behind Danni."

"Room for one more," Tom yelled to the others, pointing next to him and watching Niles sit next to Roman in the other Defender.

The remaining group looked to each other. "My car's up above," Aisha said. "I'm going with you, Ed."

Ed looked from Aisha, to Sam, Marlo, Maggie, and the Storm sisters. He glared at them. "Where's your car?"

Wendy moved forward, shoving Sandy a bit. "We parked up at the hotel," she said, lying through her teeth. "We'll follow you up and be on our way."

"You said you came from *that* end of the beach," Ed said, pointing past the garage.

"We took the far stairs down." Sandy joined in with more lies.

Ed didn't like it and knew they were lying, but he saw no choice and really didn't care as he glanced to Roman and Logan and nodded, watching the Defenders drive down the beach.

Up at the hotel, Marcus and his minions had been busy. They'd broken into the electrical boxes, cutting the phone lines and shorting the system for the entire property. But that was not all they had done, and Ed Savage and company would soon find that out.

CHAPTER 99

Niles pointed the house out to Roman, but it wouldn't have been missed if you drove down the street. Sitting in the driveway on the side of the affluent home sat a newly acquired Hennessey VelociRaptor six-door stretch limousine parked there; Roman looked at it and smiled as they pulled into the driveway. Logan parked on the street in front, and Niles got the garage-door opener and pushed the button while everyone was getting out of the other Defender. "Landon's home is four down," he said, pointing left, watching the garage door start to open.

Logan got out and looked at the shiny new VelociRaptor and was glad for it's size, but worried they were too many to fit, already planning on following in one of the Defenders.

Niles passed him and opened the door to the inside of the home. He hurried into the kitchen and grabbed the keys where Chance kept them in a drawer, and then he rushed back out from the garage, giving the keys to Roman. "Get them loaded; let's make this quick," he said.

Roman, Logan, and Tom helped Chase and Macy into the backseats of the VelociRaptor; Gabby boarded behind the drivers seats, and Maura took the row behind her. The women wanted to hold their wounded children. It was going to be tight, but they didn't care. They then helped Ty to the backseat next to Macy, while the rest of the girls went into the house to get Lucy changed.

Zolie hurried to the phone in the main room of the home. When she picked up the phone to find the line was dead, she looked at the cut cord sticking out from the plug in the wall and slammed down the phone. Turning, Zolie ran directly into the arms of the young man who was lying in wait. Dressed in a black-and-white uniform, he lunged at her, grabbing her and throwing her out of his way into a floor lamp and onto a sofa.

Zolie screamed as she hit, knocking the lamp over and falling from the sofa to the floor.

The young man dropped his pillow sack of stolen items and went out the broken window where the screen had been kicked in.

Hearing her scream, Niles came from Chance's office, and Logan and Roman entered from the garage. Tom was right behind them. The girls ran out from Chance's daughter's bedroom.

Tom saw Logan and Roman helping Zolie up from the floor; she was shaken. "A man!" she screamed, pointing to the broken window. "And the phones—they've been cut."

Logan ran to the window and didn't see anyone as Tom embraced his wife.

"Hurry, where are the guns, Niles?" Roman shouted.

"In the office. I'm looking for the key."

"Tom, get the girls in the car," Logan yelled, moving back toward the office, looking to Lucy as she stepped into the hall half dressed, holding up a shirt in front of her, allowing it to *slip* down to show him her breast, and faking surprise. "Hurry and change," he shouted; shocked at her action, he rushed with Roman to Chance's office to find Niles moving from the desk.

On the wall was a locked glass cabinet with a small, wooden box on a shelf. The gun racks were empty. "Where are the guns?" Roman barked.

"I know there's a handgun in that box. The rest must be in Landon's guesthouse; they're using it for storage," Niles said, as he fumbled the key into the lock. Pulling open the cabinet, Roman reached in and pulled down the box. He found the gun and some bullets. Picking up the box, Roman turned, and they rushed back through the garage.

Lucy was changed, and the women were getting into the VelociRaptor as they joined them.

"Here, let's share the seatbelt," Danni said after sitting next to Chase.

"Screw that; squeeze over," Lucy said, keeping an eye on Logan.

Tom eyed the small box in Roman's hand. "That's it?"

"Come on; it will have to do," Roman said.

Zolie watched Amanda squeeze in next to Ty and fasten the seat-belt over the both of them, after Heather and Ava took the smaller seat farthest back. "Girls, let me get back there with you."

Realizing the men were going to have to take another car, Roman stopped her. "Take the front seat. Tom, you drive. Niles, Logan, and I will take the Defender," he said.

"No, I want you with us," Gabby said, sounding frantic.

"There's no room. We'll be right behind you," Roman said, handing Tom the box with the gun. "Take this. We're going to stop at Landon's and get the others; now go."

Tom ran around the giant SUV, got into the driver's seat, and started the engine. Roman and Logan shut the back doors to the Ford, and Niles shut the door for Zolie. She put down her window, and Niles leaned his head in. "Tom, go left and follow the road. You'll see the main road to the hotel at the stop sign; turn right," he said.

Tom nodded. "Got it," he said. Tom put the VelociRaptor in reverse and backed out from the driveway.

Roman, Logan, and Niles watched the behemoth SUV move away and onto the street. Niles pushed the garage button, closing the doors, and they got into the red Defender.

From inside the Ford, Maura saw them moving away. "Where are they going?" she shouted.

Tom looked in the rearview mirror. "Landon's house, the guns are there," he said, handing the box to Zolie.

She opened it, seeing the only weapon they had, and looked at her husband with worry.

Getting to Landon's, Roman grabbed the remote and opened the garage door, and the three went inside. The house was empty of furniture, and they went to the kitchen where the last of the appliances were being installed. When they walked out the back sliding glass door to the guesthouse, there was a lockbox on the knob, and Niles punched in the number, opened it, and retrieved the key.

Inside, Niles had been right. There were boxes stored there, and they quickly found the guns. They each took one and made sure it was loaded. They then went back to the Defender to find the tires had been slashed. Niles panicked and ran around the back of the vehicle to look at the other side.

The shotgun fired from the house next door, hitting Niles dead in the throat. His head was almost torn from his body as he hit the driveway. Another Savage, the guiltiest of them all, was finally dead.

Roman and Logan pressed themselves up against the house, knowing the shot had come from somewhere above. Seeing Niles lying dead in the driveway, his blood painting it, shocked them. Roman started to move and grabbed Logan to follow him. They ran to the next house, staying as close to the front as they could. Stopping, they glanced back only once; then they ran all the way back to Chance's home, where they saw that the tires of the Defender left there were also slashed. They then ran to the backyard and down to the beach, heading quickly back up to the hotel.

On the far side of Landon's home, Patty leaned against her motorcycle with a shotgun in hand, admiring her work.

CHAPTER 100

At the hotel, Marlo picked up the first phone she found; it was dead. Maggie had run to another across the room. "It's not working. The phones aren't working," Maggie cried.

Sam led them to the kitchen. They picked up each and every phone as they went, but all were dead.

Stopping, Marlo picked up a large knife in the kitchen, and Sam opened the storage-room door. Inside were rows of dried goods, and in the back, another door led across a service hall to another storage room where the shotguns were stored in their boxes. Ed followed Sam to the back and ripped open the boxes, unpacking the guns and taking the locks off the handles.

Aisha looked up and saw that the shells were in other boxes higher up on the shelf. She grabbed a stepladder and leaned it against the shelf. Climbing up, she grabbed the boxes, and the ladder wobbled, causing Aisha to lose her balance and fall.

Ed tossed the empty gun on the counter and caught her. Their eyes locked again, and this time, Sam saw it; the spark between them was undeniable.

Sam turned away and saw Marlo at the door, watching. Knife in hand, her grip visibly tightened. She had seen it, too.

"Hurry!" Maggie cried out.

Marlo could feel something strange in her mind, and she followed her sister in silence.

With the guns, the others followed her out and moved quickly from the kitchen to the lobby. Marlo and Aisha ran around the front desk to try the phones. Maggie found Zolie's note about going to the Mystic Theater and held it up to Ed and Sam. "This must be old," she said.

Ed and Sam looked at it at the same time as Marlo and Aisha put down the phones. "Still dead," Aisha said, just as Marlo was about to say something similar. She shot Aisha a cold look.

Sam took the note from Maggie and tossed it on the counter. "Come on," he said, moving to the doors.

Outside, in the parking lot, Marcus Bowers was at his red Ford Explorer pulling out a shotgun from the back. He opened the front passenger door and dug in his mailbag briefcase on the seat, searching for the ammunition. He pulled them out, stuffing them into his jacket pocket, causing papers to spill out onto the seat. He looked up to see the side door of the hotel opening and quickly shut his own, running away to find the perfect hiding place.

Rushing through the side door, they hurried to the parking lot, where Ed's car was parked not far from Aisha's. They noticed all four tires were flat.

"No way!" Marlo shrieked.

Aisha looked at her vehicle. "Mine too!" she said.

Shocked, they looked to all the other vehicles in the parking lot. All tires were flat, except for one a little farther out, which Ed spotted. "Wait, that one," he said, pointing.

The red Ford Explorer was parked near an island garden, and they ran to it. The tires were fine, but the vehicle was locked. On the front passenger floor was an open messenger bag, and on the seat were papers. Part of a driver's license could be seen. On one of the papers, the last name of "Savage" was clearly printed, but the first name was covered with an envelope. Seeing this, Ed turned to the others. "Whose car is this?" he demanded, looking right at the Storm sisters.

No one knew.

Ed looked to the garden and picked up a rock. He then told everyone to stand back as he smashed the window. He reached in and hit the door locks, pulling out the papers and the driver's license. It had Ed's name on it with the photo of the captain, Marcus Bowers.

Ed showed Aisha the license, and she again confirmed that was the guy she'd been reading about. The realization that Marcus Bowers, a charlatan with one agenda, had manipulated a mentally unstable woman for the sole purpose of swindling his family built a rage inside him he had never felt before. Ed saw this clearly. He saw the simple, twisted truth of greed from a maniacally diseased mind. "He did this! He's the one that started all this!" Ed yelled in anger.

Sam opened the driver's door and looked for the keys. "No keys. Now what?"

Marlo became hysterical. "They're not letting us go. They want us here!" she said, raising her voice as panic set in. She turned into Ed's arms. "Ed, Ed! Get us out of here," she pleaded.

Ed held her, looking to Sam. "Any ideas?" he asked.

Sandy Storm had had enough. She was scared and done playing Brenda Starr with her evil bitch sister. "That's it! See you." Pulling away from Wendy, she marched off into the parking lot toward the exit.

"Where are you going?" Wendy demanded, following her.

Sandy turned and reached for her keys, rolling her eyes. "The stupid keys are in my sweater," she screamed out. "Lucy has it!"

Wendy ran to her and shook her hard, raising her voice. "We'll be fine. We're with them now. Calm down," she said.

Sandy looked at the others. "With them?" she screamed back. "They're on some psycho's fucking menu! Now who's the stupid bitch?" she screamed in Wendy's face; then she shoved her, hard, running off toward the main road.

Wendy regained her balance and looked to the others. She then chased after her sister, just as the hard rain began as the last of the light left the sky.

Sam started to go after them, but the blast from the shotgun hitting the Explorer in front of him, shattering the windows, stopped him in his tracks.

Ed grabbed Sam's arm, and he turned, running back with Marlo, Maggie, and Aisha. The five of them headed toward the hotel, and they could hear the Storm sisters screaming.

Marcus fired again, just missing Ed and hitting Aisha's car, shattering the windows. He then lowered the shotgun with a smile.

The sound of the shotgun was heard down at the beach, and Roman and Logan were at the dock when they heard it from above. They hid against the dock pilings for cover, and when it looked clear, they raced to the stairs under the wet sky.

Wendy and Sandy ran toward the gated entrance of the hotel; the gates were now closed and locked with a chain. They ran into them, trying to open them, and discovered that they had been officially locked in. The gates were tall and slick with the rain as they tried to climb them. Failing, they turned and ran back toward the hotel, not even noticing the motorcycle parked inside the property as they ran past, scared for their very lives.

Wendy and Sandy ran toward the lobby, but Marcus fired in their direction, and they took off toward the Mystic Theater. They had no paths left to choose from. And all Marcus Bowers could do was laugh as he watched them race forward to their deaths.

CHAPTER 101

Stevie Galloway woke up in the lighthouse. Hurting and angry with herself for ever falling for Marcus and his big bag of lies, she got to her feet. Eyeing the duffel bag, she opened it and emptied it out, finding the documents and learning of Marcus's scheme. She then opened the closet and screamed at seeing the dead captain. Frightened, she opened the front door and ran into the rain toward the old stairs, crossing over a raised walkway where the surf pooled near the cliff, leading from the lighthouse up to the Mystic Theater.

As Stevie was nearing the top of the old and partly rotted stairs, one of the steps broke and her foot fell through. Scared and afraid, she pulled herself up and made it to the top; she then ran up the wet grassy slope, slipping and getting to her feet, before running right into Patty. She rushed to her, grabbing on to her shoulders. "Oh, thank God. Patty, we have to get out of here. Marcus is insane!"

Patty pulled away from her, screaming, "No, Marcus is right! We have a plan. They all must die!"

Stevie's blood turned ice-cold as she finally saw the sadistic work of Marcus on her vulnerable sister's brain. "No, Patty. We need to stop this now. We need to stop Marcus," she pleaded. "He's lying to you!" she cried out in fear.

Patty moved away from Stevie and tilted her head. Her facial expression turned darker. The mad rage consumed her, and she swung the shotgun, hitting her sister in the side of the head and knocking her over, back down the slick grassy slope.

Stevie fell and rolled toward the staircase. The pain in her head was throbbing, and by the time she got back up, Patty was gone.

CHAPTER 102

Choices had to be made.

Back inside the hotel lobby, Ed and Sam led the women to the employee area behind the front desk. There was an office and, beyond that, a hallway that extended to the far exit near a two-level restaurant and bar, and serving area. They ran down the long hallway into a second kitchen. There, the empty conveyors of the dishwashing machine from the upstairs dining area sat silent, but the dimly lit room was eerily filled with shadows from the monstrous machine.

Exiting the kitchen to the main-floor dining area near the bluffs, they could see the stairs leading to where the future skeet-shooting area would be. Beyond the bluff, Ed remembered that the Mystic Theater sat silently, where he wanted to shoot a segment for one of his shows. The place would be perfect for hiding, he thought, as the lightning flashed and the rain pounded on the windows outside.

Nearing the Mystic Theater, Wendy and Sandy ran to the damaged fence and climbed up and through the bent portion. Wendy got through first and ran ahead of Sandy, who got caught momentarily when the fence tore her blouse. She freed herself and ran to catch up to her sister.

Sandy could see Wendy running up ahead as she passed an old pond, now full of mud and stagnant water. She slipped and fell into it, screaming out for help.

Wendy stopped and turned, her wet hair flying behind her, to see Sandy pulling herself up from the water. "Hurry!" Wendy screamed.

Sandy got up to see the ranger looming behind her sister. She screamed out, pointing, "Behind you!"

Wendy turned just as the ranger violently grabbed her by the throat. Pulling the knife, he plunged it into her chest.

Screaming, Sandy ran into the tall grass of the bluff, as the rain poured down and lightning struck overhead.

The ranger saw Sandy run, and he dropped Wendy to the ground. He took a few steps away as she choked up blood. He heard her and turned his head, just as Wendy opened her eyes in fear. The ranger lunged, grabbing her and dragging her to the pond. He slammed Wendy into the water face-first, suffocating her in the mud.

Her kicking died out as he pulled her head up, shoving it down again, over and over, before holding it there until her last gasp of air bubbled to the surface.

The recording device strapped to her wrist was above the water, taping the reporter's own demise.

Ed opened the doors, and the group made their way up the stairs toward the area where the skeet shooting would be. At the top, they ran into the tall grass of the bluff toward the Mystic Theater.

Sandy looked back and screamed for her poor sister and hid in the tall grass.

Roman and Logan got to the lobby and went out the side door. They saw the flat tires on Ed's Range Rover and stopped dead. But as they were about to go back inside the hotel, they heard a woman screaming and ran toward the bluff.

Ed and Sam, also hearing the screams, pushed the women down into the grass to wait.

There was no way to know where the villain was hiding.

CHAPTER 103

Down the road, on the highway, Tom was speeding in the VelociRaptor in the rain when someone's cell phone rang. Realizing they were in a service area, everyone who had their phones with them pulled them out to call the police. It was Amanda's phone that rang, but when she tried to answer it, she accidentally disconnected the call, seeing it was from her girlfriend, Jacqueline Holt.

Danni got through and was telling the police what was happening at the Vander Place Hotel, when the car behind them sped up, slamming into them and attempting to push them off the road.

Marcus's minions in their hotel uniforms were in a Pontiac Aztek, which was no match for the VelociRaptor. The Pontiac lost control when they hit the larger vehicle, and the driver slammed on the brakes, skidding on the wet pavement. The Pontiac went off the road, hitting a boulder and spinning in the air as it caught fire and turned over into a ditch. They were frantically screaming as they tried to open the doors, but the twisted metal and walls of the ditch kept them trapped inside. The fire reached the gas tank, exploding the Pontiac and turning it into their very own crematorium.

With the hit, Tom swerved lightly, but it was enough for the VelociRaptor's passenger-side tires to hit the loose-gravel embankment on the curve of the wet road. Tom tried turning the wheel, but the giant SUV leaned and rolled several times, landing at an angle on top of large boulders.

As the SUV rolled, the glass exploded inward, and the hood and doors opened, sending debris into the cab. The only one not wearing her seatbelt got the worst from the powerful crash. Gabby and Maura reached out to Chase, Macy, and Ty together, trying to hold them down in the roll. But Lucy, who was too busy fantasizing about Logan and just didn't care about sharing a seatbelt, was ejected from the door. She flew out onto the rocks, snapping multiple bones and landing in a stream, hitting her head, she struggled, and drowning in water she could have easily raised from had her bones not been broken.

As much as Gabby and Maura tried to protect their already hurt children, the rollover seemed too much. Maura screamed as she tried to wake her daughter, Macy. She looked over the seat and saw Gabby lying motionless, slumped against her son, blood dripping from her mouth, and the panicked cries of the others filled her ears.

CHAPTER 104

The rain had let up as Ed rose from the grass; he spotted the stairs leading to the lighthouse and signaled the others, and they got themselves up. Maggie looked back at the hotel; she could see her room on the upper floor, where she had left the light on, and she wished she were in the safety of the dry and warm room. When she turned back to the lighthouse, the sound exploded behind her. The shell Marcus fired hit her squarely in her back.

Marlo screamed as the warm spray of blood washed over her. *Maggie, Simon, Lisa...*Marlo's mind snapped in an instant as Maggie's dead body fell into her, knocking her back into the tall wet grass.

Sam grabbed Aisha and pushed her down to the left to keep her away from the evil that followed. He couldn't be there for Cara, but he wasn't going to let another innocent soul be taken by the madness they were trapped in.

Ed dove to Marlo; her cries were uncontrollable, and he knew they needed to be silent. It was their only way to survive this night. Ed's training had prepared him for situations like this, but the women were sitting ducks.

Marlo looked at Maggie's face; the look of terror in her dead sister's face was horrifying. She screamed as if her mission were to wake the dead. Ed crawled to her and wrapped his arms around her, placing his hand over her mouth.

Marlo kicked and thrashed, as if a demon had reached up from the ground and was taking her. Ed let go of the shotgun to handle his wife. Aisha saw what was happening, and she moved over and threw herself over Marlo's legs to help calm her. She saw Ed's shotgun and knew Marlo's screams were giving them away.

Sam kept his eye on the direction the shot had come from and stayed hidden in the grass. He watched the man he knew to be Marcus moving toward them, toward his family. He could hear the scuffle with Marlo and prayed his only chance would work. He watched, and his heart beat loudly as Marcus walked right past him without seeing him, stopped, and raised his gun at his family.

It was now or never.

Sam stood and fired. And in the silence that followed, he froze for a moment. *No, not now.* The gun jammed, and the panic took him as he tried to shoot again, causing Marcus to hear and turn toward him with his gun raised. Sam saw the crafty bastard looking right at him; his mind flashed to Cara, and the rage inside ignited.

The blast was hard, knocking Aisha back down, and she dropped the gun in the grass. It was as if Aisha were an angel, sent to the Savages from above. The wind from the shot blew past Marcus, missing him. He flinched and turned for a moment, and Sam charged, slamming into the devil, knocking the gun from his hands, and tackling him to the ground.

The two rolled, and Marcus elbowed him in his wounded right shoulder. Sam recoiled and Marcus rolled over and got on top of him and punched him in the face.

Ed got up, and as Marcus pulled back his fist to punch Sam again, Ed grabbed his arm and pulled it back with a snap. Marcus twisted around and stood, facing him, and Ed punched him in the jaw, knocking out a tooth.

Marcus fell into the grass, and Ed was instantly on him. He grabbed him by the throat and punched him in the face. Even when his fist was dripping blood, he kept punching.

Sandy Storm heard the shot and extricated herself from her hiding place, and she came running toward them. Not knowing the ranger was near until it was too late, she began screaming. The ranger was close behind her.

Sam pulled Ed back, afraid he didn't see the ranger.

Ed reached for the gun Marcus had dropped, and Sam stumbled against him bringing them both down into the grass, and Marcus sat up and got to his feet, his face dripping blood onto his shirt. He eyed the women.

Marlo and Aisha screamed. As Marcus went after them, they ran toward the stairs to the lighthouse.

The lightning flashed across the sky over the water, like it was shooting right at them. Sam pulled Ed up, with Sandy about thirty yards from them. She continued to run, screaming, when another flash of lightning came and illuminated the ranger right behind her. He threw his knife, hitting her in the back. She fell forward, and her head hit a rock on the ground.

Sam and Ed saw the ranger, but they turned and ran after Marcus. The fire in Ed's veins pushed him faster, and he was able to reach out and tackle Marcus, dropping his gun, and when they landed, Ed heard the bone snap further in his target's arm.

They rolled in the grass, with Ed landing on top of him. Ed shoved his face into the earth and pulled his right arm up behind him, twisting it behind Marcus's body with such force that more bone broke, issuing an even louder crack. The humerus splintered into a sharp shard that tore through the flesh of his arm. Blood sprayed from his limb and Marcus screamed out, the pain nearly knocking him unconsciousness. With his arm held behind him, the sharpened bone was now pointing directly into Marcus's rib cage.

Don't go, Daddy… The voice from his precious daughter filled Ed's head, and the anger inside him exploded. He threw all his weight onto Marcus's elbow, pushing his bone into his own rib cage, piercing his lung. He twisted his arm and pushed down hard, forcing his heart into his sternum.

Marcus screamed out; his chest was exploding, and he was gasping for air.

Ed rolled him over and punched him across the face. Marcus smiled as the blood spat out of his mouth. "I enjoyed your little *nugget* before we killed her."

Rage consumed Ed, and he reached down, grabbing Marcus's neck as he gasped for air from his collapsed lung. "Have fun meeting your hero in hell, you sick fuck!" Ed said, with hate in his eyes.

Twisting the psycho's neck, Ed snapped it, killing him instantly. Marcus Bowers would torment no more.

Sam had run after the women, and the ranger followed. When Marlo and Aisha got near the stairs, Patty was there, holding the shotgun.

The women screamed; they turned back to see the ranger getting closer behind Sam. They were trapped, and they turned, hearing Patty laugh as she pumped the shell into the chamber.

Stevie ran from behind Patty, knocking her down. Her shotgun went off, hitting Sam in the same shoulder that had been injured in the mountains. Sam spun to his right, hitting the ground.

The ranger grabbed Marlo and Aisha and threw them down the slick slope of the wet grass onto the landing at the top of the stairs, near the ledge. They went down a few steps; the railing Aisha hit broke off from rot, and she jumped away from it. Ed grabbed Marcus's shotgun and ran up behind the ranger, aiming at his right side. The ranger moved, and it hit him in the shoulder. He fell forward just as the old stairs broke apart and started to separate from the cliff's edge.

Ed got to the wooden landing in time. Dropping the gun, he hooked his legs under the twisted roots of one of the old, windblown trees haunting the landscape. He reached out, and both women grabbed his arms as the stairs started to break away. They fell against the cliff, holding on to him as tightly as they could.

Patty then broke away from Stevie and grabbed the shotgun, raising it just as Roman and Logan ran up behind her. They both dived, tackling her, dropping their guns and knocking her forward, breaking her back.

Logan landed on his shoulder and somersaulted over and slid down the grassy slope to the landing of the stairs, sliding feetfirst into Ed's legs, smashing a rock into his right knee with the heel of his shoe.

The pain was immense. Ed yelled out, and his vision blurred; he nearly let go of the women. Marlo and Aisha were screaming not to let them fall, and Roman got to the edge and reached down, grabbing Marlo, who was the closest.

Logan got his bearings and rolled over, reaching down to help Roman pull Marlo up.

Ed was holding on to Aisha with one hand. The pain from his knee was close to causing him to black out, but he fought it and was able to reach down and grab her with his other hand. The weight shifted from his arms, and the pain in his knee shot red-hot daggers up his leg. He yelled for help, and Logan reached down and grabbed Aisha.

Roman then reached down, and they pulled her up, pushing her to the grass. Roman and Logan turned and helped Ed up, when Aisha and Marlo screamed yet again.

The ranger had grabbed Aisha and was choking her, and the three brothers moved from the cliff. Sam crawled to Patty's shotgun and grabbed it. He got to his knees and fired, hitting the ranger in the right hip.

Melvin screamed out. Ed saw Marcus's gun and went for it as Roman and Logan went for theirs. The ranger dropped one hand from Aisha's neck to his newly injured hip, and she ripped at his face with her nails. He swung her around, letting go and dropping her, stumbling toward the cliff.

Ed raised his gun and fired, hitting him in the right side of the chest. Roman and Logan both raised their shotguns and fired, hitting him in the left clavicle and throat. Sam stood and fired again, hitting him in the abdomen as Ed shot him in the face.

Melvin fell backward, and Logan, Roman, Sam, and Ed fired in unison. He went over the cliff just as the remaining rotted staircase separated. He fell on a jagged support beam, impaling him, splitting him in half as the stairs crumbled to the rocks and raised walkway below, and burying him in the smashing surf.

Aisha got to her feet just as Sam fell backward into the grass, and she ran to him. He was bleeding badly, and she applied pressure with her bare hands. Ed got to him and took over applying pressure. Together, they stayed with him.

In the distance, red-and-blue police and rescue lights could be seen approaching the hotel.

It was about time.

PART 3
ED SAVAGE AND THE SAVAGE
HIT–SAVING SAVAGE

CHAPTER 105

Sam was rushed into surgery. Ed was also hospitalized for his knee, and Roman and Logan were being looked over along with Marlo and Aisha, when the news of Tom's rollover came in.

Ed was having his knee wrapped. He needed surgery, too, but it could wait.

Stevie and Patty had been arrested, but Patty had been taken for a CAT scan with her broken back. To everyone's surprise, Sandy Storm was alive, and she was rushed to surgery.

As the ambulances arrived one by one with a Savage in each, the panic grew. Logan was there when Macy was rushed in through the doors with a tech on top of her giving her chest compressions. Maura had thought the worst when she couldn't get her to wake up in the crash, and the hope showed on her bruised face as she was led in with Ty on a stretcher beside her. Besides his broken ribs, he further injured his ankle, breaking it to add to his pain; Maura herself, although bruised, suffered no further injuries. Logan rushed to their side, and the fright of losing Macy was insurmountable for them all.

Chase was next to come through the doors. His head was bandaged, and he was rushed right past Roman. Roman tried to get answers, but he was pushed aside and told to wait beyond the doors. Watching his son being wheeled down the corridor for tests before surgery, he turned, hearing his daughter call out for him.

"Daddy!"

Roman saw Danni's tear-filled face and her bandaged arm in a sling as she was pushed in a wheelchair beside her mother on a stretcher. Roman's shocked face filled with tears as he ran to his wife and daughter.

"She's pregnant," he yelled.

"Yes, sir, we're aware of it; now step aside, please," a paramedic said.

Danni leaned into her father's arms and burst into tears. Roman just held her as he watched his wife follow his son through the same doors.

"Mom won't wake up, Dad!" Danni cried hysterically. Roman looked to his daughter as she continued, "I tried hanging on to Lucy, but I couldn't keep her inside."

A second paramedic showed up with a gurney, and Roman picked her up and laid his daughter down on it. "She's got a broken arm, sir," the paramedic informed him as they wheeled her into a trauma bay.

"And Lucy?" Roman asked.

The paramedic shook his head.

As a nurse pulled the curtain around them to undress his daughter, Roman held in his desire to break down, scared out of his mind over his family.

Zolie and Tom were next to be wheeled in, black-and-blue from the air bags hitting them and the rolling of the vehicle. Amanda had a broken right clavicle and left forearm; for the amount of trauma she'd sustained, she was holding it together, more worried for her parents. They were lined up side by side in the trauma bays next to Danni.

Heather and Ava both came in right behind each other, each crying and scared. Ed followed the girls into the trauma bay and was listening to both sets of techs, nurses, and doctors at the same time. His mind was bouncing back and forth between the two.

Heather had hit her chin and split her lip from hitting the glass when they'd rolled; she had also suffered a broken tibia, like Simon had.

Ava had two black eyes and a busted nose, and like Amanda, she had also suffered a broken left forearm.

Marcus Bowers may have won some battles, but the Savage bloodline still remained.

CHAPTER 106

The days that followed were tough…once they were all back home. Aisha was alone, staring out her window at a city that seemed to have changed overnight. The last few days had been hard on her, to say the least. When she'd gotten home from that awful night, she had gone to Danny's apartment and let herself in with her key, only to find him in bed with his ex. She took off her ring and dropped it on the floor then and there, and ran out. Danny later tried to patch things up, but it was done. All they did was fight. She was done, and she broke it off with him, deciding to hide for a bit and keep a low profile.

Logan, Maura, and Ty stayed at their condo in the city; it was closer than Zolie's estate to Berman Medical Center where Macy was recovering once they'd repaired her pneumothorax. Her collapsed lung was so fragile that they had to keep the chest tubes in for a longer recovery than expected. Ty's ankle was operated on, and his ribs had to heal on their own, making breathing—or worse, sneezing—a nightmare.

Chase Savage was in the hospital room right next to Macy's. They were able to repair the fracture on the orbit of his eye, and he too had a long recovery. Danni's arm was operated on, and she was wearing a cast; her cheerleading was something she never thought about missing. The worst part was Gabby losing the baby. In the accident, Gabby had gotten the wind knocked out of her and passed out, and the resulting trauma during the rollover had caused her to miscarry. Roman hated the fact she had lost it but was thankful that his family was still with him.

Both Roman and Logan thought about moving once their families were well, a thought that was on all the Savages' minds.

Tom Kenowith flew home to London to attend to business at his company, leaving Zolie and Amanda at their mansion not far from Sam's and Ed's homes. Zolie didn't want to leave the grounds and was happy when her son, Liam Hart, whom she had had with Andrew Hart from one of her many marriages, arrived to comfort her. Strangely enough, she began writing as a way to let go of what had happened during those horrible few days. To her surprise, she had a novel in the making.

With Sam at home alone with Heather recovering, Ed wanted to be at his side, and when he asked Ava if she'd like to move in with them, she eagerly agreed. Ava wouldn't set foot in their old home after Ellie had been murdered there, and told her father she wanted to move like all her cousin's were talking about. Ed had Roman and Logan list his home for sale, and the repairs were underway after the murder. Too many things were happening in all their lives, including Ed's knee surgery. It went well, except he was told to use a cane for the next few weeks, a necessity he could really do without.

Marlo had a full mental breakdown. Losing her sister was the last straw, and she filed for divorce from Ed Savage. She moved back into the Four Seasons and would not see anyone except her doctors and her lawyers. The money Ed had inherited was huge, and she was going to collect big-time. That was…until Jillian York's little secret came out.

When Jillian York had cheated on Ed with Jeremy Bigelow, she had slept with Ed the night before, and the next day Ed had found her in her bubble bath, washing off the sex she'd just had with Jeremy. She was pregnant, and the baby was Ed's; she found out years later with a DNA test.

She'd left town by the time she started to show, afraid she would lose Jeremy Bigelow, and her lawyers did all her communicating. She told Jeremy she needed time away for the divorce and had the baby at her sister's. Her sister had two children of her own, and after going through a divorce, she needed money. So Jillian devised a plan for her sister to raise her son, and she sent her money each month. It worked out well. Her sister was great with kids.

Jillian had caught Jeremy with another woman later on, and she hated it. He didn't care, and he said it wouldn't matter to him if they divorced.

She had wanted out for some time, and when the news of the Savage inheritance hit the papers, she waited a bit to make her play.

Jillian's announcement hit the papers, and everyone saw it. Ed had a son older than Tucker, a son Ed was dying to meet.

Marlo Savage wasn't worried though. She now had a little secret of her own. She was pregnant. But when Marlo saw the news of Jillian's secret, the gloves came off. She told her lawyers to sue for everything she could get, and she focused all of her pain and loss into the divorce. Somehow that was easier for her to do; it was certainly better than drooling in a hospital bed.

Then there was the pregnancy. Although they had fought leading up to the trip to the mountains, on the morning UPS delivered his grill for his Challenger, they had made up and had a fun time before getting out of bed. Marlo still had feelings for Ed, and now, with a baby to think about, sometimes she would even think that maybe they could work things out. Every time she thought she had it figured out, something would change, and she was back to square one.

It was later, when Marlo had gone shopping to pick up a few things she needed at Donert's Department Store, that she'd run right into Jillian York Savage Bigelow. When the two came face-to-face, it was ugly.

Jillian was all smiles: "Marlo, so good running into you. I was hoping we could talk."

Jillian was the last person Marlo wanted to see, let alone talk with. "What in the world would we have to talk about, Jillian?" Marlo asked, really not caring.

Jillian smiled coldly. "My son, of course. He wants to meet his father, and from what I hear, Ed can't wait to meet him." Jillian laughed. "It's funny, you know. I hear you're about to divorce Ed, and here I am with his firstborn son." Greed flashed in her eyes. "Interesting, isn't it?"

Marlo had looked Jillian up and down and simply laughed. "You know, Jillian, I thought I met the top tier of crazy and delusional from a place called Black Ridge Falls. But she had nothing on you! Good thing I took notes." Marlo laughed snidely. "You really are a fool. A blind fool at that," Marlo added.

Jillian took a step back. "Oh, am I? Well, time will tell, now, won't it, dear?"

Marlo had heard stories about Jillian over the years and knew she was a grade-A bitch. She smiled knowingly. "If you think Ed would put his hands on a filthy slut like you again, you may as well take the padded cell right next to Patty's. I hear it's available." Marlo flashed her eyes at Jillian. "But you were right about one thing, *sweetie*; it sure was good running into you."

Marlo laughed in Jillian's face as she walked away from her that day, leaving Jillian York with a scared feeling in her gut that her scheme was not going to end up the way she wanted it to.

Standing nearby in the department store, Amanda's girlfriend Jacqueline Holt had arrived in the States on business and witnessed the entire exchange.

The story the reporter got from Marlo at the funeral was juicy. The contract that had gone to the now-deceased Cara Vanderran Savage for *Tycoon Wives* had been done in secret, and Marlo mentioned it unknowingly when they were talking. She told the reporter that Cara had been so excited to join the cast and that Cara had asked her to think about filming with her. The truth was, she wanted to be on the show herself, and she threw that out there to see what would happen. While it was true she didn't know it was a secret, and Cara did want to film with her, Marlo also knew Zolie's second or third husband was married to the current queen bee of the show: Marilyn Hart. Which would make it all the more fun.

The entertainment gossip shows picked it up and splashed it all over, along with all the other Savage news that week. Marilyn Hart was enraged. So was Zolie Vanderran.

Ed got a call from his agent, Rachel Shepherd, to meet her at her office. The voice mail was dry, and he didn't know what to make of it, and he was worried.

When he arrived, Rachel greeted him just as dryly as her voice mail and walked him back to her corner office. There, on the table near the windows, were stacks of fan mail. It was piled on some of the chairs and on the floor. She motioned Ed to it like a model would do with a new car. Ed looked at her, surprised. "What's all this?" he asked.

Rachel finally smiled. "Go ahead, it's all yours," she said.

Ed limped over on his cane and looked at the mail, picking up an envelope. It was all addressed to him at the studio. He picked up another and looked back at Rachel. She was glowing. "All your fans. Right after the funerals, the mail started pouring in. Ed, I did open a few at first, and they were all supportive."

Ed smiled and tore one open; inside was a beautiful card wishing him well, with comments about how they loved his shows.

Ed got choked up as Rachel moved to her desk and pulled out the contract and the recorder she'd had at their meeting with Milton.

Ed looked up from his card with a smile. "I can't believe this. I'm touched, here," he said with a smile. "What's that you got there?"

Rachel smiled. "Ed, that day at Milton's, you had a lot on your mind, and I don't think you caught it," she said.

Ed's gaze filled with questions.

"You were smart to add that clause from the *Phantom Finders* disaster."

Ed looked back in thought and then smiled.

"When Milton said they were stopping all your shows for something that had nothing to do with you, personally, he activated the escape clause built into your contracts. Plain as day, Ed, you did nothing wrong, and they acted on things done by your father decades ago. Things you had no control over. Had Milton actually *read* your contracts, he never would have said it. And I got it all on tape," she said, holding up the recorder.

Ed knew it was Niles and not his father who had started all this and wondered if that part of the story would ever get leaked, but he kept it to himself. "So where does that leave us now?" he asked.

Rachel smiled and handed him the contract.

Ed took one look at it, and his eyes lit up. "Trask Studios!" he said.

"Ed, Conner Trask himself came to my office. He's the grandson of the founder, and he's about your age. He said his studio wanted to jump at the chance to get your shows, and he made an attractive offer," she said.

Ed was beaming.

"By the way, Milton O'Malley also offered to keep things as they were once the fan mail started arriving," Rachel said.

Ed had a choice to make, and the stipulations of his father's will were in his mind.

Rachel's secretary buzzed, telling her Conner Trask was back and wanted to see her. He was sent right in. Seeing Ed Savage standing near his mail, Conner smiled. "Ed Savage, Conner Trask; good to finally meet you." He extended his hand.

"Pleasure is mine," Ed said, shaking his hand.

"I'm so sorry for what you've been through."

"Thank you." Ed nodded.

Conner picked up a handful of mail. "Rachel, sorry to stop by without calling, but all this mail impressed me last time I was here, and I came up with a thought. As a sign-on bonus, how about a contest? A fan contest to write about their dream episode, with the winner's idea not only being produced, they would also get to be on the show with Ed in a limited capacity. What do you think?" he said.

Ed was floored; he hadn't even had the time to think of anything. "I love it," Ed said, extending his hand to shake Conner's yet again. "I think it's time for some fresh energy in my circle."

Conner smiled, putting down the mail. "Great. Ed, look over the contract and get back to me; the sooner, the better," he added, looking to Rachel. "I'll have the contest contract over here in the morning. And sorry again for dropping by without calling, but now I have to be going."

Rachel smiled. "You don't ever need to call," she said, and they all shared a laugh as she walked Conner out.

"Has legal read this?" Ed asked.

"Yeah, and it looks good, but there'll be some changes, Ed," Rachel told him.

"Changes?"

"They want you in *Precinct Wars*, Ed. The ratings pushed Trask's production in the top three, and their offering you the role on the cop show as the lawyer for the next season. They also offered an opportunity to spin the character off to new series down the line, depending on the show's numbers." Rachel was watching Ed and could tell he was already thinking of the impossible workload.

"Rachel, I loved doing those few episodes, but I don't see how I could do it."

"And here it is…Ed, you need to take some time here. What they're offering is to cut your current workload, not do as many of your current shows, to make room for *Precinct Wars.*"

Ed thought of the clause he amended to his Titan Studios contract and thought of one he could add in with Trask, allowing him thirty days once the final schedule of current shows was completed to opt out, should they finally not come to an understanding. He wanted to look into the possibility of moving forward away from Milton and dealing with the will of his father.

Rachel moved to her desk. "Why don't you think on it and call me in a few days?"

"Thanks, I'll get back to you with this soon."

"Great. Oh, and get a haircut; I've got interviews set up," she said.

The Stephen Bay film was an action picture, which he was also offered. The problem was his knee injury; the filming schedule was starting too soon. He could use a body double, and the decision was made for him. With too much happening, he had to sadly decline the offer.

Quietly he left Rachel's office, not telling her of the stipulations of that damn will from hell his father had bestowed on him. Now with his father gone, it would be just him and his brothers; thoughts of a new Savage Construction filled his head on his way for a haircut.

At Berman Medical Center, Sandy Storm woke up to find a note on her nightstand. It simply stated they were sorry for her loss and her hospital bill had been paid. And it was signed with the initial S.

CHAPTER 107

arnell F. Bancroft was a smart man. At the end of the day, he thought about when he had sent over the thick folder containing all the deeds of properties and stocks and directions to Nathan Savage's will. He then sat back at his desk and lit a cigar. He turned in his chair and looked out his fifty-third-floor window at Savage Tower.

Savage Tower was busy, with reporters standing outside trying to get a story. Up in his office, Sam Savage had received the thick documents and was going through them, shocked at what he found. There was a loophole in Nathan's will concerning Ed having to stay with the company for ten years. And it actually allowed Ed to not be as involved as it sounded.

He laughed to himself. Parnell had made millions from his father over the years, and he definitely wanted to keep the relationship open. What better way than to allow such an easy mistake, a mistake Sam could easily find in the language of the ultimate contract that the pompous Nathan Savage had signed. Without knowing it, his father had put his faith in a document that actually allowed Ed to do just as he pleased as long as he stayed with the company. It was something that would most definitely have his father rolling over in his grave.

When the documents arrived from Parnell F. Bancroft's office to Savage Tower, Nathan's secretary, Sally Anne Cartwright, under directions from Nathan Savage when he was alive, made a copy and sent them to a PO box address Nathan had given her. She then delivered the originals to Sam's office.

The day they arrived at the PO box, an Asian woman entered the post office and picked them up. She then closed the PO box at the counter, telling them she was moving, and the forwarding address had already been put in. She then delivered the copies of Nathan's will to a black limousine waiting outside, to a man behind a window she could not see; only his black sleeve and gloved hand had been visible.

CHAPTER 108

At Savage Tower, in the conference room, Logan was helping Roman set up the current projects and future developments the company was working on. There were easels showing the renderings and stacks of folders neatly placed on the table.

The new mall addition was in its final phase, and a high-rise apartment tower was midway through. The Vander Place Hotel was complete, and the skeet area was under construction. Preparations for the grand opening were on hold. The Vanderran dining yacht had been towed away; they were waiting on the insurance payout to replace it. The dock was still damaged, but the construction was underway.

After his meeting with his agent and haircut, Ed Savage went back to his office. His mind was heavy with everything that had happened and the new contract he had received. He really enjoyed playing the lawyer and wanted to show Sam his contract and talk to him about their dad's will.

Getting out from the elevator, he passed the conference room and saw his brothers inside. Ed limped into the room, not noticing what they were doing. "Hey. What's going on in here?" he asked.

Logan was adjusting the rendering of the mall project on the easel, and he turned to him. "Hey there, Eastman's Mall is finishing up right on schedule, and Eastman just sent over another project for us to take a look at, one of his older malls," Logan said, picking up a folder from the table. "Got the prospects right here."

Roman was at the far end of the conference room, standing near an easel with the rendering of Donert Tower, with some folders in his hands. Don Roberts had started Donert's, a retail department store, many years ago and had grown it into one of the major retailers in the United States. The eighty-eight-story tower was to be his flagship store, offices, and hotel. There was just one problem. The contract had gone to Bigelow Construction.

Roman finished stacking the folders on the table and smiled. "Ed, glad you're here. I wanted to go over where we are on our projects, and I have some thoughts on upcoming ones as well."

Ed gazed at the mall project and then the hotel, and then he stopped at their pride and joy. The four brothers had jointly worked on a brand-new family tower. Savage Tower Two had been talked about for years, and it was nearly topped out not far from where they were now. It would be the tallest in the city, taller than Donert Tower, and the Savages' new home office. The rendering in front of him was of the building they were in, with a new name going across it: Savage Tower One.

Ed lifted the rendering and quickly peeked at their new tower behind it; letting it drop, he pointed at the Savage name. "I'm not sure on the new signage. Maybe we should just leave it? Let's render up a few more," he said and looked back to his brothers. "I trust my penthouse office will be the biggest?" Ed laughed, looking down his nose at them.

"Oh my God, I am going to jump off Savage Two if you're going to act like this," Roman said.

"Let's just push him off instead." Logan laughed.

"Sounds like a plan." Roman laughed with him.

"Ha-ha, guys." Ed sighed, moving down with Logan to where Roman was standing next to the rendering of Donert Tower, a beautiful glass building that Ed knew all about.

The property the tower was to be built on was controversial, due to the two families that each owned half the block. When the families finally sold to Don Roberts, one family member felt cheated and sued, holding up the project for over a year. Finally, it was cleared a few months ago, and construction was to begin very soon. Ed and Sam knew all this, and Ed knew the contract had gone to their rival. "Why are you looking at this? And where's Sam?" Ed asked.

Around the corner in his office, Sam had the documents of Nathan's will and had found the loophole intentionally left for him by Parnell F. Bancroft, which got him thinking.

On Sam's credenza behind his desk was a folder, a copy from Roman of Donert's Tower information, and he opened it. Looking at the adjusted bid Don Roberts had accepted from Bigelow, two things came to mind.

Sam got up from his desk and went to his files, finding his copies of Savage Construction's bid made to Don Roberts. He opened them, finding the page he was looking for, and scanned down it. He smiled. This day was getting better and better.

In the conference room, Ed wore a scowl. "Roman, why am I looking at this? I don't want to see it. You know I hate all things Bigelow," he growled. The look on Ed's face was serious. "Do this again, and you're fired!" he said, only half kidding.

Logan grinned. "Whoa, Mr. President. Someone's been drinking Dad's Kool-Aid."

Ed waved his cane in the air at Logan. "And you! You're next!" he said, as the grin returned to his face.

Logan moved back to keep from getting hit. "You better back up with the cane there, Your Highness, or I'll take out your other knee!" Logan said.

Roman laughed, agreeing, "Yeah, big man, and what was that about kicking my ass? It's two against one now, and you'll lose, old man!"

The sound of the documents slapping against the table got the lighthearted squabbling to stop. Sam was standing at the other end of the long table, shaking his head. "Nothing ever changes with you three. Good God, it's the summer at the lake house all over again!"

Ed jokingly pointed his cane at Sam. "Well, what do you expect, Sam? I got you for shooting me, Roman for nearly breaking my ribs on the yacht, and Logan for busting my knee. I should fire you all!"

Logan took a few steps toward Sam and turned back. "You know, for being the oldest, you sure are the biggest baby of all of us," he said.

Ed made a face mimicking Logan as he limped toward Sam, looking at the documents he had dropped on the table. "So what do you have here?" he asked.

Sam took a step back, closing the conference-room doors. "We need to talk about old Parnell," he said.

"What about him?"

Sam continued, "Dad's will is slightly different than Parnell first led us to believe. Now, I wasn't involved with Dad's dealings with him, so God only knows what the two of them cooked up over the years. But, Ed, you can run this company without setting a foot in here, ever," Sam said.

Hearing the news, the brothers looked to each other. Ed didn't know quite what he was hearing. "What do you mean? What did you find?" he asked.

"Parnell sent these over, the official documents of Dad's last will and testament," Sam said, opening the folder to the page with the Post-it note attached to it. "Right here, buried where Dad would never find it or read it because he trusted Parnell so much, is a clause stating that should you be drawing an earning, you can make decisions from anywhere your work takes you." Sam laughed. "It's worded to imply that whenever you are away, you are away on Savage Construction business, but it doesn't state it. Simply put, should you be drawing an earning from acting, you're in compliance with the governing rules of the will," Sam said.

Ed smiled. "I'm free?" he said.

Sam looked at him. "Now *you're* fired!" he joked.

The brothers shared a laugh, and Ed looked back to the Donert Tower rendering. His mind flashed briefly to Jillian and the son she'd kept from him. "So, I'm not tied to this place. Let's get everything signed, sealed, and finalized before going forward on anything," he said.

He limped over to the Donert Tower picture. "Roman, you didn't answer my question; what's this Bigelow project doing here?"

"That's just it, Ed," Roman said as he picked up the folder closest to him. "It seems it may not be Bigelow's after all. There was an article in the paper the other day about the 'half a block' lawsuit finally being over, clearing the project to start. Only the project start date was pushed back, and the lawsuit canceled the contract. We can resubmit a bid," he said.

Sam smiled as he took over. "Actually, Parnell had his fingers in that, too, Roman. We didn't have Bigelow's numbers until the lawsuit hit, and I looked up our original bid for Donert Tower. We were under Bigelow's number. By all rights we should have been awarded the contract, except Bigelow was able to resubmit an eleventh-hour bid, just slightly under our number. The only person who knew our number was Parnell. Now, if Parnell left this loophole for you to run the company as you wish, it wouldn't be a far stretch for him to double-cross Dad. You know money is his only friend. I don't know if Dad knew anything about this, but we *are* back in the game."

"Parnell's working with Bigelow? Dad would kill him!" The thought actually tickled Ed, and getting Donert Tower away from Bigelow Construction was an idea Ed liked.

Sam continued, "Also, I met with Don and his wife, Madeline Roberts. Cara and I had dinner with them, and they're good people. He's a stand-up guy, and once he sees this, I'm sure we can get it. Of course, the bidding will reopen to all, but I have a good feeling about this," Sam said.

Ed looked from Sam to Roman and then back to the drawing. He remembered finding the hotel-room key card on the dresser and Jillian's purse thrown against their wedding photograph. A wolfish feeling came over him, and he looked back at his brothers. "I want this building. Do whatever it takes to get it," he said.

As he started limping from the conference room, Logan stopped him. "Ed, I thought you wanted nothing to do with Savage Construction," he said.

Ed looked at Logan and then at the others. "So did I." Turning, he opened the door of the conference room and went to the elevators, hitting the down button.

Behind him, his secretary, signing for a delivery, called out to him. An elevator opened, and Ed moved away from it, taking the envelope from her. It was from Marlo's attorneys.

Ed went to his office and closed his doors, locking them. He limped to his desk and sat down, opening the envelope. The divorce papers fell out, and he picked them up, sighing. Marlo had already signed them. She didn't even want to talk about it, and Ed was crushed. He looked at the date Marlo had signed the papers; it was dated yesterday, and he felt empty inside. His entire life with her was over, and it hurt. He opened his lower desk drawer, which contained a push-button safe, and entered the code.

He was about to throw the papers in when he stopped and pulled out the VCR tape he'd taken from Patty's cabin and the one she'd mailed to Marlo, along with the book of spells and the newspaper clippings. He placed them on his desk and pulled out the fake ID Marcus Bowers had made with his picture and Ed's name.

He stared at it for a moment; then he nodded and reached farther into the drawer, pulling out his leather identification wallet and opening it to look at his badge.

Ed stared at his secret life. Without Marcus Bowers really knowing, he would never have been able to play Ed Savage for long. Because there was one very real fact that the man hadn't known.

The badge was engraved: "Agency One SIA: Savage Nine," and it had his picture on it.

If Nathan Savage thought he could keep secrets, Ed was better at it. Ed's leaving West Point had been planned, but he'd never spoken of it to anyone except Sam, not even his father, after that part of his life was over. While he did love his acting, it also provided the perfect cover for him to assist the US government.

While at West Point, Ed Savage was the third in a long line of influential men from his family. His grandfather, General Nelson Savage, had later gone into politics, and his father, Nathan Savage, was a retired air-force colonel running a high-rise construction company—a company Ed wanted nothing to do with. He spoke with his commanders and wanted to do it his way.

Ed left, like he had led his family to believe, and he did enroll in Cambridge; however, he also attended and was welcomed at the British Intelligence Agency and cross-trained as an American agent.

It was the year of the shaving-cream commercial that his first assignments had started.

Ed Savage, Secret Intelligence Agent: Savage Nine, went to quit Agency One after his last case. Ed was on location shooting a movie in the Mediterranean about a lost treasure submerged in a long-ago city that archaeologists had found beneath the sea. His case involved a kidnapped American woman and her daughter being held in a city near the filming location. Since Ed was popular with fans around the world, it was easy for him to gain access to places for reconnaissance missions and get invited to the best parties.

When Ed got word that the kidnapped woman and her daughter were indeed held on the grounds of an estate next to a party he was invited to, he accepted. The plan was simple enough, or so it had seemed at the time: Ed was to attend, and when another agent started the fire, he was to slip over the wall and grab the women.

With the attention on the fire and the panicked guests leaving the estate, all hell broke loose. Ed made it over the wall, and it felt too easy; that was the problem.

Ed saw the guard at the back guesthouse get shot and fall to the ground. Agent Miller, an agent Ed had known, who wasn't planned in the assignment, appeared and waved him over, holding his gun with a silencer in his other hand. They went in, untied the women, and ran to the back toward the water, to the dock where Agent Miller had a small motorboat waiting. Agent Miller helped get the women on board and started the engine. Freedom was a short ride away, but Agent Miller had been keeping a secret of his own.

With the boat moving away from shore, Ed jumped from the dock to the boat, and that was when Agent Miller made his move. He pulled his knife and swung it at Ed, but Ed saw it coming and moved, grabbing his arm. The men fought and fell into the water, where Ed was able to get the knife from him and stab him in the chest.

When he came up for air, the boat was farther away, and he started to swim toward it. In Agent Miller's dying moment, he detonated the trigger, and the boat was blown from the water, killing the woman and her daughter.

When the movie had wrapped and the mission had failed, Ed went home completely defeated. One of his series was just starting to film, and that was when Marlo had had enough with him being gone so much. The fighting began, and life became miserable.

Ed flew to Washington, DC, and met with his boss, handing in his badge. The case weighed on him, and he had nightmares of the women's faces, the hope in their eyes that they were finally headed home to freedom...only to be killed so horrifically. Ed's boss took one look at his badge and would not accept it. Instead, his boss froze him out temporarily, telling him to concentrate on his marriage and not worry about Agency One, and when he was ready, he would be welcomed back.

Ed had left and worked on his marriage. They were in a rough spot, but they'd loved each other. That was too many years ago, and he wondered now if he should go back to Agency One.

He sat there, staring at his badge. Pulling out his cell phone, he selected "speaker" and then placed it on the desk, punching in the familiar number. The call was answered immediately by the electronic voice: "Enter passcode." Looking at the divorce papers, Ed shook his head and hung up the phone. He wasn't ready yet.

In a Washington, DC, control room, buried deep inside a very stately, important-looking building, a monitor alerted Agency One that Savage Nine had just accessed the phone line.

CHAPTER 109

Jeremy Bigelow was furious. It had been weeks since he had found out who was behind that damn newspaper article that had started this whole Donert Tower rebidding nonsense.

The time and money spent waiting on the lawsuit, the renderings and the scale models, not to mention permits, equipment, storing building materials, and everything else—it all had been costing him millions. Now, with the rebidding underway, the thought of Savage Construction attaining the contract burned his blood.

The meeting he had just come from with Don Roberts hadn't gone as he had hoped. He had planned on smoothing things over and retaining control of Donert Tower. But now with the time that had passed, things had changed, and Don Roberts seemed to have information he was not sharing.

Bigelow stormed into his office and ordered all his calls to be held. He had paid Parnell a hefty sum to get that information—Savages bid on Donert Tower—and now he was questioning everything.

Sitting at his desk, he opened his drawer, pulled out a file on the lawsuit that had held up the project, and flipped through the papers. He pulled out the document with the newspaper article copied to it and the reporter's name and sources. Parnell F. Bancroft had been in the courtroom the day the "half a block" lawsuit was cleared, and he was the source of this story to the press, the flame that lit the fuse that blew his contract sky-high.

CHAPTER 110

E d placed everything back inside the drawer safe and took one last look at the date Marlo had signed the papers. He sighed again, stuffing them into the drawer safe and locking it. Getting up and grabbing his cane, he pulled his contract from his jacket pocket and threw it on his desk. He then left his office, heading back to the elevator.

When the elevator doors opened on the lobby, Ed was by himself inside the elevator car, finishing a phone conversation. "Okay, I'm in." He put his phone in his pocket, but instead of going to the garage elevators, he exited the building and took a walk to clear his head.

It was a beautiful early evening, and he missed just being outside in the crowd of normal people on the street. When he was stopped at a crosswalk, he glanced up at the tower down the street where Parnell F. Bancroft's law offices were, and he smiled. Turning, he continued on his way.

On the fifty-third floor, still in his office, Parnell sat in his high-back chair and turned to his desk to put out his cigar. He smiled as he made his way over to his bar to make himself a celebratory drink. Returning to his desk, he lit another cigar and stood looking out the window.

He did not notice his office door opening, nor the gloved assassin dressed in a black suit stepping inside and raising a gun, with silencer, from under his coat. Just as Parnell turned from his window and saw the assassin, he was shot twice in the forehead.

The bullets went right through Parnell's skull and shattered the glass, sending him plummeting out his window to his death.

Ed was now several blocks away at a newspaper-and-magazine street vendor. He looked at the clock behind the clerk he was making conversation with about the Giants, his favorite team, and asked if the time was correct. He then bought a couple of magazines and a newspaper and paid with his credit card at the exact time Parnell was shot.

He eventually made his way on to his favorite pub, put down a few twenties, and ordered a whiskey, downing it in one shot.

The bartender was about to pick up a twenty when Ed asked for another, and when it was served to him, he stared into it, thinking of the monumental decisions he had before him. The divorce papers were really messing with his mind, and he was tired of trying. He loved Marlo, but with everything she was throwing at him, he couldn't take it anymore. He figured she must have finally come to terms with everything that had *really* happened that ugly night in the mountains, and to be honest, he was disgusted with it too. He had only wished she had talked to him about it first before signing their life away. Maybe they could have worked through it. He thought of her signature on the dotted line, which was dated only yesterday. To Ed, his marriage had ended twenty-four hours ago without him even knowing about it.

The bartender reached for his money when Aisha came up behind him.

Handing money to the bartender, she laughed. "I've got this."

Ed smiled as he got up to greet her. "Yes, you do," he said, and they enjoyed their first kiss.

CHAPTER 111

Ed Savage was standing naked in the upper-floor window of Aisha's apartment. The moonlight lit the sky, and he lifted his arm, rested his head against his forearm, and sighed. His head was heavy from the whiskey, and tomorrow's hangover was going to be a whopper. His thoughts were on his marriage—or what was left of it, if anything was. He looked back at Aisha sleeping in her bed and looked back out the window. He thought of Marlo and those damned divorce papers she had signed, and the weight of it was crushing him; his heart was filled with hurt.

Deep down, he had known this would happen when he decided to meet up with Aisha. Even though all the warning signs were there, the rumbling volcano and the receding tide of the tsunami be damned; he had brushed them aside and ordered more whiskey. He'd known he wasn't thinking clearly, and who could blame him with his entire family enduring such trauma? Yet, it was too soon, and it felt wrong—something was missing, like he was forgetting something and didn't have all the facts. And now, the guilt was everywhere—even though he loathed the ugly truth of that night.

A single tear emerged from his eye, and he wiped it away and looked out to the city. He could see the lit sign of the Four Seasons, where Marlo was now living.

CHAPTER 112

I n her bedroom at the Four Seasons, Marlo was having another restless night's sleep. She tossed and turned and was in a dream reliving that horrible first night at Black Ridge Falls.

The images flashing in her mind were new ones, images she had not remembered since waking up in that mountain hospital. She was confused, and her dream was adding more confusion to what she had remembered and told her doctors.

In her dream she flashed to being inside the RV, being pushed back onto the bed and fighting that horrible man wearing that filthy hunter's mask over his head. She remembered him tearing her clothes with the stick and ripping open her pants—but that was outside her mind told her. She thought she remembered grabbing the mask and pulling it from him and seeing his face for a brief moment, before he smacked her across the face—or had she seen it somewhere else?

Marlo stirred in her bed, and her dream blurred to being inside the RV as it caught fire. She remembered the flames shooting up from inside the RV and the loud explosion that followed. Her dream blurred again, and then she was running in the woods. She could hear him behind her, that hideous beast hiding behind the mask who had attacked her inside the RV. She turned a corner on a path and looked back to see him as he turned it himself, getting closer. She screamed, and when she turned away from him, she stopped in fear as another was now in front of her.

Her mind snapped. *No, it can't be.* It happened too fast; she didn't have time to react when the giant, bearded man grabbed her and laughed, turning her around to see the hunter coming at her, growling under the mask. There were two of them!

Marlo thrashed in her bed, reliving the dream.

She screamed, and the second man pushed her into the arms of the first man, and he threw her to the ground. He got down on top of her, and she reached up and pulled the mask off and saw him. He was the same, except...He was *clean-shaven.* He let go of her and slapped her across the face. He was too strong, and then the other one was there.

"She's a fighter," said that evil human being who wore the beard as he joined the nightmare she wanted no part of. He was then beside the other and on top of her, when he pulled his pants open.

The other man laughed and began kissing at her neck; the second one then laughed in her face as he pulled at her clothing. *She's a fighter...*

Marlo rolled over in her bed, pushing away the pillows as her dream blurred back to inside the RV, hearing Lisa call for her and hearing..."They lost her."

Marlo's eyes shot wide open from her nightmare, and she cried out in the darkness of her hotel room.

*She's a fighter...*The words echoed in her mind as she pulled her thoughts together and reached for the bedside light. She sat up in bed and *remembered.*

The tears were uncontrollable as the memories of what had happened—what had *really* happened—that horrible night filled her head. They'd raped her. They'd both raped her.

*She's a fighter...*It wasn't her doctors who'd first said that; it was her attackers. She remembered listening to her doctors at both hospitals. She still couldn't remember much from being at the smaller facility in the mountains, but after, after she got home, she had been checked into the hospital for tests. Her doctor had told her! Ed had been there! But somehow she hadn't heard it. It was now like hearing his voice for the first time, and it was all sinking in.

Marlo opened the palms of her hands and studied them like she was looking at them for the first time. Her vision was blurry from her tears, and she started shaking as her mind asked her over and over, *Where have I been?*

It was like cutting through a giant sheet of blurry plastic tarp, stepping to the clarity of the other side, and seeing the ugliness that was all around her for the first time. The emotion of the vile truth had finally broken through, breaking the numb veneer she had somehow built around her. "Oh God, Ed," she cried out as tears poured from her soul.

She gasped for air as the ugly truth was finally being purged from her body, and she choked on her tears. She fell back into the bed and clutched the pillow and screamed into it as she finally felt the pain from that night start to lift from her body.

"Oh God, Ed! Ava! What have I done?" All alone in her giant bed, she opened her eyes and thought of Lisa, Maggie, and Simon, and she pushed herself up against the headboard and pulled the pillow to her. She rocked herself in tears and looked across the room toward the window, seeing the lights of the city beyond. She then put her hand over her stomach and cried as the memories of the nightmare reminded her of that night...He had said, "They lost her."

CHAPTER 113

E d Savage woke up in Aisha's bed alone that morning. He stirred as his vision blinked to reality and saw the bottle of aspirin and the bottle of water on the nightstand. He reached for it, took three pills, and washed them down, almost downing the entire bottle of water.

Hearing her in the kitchen, he pulled the blankets off and spotted his boxers on the floor near the bed. Getting up and putting them on, he went to the kitchen to see Aisha pouring coffee. She had prepared breakfast and had the orange juice waiting. "Good morning," he said with a wink, grabbing a piece of bacon from one of the plates.

Aisha moved around the counter into his arms, and he hugged her. "Glad you answered your phone yesterday," she said.

Ed closed his eyes and remembered answering his cell in the elevator as he left the office. "When you called, I was a bit of a mess. So yeah, I was up for meeting you for drinks."

Aisha pulled away from him and looked down at his boxers. "I see you're still up," she said, blushing. The toaster popped the bagel, breaking the stare between them, and she went and placed it on a plate. She started to spread the cream cheese on one of them; then she stopped and looked back at him. "Ed, we shouldn't have done that."

Ed wasn't surprised to hear her say that, but he kept it to himself. "What do you mean? Didn't you enjoy it?"

Aisha smiled and looked Ed up and down. "Oh no, it's not that; you were just what I needed." She smiled, feeling the blush return to her face as she looked back and noticed she had spread a little too much cream cheese on the bagel. "I'm still a mess over Danny, and technically, you're still married, divorce papers signed or not. Ed, it's just too soon."

Ed sat on the stool at the breakfast bar, picked up his orange juice, and took a healthy drink. The thought of Marlo last night was still on his mind, and he blinked it away and stared intently at Aisha. "You're right. But I'll tell you something, Ms. Thomas. You sure brought back the magic into my world last night."

Hearing his words and thinking of the hurt she had been feeling since finding Danny in bed with his ex filled her heart. She picked up the bagel and moved over to him and stood between his bare legs. She fussed with his hair and held up the bagel to feed him. Ed took a bite, and she smiled, seeing the cream cheese on his nose. Ed could see it on his face; he pulled her to him, and they kissed.

She pulled back, laughing, and smiled with a look of admiration in her eyes, wiping cream cheese from her own face. Then her smile turned to fear when she noticed what was on the television behind him. The TV was on low, and the news was reporting the death of Parnell F. Bancroft. Ed noticed her look change and followed her stare. "What?" he asked, turning to see.

Aisha picked up the remote and turned up the volume. On the screen they saw the report of the broken upper-floor window of the unmistakable tower where Parnell F. Bancroft's office was. The reporter covering the event was a professional and nothing like the stupid Storm sisters. Ed and Aisha watched the reporter nod to her cameraman.

"As first reported, lawyer Parnell F. Bancroft was killed yesterday after jumping from his fifty-third-floor office. Now we have learned he was murdered; police have stated the victim was shot and fell through his window. Neighboring office workers are being questioned, and thus far, no one heard anything. Should police make any further statements, we'll be covering it live…"

Ed grabbed the remote and turned off the TV. He and Aisha just looked to each other. "It can't be, Ed. They're all dead or in jail," Aisha said.

Ed got up from the breakfast bar. "Sorry, I have to go." Ed went back to the bedroom to finish getting dressed. He then grabbed his cane for his limp of shame home.

CHAPTER 114

Exiting the building, Ed hailed a cab back to Savage Tower to get his Jaguar and headed to Sam's, where he was now living with Ava and Heather.

Ed pulled into the driveway, got out, and rushed inside to find Sam watching the news. "Sam, I just saw this! I can't believe this is happening. Where are the girls?"

Sam looked over the sofa toward him. "Danni picked them up this morning to go to the hospital to visit Chase and Macy," he said, finishing his coffee. "This shit isn't ending."

Ed moved closer to the TV. "Have they said who did this yet?"

Sam got up with his empty coffee cup and moved toward Ed; his shoulder bothered him, but he was dealing with it. "No, I thought it was suicide at first, but now...who knows?"

He brushed past Ed and could smell the limp of shame on him. "You unscrupulous whore! You smell like perfume, bacon, and sex! Glad the girls are gone here, Whorezilla!" Sam said with a playful grin.

Ed gave Sam a funny look and headed to his room to shower.

After his shower the hangover was lingering, and he skipped shaving. Ed rushed to join Sam in the kitchen, where he was packing his briefcase. "Any further news on Parnell?" Ed asked.

"Nope, same stuff over and over. You know how it goes with the media. Oh yeah, they've now tied Dad's will into it, so we're being rehashed on the air with everything else that's happened."

"I figured as much. I left my new contract with Trask Studios on my desk, and I want to run that by you and get that finalized today."

"Trask Studios?"

"Oh yeah, I'm leaving Titan. I'll tell you about it later. I'm about to head in; do you want to drive in together?"

Sam looked up from his briefcase. "Can't. I'm meeting Don Roberts on my way in, and with this now happening, I really don't want to reschedule."

Ed frowned. "You think this will keep us from getting Donert Tower?"

"I don't know what to think anymore, Ed. This seems to just never end," Sam said as he closed his briefcase. "Roman called Don yesterday, and he agreed to meet with us. We're going to tell him what we found and take it from there." Sam picked up his keys. "I have to get going. I'll see you at the office."

Ed grabbed a bottle of water from the refrigerator and looked back to his brother. "Sam, one more thing: I don't want anything said about—"

Sam cut him off with a knowing grin. "About you being a giant whore? I'm glad for you. We've been to hell and back. Not another word from me," he said, and he opened the door to the garage.

Ed looked to the TV, where the story was now focused on Savage Tower and the tie to their father's will. He picked up the remote and shut it down.

Outside Savage Tower, the black limousine pulled up front, and the front passenger door opened. A lumbering man in a black suit got out, looked around, and opened the backdoor of the limousine.

CHAPTER 115

When Ed arrived at Savage Tower, he could see the news vans. He parked in the garage and took the elevator to the lobby. Security had barred the reporters from entering the building, and he was happy with that. He grabbed the next elevator and hit the top floor.

As he exited the elevator, his staff was huddled around a large TV monitor, watching the news and gossiping. Ed limped in, and they all scattered to their desks. "Back to work, people," Ed said on his way to his office.

Ed's secretary was not at her desk, and his office door was ajar. He pushed the door open farther to find a woman with silver hair and dressed in Chanel sitting at a chair near the window. Her bodyguards stood at attention by her side. "Tallulah Tuesday," Ed said, frozen in the doorway. "How did—? Never mind. Where's my secretary?"

Tallulah gave a slight smile, stuffing the tabloid into the newspaper and putting it under her arm. "The little mouse had car trouble this morning. I'm sure she'll be in shortly," she said with a knowing glare as she rose to greet him.

Ed closed his office door and looked at her with suspicion. "Car trouble, huh?" he said, returning the glare. "You're forgetting we've done this dance before. Now, what brings..." Ed stopped himself, re-membering, and then he continued, "The phone call."

"Yes, Savage Nine. You accessed the phone line, and it's been long enough since you left. And with your—shall we say—little adventure last night, well, I figured you were ready to come back," Tallulah said, eyeing him sharply.

"You're tailing me?" Ed shot back.

"You know all calls to *that* number are traced; agents were sent out immediately. But *that's* not why I'm here."

Ed limped to his desk and noticed his desk-drawer safe was open, and he looked to her. "Really, Tallulah?"

"I wouldn't be my charming self if I didn't, now would I?" she said, moving closer to the desk. Tallulah waved her hand over her shoulder. "That will be all; I'd like a moment with Savage Nine," she said, never taking her eyes off him. The bodyguards quietly moved to the door, closing it behind them.

"It's good to be working together again," she said, studying him. "I knew you would come back."

Ed sat back in his chair, placing his cane against his desk and the open drawer containing the safe. "I'm not back, Tallulah." Ed let that set in for a moment. "I'm not coming back, not after what happened. Besides, too much is happening in my world right now, and I just can't, even if I wanted to."

"You thought he was dead. You can't blame yourself; Agent Miller detonated the explosives after you stabbed him. When are you going to stop blaming yourself?"

With everything that was happening in Ed's life at the moment, having to relive that dreadful night, watching those two women be blown from the water so long ago, was a slap to his face. "Tallulah, I can't do this," Ed said. "But I will ask, is Agency One involved in Parnell's shooting?"

Tallulah just stared at him for a moment. "You really don't know?"

Ed searched his mind, and that feeling he had yesterday of missing something was back.

The documents found at the lighthouse were quite invasive. It seemed Marcus Bowers had been able to siphon funds from one of Niles and Charlotte's accounts to an offshore bank. Further, a bank account had been set up in Ed's name using the false identification, but they had frozen everything associated with Marcus's scheme. Even the prescription photos he had sent Tallulah came back; nothing other than the medications Patty Galloway was taking were listed, and nothing seemed out of place—for Patty, anyway.

"The prescriptions?" Ed eyed her with hope.

"Agent Thrasher dug deeper," she said, not taking her eyes off him.

"Agent Thrasher? Never heard of him."

"You know him; Wes Thrasher, he's been with me almost as long as you."

Ed thought for a moment, "Oh, Winston Weston Thrasher III. Now I remember that pretentious fuck. I never called him by his last name."

Tallulah smiled. "He hasn't changed. Anyway, the prescriptions were traced back to a pharmacy in the town of Black Creek, just before Black Ridge Falls. I'm sorry this took longer, but after some checking, a new prescription for asthma medication was processed the day after Lisa went missing. I just got the report this morning and flew here right away."

Ed leaped up from his chair. "Where's the address associated with the prescription?"

"Not far from the farm Marcus Bowers had been arrested at. We have agents there now."

Ed grabbed his desk phone and punched in an extension. "Have the helicopter standing by," he barked, slamming the phone down.

"Savage Nine, we have a team assembling at a warehouse in Black Creek, not far from the location. Agents will be there to assist you," she said; then she pulled the paper from under her arm. "I'm sorry, Ed, but you need to see this too."

Tallulah lifted the tabloid from the paper and showed it to him. The headline read, "Bastard Son Wins Daddy Lottery."

"I'm sorry, Ed. But you'll have to deal with this when you get back."

The newspaper was bad enough, with Jillian York's story of his first-born son being splashed right below the nasty murder headlines. But the tabloid was a salacious disaster.

Ed took the tabloid, and Tallulah moved from Ed's desk back to the window and looked toward Bancroft's office building. "We had nothing to do with Parnell's shooting, by the way. Why would we?" She paused, picking up her bag. "This could be coming from your father."

The beeping from inside Tallulah's bag alerted her that she had a message. She pulled out a small tablet and tapped the message. "She's alive, Ed; look." Ed came around his desk, and together they looked at the satellite image of the two little girls carrying laundry in the backyard of the farmhouse. "Here, take this with you." Tallulah handed him the tablet. "Agent Thrasher will meet you there," she said, moving to the doors and opening them. "Ed, I've missed you. Now go get your daughter and bring her home."

Tallulah left the office with her bodyguards and headed toward the elevators.

As the elevator doors opened, Marlo came rushing out, going right past Tallulah and straight for Ed Savage's office. Tallulah turned to see Ed come out as Marlo frantically moved him back inside.

"Ed. Oh my God, Ed. I'm so sorry for everything. I remember now. I remember everything that happened that night. There were *two* of them. He said, 'They lost her.' Ed, you were right all along; we have to go back! We have to go find our daughter!" Marlo cried with the realization of hope beaming from her.

Ed looked at his wife, and his heart melted, seeing her as he had *always* seen her—with love. "Marlo, listen to me. Lisa is alive. I just now found out, and I know where she is. Now come on; you're coming with me."

Ed held her arm, and together they rushed to the elevators, his knee throbbing from the sudden motion. Fumbling for his keys inside the elevator car, he handed his cane to Marlo, inserted the roof-level key into the slot, and turned it.

On the roof of Savage Tower, the helicopter was on and ready. Ed escorted Marlo to it and boarded. Moments later, the helicopter lifted from the roof in the direction of Black Creek.

CHAPTER 116

L ocking the car at Donert's Department Store, Sam and Roman entered the store on the way to the executive offices. They spotted Don across the store in the women's shoe department and made their way over to him.

As they neared, they noticed he was in a meeting with a brunette woman, and to their surprise, Amanda Kenowith was sitting down next to them, writing away on a clipboard the notes of their meeting.

Don looked over and greeted them immediately. "Roman, Sam, good to see you." He reached out to shake hands.

Amanda was surprised. She put her clipboard down beside her and stood up. "Uncle Roman, Sam, I didn't know you were going to be here today," she said quickly, and she included an introduction to her good friend. "Sam, Roman, I'd like you to meet my business partner, Jacqueline Holt. Jacqueline, this is my uncle Roman and my uncle Sam," she said, pointing to each.

"Very nice to meet you both; I've heard so much about you, and I'm so sorry," Jacqueline said as she reached out and air-kissed Roman and then Sam. As she pulled away from Sam, she immediately felt something; an emotion stirred inside her, and she pushed it away.

"Thank you," Sam said, eyeing the young, beautiful woman.

"Yes, thank you," Roman said. "How are you feeling, Amanda?"

Amanda lifted her wrapped forearm up, covered in a tasteful print to match her dress. "I'm fine; Mother, of course, selected this for me."

Everyone shared the laugh.

"Sorry to crash your meeting, Amanda. We're a little early ourselves and spotted Don across the store," Roman said, looking to the girls.

"No worries," Jacqueline said. "We were just finishing up, so your timing was perfect." She looked from Sam to Roman. "He's all yours, guys." She laughed.

At that moment, Madeline Roberts came out from the back area with some photographs of the display units they were having installed.

"Madeline, you remember meeting Sam Savage," Don said, introducing his wife to Sam and Roman.

Madeline's heart sank as she approached Sam and reached for his hand. "Oh, Sam, I'm so sorry; Cara was such an amazing woman."

"Thank you," Sam said.

"This is Roman Savage." Don continued the introductions.

"Hello, Roman, my heart goes to you and your wife and your family," Madeline said, holding the photographs against her chest. "And it's a pleasure to finally meet you."

Roman nodded. "Thank you. Pleasure's mine."

"Honey, I'm going to let you take the lead on this one, and I'll take the guys to my office. I'm out of my league here," Don said with a laugh, looking at the ladies' shoes.

Roman gazed at all the shoes. "I think my wife has one each of all these." He laughed along.

Madeline smiled at the men and gave Sam a hug. "If there is anything we can do, you reach out; you hear me?" Madeline looked at Sam with genuine concern, and he could tell she meant it.

"I've got it handled here," Madeline said. "Go on, Don; I'll see you upstairs."

"Guys, this way," Don said as he led them toward the escalators.

As they stepped onto the escalators, Sam leaned against the railing and glanced back at the ladies; to his surprise, Jacqueline Holt was looking his way.

In the upper floors of Donert's Department Store, Don led Sam and Roman into the executive offices, and the men went into one of the conference rooms, where coffee and soft drinks were laid out for their arrival.

"Guys, help yourselves," Don said. "I need to grab something."

Sam and Roman each poured themselves a coffee and sat down when Don returned with his briefcase. He set it down on the table and opened it, pulling out a rather large folder containing all the legal documents pertaining to the bid submitted by Savage Construction.

"Before we get going here, guys, I just wanted to say how sorry I am for everything you have been through," Don said, opening the large file.

Both Roman and Sam nodded, and they pushed away the hurt and tried to focus on the business at hand. They both could see the rendering of the eighty-eight-story glass tower propped up at the end of the room, like they had of their projects in Savage Tower.

"That damn court case cost me a fortune," Don finally blurted out, changing the subject, which both Savage boys appreciated.

"I'll bet," Roman said, thinking of the delay and the costs associated with it.

"Now that we're clear to proceed, the bidding window will be open for a very limited time, gentlemen," Don said. "I've talked with Bigelow, and there are other outside companies that want a shot at it, so I'm all ears."

"Don," Sam said, "we have reason to believe our lower bid was leaked to Bigelow, explaining his eleventh-hour change of bid to you."

"You know, I'd met with Parnell several times over the years, and I never came to terms with doing business with him for whatever reason," Don said.

Sam was shocked, "Parnell? I didn't mention him."

"You didn't have to. I'd seen him leaving Bigelow's office after the contract went through, just before the lawsuit started. At that point, I didn't know what to make of it; now it fits."

"If Dad were alive, he'd…" Roman stopped himself.

The men pondered that statement, knowing of Parnell's death, and an awkward silence fell in the room.

"What's in the past I'd like to leave there and start this thing fresh," Don finally said.

"I like the sound of that myself," Sam agreed.

Roman was also nodding. "Yeah, no more skeletons for me."

The men shared a laugh, and Sam opened his briefcase and pulled out a folder. "Don, we worked on a new bid, and here it is." He slid it over to him.

Opening it, Don scanned down to the bottom line. He pursed his lips and tapped the tabletop with his fingers in thought.

Both Sam and Roman looked to each other and didn't know what to think.

Don closed the folder and looked up to the guys. "Looks good; I don't have anything further at this time, except to say I'll be in touch."

Roman was a little surprised. "Don, I wanted to let you know that Savage Construction is solid in every aspect. The slowdown at the Vander Place Hotel and the housing-division project has reversed, and sales are climbing."

Don chuckled. "Roman, it's all good. If I didn't believe Savage Construction was a viable company, you wouldn't be here." He looked to Sam. "Really, with everything that's happened and what I've read, I'm not worried. And you shouldn't be either. And, by the way, Sam, that evening we had dinner with you and Cara, I felt good about all this then. Now let's see how the numbers come in, and I'll give you a call."

"Thank you, Don," Roman said, standing up.

"Yes, thank you." Sam also got to his feet.

Don stood and shook their hands. "Now, I better go see how Madeline is doing, or I'll go bankrupt buying shoes." They laughed as he walked the men from the office.

CHAPTER 117

T he helicopter landed at the warehouse on the far side of Black Creek, away from any prying eyes of the farmhouse. Ed and Marlo had been told this was a secret operation, and only unmarked cars would be on hand. When they got to the warehouse, Marlo was amazed at all that was going on in the makeshift command post.

A large delivery truck was parked, and in it were more computers than she had ever seen. Ed kept an eye out for Agent Thrasher as they were led to a large table with printed photos of the satellite images taken of the two little girls in the backyard. Marlo picked one up and fell against her husband. "My baby," she cried out.

Ed felt the same pit in his stomach his wife was probably feeling.

"Mr. Savage." The stern voice came from behind them.

Ed tuned to see the lead detective approach with his hand extended.

"FBI Agent Stan McArthur. Let me bring you up to speed."

The men shook hands, and Marlo was introduced. "This should go smoothly. We've been watching the place, and it's quiet. We've shut down mail delivery in the area and have a decoy ready over there," he said, pointing to the other side of the truck filled with computers, as a female agent brought new images to the table.

"Should go smoothly?" Ed questioned, hating having to keep his security clearance in the dark.

"Their usual mail-delivery time window is fast approaching; we'll get the children out safe. You have to let us do our jobs. Now, we'll need you both to stay here, out of the—"

Ed cut him off. "Over someone's dead body am I staying here."

Seeing this was about to get heated, the female agent handed the images to Marlo. "Excuse me, Mrs. Savage; can I get you to look at these?" She led her over to another table where she could sit down. There, Marlo saw the laptop computer showing the farmhouse, and she stared into the screen.

"Walk with me," Ed told the agent.

Marlo looked back to Ed to see him talking with the agent; she then looked at the new photos. On the laundry line in the back-yard of the farmhouse, she spotted it immediately. It was a shirt Lisa loved, and she was wearing it the night she'd been taken. Marlo's heart dropped.

"Ed!" she said in a raised voice, getting up from the table and rush-ing to him with the photo. "Ed, look. It's Lisa's shirt on the clothesline."

Ed took one look at the torn shirt and knew it was his daughter's.

"Give us a minute," he said to the agent.

Ed led Marlo away from him toward the mail truck at the far end of the warehouse.

"Marlo, I want you to listen clearly. We're leaving shortly to go get her. I'm going to need you to stay here and trust me that I'll bring back our little girl."

"No, Ed. Let them handle it. I can't lose you. Not now," Marlo said with wet eyes.

"I'm going to be fine. I'm riding in a backup car. I'll be far enough away when they go in," he said, telling her the same lie he'd told the agent a few moments ago.

"Ed." Marlo grabbed on to him. "Ed, I remembered everything that happened…they…"

"Shush…honey. I know; the doctor told us. I was waiting for you to accept it."

"I couldn't, Ed. I didn't know until last night."

Ed instantly knew his wife was suffering more than he could have ever imagined; he also knew she was coming back to him, and the thought of sleeping with Aisha was haunting him. He grabbed her and held her tight. "We're gonna get through this, baby, all of us," Ed said, his eyes becoming wet like hers.

"Ed, I'm scared."

"Don't worry, honey; we're going to get her."

"Yes, but I'm pregnant..."

She burst into tears in his arms, and the weight of what she was telling him was killing them both. He knew she had been raped, and her complete block of the incident was something her doctor had told him he had to let her come to terms with on her own. Now he not only knew of her pain; he also shared it.

Holding her in his arms, he noticed two men talking near the mail truck as he comforted his wife.

"Have you worked with this guy Tallulah keeps going on about?" the younger agent said to the older one.

The name "Tallulah" got Ed's attention.

"A few times, but it's been ages; he's a washed up has-been that left to be some giant Hollywood douche after fucking up a case, the guy's full of himself. No wonder he couldn't figure it out."

Ed zeroed in on the little fucker talking shit near the open side of the mail truck. He immediately knew who that was. "Wait here, Marlo," he said sternly.

Marlo watched her husband walk over to the men talking near the mail truck; he was barely using his cane.

Knowing this little punk needed some negative reinforcement "Savage style," he slammed his hand on the man's shoulder, grabbing him by his neck. "You're with me, jackass!" Ed barked, pulling the man he knew as Agent Thrasher away from the other agent.

"Hey!" Thrasher yelled as other agents looked to see what was going on.

Ed swung him around and pinned him against the mail truck with his cane.

"Oh! Sorry, Mr. Savage. I didn't know you were here yet," Agent Thrasher said, scared shitless.

Ed took his open hand and smacked the side of the guy's face. "I know you didn't." He let go of the man as others surrounded them.

"It's okay, guys," Agent Thrasher said. "We're old friends," he continued, shooting Ed a look as he waved to the others.

"It's time," FBI Agent Stan McArthur said.

As if a gong in the bowels of hell were ringing, agents rushed in all directions, and Ed reached over to Agent Thrasher and grabbed his arm. "Don't you move; you're coming with me. I just need a second." Ed then limped over to Marlo, who was being led away with the female agent.

The man Agent Thrasher had been talking to went over to him and laughed. "Ha-ha! That's what you get for talking shit on Ed Savage."

"Ugh!" Agent Thrasher groaned, seeing the guy's smug face.

"Marlo, everything's going to be fine. I love you," Ed said, grabbing her and kissing her. He reached down and placed his warm hand on her stomach. "That's my baby. I love you. Don't you forget it."

"Ed, we have to go!" Agent Thrasher yelled.

Ed kissed his wife, and Marlo watched him turn to run back toward the truck; she could see his limp was bothering him as she was led away.

On the other side of the mail truck was a Toyota 4-Runner. Agent Thrasher got in and started it, and Ed opened the door next to him.

"Nope," Agent Thrasher said, pointing to the backseat with his thumb. "You can't go like that; you'll need to change."

Ed looked in the backseat and saw the clothes sticking out from the duffel bag.

"Tallulah had me bring 'em. Hope they fit; you look like you've gained a few since your last weigh-in," Agent Thrasher added with a sarcastic smirk.

Ed slammed the door shut and got in the backseat, eyeing the boots on the floorboards. "You really are a dick. You know that?"

"Yep."

Ed reached into the bag and found a watch; putting it on, he tapped the screen, but nothing was happening.

"Just flex your wrist," Agent Thrasher said, seeing what he was doing in the mirror.

Ed flexed his wrist, and the screen turned on, showing the satellite image of the farmhouse. He looked up to see Agent Thrasher's eyes laughing at him in the mirror.

"Keep your eyes on the road; you're not my type," Ed growled.

Agent Thrasher laughed and put the Toyota in drive.

Marlo watched the vehicles drive out from the warehouse and turned to the laptop on the table. Next to it were photos of a tan van and the people who owned the place. She picked them up and looked at the fiends who had her daughter.

CHAPTER 118

Lorna Smutty had left Charlie at the house to run into town on errands. She hated the first few months of any new arrival at the house, with all their damn crying. Starvation seemed to do the trick to shutting the little bastards up. But this new one...What a little bitch this one was.

Lorna pulled her nasty-looking tan van into the pharmacy and saw that Pete was alone. "Hey there." She waved.

"Hey, Lorna," Pete said, noticing the red mark on her hand under the bandage. "What happened?"

"Oh, the cat bit me," Lorna lied, remembering Lisa biting her when she had slapped her. "I'll be needing some stronger pain meds," she said, rubbing her hand over the bandage.

"Give me a minute," he said, moving behind the back counter.

Lorna picked up a chocolate bar and opened it, stuffing it in her mouth. *I think I'll show that hungry little bitch the wrapper when I get home.* She smirked, placing the wrapper in her ratty bag next to the small handgun.

CHAPTER 119

E d Savage and Agent Thrasher got out of the 4-Runner on a wood-
ed road near the farmhouse, grabbed the long-range assault rifles
from the back, and loaded the magazines in the handguns. Placing
the knife in his belt, Ed followed Agent Thrasher along the woods behind and above the farmhouse. They soon spotted the backyard with
the clothesline drying Lisa's shirt.

From above, Ed used binoculars to see the windows to the farmhouse; they were shaded with curtains, and he wanted to get closer.

"I'm going in," he said.

"Ed, I don't think that's a good idea."

Ed shot him a look. "It's Agent Savage. And I don't care what you
think, Winston."

"It's Wes. Now who's being a dick?" Agent Thrasher said, watching
Ed as he moved down the hill in the brush.

Ed made his way closer to the farmhouse, and as he got near, he was
reminded of his last mission—the one that he had walked away from
Agency One over. He looked at his watch and begrudgingly flexed his
wrist. The screen illuminated, showing the mail truck pulling into the
long driveway of the farmhouse. The time was now.

CHAPTER 120

Back at the warehouse, Marlo moved from the table to the large truck filled with computers and climbed inside. The agents there didn't mind her taking a look at the surveillance they had on the screens. "What am I looking at?" Marlo asked, glancing at the many screens.

"Ma'am, we've got all the traffic cams, banks, pretty much any camera in the area patched in here," the agent said. "Along with the satellites."

Marlo noticed the mail truck and pointed at it. "Isn't that the truck that was just here?"

"Yeah, we have a car behind it."

Marlo watched in silence as the mail truck turned down the driveway to the farmhouse.

On another screen, a movement caught her eye, and she saw the tan van from the photos on the table parked at a pharmacy. A truck had driven by, causing the movement just as a large, fat woman exited the store and got in the van.

"That van!" Marlo shouted. "That's the van they're looking for."

The agent waved his hand toward her. "Shush, ma'am! It's going down now."

Marlo looked to the other screen and saw the mail truck park at the farmhouse. She then looked to the other screen and saw the tan van pull away from the pharmacy. Scared, she got up and climbed out from the truck to search for the female agent.

She hurried over to the table where the laptop was and saw the keys at the far end of the table. A large map to the farmhouse hung on the wall, and smaller copies of it were on the table. Seeing everyone huddled over at another table looking at computers, she grabbed the keys and a map from the table and made her way out from the warehouse. Clicking the door-unlock button, she heard the beep and saw the lights flash to the Ford Focus parked at the end of the lot.

CHAPTER 121

The agent dressed as a mailman walked up to the house and rang the doorbell while Agent Thrasher watched through the telescope of his rifle from above. When no one answered, he knocked on the door.

Ed had moved to the side of the fence and flexed his wrist to see the image playing out when he heard it—the muffled sound of a silenced child's scream from inside. Quickly, he eyed the stump next to the fence and used it to climb over and drop to the backyard, landing on his good leg and ignoring the throbbing pain from his knee. Lisa's torn shirt was blowing on the clothesline.

He heard the knocking from the front door and the sound of a man scolding the girls. Getting to the window, he saw her. Lisa Savage was sitting on a mattress with another girl with red hair. Ed felt his life return to him at once, just as the dog came running around the corner of the house.

The wolf-dog hybrid charged, growling as it lunged at him. Ed reached for his knife just as the dog collided into him. As it growled and snapped at him, Ed held the knife to the dog's breast, and as the dog advanced, it howled, knocking Ed into the house and alerting the bastard inside that he was there. The dog then whimpered and bled as it ran to the backyard.

The man grabbed the girls. The older one kicked him, and he dropped her, but he was able to keep Lisa in his grasp. Ed could hear the girls crying, and he pulled his gun back and broke the window as the man disappeared from the room with his daughter.

The agent at the front door kicked down the door and barged inside as two other agents from the mail truck jumped out and ran into the farmhouse. Agent Thrasher kept searching each window of the back of the house for any movement with the telescope of his rifle when the call came in. Answering his phone, he learned Marlo had taken a vehicle, and GPS was alerting them she was en route.

Ed broke the rest of the glass away and slid feetfirst through the small window down into the basement. The red-haired girl screamed, and he noticed her arm was bandaged, and blood was dripping down her arm. He told her he was there to save her. Instinctively, he picked up the girl and hugged her; then he put her down and said to hide by the washer. He then moved to the door the man had gone through, and it was locked. Ed heard the men upstairs, and he shot the door lock, charged through, and moved up the stairs.

"Basement's clear," Ed yelled. "I'm coming up."

The blast from the gun hit the first agent, and he tumbled down the upper stairs down to the first floor as Ed got to the top of the basement stairs. The sound of a door slamming shut upstairs and his daughter screaming haunted his mind. Ed moved into the kitchen, following the other officer and looking for another way to the second floor, when the shot came through the kitchen ceiling, hitting the second officer in the shoulder.

Ed jumped back, aiming his gun to the ceiling, and moved out from the kitchen.

He then grabbed some books off a shelf in the front room and returned to the stairs. He threw them into the kitchen and made his move. The sound of the books hitting in the kitchen caused the freak upstairs to fire at random through the floor into the kitchen and Ed signaled the third agent, and they climbed the stairs.

Seeing the closed bedroom door, the agent signaled Ed to take the side bedroom next to it. Ed got to the wall and leaned against it, with thoughts of his daughter just on the other side. The agent then signaled to Ed, and he kicked in the door and dived away into the bathroom across the hall. The shots blasted into the bathroom, and when Ed heard his gun empty, he came around the door and fired, hitting the man in the chest.

The man fell back pulling a handgun, and Ed emptied the gun into him, seeing Lisa on the far side of the room. The man's corpse fell to the ground, and Lisa was screaming and crying. Ed dropped his gun, grabbed his daughter, and wrapped her in his arms. Tears streamed out from his soul as he held her, not wanting to ever let her go.

"Shush, my little nugget. I'm here. Oh my God! My baby! I love you so! Shush," Ed kept telling his daughter as his body weakened, and he sat on the bed rocking his baby girl.

The other agent in the bathroom radioed that the area was clear, and Ed turned to him, looking over his precious daughter. "There's another girl downstairs; she's hiding by the washer."

The agent took one last look at the father holding his beloved and knew there was another father waiting for the child downstairs.

CHAPTER 122

A ll Marlo could think about was how awful she had been to everyone around her, and the guilt weighed heavily on her. Her thoughts were scattered, and somehow she believed she was doing the right thing by warning Ed of the tan van—that was, until she saw it.

As she drove up the road, it passed on the crossing road in front of her, and she turned to follow it. Everything that had happened to her was flashing in her mind; the loss of Simon and the horrifying way she had lost her sister were at the forefront. She narrowed her eyes on the van and floored the accelerator.

The Ford Focus shot up the road, gaining on the van, and Lorna never saw it coming. Marlo pulled up alongside the van, and before Lorna knew what was happening, Marlo turned the wheel into the van. The cars crashed off the road into a neighboring farm, and the dust blew into the sky.

The air bags deployed, knocking Marlo against her seat. Tearing at them and reaching for the seatbelt, she unlocked it and opened the door and fell out from the car. Getting up, she ran to the van, which was tilted with the passenger side down on the uneven ground. She pulled open the door and swung it wide to find it empty.

The door then slammed shut in front of her, and Lorna was there. Lorna pushed Marlo into the side of the van and slammed her head against it. Marlo kicked her and reached up, digging her fingernails into her face and eyes, and would not stop as the adrenaline shot through her. Lorna screamed and stepped back, pulling Marlo with her, and both women fell and rolled, loosing each other's grip.

Lorna wiped the blood from her face; her vision was blurry from Marlo's attack. But she was able to spot her ratty bag, which had flown from the van in the crash, and she crawled to it, reaching inside and grabbing her gun just as Marlo got up and ran toward her.

Marlo didn't see it coming. Lorna rolled over, her eyes stinging from the blood, and aimed the gun and fired, hitting Marlo in the left shoulder. Marlo spun to her left and fell to the ground.

Ed was carrying his daughter from the farmhouse when he heard the shot and looked in the direction it had come from. He could faintly see a small dust cloud dissipating in the field at the next farm.

The other agent was there with the red-haired girl, and Ed looked to him with questions in his face.

"Mr. Savage, there's a report that your wife took a car."

Ed handed his daughter to the officer. "Don't you let her out of your arms," he ordered. Ed then took off running in the direction of the gunfire; his knee was hurting, but nothing was going to stop him.

"Don't go, Daddy!" Lisa cried.

Ed heard her behind him and squeezed his eyes shut; then he opened them and ran, ignoring the pain in his knee.

Lorna rubbed the blood from her bleeding eyes, and her vision went dark. Flashes of light seemed to strobe in her eyes. She screamed, "You bitch! You blinded me!" She rolled over and rubbed her arm across her eyes; her vision blurred, and she could see. She got to her feet and lumbered over to where Marlo had fallen, watching her cry on the ground. "You bitch. Look what you've done!" she screamed, raising the gun. She picked her up and slammed her against the van. "I am going to kill you and your little bitch daughter." Lorna's bad breath sprayed into Marlo's face.

In the distance, Ed could see some fat woman struggling with another. "No, please, God, no," Ed begged as he ran, holding up his other gun and aiming as his foot hit a pothole, tripping him on his bad knee. As Ed fell forward, Lorna brought the gun up and pushed Marlo away from her to aim, and Ed heard the gunfire.

The semiautomatic shots blasted into the woman from the woods, and the fat woman was dead before she hit the ground; her brains were splattered all over the nasty tan van.

Marlo fell to the ground, the adrenaline evaporating from her body in a flash, and she screamed out.

The sound was terrifying, and Ed picked himself up in tears. He ran to the crashed vehicles and found Marlo, shot in the shoulder but alive. He could see that the fat woman was indeed dead, and he bent down to his wife and picked her up into his arms.

"Ed, I had to warn you," she sobbed.

"You did good, Marlo," Ed said, kissing her on her head.

The sound of agents arriving was all around them, and Ed picked up his wife, his throbbing knee be damned; not wanting Lisa to see the carnage, he carried Marlo to the other side of the vehicles toward the agent carrying their daughter.

"Look, honey. Look."

Marlo lifted her head, and she saw the agent put down the little girl, and she heard her daughter call out her name.

"Mommy! Mommy!" Lisa yelled, and she ran to her mother and father.

Ed put his wife down, and Lisa ran into their arms. Tears of pure love filled each of their hearts. Ed held on to his family, not wanting to ever let any of them go, when Agent Thrasher appeared with his semiautomatic rifle. Ed looked at the guy, and the asshole actually had tears in his eyes. He nodded at Ed and turned and walked back toward the farmhouse, and Ed held his family tighter.

CHAPTER 123

T he little girl with the red hair told Agent Thrasher that the dog at the house had bitten her arm, and animal control was called. They kept the backyard sealed until they got there, and they were glad they did. The dog wasn't going down without a fight and was finally tranquilized after taking two shots.

The girl had been there for two years, and she was returned to her parents after they had lost her in the mountains of Black Ridge Falls.

Agents then swarmed the pharmacy and arrested Peter Andrews, and they closed the place down. They searched the place for anything that could be related to other missing children and took the computers and all the records to check for any bogus prescriptions associated with the missing.

Marlo's bullet wound went right through her shoulder. The paramedics bandaged her and wanted to take her back to the hospital she was first taken to, which seemed so long ago. Instead, Ed called the pilot of his helicopter and had him come to them. He then paid the paramedic to fly with them back home and watch Marlo during the flight.

CHAPTER 124

The homecoming was well overdue.

A few days later, when Tom returned from London, Zolie Vanderran insisted that Ed and Marlo move into her mansion with Ava and Lisa. Seeing that innocent child safe was all she could think of, and Marlo's silly interview seemed like nonsense at this point. Marlo was recovering from her bullet wound and was thankful for the invitation. The grounds were walled yet expansive and included two guesthouses and, of course, a pool house. After getting Lisa back, she also insisted on hiring extra security.

She extended the invitation to all the Savages, and to her surprise, Sam and Heather; Roman, Gabby, and Danni; and Logan, Maura, and Ty took her up on her offer. Between the main house and the pool and guesthouses, they had plenty of room. And when Chase and Macy were released from the hospital and brought to the estate to recover, it made it a true homecoming.

Lana and Kate Savage were excused from West Point and were on their way home for a visit, and Tucker and Chet's flight from the aircraft carrier in the Atlantic would have them home soon.

Maura talked to her sister Zolie about Cara's will mentioning Marlo, and after she got settled, they broached the subject with her. Marlo told them she and Cara had been planning a restaurant called "Savages" and had looked at a few locations, and although they had narrowed it down to two locations, she didn't know Cara had purchased the one Marlo liked better.

Marlo also got an interesting phone call from the man himself behind the *Tycoon Wives* juggernaut. She was told to rest up, and when she was up to it they'd like to schedule an interview for the show, and Marlo kept that phone call to herself.

The healing was beginning for the Savages after what seemed like an unending nightmare, and when Ed took a meeting at Trask Studios to go over the contract he had amended and sent in to Conner Trask, he was delighted at the outcome.

With everything that had happened, Ed felt it was time for more than a change of studios and signed on to *Precinct Wars*. A move Conner Trask wanted above all others. Ed also decided to be more involved with Savage Tower and needed a lighter schedule.

KBEX-Cable was able to get the unaired shows released from Titan Studios, and what they had in unaired episodes, they repackaged under his main show title—*Savage Mysteries*—and added a subtitle. With *Precinct Wars* wrapped for the season, it was decided *Savage Mysteries* would air in the summers on a lighter schedule.

Archive Raiders had been in its last year, and had been advertised, so letting go of that one wasn't as hard on him or his fans.

Then Don Roberts called Roman to tell them they had the contract to Donert Tower, and the family celebrated.

But the best news of all was the fact that Lisa had never been touched in an improper way, and the results of Marlo's pregnancy. Ed felt this was a chance at a fresh start. The day he got those damned divorce papers he felt it was over, and figured Marlo had known she'd been raped, and as much as he wished, he could not change the past.

He had guessed at her knowing and was tired of the constant attacks when he'd met with Aisha. He had given up, and now he hated himself for it. He also hated the fact that those two men had had their hands on his wife; that bothered the hell out of him. He knew they were going to have to talk about all this, but for now, the time was for healing.

When she remembered being raped, the thoughts of the baby not being Ed's haunted them both, and she wanted to know for sure.

When her doctor told her she was farther along by a couple of weeks than the day UPS had delivered Ed's grill, they knew. But she told Ed, that once the child was born she would schedule a test for peace of mind. One way or another, she needed to be reassured that her husband was going to be a new father, which made Ed love her even more, if that was even possible.

The murder of Parnell F. Bancroft was still unsolved, and perhaps it was unrelated to the hell the family had gone though. Ed hoped to God that was true and planned on calling Tallulah to open an investigation into it.

The family had endured the worst thing that had ever happened in their lives, and together the Savages were strong. Of course, when it came to who stayed in the mansion and who got which guesthouse, the brothers were back at it once again. Even Sam whined, wanting to stay in the mansion due to his injury. Ed was being grumpy and being a true "Squidward," wanting it for himself. The ladies got a good laugh, watching them squabble over who got what.

That evening, Zolie had the most amazing dinner prepared for all of them, and for the first time in what seemed like forever, nothing but good things were coming for Ed Savage.

A NOTE FROM YOUR AUTHOR

Dear Reader,

Like a season finale of your favorite TV show, it was with intention that I left a few minor lingering threads in wrapping up Volume One of this trilogy.

I hope you enjoyed meeting Ed Savage and his family as much as I did creating them, and be aware that Volume Two will pick up right where this journey left off. I look forward to having you take this incredible adventure with me!

And while I can easily admit in wanting to keep the story going, the word count Gestapo was haunting this first time writer's thoughts and dreams.

To see some visually exciting advertising for my work and more information on my next novel please check out my website: www.SavageRobertsPublishing.com

And finally, what a different animal songwriting is. For months nothing would come and then *it* happened. The song, "Savage Night" you can also find on my website: www. SavageRobertsPublishing.com

And I will say, storytelling seems to come freely to me, and to the songwriters out there; you rule!

—Bryan Roberts

Author Biography

Bryan Roberts has always loved writing—but only thought of it as a hobby. Recently, he has taken his hobby and turned it into an avocation. He has a flair for the dramatic, and it is no wonder. When he's not writing, he's in an operating room working in health care and the extraordinary world of trauma; he also has a love for historic places.

Once while volunteering as a stagehand at the closed Ambassador Hotel, he was in the kitchen; he saw where the walls had been stripped bare and was told the FBI had taken everything to reconstruct. Looking at the floor and imagining Bobby Kennedy had just been shot was one of the most haunting things he had seen, and one memory is written in this novel from that kitchen.

With his curiosity in overdrive, he snuck off alone, seeing the dust-covered lobby, empty mailbox slots, and the blocked-off grand staircase piled high with tangled furniture, making it impossible for him to go any further. Retreating in a frightened run, he ran back down the long abandoned hallways back to the stage.

Roberts's experiences have exposed him to amazing places and people. These elements surely inform his writing. With his imagination spurred, he has invented a completely new style of storytelling that blends the drama of reality TV with the adrenaline-pumping style of the murder-mystery thriller in a genre mashing adventure that works well.

His enthusiasm for his latest work is evidenced by his multimedia approach to marketing. He has written and filmed both an original song and short video that complement his writing. Look for the song, "Savage Night" on Bryan's Author page on Amazon and his website: www.SavageRobertsPublishing.com